NO MERE ZOMBIE

DEATHLESS BOOK 2

CHRIS FOX

CHRIS FOX WRITES LLC

For Yukon. You are missed, my friend.

PREVIOUSLY ON DEATHLESS

Whenever I pick up the 2nd book in a series I'm always torn. Should I re-read the first book, or just dive right in? I usually want to do the latter, but I can't always remember what happened in the previous book. This page is for all those people like me who can't quite remember everything that went down in *No Such Thing As Werewolves*. I've decided to re-cap it just like a TV show. For those that just finished *No Such Thing As Werewolves* feel free to skip to the prologue.

In an announcer voice "Last time, on Deathless..."

A giant black pyramid bores from the earth in Peru, and a team of soldiers have been dispatched to investigate. They encounter a were-wolf dressed in Egyptian-style clothing, which tears through their ranks before escaping. They bring in a team of scientists to help them investigate the pyramid, and quickly find that the central chamber is full of very lethal radiation. They desperately seek a way into the pyramid's control room, while the escaped werewolf with the bad fashion sense (Ahiga) begins slaughtering innocents. Some of those innocents rise as werewolves, and a plague begins spreading across South America.

The desperate team of scientists recruits Blair Smith, a brilliant anthropologist working at a local junior college as a teacher. Blair finds a way into the inner chamber, where the team discovers a woman sleeping inside of a high-tech sarcophagus the ancients called a rejuvenator. Unfortunately, the act of opening the door to the inner chamber injects Blair with an unknown virus and Blair dies (it's all very sad, really). Within hours he rises again as a werewolf and begins slaughtering his former companions.

Blair wakes up in a small Peruvian village not far from the pyramid where he meets Liz, a beautiful young redhead from the United States. The pair are pursued by Commander Jordan, the leader of the forces controlled by the mysterious (terribly mysterious) Mohn Corp. Liz is killed and brought back by Blair as a werewolf, and we learn that female werewolves are much larger and much scarier than males. The pair flees north, deciding that if they can get to California, Liz's brother, Trevor, might be able to help them find some sort of cure.

Meanwhile Ahiga tries to catch up, because he realizes that Blair has inadvertently stolen the key to the Ark (the pyramid). That key is required to wake the woman inside, who Ahiga refers to as the Mother. It turns out she's the progenitor of the entire werewolf species, and when Ahiga finally catches up to Blair he tells him that without her the world is doomed. He explains that the world is about to enter a new age. The sun will go through a Coronal Mass Ejection, which will wipe out nearly all technology. This CME will also activate a virus that will turn all the people who currently have it into zombies (oh crap).

Blair decides to be a dumbass and tells Ahiga to go screw himself. He and Liz continue on to California where they meet up with Trevor and begin investigating the werewolf virus. It turns out that Trevor is a helio-seismologist who just so happens to be investigating a giant sunspot (what a coincidence, right?). He confirms that a CME could royally screw the entire planet, and agrees to help Blair and Liz get back to Peru to wake the Mother.

Before they leave, Commander Jordan and his comic-relief side-kick, Yuri, show up with a bunch of soldiers in power armor. They blow up Trevor's house and his '67 Mustang, but fail to catch Blair. The werewolves escape back to Peru where they gather some furry allies and invade the Ark. They battle Mohn Corp.'s ever growing army, and there are casualties on both sides. The werewolves win and wake the Mother, who slaughters poor Commander Jordan and every soldier under his command. It's very sad, because by this point we feel bad for poor Jordan.

In the epilogue the asshole author (that's me) dropped a really, really messed up cliffhanger. One of the scientists had the virus that would cause her to turn into a zombie when the CME hits. Not only does she turn into a zombie, but Trevor gets bitten within the first 30 seconds of the zombie apocalypse. Poor readers were left wondering what happened to Trevor. Fortunately, you're holding the sequel and are about to find out. I hope you enjoy it...

If you do, please consider leaving a review both for this book and for *No Such Thing As Werewolves*. I'm an indie author, and reviews are vitally important to my success. You might also consider signing up for the mailing list to hear when future books will be available. If you do, I'm happy to give you a free copy of *The First Ark*, the prequel that explains a bit more about who the Mother is and where the zombie virus comes from.

Okay, enough rambling! On to *No Mere Zombie*...

PROLOGUE

I rakesh shook the chill rain from his cloak, handing it to the pale-faced thrall by the door. The frail old man gave a bow, leathery skin sagging around sunken eyes. Such an embarrassment. The worthless servant was a stark contrast to the majesty of this place, one of the oldest structures in the world. Ptah's temple predated all others save the Ark, or so Irakesh had been taught.

He strode up the wide marble entryway, ignoring the handful of thralls who peered anxiously around columns. None were brave enough to challenge his passing. Not that he expected them to. They were not warriors and the na-kopesh riding at his hip was a warrior's weapon. A Sunsteel sword, one of only a handful in existence. An honor no other deathless his age had ever been accorded.

Irakesh moved confidently down a side passageway, idly gazing upon the elaborate murals depicting their creator's earliest feats. Such a pity that Ptah's greatest works were long behind him. The ancient deathless should have had the grace to take his own life, rather than fade into obscurity. Yet it was to Irakesh's benefit that he still lived, if their existence could be called life.

He finally stopped before a wide chamber with a low stone table. His target sat alone, hunched over a faded bronze chalice. Irakesh sat down across from him, surveying his target. Ptah's dark-skinned face was made for scowls. Excessive unibrow, crooked nose. His shimmering white cloak was rumpled and the golden lion clasp needed time with a rag and polish. His thralls were doing a poor job attending to his appearance, though from the look of the wretches they themselves were just as worn.

From the way Ptah leaned into the table, he'd already enjoyed several cups of fermented blood. He didn't even glance up when Irakesh sat, though Irakesh could have been an assassin dispatched by a more powerful deathless.

Yes, he could see why this once great man had fallen from the lofty heights of power. Deathless Ptah, a man older than he by millennia, yet one who'd never managed to accumulate a power base. He was forever trapped at middling rank, his monumental creations little more than ancient tales, eclipsed by those like Irakesh, who were bold enough to take risks at a young age and thus catch the attention of more powerful masters.

Careful, my host. Do not underestimate him. He is old but cunning. The Risen's voice buzzed like a fly in the corner of his mind. Irakesh ignored it.

Ptah looked up from his chalice, swirling the thick scarlet contents. "What do you want, boy? Let me enjoy this age's final weeks in peace."

"My apologies for the intrusion, mighty Ptah. I'm hoping our meeting will be both brief and profitable," Irakesh assured him, all smiles. He rested a friendly arm on the stone table. "Ra asks your cooperation."

Ptah paled, setting his cup on the table with more force than he'd probably intended. Its sticky contents sloshed over the side, adding to the layer of grime on the pitted stone. He gave Irakesh a sidelong glance. "Ra? I refuse to grant her that title. What could *Sekhmet* possibly want from me? I have no power. No influence. No one will grant me a place in an Ark."

"*Ra* may," Irakesh corrected, horrified by the man's use of his mother's true name. Such usage was forbidden, punishable with an excruciating death. He gestured to the thrall standing behind Ptah. The woman scurried over with a second chalice, squeezing a tiny spigot placed in her wrist. The wooden cup filled with her warm blood, potent with the alcohol that she'd imbibed. It was the fastest and most enjoyable way for a deathless to get drunk, something it appeared Ptah knew intimately. "If you aid me, there could be a place for you in the Ark of the Cradle."

"So Sekhmet dangles the carrot then," Ptah snorted, eyeing him suspiciously, as expected. Ra controlled the Ark and would make the final selections. Those she favored would live to see another age of the world thirteen millennia from now. A full half of the longest count. Those she didn't would wither and die when the sun went through its change, denying them its life-sustaining energy. That momentous event was nearly upon them.

"She'd add me to her pantheon then?" Ptah asked, a glimmer of hope flitting across his features before he brutally repressed it. "Not without a high blood price, I'd wager. What does she wish of me?"

"You are a man of little influence, Ptah. We all know that," Irakesh said, a slight smile slipping into place. He might be enjoying this just a little too much. "What you do have is an incredible talent for shaping helixes. We owe much to your discoveries. Ra asks that you shape mine in a very specific way. You were one of those responsible for the discovery of the Ark of the Redwood, were you not?"

"It was my hand that shaped that Ark's access key, yes. I did it at Isis's direction, but I hold no loyalty to her. I am neutral in this eternal squabble," Ptah said, eyes growing dangerous. Like a rat who'd been cornered.

"Peace, Ptah. I'm not accusing you of anything," Irakesh said, holding up his hands in a gesture of friendship. He savored a sip of blood before continuing. "I care nothing for your loyalties. Only for your ability to shape."

"What is it you desire? Speak plainly, boy. I've no patience left for games," the man growled, picking up his cup and downing the contents in one defiant swallow. He stood higher than Irakesh, but that was overshadowed by Irakesh's matron. Everyone feared Ra. Even Isis.

"I need to fool the access key to the Ark of the Redwood. It must believe me of Isis's bestial get," Irakesh explained, then took a small sip of his own beverage. It was warm and tangy, not up to his usual standards. Hardly surprising in this forgotten corner of the world.

"You what?" Ptah asked, slack-jawed. Then he began a dry wheezing laugh. It went on for long moments before he calmed enough to continue. "Boy, you are wasting my time. Even if I could do the shaping, there's no way you'll ever lay hands on that access key. It's protected by Isis herself, deep within her stronghold on the jungle continent."

"How I lay hands on the key is my business. Can you do what I ask?" Irakesh demanded, leaning over the table and resting his hand on the hilt of his na-kopesh. Ptah's flat smile seemed more amused than threatened.

"I taught Sobek to become one with the crocodile. Gave Anubis the blood of the jackal. Of course I can shape your helixes. It's a trivial matter," Ptah allowed, throwing back his cloak to expose broadly muscled shoulders. The physique surprised Irakesh. It seemed that he had *some* pride remaining. His gaze became calculating, though still fogged by drink. "If I do this, I want more than some vague assurance about a place in the Ark of the Cradle. Tell me your plan and if it amuses me, I may do as you ask."

"That's a dangerous question, Ptah. A deathless could be concerned that you intend to sell this information to Isis," Irakesh said, tightening his grip on the hilt of his sword. He doubted that he'd need it, but one could never be sure. Even Ptah might attack rather than be taken for interrogation. Irakesh was one of the finest swordsmen in the world, but who knew what hidden powers Ptah might possess?

"There's no time left for that," Ptah scoffed, slamming his empty chalice down with a metallic clink. "I want to know, because if Isis catches you, she'll know that I did the shaping that let you take the key. What do you think will happen to me then? Not very forgiving, that one."

"If you're in the Ark with Ra? Nothing. She'll protect you," Irakesh answered smoothly. The man's concern seemed legitimate, but something about it rang false. He'd probably been working with Isis for centuries, quietly passing secrets and betraying his own kind. "Very well, I'll share the plan. Assuming you can do the shaping right here. Do your work and you'll have the entire plan, my word as a deathless."

Ptah studied him carefully, then gave a tight nod. No deathless with a shred of honor would break their word. Besides, Ptah must know that Irakesh could haul him before Ra, if needed. That would be unpleasant for them both.

"Very well, give me your palm," Ptah demanded, extending a leathery hand with his palm facing up. Irakesh obliged, laying his palm against Ptah's. It was clammy, a decidedly undeathless-like trait. "Hold still. There will be pain."

Fire flooded up through Irakesh's hand, spilling into his arm as it raced through his entire body. It was agony, the sort that could crush a lesser mind. Fortunately, Irakesh had endured far worse. His mother had seen to that. For him this was a pleasant diversion, a reminder of his own power in the face of pain. He allowed the waves of energy to course through him, gritting his teeth but refusing to cry out.

The entire process lasted perhaps a dozen heartbeats. By the end, a sheen of sweat had broken out on Ptah's face. If he were still capable of breathing, the man would have been panting.

"It is done. The key will accept you as one of Isis's get," he said, releasing Irakesh's hand and leaning heavily against the table. It was an impressive feat, showing a glimmer of the power that the man had once possessed.

"Very well, you have done as asked. I will live up to my end of our bargain," Irakesh said. He was ambitious and willing to cut corners on his rise to power, but even he wouldn't break his oath. Without his word, man was no better than beast. "I am going to slipsail to the jungle continent and sneak into the Mother's Ark. I have already arranged for an 'accident' to cause significant damage, so she'll be occupied with repairs when I enter. I'm quite skilled at shadow dancing, as you're well aware."

"Ha," Ptah snorted, waving at the thrall to refill his cup. "It won't save you. That will get you inside and if you're lucky she won't notice you using one of her rejuvenators. But what of waking? When the longest count ends and the Ark returns to the world, you'll have to not only sneak past Isis to steal the key, but then escape and flee across two continents before you can use it."

"The rejuvenator will wake me one week after Isis's slumber ends," Irakesh explained, voice pitched low so not even the thrall hovering over Ptah could hear. Many dismissed thralls, but Irakesh knew that they had ears. He'd purchased the services of many. "By that time, she will have assumed that her Ark is safe. She will emerge and begin consolidating her holdings. I will wait for her to leave, then simply steal the key and run. She might be able to catch me, but if her Ark is damaged, she won't be able to leave it. She'll have no choice but to stay and defend, while I claim the Ark of the Redwood."

"A bold plan. One that might even work," Ptah allowed. He downed the contents of the fresh cup, rising from his stool as he set the empty cup on the table. He swayed like a man newly at sea. "I've lived up to my end of our little bargain. See that you do the same. I want a place among Sekhmet's pantheon."

"You're lying," Irakesh said, rising smoothly to his feet and drawing his na-kopesh. The curved blade caught the sun glinting through the high windows. "You have no intention of joining Ra. You're off to report to your real master. To tell Isis of my plan."

If he was correct, Ptah would try to kill him, confirming his suspicions. If he was not, then Ptah would protest his innocence loudly and longly. Either way he needed to die. He was no longer of any use and if he found out that Irakesh was acting on his own, he'd warn Ra. That would end *badly* for Irakesh.

Ptah wrenched a bronze dagger from its belt sheath, aiming a clumsy strike at Irakesh's heart. Irakesh flowed backwards, casually allowing the blade's point to touch his tunic. Then he lunged, ramming his blade through Ptah's chest in a parody of the same strike the man had just attempted. It was the ultimate insult. Ptah's chest began to smoke and smolder as the blade did its work, bright pulses of sickly green essence flowing up the blade and into Irakesh.

The once-great god glared hatefully at Irakesh as his second life faded. "Isis will stop you."

"Not so," Irakesh said, shoving Ptah's smoking body heavily to the ground. He wiped his na-kopesh on the rumpled cloak, though Sunsteel never needed cleaning. "I will steal the key. The Ark of the Redwood is mine and you're the one who gave it to me, Ptah."

1

WAKE UP

Jordan awoke screaming into the frigid morning, a harsh series of ragged cries. The phantom pain of his arms being torn off was still very real, though a quick glance showed that both were intact. He scrambled to his feet, whirling as he tried to understand where he was and what had just happened.

The last thing that he remembered was dying in the Ark. He'd been torn apart by the Mother, an ancient being that was for all intents and purposes a god. She was the progenitor of the were-wolves, and his entire mission had been to curtail their spread. They murdered innocent people, who rose and murdered more people in turn. Yet he'd failed utterly to stop them, and Professor Smith had led his companions into the Ark and successfully woken the Mother.

He looked down at himself. Jordan was covered in blood, most of it dried into thick, flaky patches. He was also naked, and it was damned cold. A quick glance around showed that he was at the base of one of the Ark's sloped sides. The pyramid towered above him, stabbing into the sky like a too-smooth mountain. The place was deathly silent, and other than the cry of a wheeling hawk, the wind was his only companion.

Not your only companion, Ka-Dun. I am here.

Jordan whirled again, reaching for the pistol no longer belted at his side. "Who the fuck are you?"

The words were strange. They were inside his mind somehow.

I am your beast, Ka-Dun. I serve as guide and protector. Turn towards the Ark's mirrored finish. Study your reflection there and I will show you the truth of things.

Jordan knew he wasn't going mad, though he wished he were. He was alive when he should be dead. He was naked and covered in blood. He had no memory of coming to this place, because he'd died within the Ark. All of that painted a very disconcerting picture.

He did as the beast asked, turning to face the pyramid. As the voice had said, he could make out his reflection in the dark stone. He looked like hell, close-cropped blond hair now matted with dirt. His entire body was a mass of dust and blood.

Watch, Ka-Dun, the voice said.

Jordan felt something stir within him, a tingling energy akin to static electricity. It flowed down his body, beginning in his chest and moving outwards through his limbs. The tingling grew hotter, becoming a torrent of very painful fire. Then the change began. It wasn't the agony that really bothered him; it was the knowledge of what he was seeing.

Bones popped and limbs elongated, even as blond fur sprouted from every part of his body. His back arched, body contorting at the mercy of the change. A lupine muzzle burst from his face, his teeth lengthening as it did so. He grew taller, now nearly eight feet as fur covered the last of him.

The reflection staring back at him was unmistakable. He'd become the enemy. Jordan was a god-damned werewolf. Part of him was thrilled at still being alive, but most of him was horrified. In a way he'd sold his soul, had become the very thing he'd sworn to fight. For what? And what could he possibly do about it?

Prepare yourself, Ka-Dun. It begins.

Jordan wasn't sure what the voice meant, but he felt something all around him. A gathering energy like the moment before a lightning strike. Then tendrils of fire veined across the sky, lighting the valley as if it were noon. He didn't know what it was, but he could feel that energy. Draw strength from it. Part of him sensed that whatever it was would forever change the world.

It is the great change, Ka-Dun. The sun-sign that shows that we have entered the next age. Your powers will increase, and you will need them. For in the wake of this cleansing fire, the ancient enemy will rise again.

2

THE END OF THE WORLD

Director Phillips ignored the whispers rustling through the knots of technicians as he stepped off the elevator onto the lowest public level of Mohn Corp.'s Syracuse installation. They found excuses to scurry off on whatever business they were supposed to be about, taking great care to avoid his gaze. He abided his side of the social contract, ignoring them as he would ants. Was it wrong that he'd grown used to doing that, used to thinking of himself as the Director instead of just Mark? He wore the title like a mask, a very powerful mask.

He passed under the high ceilings with their halogen lights, by the impersonal concrete walls and the watchful eyes of security cameras. None of the Kevlar-clad security guards challenged him as he passed through checkpoints, though policy said they should. They too avoided his gaze. In a way it was as if he didn't exist, a ghost surrounded in this tomb of an installation. Until he chose to be noticed.

A precise seven minutes after exiting the elevator he finally arrived at Ops, a fishbowl of a room flanked by wall-sized windows on three sides. Banks of monitors lined stations within, each manned by a white-garbed tech monitoring a stream of information that he'd deemed critical. The room's far side was dominated by a monitor larger than the aquarium he'd visited in Monterey the previous summer. It was dark now, waiting for his arrival to spring to life.

"Get me feeds on the twelve primaries," the Director barked before the glass doors had even finished sliding open. Dozens of heads swiveled briefly in his direction, then dropped back to their respective tasks as he strode boldly between the yellow strips marking the pathway to the pit.

They looked haggard and more than a little terrified, and he couldn't blame them. Their world was about to end, and they were no doubt wrestling with a mixture of fear and guilt. Here they were in the only secure facility left in the world, the one place where technology would survive the sun's fiery wrath. If any of his personnel had family outside this place they'd almost certainly never see them again.

The people would be fine, so far as they knew, but the CME would devastate the world's power grid. There would be no internet, no cable. No food being transported in daily. No modern conveniences. That would lead to a very scared, very aggressive populace and every one of his people knew they were exempted from that chaos. They'd be safe while the rest of the world tore itself apart.

By the time he'd descended the three steps and entered the spacious ring at the foot of the massive wall display a dozen feeds had already sprung to life. He barely noticed as an Asian woman slipped a tablet into his hand. It was the control interface not only for the display, but for the entire complex. Using the simple device he could find data, issue commands or even shut down power. The biometric sensor was keyed to his thumb, of course.

He took a moment to survey each of the twelve feeds, a brief twinge of satisfaction rising as the low hum of conversation resumed behind him. His command crew were the best at what they did, far too professional to allow a superior's arrival to intimidate them for long. They had jobs to do and every one of them knew failure could cost countless lives. Most probably took solace in the work, focusing on it rather than on what they were about to witness.

"What am I seeing on number six?" he barked, tapping the feed on the tablet and swiping to the data screen. "These metrics are outside tolerance. Get it locked down. Seconds count, people."

Eleven of the twelve satellites were in the final phases of lock-down, the feeds showing enormous clam-like shells that were slowly covering their vital components. Those components would be cooked instantly if exposed to the fury the sun was about to unleash on their world. Number six, on the other hand, sat perfectly still. Its feed was still being received, but the protective casing remained retracted.

"Sir," one of the techs piped up, a sandy-haired kid who looked as though he should be serving french fries. "Number six has a damaged servo. Time to repair is just under two hours."

"Noted," Mark shot back, turning his attention back to the tablet.

He pinched the IRIS feed, dragging it open to cover the entire screen. The deep-space satellite belonged to NASA and had been designed to study the sun. It had been deployed a bare handful of months before, a timely addition to their data-gathering abilities. Gasps sounded behind him as some of the technicians saw the feed he'd pulled onto the main screen. He couldn't blame them, even if they were supposed to be professionals. No one had ever seen anything like this, at least no one in the last thirteen thousand years.

A fiery wave blanketed space, hurling towards the camera with incredible speed. It drowned out the sun behind it, a glob of plasma that undulated and pulsed as it approached. The image provided no real context, but Mark knew that the coronal mass ejection was many times the size of the earth. That made it far larger than anything in recorded history, and he prayed that their projections of the catastrophic damage it would wreak to the earth's power grid were wrong.

"Get me an estimated time of impact," he bellowed, pivoting to face the sea of technicians. Most typed furiously on their keyboards, but a few shot him terrified glances. One woman was crying, a young blonde with close-cropped hair and swollen eyes. "Now, people."

"Eighty seconds until it hits satellite six, sir," an Asian woman with wireframe glasses spoke up, rising from her desk so he could meet her gaze. It was the same one who'd given him the tablet. Benson, the name tag read. "We have another forty before it reaches us here. It will blanket the entire planet in just under four minutes."

"At least one of you is competent," the Director growled, attempting to suppress the irritation at how powerless he felt. "Keep six broadcasting and record all data. If we're going to lose it, let's at least get what we can. Shut down all monitoring as soon as it goes dark."

He strode from the pit towards the wide glass desk on the far side of the room. It was slightly elevated over the others, giving him a commanding view of the technicians. It had been placed there to further reinforce his authority, though it did little to help his mood. He slid into the high-backed leather chair behind the desk and keyed in a sequence on the silvered keyboard. His monitor flared to life with the lime-green connecting icon.

"What is it, Mark?" a familiar voice answered almost immediately. The picture showed a stocky blond-haired man with piercing blue eyes, hands steepled on his desk as he stared at the camera. Leif Mohn himself, a man even Mark found terrifying.

"The second wave will be here in three minutes. We're going to lose satellite six, but the other eleven are protected," he explained, pausing while he awaited a response. Mohn's face revealed nothing.

"That's a shame. Six is responsible for north Africa, isn't it?" Mohn asked, tone neutral.

"It is. We can bridge the gap if we alter five and seven to cover a wider radius, but that leaves thin coverage in all three areas," Mark replied. It wasn't the best solution, but it was the best they had.

"As soon as the wave is over, have the artifacts brought below. I want to see if the wave has any effect," Mohn instructed, reaching for something off-screen. He turned back to the camera. "Do we have an update on the situation in Peru?"

"No, sir," Mark admitted, though he hated doing so. It made him look incompetent for trusting subordinates. "Last we heard, Commander Jordan was in place and awaiting the package, but he hasn't reported in since this morning. That's unusual, but given the impending wave we couldn't send a team to investigate."

"Inform me if anything changes. Also, I want to be notified the second we've compiled footage from the aftermath of the wave," Mohn said. He didn't bother awaiting a response, simply terminating the feed.

If the Old Man had been upset about losing an eighty-billion-dollar satellite moments before they were knocked back into the Stone Age, he certainly didn't show it. Mark compartmentalized the conversation. He had to focus on the situation. Time was critical.

"Sir, wave impact in fifteen seconds," Benson called from her desk. She'd be one to watch in the coming days. She seemed to be keeping it together better than most of the techs.

Mark rose from his desk, watching the feed from six on the giant screen. The wave had blotted out everything, leaving the screen filled with the sun's fiery wrath. Had the first civilization witnessed something similar thirteen thousand years ago? Or had they lacked the technology and simply been eradicated? He would give anything to know more about that civilization. Mohn had gleaned so little from the pyramid in Peru and even less from Göbekli Tepe. The only solid information they had came from the artifacts, and that was extremely limited.

The screen went dark. Satellite six was gone. The room fell utterly silent, save for the low hum of computers. No one spoke or even tapped away at a keyboard. They all knew that when the feed returned, when the wave was over, they'd find themselves in a strange new world. There was no way of knowing just how it would affect them.

They had projections, of course. The world's power grid would be severely damaged, though there was no way to predict the exact magnitude of that damage. People would be left in a dark aftermath, fighting for food and possibly shelter as the civilized world tore itself apart. That would leave them unable to respond to the true threat, these werewolves that had begun appearing several weeks after they'd explored the pyramid.

Had that been their true plan all along? Start the plague just before the world faced its worst calamity in recorded history? If so, it was utterly devious. It would give the werewolves the time they needed to spread unopposed. Mohn Corp. would resist, of course, but how much resistance they could offer remained to be seen. They had less than three thousand personnel in Syracuse, and every other installation lacked the elaborate shielding they had here. The other facilities would suffer severe damage from the wave. They hadn't the faintest idea as to the werewolves' motives and were woefully unable to respond to the threat.

The lights flickered for a split second and then came back on at a slightly reduced intensity. It was the only sign that they'd switched from the local power grid to their own nuclear reactor. That switch was intended to be permanent, since they had no idea how long it would take for the local government to rebuild, assuming that it even survived the disaster.

"Sir," Benson called. She waited for his attention before continuing. "Satellites are beginning to redeploy. We'll have feeds in sixty seconds."

"Excellent," Mark replied, leaving the desk and heading back into the pit. He studied the black screen for nearly a full minute before it flickered back to life.

It now showed eleven feeds, with a conspicuously black spot where six should have been. He tapped a series of commands on the tablet and watched as each of the satellites altered their cameras from the sun back to the earth. The feeds revealed familiar images showing every continent. Those in daylight time zones looked exactly the same, but those on the far side of the earth were dark, save for a thin band of lights around the equator. Every city outside that belt had been extinguished. Power was gone in the blink of an eye leaving them, so far as they knew, the only organization in the world with both satellite access and electricity.

The latter would return in time, but no nation would be able to recover satellite access. Every last one, save for those belonging to Mohn Corp., had just been obliterated by the coronal mass ejection.

The world was blind, naked before whatever apocalypse the ancient myths had tried to warn them about.

"Give me points of interest, people. What can you show me?" he asked, folding his hands behind his back. It galled him to know so little, but there was nothing for it but patience.

"Sir, feed five is making a pass over northern Africa. Cairo was listed as a potential point of interest. I think you're going to want to see this," a young man with a shock of black hair and a cleft chin said. Mark was close enough to read the name tag. Jacobs.

He called up feed five, which dominated the main screen. The camera was aimed at the Giza plateau and provided a spectacular view of the Pyramids and the Sphinx. The ground shook and trembled, sending temple columns and a few stones from the Pyramids tumbling to the earth. Odd, since Egypt wasn't seismically active.

Then a jet-black point jutted from the earth between the first and second Pyramids. It grew larger and larger, boring up through the earth just as the one in Peru had. Only this one was far, far larger. The ground around it roiled and bucked as it continued its ascent. Eventually, the structure hit both the first and second Pyramids, knocking them out of its path like children's blocks. Five thousand years of human history were obliterated in the blink of an eye, leaving nothing but rubble at the feet of what must now be the largest man-made structure in the world. Assuming it *was* man-made.

Only the Sphinx had survived the destruction, now perched at the very foot of the newly arrived pyramid, as if it had been made to sit there. Odd that. The pyramid's obsidian surface was different than its counterpart in Peru. It was decorated with elaborate golden hieroglyphs as large as a man. Thousands upon thousands of them. What did they mean? Who had created them? There were so many damned questions and precious few answers.

"Sir," Benson barked as she shot to her feet. "There are more of those things. One in Australia. Another in Cambodia. There might be others but those are the ones that we've identified thus far."

The Director walked back to his desk and called the Old Man.

3

ZOMBIES

"Director Phillips?" a voice blared from somewhere outside the dream. Mark struggled awake, sitting up in bed. He glanced at the clock. 2:43 AM. He'd only been out for about forty minutes. It was more than he'd expected.

An insistent red light flashed at the base of the wall screen. He tapped it.

"I'm awake. Report," he said, still groggy but already processing. If they'd woken him this quickly after he'd left Ops, something monumental must have happened.

"Sir, I'm piping you the footage from satellite five now," a female voice said. It was the Asian tech. Benson. "I've concatenated the most important parts, complete with our initial analysis."

He was impressed. She hadn't apologized for waking him, which most other techs would have done. If it was important enough to wake him she was smart enough to realize no apology was needed, because she was simply performing the duty he'd assigned her.

Mark picked up the tablet from the nightstand and propped the pillow up against the wall. He leaned back, swiping to wake the device. It took a few moments to browse to the footage Benson had indicated. There were four videos, one from Cairo, another from

London, the third from Berlin, and the final one from Paris. He started with London.

It was a top-down view of downtown, just outside a hospital. Police stood in the street, directing crowds of people. Abandoned vehicles clogged the street and thousands of people streamed between them. It was his first look at a large city after all power had been lost, but beyond the expected chaos he didn't see anything remarkable.

A figure staggered out of the hospital. Then another. Then a third and a fourth. They lurched drunkenly towards the crowd, where they began to attack people. At first most of the crowd barely noticed, but then some of those attacked rose and began attacking others. The violence spread like wildfire, ripping into the crowd in several places.

People were finally aware. They began stampeding away from their attackers, more than one poor soul trampled as people flooded past. The camera zoomed in, focusing on the spot where the violence had begun. Several figures knelt over the fallen. Were they...feeding?

A window popped up on the far side of the screen, listing behavior observed over the next two hours. Extreme violence. Immunity to pain or injury. Inability to speak or reason. Extreme and lethal aggression. Benson had included a great deal of data but drew no conclusion, though it was obvious to any observer. He'd just witnessed a scene that could have come from a Romero movie. Those people were zombies.

Mark turned off the tablet, setting it on the pillow beside him as he considered the implications. He could assume the other three videos showed similar incidents. That suggested this might be global, though he couldn't confirm that without more evidence.

The Old Man had hinted for years that some sort of apocalypse was coming, but Mark had assumed that it must be the CME. It was only recently that he'd modified that hypothesis to assume that the werewolf outbreak in South America was somehow part of a master plan set in motion eight millennia before their recorded history began. What if he wasn't seeing the whole picture? What if this zombie outbreak was the real apocalypse? Who had set it in motion and what did they stand to gain from it? How did the werewolves figure into it all? Most importantly, how much did the Old Man know and why wasn't he sharing that knowledge?

Mark turned the tablet back on and browsed to the Cairo video. The pyramid was significantly larger than the others and the fact that the world's oldest known pyramids had been built virtually on top of it was suggestive. Were the ancient Egyptians the distant descendants of the people who'd built that pyramid?

The footage was from a higher vantage than London, showing pandemonium sweeping the streets of Cairo. Some people ran, some fought, and others huddled on top of buildings. Those in the streets were pulled down by growing hordes of shambling corpses, soon rising to join their attackers. It chilled him, but what came next was even worse.

As one, the corpses froze. Thousands of bodies all at once. Then they began a slow orderly walk towards the massive black pyramid. He sped up the footage, watching as they marched like ants towards the base of that structure. An army of the dead in neat, even rows. Waiting, but for what?

It was time to alert the Old Man. He swiped to his contacts and tapped the connect button next to the Old Man's dour picture. The tablet beeped twice and then went to voice mail. Mark checked the time. 3 AM. Mohn would have picked up, unless he was on a call. Who could the Old Man be talking to?

Mark logged into the admin panel, delving down into the call logs. Odd. The Old Man had placed six calls to London in the last four hours. Who the hell was he talking to in the middle of the night? The London facility was small and held little tactical value right now. The woman in charge there wasn't even a top-level executive. In fact, Margery probably knew less about what was happening in her own city than Mark did. So why would Mohn be calling there?

4

THE DEAD RULE

The dead ruled Cajamarca. Blair gazed down at the moonlit city from his perch atop the steeple. The church sat midway up a hill at the city's edge, looking down on a sea of churches, skyscrapers, and homes. Not a single street light or friendly glow from a residential neighborhood could be found. Whether the people had lost power when the second wave hit or were merely trying to hide, no one seemed willing to advertise their presence with so much as a flashlight.

Yet they were down there. He could smell a dozen competing scents, all tinged with fear. There were survivors and they'd wisely chosen to hunker down and wait for help to arrive. Blair was that help.

"Look, down there by that grocery store," Liz said, materializing next to him. Her copper hair was bound in a tight ponytail and she wore a pair of black yoga pants with a matching jacket. Simple night camouflage. "Something moved in that window."

"You know, I hate it when you do that," Blair said, eyeing her sidelong. She'd taken to using a new trick the Mother had shown her. Something she called shadow riding. That usually meant she was lurking in *his* shadow. Literally. "It could have been a zombie. Or a pet."

"Maybe, but it's worth a look," Liz replied. She turned to face a neighboring apartment building, beckoning.

A figure blurred into view, crossing the distance between them in three quick hops. A tall man in a black t-shirt and dark canvas pants landed on the roof below them, his blond hair covered by a tactical helmet with a glass visor. He cradled an assault rifle in his arms, scanning the darkness for threats. Part of Blair still panicked at the sight of Commander Jordan, memories of fleeing Mohn's chief executioner still fresh in his mind. No. That had all changed.

The Commander was on their side now. He'd risen just a few hours after the Mother had torn him apart, a blond werewolf a good six inches taller than Blair's silver form. Not that Jordan wore his bestial form often. The soldier definitely preferred conventional weaponry to claws, but he seemed just as effective without them. They could use their increased strength and speed while in human form, and Jordan utilized both with terrifying lethality.

"Sit rep?" Jordan asked, all business. Blair still didn't trust him. It was hard trusting a man who'd blown up houses to hunt you down.

"Movement down there in the grocery store. Blair and I will check it out. I want you and Bridget to wait here," Liz ordered. Blair was amazed at how easily command came to her now. She'd already adopted the Mother's doctrine of the Ka-Ken being the battlefield commanders. The role fit her.

"We can do that," Bridget said, emerging from the shadows behind Jordan. She was comically short beside him, though those roles would reverse if she shifted. Bridget wore the same black yoga pants as Liz, with a black tank top that left her pale shoulders exposed. She caught his eye. "Be careful, Blair."

"It's probably nothing, but we have to check," he said, shrugging. He turned towards the building, eyeing the route in between. "Four jumps. You going to hitch a ride, Liz?"

"Sure, faster that way," she said, flowing into the darkness like inky mist. Damn, it was eerie. He couldn't feel anything, not the slightest hint that she was in his shadow. Yet he was positive she was there.

He bounded down the slope, drawing on the moon's strength to fuel his blur. The wind whipped at his clothing, blowing his hood back and plastering the jacket to his body. He landed just outside the grocery store in the middle of a near-empty parking lot. He raised his nose, examining the scents. Soap. Sweat. Urine.

"You were right. There's someone alive in there," he whispered, moving to the door in a low crouch. He peered through the glass, scanning the dark aisles. A normal person would be blind, but the thin moonlight lit the place like day for his eyes. He could clearly make out several figures. "Look, crouched there in the produce section. Four of them."

"Shall we introduce ourselves?" Liz's disembodied voice asked, still wrapped in shadow.

"Okay, I'll go inside. Stick to the shadows unless I get into trouble. We don't want them to feel threatened," he replied, rising to his feet. He rapped lightly on the glass.

Two of the four figures drew together, whispering. He couldn't quite catch their heartbeats, but the words were plain. A young man was speaking in Spanish. "We should let him in. He could die out there."

"We barely have enough food as it is," an older woman hissed. Mother maybe? "Besides, what if he's been bitten by those things. We can't take a chance."

"I'm letting him in," another man said, this one older. He rose and started walking towards the door. Blair did his best to look harmless as the man approached. He stopped at the door and turned the bolt, then heaved until the glass slid open. He peered out at Blair. "Get inside and be quick about it. Those things can show up at any moment."

Blair ducked inside, waiting near the grocery carts while the man slid the door shut. He hurried back to the produce section, gesturing towards Blair to follow. The man led him to the back where the other three figures all squatted in darkness.

"I'm Miguel, this is Yvessa, her son Juan, and that's Carlos," Miguel explained. He leaned forward, the moonlight illuminating the left side of this face. "Listen, you ain't been bit, have you? By those things."

"No, I haven't," Blair replied.

"How did you get past them then? They're everywhere," asked the woman Miguel had introduced as Yvessa.

"You wouldn't believe me and it's not that important. My friends and I are doing our best to clear the city, but like you said those things are everywhere," he said, unsure how much he should reveal. He wished they'd discussed what to actually say before approaching survivors. Too late now.

"You're one of those wolf things, aren't you?" Juan said, a bit louder than the others in his excitement. "I told mom that I saw one of them fighting the zombies. She didn't believe me, but it makes sense. Everyone just sort of forgot all the werewolves when the zombies came, but they're still out there. A lot of them. They stopped killing us and started killing zombies. Guess they hate them even more than they hate us."

"Yes, I'm one of them," Blair admitted. Maybe it wasn't the smartest move, but they were going to find out soon enough. "Listen, I know the werewolves went crazy and a lot of people died. That's over. Werewolves will kill the zombies and protect you."

"You expect us to believe that? You eat people," Yvessa screeched, voice echoing through the store.

Everyone froze. They waited for several long heartbeats, but there was nothing. Maybe the zombies hadn't heard.

"I know you've got no reason to trust me, so judge me by my actions. There's a church up on that hill with a tall gate around the grounds. We've already cleared the zombies there, and we've stock-piled guns and food. If we can get you inside, you should be safe," Blair explained, praying they'd accept his help. "If you stay here, sooner or later they'll get in. We can't protect humans everywhere, so we've got to get you to where you can protect yourselves."

Silence reigned for several moments as the people eyed each

other in the darkness. No one seemed willing to make a decision until Miguel finally spoke. "My brother was killed by those were-wolves. Hell, for all I know, it could have been you that killed him. I'm not going anywhere with you."

"So what do you suggest?" Juan asked, glaring up at Miguel. The little kid had spunk. "If we stay here, we're going to die. Besides, if he wants to kill us, what are you going to do about it?"

"He's right," the quiet one finally said. Carlos, that was his name. He stood, hefting a backpack and settling the straps over his shoulders. "There were six of us yesterday. Ten a week ago. We've got to do something or in a few days there won't be anyone left. What's your name, mister?"

"Blair. Blair Smith," he said, offering Carlos a hand. The man had a firm grip. "My friends can be a little frightening, but I want to remind you that we're here to protect you. Follow me."

Blair moved confidently to the door, hoping that Liz wouldn't reveal herself just yet. He'd just gotten through to them, but his control was tenuous. One sudden shock and these people would scatter like a flock of birds.

They made it into the parking lot, a dim expanse of cracked asphalt bordering a two-lane road that led back to the church. Getting there was going to be a lot harder on foot with refugees in tow. Blair turned to face his charges. "I'm going to start by introducing one of my friends. Her name is Liz. Don't be startled when she appears. Liz?"

Liz shimmered into existence, stepping from the shadows. It helped that she'd remained in human form, a beautiful redhead in tight clothing was a lot less intimidating than a nine-foot werewolf. She gave their new friends a warm smile. "Hi there. Like he said, my name is Liz. I'm going to help you get to safety. Just stay between the two of us. Move quickly and quietly and we'll all get through this."

They gave her the deer-in-headlights look, all except Juan, who was just old enough to be ruled by hormones and therefore far more interested in Liz's figure than the fact that she'd just stepped out of thin air. Blair found himself liking the kid.

"This way. Quickly," Blair said, moving up the middle of the street. Juan filed after him immediately, the others a few moments later. Liz brought up the rear as they wound around a low squat building that looked like a school. The road grew steeper until they rounded a block of apartments and finally spotted the church.

Blair scanned the roof until he located Jordan. Line of sight was a limitation for his abilities, as was distance. This was within range, though. He concentrated, sending a thought towards the beefy soldier. *We're coming up the main thoroughfare. Send Bridget to meet us, but hang back with your rifle and pick anything off that gets too close.*

Blair didn't wait for an answer. Jordan was having trouble adapting to his mental abilities, and hadn't learned to send responses yet. He kept moving, slowing a bit as the breathing behind him grew more labored. Sometimes he forgot how much being a werewolf had changed him. Blair had never been in great shape, but since the change things like this were effortless. He could sprint uphill for miles without growing winded. He glanced over his shoulder to see Juan helping Yvessa up the hill. Carlos and Miguel seemed to be faring better, the pair darting nervous glances into darkened apartments.

Something screeched in the distance, followed by the slap of bare feet on pavement. Blair leapt to the top of a neighboring street light, catching the metal with one hand and flipping on top of it. He scanned the dark park between them and the noise.

"Zombies," Blair muttered, scrubbing a hand through his hair. "Why did it have to be zombies? The ancient enemy couldn't have been lawn gnomes or something?"

A mob of pale figures was sprinting in their direction, far more quickly than any zombie he'd seen so far. Damn. A number of movies used fast zombies, but he'd hoped that was just enthusiastic story-telling and that the garden-variety slow walker was all they'd have to deal with.

"Incoming," he called down to the group. Liz looked up to meet his gaze. "There are at least six of them, all coming this way."

"I'll intercept them," Liz called, loping off in that direction. She paused behind a tree to strip off her clothing. Juan wasn't the only one staring.

"Blair," Yvessa screamed, pointing behind him. "There are more of them."

He dropped from the street light, landing in a crouch. A dozen figures emerged from a shattered store front, these ones moving more slowly than those he'd seen in the distance. They were still a threat, though. Blair blurred, starting with a tourist in a Hawaiian shirt on the far left. He severed the spinal cord, then charged a desiccated woman wearing only a single sock. A quick swipe dropped her as he moved on to the next target. The work was swift but grisly.

Yvessa's screams continued unabated, though he could hear Juan pleading with her to be quiet. More and more zombies emerged from buildings. Some drifted out from under the trees in the park. There had to be at least a hundred, maybe more.

Then the runners came into view, too-white bodies barreling through the park in their direction. Liz disappeared into the shadows, reappearing directly behind a runner in the back. She leapt on the pale creature, bearing it to the ground and crushing both skull and spine under her weight. Blair fell back to the group, watching in horror as the other five runners approached. They were so fast, too fast for him to take the time to shift into wolf form.

Liz leapt on top of a second one, bringing it down. There was no way she'd be able to stop them all. A gunshot cracked and a runner's head exploded. Then another. Suddenly Bridget's nine-foot silver form was there, dismembering another. The last one was almost upon them, but Blair glided forward to meet it. Its scarlet eyes glared hatefully at him, and its razored teeth sent a chill coursing down his spine.

Blair blurred, dodging to the right and then back to the left. The move caught the runner off guard, and he seized its head between his hands. A quick jerk snapped the neck and the thing dropped bone-lessly to the ground.

"Nooo," came a shriek from behind. Blair spun to see a group of walkers surrounding the refugees. Miguel stabbed a walker with a long knife that he'd pulled from somewhere, but he was too slow to reach Yvessa. One of the creatures had seized her arm. It bit down on her shoulder, clinging there like a bulldog as it gnawed her flesh. Her shrieks split the night around them.

Blair finally shifted, destroying his clothes as he grew taller and stronger. Fur erupted from his skin as his snout elongated. Then he leapt forward, decapitating the zombie with one blow. He barreled into the next and the next, a single second stretching as he blurred through a sea of zombies. Then it was over, the refugees left amidst islands of bodies, with Bridget, Blair and Liz standing in a protective triangle.

"We all know what happens next," Miguel said, gesturing at Yvessa. "She's going to become one of those things."

"Not like this," Yvessa moaned, sinking to her knees. She cradled her mangled arm in her lap. "It can't end like this. There must be something we can do..."

"Don't look," Liz said, gathering Juan and moving him away from the group.

The boy began to struggle, straining to reach his mother. "No, there has to be something we can do. There has—"

Liz's hand clamped around his shoulder, pulling his face into her chest. "Shhh."

Blair knew what he had to do, and it had to be done while Liz was comforting the boy. He stepped forward and snapped Yvessa's neck before she was even aware he was moving. It came more easily than he'd expected, the first time he'd ever had to kill a defenseless person. Was that the beast's influence, or had he changed more than just physically?

Juan spun away from Liz, giving a shriek as he dropped to his knees next to his mother's corpse. Blair hated himself, but what choice was there?

None, Ka-Dun. His beast rumbled, somber and subdued. It didn't speak often these days, not since they had truly joined.

They'd been gone from the Ark too long and they needed to get back.

5

NAMELESS

The shambling corpse had lost his name. It hovered just out of reach, as distant as the stars. It bothered him, this lack of a name. Bothered him a great deal. Almost as much as his imprisonment, an unwilling passenger in a body that seemed to have its own agenda. That body shambled forward, weaving through the deserted street. It passed unfamiliar houses, odd structures set atop two-foot stilts. They were different than the houses the nameless corpse knew, with thinner walls and thatched roofs. It would have been interesting to inspect them more closely, but his body shambled forward with no regard for his orders.

It staggered, tripping over a shape in the darkness. His body looked down at the obstruction. A corpse, or what remained of one. The flesh had been meticulously stripped clean. The bones cracked, already drained of marrow. The tide of hunger rose, threatening to overwhelm him as it had so many times over the last week. It never abated unless he was feeding, resuming the very instant he stopped chewing.

His body turned its gaze back to the town, studying the line of houses. The flickering light of a candle came from a window four houses down on the left. The darkness obscured any differences, making the house identical to its neighbors. His body shambled towards it, slow and awkward. That frustrated him too, though he didn't know any other way of walking. It felt...wrong.

His leg shook violently as he raised a foot, but he avoided toppling as his body set it on the first step. The worn wood creaked loudly under his weight, but it held. He attempted the second. Then the third. A fourth step carried him to the door, faintly illuminated by the glow in the living room window. A gasp came from inside. The light winked out.

He listened. Breathing came from behind the door. There were heartbeats. Two of them. Both rapid. Should he be able to hear heartbeats? No, he was positive that was wrong. Different. New.

His body raised a trembling hand to the door handle, wrapping a weak grip around it. It turned with a click, the door creaking open with a little urging. Shouldn't they have locked the door? Or at least blocked it with a dresser or bed?

His body staggered inside, gaze sweeping the room. It was gathered in darkness, except for the patch of bamboo planks in the pool of moonlight. The heartbeats were more frantic now, thundering from the corner of the room. He could just barely make out a pair of shapes huddled against the wall. One taller, sheltering the smaller one. A woman and child. Horror bloomed, giving way to panic. Every fiber of his being yearned to warn them, to scream that they should run. All that emerged was a low wail, the first time that he'd been able to force his body to do anything.

It shambled across the room, moving towards the doomed family. Why didn't they run? They could probably make it past him. He was slow, ungainly. Yet they cowered there, praying he wouldn't notice them. His body crossed the gap in three awkward steps, then lunged at the larger figure. An old woman with short white hair. She flinched, but made no attempt to run. Instead she shoved the smaller figure forward. "Antonio, corre!"

The little boy shot to his feet, bolting across the bamboo floor like a deer as he burst from the room into the night. The nameless corpse turned to watch the boy's flight, then turned back to his prey. He seized the woman's arm, biting savagely into her shoulder. His weight bore her to the wooden floor with a hollow thump as he began to feed. At first she screamed and thrashed, but that grew weaker as he tore loose mouthful after mouthful. The hunger faded for the first time in days. In its place came clarity. He remembered.

There had been a pyramid, surrounded by bright lights. Men with guns. Werewolves. That couldn't be right, could it? There were no such things as werewolves.

6

THE RING

Blair scrubbed a hand through sweaty hair as he trudged towards his chamber, somewhere past exhausted.

"Blair," Bridget called from behind him. He turned to find her hurrying down the passageway. She gave a dazzling smile when he stopped and waited for her. It brought back so many memories, most of them unwelcome. "I'm too keyed up to sleep after that mess in Cajamarca. I was thinking maybe we could do a little sparring."

"You mean you're looking for a punching bag," Blair said. He returned the smile, focusing on one of the better memories. It was nice to relax, just a hair. He'd been on edge since the second wave hit—hell, since he'd first come to the Ark almost three months ago.

Being forced to leave behind survivors didn't help. He knew no one was happy about that, but he'd been the one to argue for it. The Mother was right. They couldn't get bogged down by a small group. They had to think big picture, as much as it killed him to do so. "I always get my ass handed to me. I've never been able to catch you with any of my tricks. Guess I'm not much of a Jedi."

"You'll never win with that attitude. I've never known you to give up. Isn't your manhood at stake being beaten by a girl?" she teased, linking an arm through his as they strolled towards the sparring ring the Mother had none too subtly demanded that they practice in daily. He knew he should disengage, but damn if it didn't feel good. He deserved a little gratification. She smelled heavenly, familiar and warm.

"Being beaten by a girl? You mean having my throat torn out by a nine-foot werewolf who can vanish at will?" Blair asked, shaking his head. "Trust me, my manhood is intact. It's not a fair fight. Girl were-wolves shouldn't hit boys."

Bridget laughed, jeans clinging to her like a second skin as she skipped ahead into the sparring ring at the center of a cavernous chamber. It was a fascinating invention. A glowing white ring bordered a wide black swathe of obsidian, raised about two inches above the surrounding room. The moment Bridget entered it the ring began to pulse in time with her heartbeat. She crouched at the far side, a predatory grin on her face. How stupid was he, doing this yet again?

Bridget pulled off her shirt and dropped it on the stone just outside the ring. The bra came a moment later, followed by the jeans. At least there were some perks to this. He pulled off his own shirt, adding garments until they both stood naked. That had been the most awkward part the first few days, especially when they all sparred together. Now he was used to the nakedness, no longer embarrassed. It was hard to be, after the werewolf virus had reshaped his body into something any gym rat would envy.

"All right, let's get this over with," he said, forcing himself to take the final step into the ring. It flared brightly, veins of light running inward towards the center of the ring. He shifted as he moved, the change like breathing now. In the span of three spaces he gained two feet of fur and muscle, the silver mirrored in Bridget's coat as she shifted too.

Then Blair was elsewhere. There was no ring, just a vast jungle. The Amazon this time. He hadn't seen this level before, but he couldn't waste time gawking. Bridget would already be studying the ring, learning the terrain. She'd find the best place to ambush him and then strike, when he least expected it. It always began this way. How could it not? He couldn't hide from a female and she could effortlessly fool his senses. The only advantage he had was speed.

Blair blurred to the top of a wide, bowed tree with thick drooping fronds. He'd never seen it before, but then he'd also never been to the Amazon. The bark was leathery against his bare feet. It smelled bitter. There was flash of movement in the corner of his vision. He spun, leaping to another branch to get a look at the cause. A pair of squirrel-sized monkeys chittered quietly on a branch. Their black and white fur and drooping mustaches lent them a dignified air.

Macaws shrieked from neighboring trees, a counterpoint to the intermittent drone of insects. In the distance a jaguar roared. The jungle flowed around him, unaware of the predators in its midst. Maintaining that advantage was critical. If the animals fell silent it would alert Bridget to his presence, whereas he'd get no such warning. The animals were simply incapable of detecting a shadow-dancing female.

Blair blurred forward, grabbing a thick branch with both hands. He swung, using his momentum to carry him to a neighboring tree. He cushioned his landing as much as possible, but the monkeys in the neighboring tree still fell silent. Hopefully Bridget hadn't heard that. He scanned the surrounding jungle, layers of shadow obscuring the jungle floor. Only a few rays of sun broke the canopy, isolated pools of light in a greater shadow.

He released the limb, dropping silently onto a fern below. It cushioned his fall enough that the droning insects continued uninterrupted. He dropped into a crouch, back planted against the tree. There had to be a way to detect her. He couldn't see or smell her and he couldn't probe her mind, at least not effectively. Her defenses were too strong. So what were his options?

Shaping had to be the key. It was his one advantage. The Mother wouldn't have left an entire gender defenseless, so there must be a way to compensate for a female's stealth. Hmm. He couldn't pierce Bridget's mind when he probed her, but he *could* feel resistance when he tried. How could he use that? Maybe he could somehow broadcast his will in all directions like a sonar burst. A sort of ping.

This is possible, Ka-Dun. Dispersing your will weakly in all directions. Ingenious, the beast rumbled. It spoke rarely these days, now that they'd joined fully.

Disperse his will. He considered the problem for a moment, blurring to another tree trunk, then another so quickly that he hoped Bridget couldn't follow. How could he do that? Visualization. That seemed to be how all their powers worked. Blair imagined his will as a giant balloon, slowly filling as he pushed harder. It grew larger and larger, bulging around him in a shimmering wave he suspected only he could see. He pushed harder, straining until it was as large as he could make it. Then still further. Finally it burst, spraying bits of his will in a blast around him. It washed harmlessly through the jungle in every spot. Except one.

He met resistance in a neighboring tree, just a few feet behind him to the left. Blair blurred, diving into a roll as Bridget's claws raked the space he'd just occupied. He flipped to his feet, spinning to face her as Bridget melted back into the shadows.

"That's the first time you've anticipated one of my attacks," her disembodied voice came from the shadows. "What did you do differently?"

"Trade secret," he replied, grinning as he repeated the trick. *There.*

He lunged at the darkness, his swipe connecting ever so briefly with flesh. His claws came back tinged with blood, but there was no sign of Bridget.

"Clever, whatever it is. You can find me now. And here you didn't want to spar," she teased from the shadows.

Furry arms shot from the darkness behind him, wrapping around his midsection as Bridget's much heavier body bore him to the ground. He struggled briefly, but now that she had a hold of him there was no escape. She was much, much stronger.

Then she began the worst form of torment, the kind she knew better than anyone how much he dreaded. She tickled him. He thrashed back and forth, struggling to free himself as he wheezed out laugh after laugh.

"A-all right," he panted, going limp. "I yield."

The jungle vanished, replaced by the obsidian ring with its bright border. Bridget's form wavered, shifting back into a *very* naked woman. Her impossibly soft breasts pressed against his back, her face buried against the fur behind his neck.

Blair shifted too, rolling onto his back. Bridget snuggled up to him, draping an arm across his chest and nestling her head on his shoulder. It brought him back to countless mornings in bed, long conversations about interesting topics after hours of lovemaking. The longing warred with the pain of betrayal. Part of him recognized this as an invitation to more pain, but he stayed where he was. Her scent was overpowering.

"I'm sorry, Blair. For everything. I hope you understand that," she murmured, burying her face against his shoulder. It actually sounded sincere. Maybe it even was. People could change, couldn't they?

"It looks like the ring is already in use, though not for sparring," Cyntia's thickly accented voice came from the doorway.

"We'll just have to wait our turn," Liz replied, tone dry as the Sahara.

Blair scrambled to his feet, blushing in embarrassment and guilt, though he wasn't sure why he should. It's not as if he were dating Liz, though they'd certainly grown close during their mad flight from Peru. Bridget leapt to her feet, snatching her shirt from the ground and covering her chest with it. She refused to meet Liz's gaze. He was a little ashamed of standing there naked, but he squared his shoulders anyway.

"We just finished," Blair offered. Lamely.

"I'll bet you did," Liz muttered, expression unreadable.

"Blair learned a new trick," Bridget said, obviously attempting to change the subject. She glanced down at her nakedness, blushing scarlet. "He can find us even when we're hiding in the shadows."

"Interesting," Liz said, striding purposely towards the ring. She'd already regained her composure and if she was angry, she certainly didn't show it. "How do you do it, Blair?"

"I send out a sort of 'ping.' Like radar," he explained, exiting the ring and meeting Liz and Cyntia near the edge. He picked up his shirt, but didn't put it on yet. He'd be damned if he was going to act embarrassed, no matter how he felt. Bridget stood a few feet away, still avoiding Liz's gaze. "I can't easily invade your minds, but I feel the resistance when I try. If I send out a weak ping in all directions I can sense where you are."

"Impressive," Cyntia said, crossing her arms over a more than ample chest. The gesture seemed deliberate, so Blair studiously avoided looking. He was already in enough trouble, though he wasn't sure why he should be. "Did you discover this technique, or did your beast reveal it?"

"It was my idea. The beast seemed rather surprised," he replied, eyeing the safety of the door. "I'm going to go grab a shower. I'll see you all at dinner."

Bridget started to follow, but Liz touched her arm. "Would you stay, Bridget? I was hoping we could spar."

Bridget's creamy face paled. She shot Blair a worried look and then turned back to Liz. "Of course. There's still a lot you can teach me."

"Great. Cyntia, why don't you help Blair get dinner started? We can spar later. Bridget and I need some time alone."

7

HIGH SCHOOL BULLSHIT

L iz stepped across the glowing line into the circle, dropping her sports bra onto the stone outside, along with the rest of her clothes. She rolled her neck, unlimbering for the fight. Then she shifted, marveling in the miracle of it.

The process still hurt. How could it not? Bones snapped and popped as her body rearranged itself, limbs lengthening and muscles swelling. The worst part was definitely the muzzle splitting her face, and she teared up briefly in the same way she had when a girl had broken her nose back in the fifth grade.

When the process was complete she'd gained over three feet in height, and a thick auburn pelt covered her nakedness. That had been a mercy when she first started, but constant combat and the burdens of leadership had burned the embarrassment out of her.

She paused, turning to face the shorter woman. Bridget had dark wavy hair, beautiful eyes, and a dazzling smile. There wasn't a wasted ounce anywhere on that perfect body. She could see why Blair was interested, but it still stung. Liz felt frumpy beside her.

"I'll be the target," she said, walking to the middle of the ring. The lights began pulsing in time with her heartbeat.

Bridget shifted as well, becoming a majestic silver just a few inches shorter than Liz. She stepped into the ring, but the scenery didn't change. That was a first.

The ring senses purpose, Ka-Ken, Liz's beast rumbled. *You seek a direct confrontation, a battle of strength. Trickery is not needed, and so the ring offers no distraction.*

Was she really picking a fight over a man? Maybe. It seemed like exactly the sort of thing she'd have chastised her brother for doing, a fistfight over a girl. Her desire to do exactly the same thing was testament to how much the virus had changed her.

"So have you known Blair a long time?" she asked, turning to face Bridget as the smaller wolf wrapped the shadows about her. She was gone a heartbeat later, undetectable save for her disembodied voice.

"Yes, for a long time now. We went to Stanford together. Him, Steve, Sheila and I," Bridget's voice explained. It circled slowly around Liz as Bridget moved. "We dated for three years, most of it spent at school or later at a dig site in China."

There was a moment of silence and then a flash of silver as Bridget lunged from the right. Liz flowed into one of the combat forms the Mother had taught her, catching Bridget's neck with one hand and her right arm with the other. That left one of Bridget's arms free, and she raked Liz's chest in a spray of blood.

Liz responded by slamming Bridget's face into the obsidian, then rolling away and disappearing into the shadows. Now it was her turn to attack from the shadows. They'd alternate until they grew tired, the idea being that they could practice both attacking and defending. Liz had taken to the exercises with a surprising fervor. She really enjoyed losing herself in the activity, the primal joy of combat. Usually she did, anyway.

"But you broke up?" Liz asked, circling Bridget. Her opponent shifted slowly, ears twitching as she sought Liz.

"A long time ago, yes," Bridget said, dropping her gaze to the stone. If werewolves could have blushed, Liz had the feeling that Bridget would be. "Steve was his best friend, and Sheila was mine. Blair took a job heading up a dig and it took all of his time. He didn't come to bed. Didn't eat with me anymore. I didn't see him for months. Steve..."

A wellspring of rage bubbled up in Liz as she understood where Bridget was going with this. She lunged from the shadows behind Bridget, wrapping one arm around her to pin both arms while the other tore out Bridget's throat. Liz shoved Bridget to the stone and then rolled back into a crouch while she waited.

"You slept with his best friend?" Liz asked, more than a little satisfied by the amount of blood. What a mind fuck. That explained so much of the subtext, why Blair seemed interested in Bridget one moment and angry the next. "I'm amazed he still speaks to you."

Bridget struggled to her feet, the terrible wounds healing almost instantly. Her ruined throat knitted itself back together as she slipped into the shadows.

"So am I," Bridget agreed, sounding embarrassed as she circled Liz. "I don't deserve it. I cheated on him. The worst part is that when he came to the dig...I abandoned Steve. We'd been on the rocks for a while, but that's no excuse. He was dying from radiation sickness, and I ran to Blair for comfort. I didn't deserve either of them. I still don't."

"But you're pursuing him anyway?" Liz asked. She kept her tone even, but was willing to bet that Bridget sensed her disapproval.

"I shouldn't, but Liz, I can't help it. I love him. I always have. Even when I was with Steve I never stopped loving Blair. If he told me to leave him alone I would, but he hasn't. You can't blame me for trying," she said, voice still moving as she continued to circle. Liz got the sense that she was looking for some sort of absolution, but she wasn't the one who could offer that. "I know it's wrong. I know I should just let him go, but I feel like I have a second chance. To be a better person. The woman he deserves. He's an amazing man."

"A man you don't deserve," Liz growled, flexing her claws. "If you hurt him again, there will be hell to pay. I promise you that."

8
_____

MOTHER'S RETURN

"You are a very stupid man, Blair Smith," Cyntia said, nose slightly upturned like some South American parody of a Valley girl. The statement was made while she filled a battered pot with water, then set it gently on top of the Coleman camp stove they'd liberated from the installation outside. The Mohn Corp. soldiers who'd occupied it were all dead, slaughtered by the Mother in her seemingly infinite fury.

"You won't get an argument from me," he agreed, opening the dented cabinet that they'd used to store their dwindling supply of food. Well, processed food anyway. They could always go hunting, but that still felt incredibly odd despite the fact that Blair enjoyed it. "How about beef stroganoff tonight?"

Blair picked up a large packet and tore the seal. He set it on the marble next to the camp stove, marveling at the veins of gold that shot through the rock. Its value was incalculable and it could be found throughout the Ark.

The powdery substance inside the packet smelled like preservatives, but at least it was better than the smell of his own sweat. He would have made time for that shower, except that he had a feeling

Cyntia would have insisted on joining him. She had an odd idea about what constituted boundaries.

"Do you know why you are a very stupid man?" Cyntia asked, unperturbed by his attempt to change the subject.

"I have a feeling you're about to tell me," Blair said, suppressing the sigh. It was like a bad anime show, one male character surrounded by women. There was Jordan of course, but somehow he managed to sidestep this crap. Blair missed Trevor.

"You are a fool because Liz desires you. She is a much better match than that little vixen with the shifty eyes. Liz is strong. You need a strong woman, Blair Smith," Cyntia explained, lowering the temperature on the camp stove as the water came to a boil.

"I'd love to hear you call Bridget weak to her face," Blair retorted, pulling the mouth of the packet wide so that Cyntia could pour in the water. Once it was full, he used the strip at the top to reseal it. It would cook for the next few minutes, but the others would arrive long before then. Their enhanced senses allowed them to smell cooking anywhere in the Ark.

"You dance about with words. Do not play such games. You know I am right," she said, giving him a measured glance. She began setting bowls around the wide marble table. It was flanked by a pair of benches cut from some sort of foam. There was enough room to seat twenty, so they only took up a very small corner.

"You're right," Blair admitted, surprising himself. He picked up the packet of stroganoff by the top edges and carried it to the table. "Bridget is bad news. I know that."

Cyntia stopped, turning slowly to face him. She gestured with a fistful of plastic spoons. "Then you have no business cavorting with her. She is a harlot. You should tell her you will never be with her again."

Realization struck like a bolt of lightning. He'd never told Bridget to leave. Or even to leave him alone. He'd accepted, even welcomed the attention. Why? It wasn't fair unless he wanted to get back together with her. Did he?

"Stroganoff again?" Jordan boomed as he strode into the chamber. He was almost as menacing in human form, all muscle and stubble. "What I wouldn't give for a sixteen-ounce cut of prime rib."

"You are a stupid man too, Aaron Jordan," Cyntia said, a grin slipping into place. She sat languidly at the table, placing the last spoon next to her bowl. "But you are very easy on the eyes. Not so easy as Trevor, but he would not mind me looking, I think."

"There you go again," Jordan said, sliding his massive frame onto the bench across from Cyntia. He shook his head, giving her a warm smile. "You're a passable soldier, but you're not at all my type."

"Stroganoff again?" Liz said, striding into the room with the grace of a panther. She really was beautiful, in a wholly different way than Bridget. Liz's long copper hair was more honest, her sapphire gaze something he could imagine waking up to. That said nothing of her figure, even wrapped in the baggy green fatigues that Mohn had unintentionally provided. She was a lot taller, almost eye level. That had really grown on him.

Bridget strolled in afterwards. She darted Blair a shy smile, then quickly looked away.

"Yes, it is just about ready. Sit and I will serve you," Cyntia said. She took the role of hostess very seriously, something that could almost never be said of her. She popped open the packet, using a large plastic spoon to ladle the steaming stroganoff into bowls. It smelled heavenly despite being freeze dried, but it didn't satisfy the primal urge for meat that he'd been saddled with since his transformation.

Liz and Bridget dropped onto the bench next to Jordan, so Blair slid in next to Cyntia. He picked up his spoon, but it would be several minutes before the food was cool enough to eat. "It's been a week now. I wonder what things are like back in the States."

"Bad," Jordan said. He shoveled a spoonful of stroganoff into his mouth. "Oww. Hot. Yeah, it will be bad. The power would have gone out even without the second wave. It takes people to run power plants and zombies would have made that impossible. So you've got isolated groups everywhere because no one can communicate. Food will be a serious issue. So will medicine. Not to mention the zombies themselves."

"I could have told you that. I watched *The Walking Dead*, too," Bridget said with a little smirk.

"The writers of that show were wise men," Jordan replied, shoveling a second spoonful.

"I have to wonder how far the werewolves have spread," Blair added. He took his first tentative bite. Still hot, but good. "Peru was the epicenter and we still have problems with zombies. There were less werewolves in the United States, especially the east coast. They've got to be in bad shape."

A figure glided into the room, snuffing the conversation like a candle. The Mother had returned. Her ivory garments were spattered with blood but were otherwise undamaged. He still hadn't figured out how she shifted with her clothes. Was it the garment or some power? A waterfall of silver locks flowed down deceptively delicate shoulders, framing an oval face set with emerald eyes. She was both breathtaking and otherworldly.

"You still insist on eating that goop," she snorted, sitting crosslegged on the bench next to Blair. She slapped a haunch of meat from what he guessed might be a goat on the table before her. "We are carnivores. We eat meat. You need to hunt."

She seized the haunch with both hands, ripping off a mouthful and chewing blissfully as the rest of them gazed on in a mixture of horror and jealousy. His stomach rumbled.

She opened her eyes and blinked twice. "Why are you staring at me?"

"It's not important," Blair interjected, surprised again at the vast gulf between the Mother's culture and their own world. "We found survivors in Cajamarca and did our best to set up a sanctuary for them. While we were there we ran into something strange. Zombies that were faster and stronger than the others. A more evolved version of the walkers."

"Evolved," the Mother replied, cocking her head as if tasting the word. She picked a piece of fat from between her teeth before continuing. "That doesn't quite fit. They have fed upon the flesh of others, which gives them strength. The more they feed, the stronger and smarter they become. This is why they were a more challenging opponent than the shamblers you first encountered."

"How large can they get?" Liz asked.

"I've seen a deathless 30-spans high, this one a primate from the Cradle. It took Ra two millennia to grow it and me another six to destroy it," she said. Blair's jaw dropped at the cavalier way she discussed such a time span.

"Mother, I know this might be rude but how old are you?" he asked, bracing himself for a possible explosion.

"I have seen the length of an entire longest count, roughly twenty-four millennia," she said, continuing her meal.

Blair's wasn't the only amazed face. "We must be like children to you. The oldest living human is barely a century. Our entire recorded history is around five thousand years. You've seen nearly five times that amount of time."

"Not truly," the Mother replied between mouthfuls of raw meat. "I was only awake for eleven millennia. I slept for thirteen between ages, when the sun was dim and cold. But enough of me. Tell me more of your journey. You say you've helped these survivors find sanctuary? How many are there?"

"We only located a handful, but there are almost certainly others," Liz interjected, eyeing the Mother as she waved steam away from her bowl. "We wanted to stay and find more, but you insisted we return. I'm still not sure I agree with that. We should be out there protecting people, but instead we're back here relaxing."

"I understand your feelings," the Mother said, heaving a sigh. She stopped eating and divided her attention among them. "You want to protect and that is to the good, but you must learn to take a longer view. I'm afraid I *do* see you as children, though there is no insult in that. You think in years or perhaps in decades. I ruled this continent and the one to the north for sixty centuries, and spent another fifty in the land you call Africa. I have learned the ugly patterns of our race. The people in this city are important, but not nearly so important as your learning to hone your abilities. I cannot risk you being overwhelmed when you are untrained. That is why I needed you to return, why you are not there protecting those who cannot protect themselves.

"Fear not, though. On the morrow we will return to Cajamarca and I will create champions from those willing," the Mother explained. "They will help protect the city as you watch over this Ark."

"Can't you watch over the Ark?" Bridget asked, eyeing the Mother sidelong. "I mean, you're stronger than all of us. We could help the city while you protect this place."

"Would that I could," she said, heaving another sigh. "The central chamber is damaged nearly beyond repair. I must create new control rods and I can find the material I need in only one place. There is an island to the east, far out to sea. I must find a ship and journey there to obtain the stone. We will need the Ark's full strength in the years to come. Tomorrow I will return to Cajamarca. Liz and Blair will remain. The rest of you will accompany me."

"Mother," Cyntia said, clearing her throat before continuing. "I wish to search for Trevor, the friend we lost during the second wave."

"This is the one you fear may have fallen prey to the deathless?" the Mother replied, smile melting. She rested a sympathetic hand on Cyntia's shoulder. "It is possible the man you knew still exists, but that is extremely unlikely. You are most likely to find a shattered husk with no memory of the man he once was. If you must seek your lover then do so, but steel yourself for what might come. The path you choose is difficult to walk."

"Thank you, Mother," Cyntia replied, eyes falling to her bowl.

"So you want me to go with you?" Jordan asked. It was the most uncomfortable Blair had ever seen him. Not surprising. The Mother *had* ripped his arms off just a few weeks before.

"Yes," the Mother said, giving a mischievous smile. "I can smell your fear, but you contain it well. I know you remember well our last encounter, but rest assured, you are one of my children now. I would have you serve as Ka-Dun to Bridget. Ka-Ken need the support of a Ka-Dun and I believe Liz has already laid claim to Blair."

The table fell silent. Blair's cheeks heated and he suddenly found his stroganoff very interesting.

9

RETURN TO CAJAMARCA

J ordan slung his pack over his shoulders, cinching the straps around his waist and chest. It carried perhaps two hundred pounds of ordinance, enough to make him the center of a massive fireworks display, should it come anywhere near open flame. He studied his reflection in the mirrored door. His close cropped hair was orderly, his black t-shirt comfortably tight. He *looked* the same. But he wasn't.

He'd died back there, torn apart by the Mother when she'd shredded Mohn's forces. Curiously, of the two hundred people she'd killed he was the only werewolf to be found. There were many sets of tracks leading away, but he had no idea where the others had gone or why. Perhaps it was some animal instinct, some survival reflex that made them flee a predator like the Mother. One he apparently lacked.

He touched the smooth stone door and it slid silently open, revealing the colorful corridor he was already growing used to. He strode boldly down the western passage, passing small diamond-shaped lights every ten feet. They afforded an excellent view of the hieroglyphs, though he appreciated them more for the tactical knowledge they might provide than any beauty they might possess. Many recounted battles with the zombies.

"Jordan," Blair called, trotting towards him. He pulled up a few feet away. "So you and Bridget are heading out with the Mother this morning?"

"Back to Cajamarca, yeah," he said, falling in beside Blair. The pair made their way towards their hastily erected mess. So odd to be walking next to someone he'd battled to the death only a week before. "Hopefully we can find more survivors and get them to the church. No idea if any will accept her offer, but I suspect a few will be desperate enough to try."

"Let's hope so. We're going to need all the help we can get," Blair replied. They entered the mess to find everyone else already there.

"Morning," Bridget called, giving a little wave. She was sitting next to Liz, whose hair was loose today. It looked good on her. The Mother sat across from them, cross-legged on the bench. She ate nothing, eyeing the food distastefully. There was no sign of Cyntia, but Jordan could smell her. She'd probably just left.

"Eat your muck swiftly," the Mother ordered, gesturing to the empty seat next to her. A pair of bowls had been set out, the pleasant aroma of maple oatmeal steaming out of each. "We'll leave as soon as you finish. I want to reach this city by midday."

"That's not possible," Jordan said, sliding onto the bench next to her. He picked up his spoon and stirred the oatmeal. Maybe it wasn't smart to contradict her, but the words were already out, so he forged ahead. "It took us two days to get there last time out."

"Just because you have not done it doesn't mean it isn't possible. I will teach you to blur over long distances. This ability is like a muscle and will get stronger through use," she explained, crinkling her nose as Jordan took his first bite. He still found it odd that she survived solely on meat. He was as much a carnivore as any man, but one needed chocolate and coffee too.

"What about Bridget?" he asked, nodding towards the petite brunette. "She can't blur."

"She will ride your shadow," the Mother explained, as if that settled the matter.

Bridget paled and he could guess why. Liz had already learned that trick, but Bridget seemed slower on the uptake. Not that she wasn't intelligent, but whatever gave them their power was harder for her to use. It was the same for him. Blair picked up all this shaping crap with ease, yet for Jordan it took concentrated effort to do things that Blair considered simple.

"I'm ready," Jordan said, dropping his spoon in the empty bowl. No sense putting it off. They had work to be about.

"Very well," the Mother said, rising lithely from her seat. Bridget stood as well, hefting her black nylon pack.

She glanced at Liz and her eyes hardened with determination. Then she turned back to Jordan. Her whole body began to tremble, and a moment later she flowed into the shadows. Into his shadow, to be more specific.

Jordan hefted his own pack, feeling more than a little uncomfortable that Bridget and her pack had vanished so completely. He rose from the bench and followed the Mother as she made her way up the northern corridor towards the surface. The Mother glided into a run, swift but not quite a sprint. Was this the pace she planned to set for the whole trip? It had that feel. Could he maintain it?

Of course he could. He was a god-damn killing machine. He could run for days as a human. Now? Jordan pushed himself, bouncing past the Mother and into the lead. The Mother shifted, suddenly nine and a half feet of silver fur. She bounded off the wall, retaking the lead. He matched her shift, his shirt and pants shredded by the move. Damn it.

Try as he might, he couldn't catch her. She shot a grin over her shoulder. It was alarmingly childlike for a woman who'd lived forever as a goddess. They burst from the tunnel into the bright morning light, blazingly hot but pleasant nonetheless. They loped southwest, heading back the direction they'd just recently come. Jordan didn't know what to expect, but if nothing else, this trip would be interesting.

10

IRAKESH

I rakesh snapped awake, blinking rapidly as his eyes adjusted. Dim splashes of ruby and emerald danced on the walls, cast by the gems powering the rejuvenator that had carried him into this new age. The entire structure vibrated as the crystal became a thick viscous liquid that pushed him up through the top. It hardened underneath him, leaving him atop its warm surface.

He dropped lightly to his feet as his gaze darted frantically around the secondary rejuvenation chamber. There were six other rejuvenators, none of the gems active. The silver door was sealed, the Ark glyph on its surface dark. Odd. That should have been lit, even if faintly. Had the Ark run out of power? That couldn't be or he'd have never awakened.

Perhaps he'd been detected and Isis had locked down the chamber. If that were the case he'd be dead in minutes, assuming he could evade her that long. If he'd had a heartbeat, it would be thudding frantically in his chest. He struggled to calm himself. She wasn't going to catch him. He was as safe as he could be nestled in the very heart of his enemy's stronghold. Irakesh had reservations for the first time since he'd concocted this mad plan. Could it be done?

Such thoughts were useless. He was committed to this course

now. If he failed, he'd die in the attempt and even if he somehow lived, Ra would flay him alive as an example of those who failed her. A harsh mistress, his mother.

He padded silently on the supple soles of his boots, creeping to the doorway that led into the corridor beyond. All was dark out there, hardly a surprise given the sabotage he'd arranged just prior to the Ark's internment. All sorts of systems would be failing, though he'd been excruciatingly careful to ensure that the rejuvenators were safe from his tampering.

Irakesh channeled a bit of energy to his eyes, drinking in the near darkness as if it were lit by the full moon. He crept down the corridor, straining for the faintest of sounds. There was nothing this far down. He was on the Ark's nineteenth tier, a full eight tiers beneath the surface. Either Isis hadn't made it down this far, or had sealed it off after her exploration. There was no movement; not even the air stirred.

He was completely sealed off. Had he needed to breathe, such a thing would have been the end of him. Ptah's shaping ensured that the Ark would see him as a champion, which would normally mean life support. Yet he'd blinded the sensors in this area, so the Ark had no idea that someone was alive down here.

Irakesh padded silently up the corridor, marveling at the fantastic hieroglyphs. They told a tale he was familiar with, that of Isis's exodus from the Cradle. Yet there were many differences from the narrative Ra had circulated. These glyphs painted Isis as a savior of her people, the creator of champions who shielded the unblooded from the depredations of the evil deathless. How quaint. So near the truth and yet not.

He reached a wide stairwell leading to the next tier. Each step was a struggle, because they'd been created for the much larger champions. The males topped seven feet and the females were even larger. Most deathless, like him, retained a near-human form. Some could reshape their bodies, though that was generally reserved for those much older than Irakesh and was a more permanent process.

A wide silver door blocked the corridor, set with the glyph

meaning Ark. He hesitated before placing his hand on the warm
metal. This was the moment of truth, the time during which he'd be
discovered or would know that he was still cloaked by the shadows
and by his subterfuge. When the door opened it would trigger an
alert. Anyone linked to the Ark would know that he was moving
down here. If that someone was Isis, then his very short life was
about to end.

Irakesh pressed his palm into the silver, waiting an eternity as it
opened. He blurred up the hallway, using some of his dwindling
energy reserves to get some distance from the door. He stopped near
a statue of Ka-Ket, the Mother's favorite daughter. He'd never met her,
but battle legends said she was an implacable foe. Often called
Jes'Ka, or 'eater of death' in the old tongue. She towered over him,
spear held in both hands. Beautiful. He wished he could have met
her in person.

He waited at her feet, listening for the sound that would herald
his death. None came. Perhaps Isis had already departed and was
securing the area. That had been the plan, after all. Something must
be occupying her attention or she'd have felt his presence moving
through the heart of her sanctuary and come to investigate.

Irakesh trotted silently down the corridor, taking the most direct
route across this tier. He repeated this five more times, gliding
through silent rooms that hadn't known the sun in thirteen millennia. It was a tomb, this place. He exited the corridor into the Ark's
central chamber. This would be the most dangerous place. If there
was opposition, it would be here.

He gathered the shadows thick about him, enveloping him like
the womb of the very night itself. It wouldn't stop Isis; she was too
canny for that. But it would fool any of her Ka-Dun, had she any left
in the Ark. Irakesh crept between the monoliths, gawking at the
catastrophic damage around him. The entire chamber had been torn
apart by some unknown weapon. Gouges marred walls and floor. The
obelisks that powered the place were shattered, only three of five
intact. This was why Isis hadn't detected him. She'd been unable to.
This Ark was damaged past usefulness. Unless she repaired it, one of

the greatest wonders the world had ever known was little more than a fancy cave.

Was this somehow his work? It couldn't be. His sabotage had only damaged a few critical systems. This place had been through a protracted battle with a level of violence he'd never witnessed. Though it made his job easier a part of him cried out at the destruction. This place was more than priceless. It *was* power.

He crept closer to the access key, a statue of Isis, life-sized and incredibly intricate. He could feel the power matrix within, thrumming with the life the Ark somehow still clung to. It was enough for his purpose. He reached for Isis's outstretched palm, wrapping his cool fingers around the warm stone. It pulsed, sending a jolt shooting up his arm. It hurt, but he didn't dare release the hand before it had done its work. Another pulse, then a third and fourth in rapid succession.

Just like that it was over. He stared down at his hand in wonder. He'd done it. He'd stolen the access key for the Ark of the Redwood. If he could make his way to the northern continent he could finally show them all. He'd become one of the most powerful Ark Lords the world had ever seen.

11

DEATHLESS

If staring at a woman's ass were illegal, then the police would already be on their way. Blair gaped openly as Liz bent over to pick up a stack of heavy plastic crates left behind by Mohn Corp. She wore a tight-fitting pair of black fatigues—not the sexiest clothes, but still impossible to ignore on a woman like her. He felt a brief twinge of guilt given his recent flirting with Bridget, but only a twinge. It's not as if Liz even knew he was looking.

She easily hefted three of the crates, each weighing sixty pounds or more. Liz began walking back to the Ark, peering around her burdens since they were taller than her head. Blair picked up two of the crates knowing the limits of his strength. He still found it odd that women were so much stronger than men, but it provided a strange sort of balance to the traditional world.

"Let's make this the last load," Liz called over her shoulder. A sheen of sweat made her shirt cling to her back, highlighting the muscles as they moved. "We've been at this all day. There's enough food and medical supplies down there to last us for months."

"You're not getting an argument from me," Blair replied, following after her. It was easier to go single file through the Ark's confines, at least when carrying this sort of burden. "It looks like we've raided almost everything we can from their camp anyway. Pickings have been slim for the last few trips."

"Maybe we can actually relax for a bit after we finish," Liz suggested, beaming one of those smiles over her shoulder.

"I found a bottle of rum yesterday," Blair said, shooting back a grin. "We ought to crack it open and celebrate. You realize this will be the first downtime we've had since we became werewolves? We didn't even pause after the end of the world."

They entered the comforting shade of the tunnel, winding down into the Ark. It amazed him how differently he'd come to view it since the day he'd arrived. That had been less than three months ago, and yet the gulf was wider than any lifetime. The corridor sloped down as they passed the first row of antechambers.

"So can I confide something?" Liz asked, slowing until he could walk with her.

"Of course. After the things we've shared? You can tell me anything," Blair replied, adjusting the weight of the crates.

"I'm having trouble sleeping. I haven't been able to since that day we woke up naked. The day I—well, shit, I can't even say it," she finished lamely, quickening her step again.

"The day you killed that man when we were on the run," Blair finished for her. He quickened his pace to match. "Liz, you're a doctor. A healer. You're kind and everything I've seen you do is aimed at helping the people around you. I get why this is hard for you, maybe better than anyone."

"Do you?" she asked, eyes sharp. "Blair, I wanted to heal people. Make the world a better place. Now I kill. Relentlessly. I'm a death machine, the ultimate warrior. That's my lot in life now, to slaughter every day. To fight. It isn't me, Blair. It isn't fair. This isn't who I was supposed to be."

He didn't have an answer. They walked in silence until they reached the eastern wing. Then he cleared his throat, finally sorting out his thoughts enough to speak. "Liz, neither one of us wanted this.

I was a teacher. You were a healer. We can still be those things. For you? Cleanse the land, Liz. Just like you said you wanted to. Kill the zombies. Wipe out the undead. Help a new and better world rise from the ashes. That's your purpose now."

"How can you accept it so easily?" she asked, setting down her crates as they finally arrived in the mess. She turned to face him, ponytail swishing across her shoulder. "I just can't get my mind around it. I can smell blood. Hear heartbeats. But what's worse? I *want* to hunt, Blair. I want to kill. I want to let it out and slaughter everything around me. How do you reconcile that with the teacher in you? Because the doctor in me is horrified."

"Because I've come to understand that the world we lived in only existed because some had to sacrifice to make it so," Blair explained. It was something he'd thought long on. He set down the crates before continuing. "Soldiers fought to secure oil so America would be wealthy. Our standard of living was paid for in their lives. We're safe from fires because firemen put themselves in harm's way. We don't have the luxury of being doctors or teachers anymore. We're soldiers now. Either we take back this world or the zombies snuff it out. Does it suck? Sure. But we don't have a choice. I square the beast in me, because I need it to fulfill my role. To do the things no one else can."

"I hadn't looked at it that way," Liz admitted, moving to sit on the edge of the long table. "We really are necessary. I think about what would have happened without this place. What if Mohn had won and the werewolves were stopped? Where would the world be? Overwhelmed by zombies and out of power. You saw what those fast zombies did and the Mother says that's just the beginning."

Her expression softened and his mouth went dry as he stared into her eyes.

"Listen, Blair. I wanted to talk to you about Bri—" Liz began, trailing off as he whirled to face the corridor.

"We're not alone," Blair said, peeling off his shirt and dropping it to the marble. He shucked out of his pants as well. They were comfortable and he didn't want to replace them. Again. "Someone is accessing systems in the central chamber. I can feel it, like something whispering in my ear."

Only one of the Mother's near progeny could access the Ark. There is another champion within these walls, perhaps from the secondary rejuvenation chamber.

"It's another werewolf, someone like us," Blair explained, turning to face Liz, who was also stripping. He tried not to stare. Focus. "I'm going to go delay her so she doesn't get away. Get there as quickly as you can."

"Blair that's—" Liz began.

No time. He blurred, all the way up the corridor and down another. Blurred again to reach the central chamber, crossing the distance in a span of heartbeats. He leapt through the doorway, rolling down the ramp and behind one of the damaged obelisks. The room was empty, or at least it appeared so.

"You're not Isis," a male voice called from the shadows. It was clearly amused, clipped with something akin to a British accent, though he knew that wasn't quite right. "So she sent a single Ka-Dun? A poor decision on her part unless you are a good deal more powerful than you appear. Why don't you tuck your tail between your legs and scurry away? I'll let you live."

"Why don't you come out where I can see you? I'd be happy to show you just how powerful I am," Blair roared. Why couldn't he hear a heartbeat? Or smell the intruder? He was perfectly cloaked, like a female.

"Of course," the intruder said, right behind him. Blair began to spin but even as he blurred, so did the intruder. Blair caught the impression of ebony skin and a shaved head, but what drew his attention were the smoldering green eyes and the razored teeth. The same teeth as the fast zombies.

The stranger brought the palm of his hand up, mere inches from Blair's chest. It glowed the same sickly green as the eyes and then discharged an arc of energy. The bolt took Blair in the chest, hurling him against an obelisk with a sickening crunch and a flash of agony. The blow shattered his back, erasing feeling below his waist.

"I have appeared," the man said. He loomed over Blair, grinning cruelly. His age was indeterminate, perhaps early thirties. He wore a shimmering white vest and flowing white pants similar to the Mother's garb. Both wrists bore golden bracelets and he had an elaborate neck torque that could have been found in an Egyptian tomb. His skin suggested Nubian ancestry. "Where is this power you were going to show me? All I see is a pup with a broken back, yipping at something it cannot understand."

Be wary, Ka-Dun, this is not a champion. You face one of the deathless. They command the shadows as females do.

He blurred too, Blair thought.

Deathless possess many powers. They also possess a breed of shaping, different from your own but very powerful. That is the source of the bolt of unmaking he unleashed.

"Lovely," Blair muttered. He flooded his body with energy, healing his broken back and leaping to his feet. The deathless stood calmly, an infuriating smile still pasted on that too-handsome face.

Blair blurred forward, dropping low and swiping at his opponent's calf. The deathless flowed backwards, narrowly avoiding his claws. He ripped a strange sword from a sheath at his side, the golden blade oddly curved in a way Blair had never seen. The blade hummed as it came for Blair's head. He ducked under the blow and raked the deathless with his claws, catching his opponent in the chest. His hand came away bloody as the man melted into the shadows.

"Impressive. You're quick," the voice said, clearly amused. "I am Irakesh, of the Cradle. How are you called, young Ka-Dun?"

Blair considered ignoring him, but the longer he prolonged this fight the greater the chance that Liz would arrive. "My name is Blair."

"You are of this new world then? Interesting. Isis has been busy. I hadn't realized she would begin recruiting so quickly," the voice said. It had moved to another section of darkness, somewhere near the central obelisk. "She left you behind while consolidating territory, and I can feel her access key within you. That should have been

Ahiga's responsibility, jumped-up urchin that he was. Does she trust you, or was she desperate?"

Something flashed behind him again. Blair blurred forward but wasn't fast enough. Claws scored his back, sending lines of pain through his entire body. Were they poisoned somehow? It didn't feel like a normal blow. Why hadn't the deathless used his sword?

Irakesh vanished back into the shadows. "You're outmatched, little wolf. Hamstrung by Isis's paranoia. You cannot command the shadows. Do you know why that is? Because when she created your kind she didn't want one person to have access to the full power at her disposal. So she segregated those powers, allowing only a fraction to be possessed by each gender. My kind has no such weakness."

Blair leapt on top of the central obelisk, its surface scored from the battle with Mohn. He scanned the darkness. Was this Irakesh lying? Or had the Mother really done as he said? It made a certain sort of sense. It made the sexes reliant on each other, forming an excellent check on the power of any one individual.

"What will you do? You cannot find me, but I can easily find you," the voice taunted. A green flash came from behind and to the right. This time Blair blurred away, narrowly dodging the bolt as it rippled across the obelisk. The obsidian absorbed it, seemingly undamaged.

Blair rolled behind another obelisk, taking a moment to focus his will. He had to find the bastard or this game of cat and mouse was only going to end one way. He sent out a pulse, just like he'd used while sparring with Bridget. There, resistance a few feet to his left.

He lunged, wrapping his arms around the patch of darkness. Something strong wriggled in his grip, but Blair fought to hold the deathless. He bit down hard, savaging Irakesh's shoulder with a mouthful of fangs. The blood tasted sour, like wine turned to vinegar. He resisted the urge to spit it out, tearing further as he tried to sever his foe's arm.

A wave of green energy burst from Irakesh, washing over Blair's entire body. He tumbled backwards, muscles spasming as if he'd been subjected to a massive jolt of electricity. His body lay there twitching, refusing his commands to rise and fight. It was similar to the power that Ahiga had used back in Acapulco, but much more painful.

"Now that was truly impressive," Irakesh said, clutching his shoulder with his good hand. The flesh was already knitting back together. "I didn't know a male could find someone shadow dancing. That's either a new talent, or a very closely held secret. I almost regret having to kill you without learning the answer."

12

HELL HATH NO FURY

Liz sprinted down the corridor with the long strides afforded by her lupine form. Sweat trickled through her fur as she bounded off a wall, using her momentum to fling her around a corner. Yet as fast as she moved it wasn't fast enough.

In the distance she heard the grunts of combat, steel scraping against stone. Blair's heart beat swiftly, his breathing ragged. He was fighting someone or something and she knew nothing about what they were dealing with. Damn him for running off. He was so damned impetuous.

She redoubled her speed, running low along the corridor. The combat continued, Blair giving a pained yelp that echoed from the room ahead. She rounded the last corner, dashing down the ramp and into the central chamber.

A bald man with dark skin stood over Blair's crumpled form, his shimmering ivory clothing eerily familiar. The style and cut was too similar to the Mother's to be a coincidence. The flowing white fabric draped over an athletic body, exactly the type of guy she preferred to date.

"I almost regret having to kill you without learning the answer," the man stated, his arrogant voice still somehow friendly.

The ancient enemy, the beast rumbled, low and hostile. *End him, Ka-Ken.*

Liz pounced, claws extended as the shadows gathered about her. She came down on the man's back, bearing him to ground with the heavy crack of bone breaking. She pinned him in place with both hands, tearing out his throat then ripping into his face with a savagery she hadn't known she was capable of.

He screamed, his right eye punctured by one of her canines. Then he dissolved into a cloud of green mist. Not shadow, but something electric and insubstantial that made her fur stand on end as it flowed away from her. Liz spilled to the ground, clawing uselessly at the air. It dispersed the cloud, which flowed into the shadows and disappeared.

Where had the bastard gone? She scanned the area, but there was no sign of him.

Deathless are tricky, even more so than the Ka-Dun.

"Blair?" she asked, turning to face him. He staggered to his feet, leaning heavily against the wall. At least he was alive.

"I'm all right," he panted. He didn't look all right. Raw pink wounds dotted his fur where his skin had been burned away. "We have to stop him. He took an access key, one linked to another Ark."

"What is he?" she asked, scanning the darkness. There was still no sign of the intruder.

"He's a deathless," Blair explained, rolling his neck. It cracked and popped as vertebrae reset to a more natural position. "I'm guessing he's been hidden here the entire time. Sleeping just like the Mother. He must have just awoken. He was about to kill me when you showed up. Thanks. That's another one I owe you. It's becoming a habit."

"Yeah, well, just remember how much you owe me when someone has to wash the dishes tonight," Liz said, giving him a half smile as she continued to scan the darkness for their new friend.

"I don't know where he went, but I doubt he'd stay here. If it were me I'd flee the Ark before the Mother returned. It can't be accidental he waited until she was gone," Blair said, hobbling towards the ramp leading back to the surface. His theory made sense. "Let's see if we can pick up a trail. He can use the shadows, but I bet he still leaves footprints."

13

THE HOUSE OF MOHN

Irakesh quickened his pace, blurring up the ridge line to its peak. The bare granite jutted up into the night sky, overlooking both the way he'd come and the route forward. Behind him lay the gleaming black surface of the Ark, massive and silent. Ahead was a gentle slope with a narrow dirt road. The hillside was covered in scrubby brush, a stark contrast to the fields of ice when he'd invaded this place all those millennia ago. Apparently the climate had changed dramatically, the first sign that he'd emerged into a different world.

He studied the path, which wound down the hillside to a valley nestled between several hills. Beyond lay a wall of thick green vegetation. The jungle, where he could easily lose himself. Excellent.

Something much closer drew his eye. A strange metallic shape caught the moonlight, perhaps a hundred yards down the slope. He studied it from a distance, but could make no sense of the thing. It looked like scattered debris, as if a slipsail had been dashed against the side of a mountain and this was all that remained.

Irakesh blurred closer, blending into the shadows as he approached. Up close the place reeked of some unnatural substance, something sharp that burned his eyes. He'd never encountered anything like it. A four-foot section of a strange white material lay at his feet, the main body of the craft a few feet beyond. It was primarily metal, though parts were molded from a smooth substance he'd never seen.

He picked up the long blade, amazed by its lightness. It was strong like metal yet far lighter. What could it possibly be? He dropped it and investigated the craft itself. The front had impacted with the hillside, crushing the area he presumed the pilot must lay. The slight stench of decay confirmed this, and as he knelt to examine further he saw a crushed hand jutting through a break in the strange transparent material that so closely resembled glass.

Irakesh circled the craft, coming to the side where a large portal lay. He could smell more decay within, so he ducked inside. A body lay at his feet, clothed in strange green clothing with a weave far too tight to belong to a peasant or even a common soldier. He knelt next to the body, smiling when he realized it was primarily intact.

He seized the corpse by the neck, dragging the head into his lap. Two claws in the ocular cavity let him pry open the skull, exposing the spongy grey matter within. It was old, but intact. He might be able to glean memories from this poor fool. Irakesh carefully peeled away the prefrontal cortex, devouring bite-sized morsels until it was gone.

His eyes closed as the rush of memories washed over him. So much, all of it new. This man was an officer in the military of some house known as Mohn. He'd been second in command here, an observer dispatched to watch over the real commander and to report back to his masters. The craft he'd crashed in was a helicopter, which had been bound for a kingdom called Panama. Mohn possessed a stronghold there. A stronghold with powerful weapons.

Wait, what was that? Irakesh focused on a recent memory, some sort of communication with this man's masters despite the fact that he was thousands of miles away from them. He'd been ordered to retrieve a weapon of incredible power. The soldier didn't understand precisely how this bomb worked, only that it split the atom and generated a massive burst of radiation and explosive force. Irakesh's jaw fell open as he considered the implications.

He *must* obtain this weapon. More, he could use the strange transports contained at the stronghold in Panama. They would allow him to travel far more quickly, potentially reaching the Ark of the Redwood in days instead of months.

Irakesh rose to his feet, dropping the body as he exited the craft. He needed to be away before the Ka-Dun and his vicious Ka-Ken caught up with him, but first he'd leave a trap to occupy their attention while he gained room to maneuver. Irakesh smiled wickedly. He had just the thing.

14

ZOMBIES

Mark exited the elevator and strode briskly down the hallway toward the holding cell. Benson was already waiting, studying his approach as she removed a pair of blue latex gloves. They left a powdery residue on her hands, but if it bothered her she didn't show it. He found that sort of pragmatism attractive. She wasn't concerned with appearances, just data.

That was further reinforced by her short black hair, cut just above the shoulders. It was all about function rather than form, and offered nothing an enemy could take advantage of.

"Right this way, sir," Benson said, spinning on her heel in a way that suggested time in the military. He followed her up the hall, her heels clicking on the tile as they approached a wide window. It looked down into a well-lit room with a single figure strapped to a steel table.

"You vivisected it?" he asked, peering at the still open chest cavity. The thing had once been a young man with dark, curly hair. The bloodshot eyes roamed the room, though his head was strapped to the table.

"Yes, sir," Benson replied. She picked up a tablet from a cubby next to the window and handed it to him. "I've compiled all available data, but I'll give you the highlights. The body has been taken over by a virus. The flesh is necrotic, but the nervous system is still active."

"The virus reproduces through a bite?" Mark asked, scanning the data on the tablet.

"Or through any fluid exchange. Blood or saliva can transmit the virus as well," Benson replied, leaning towards the glass as she studied the figure. "The real mystery is the cause of the virus. We know that it activated when the CME hit, but we don't know its origin. Our assumption is that it's been present all along, dormant in the hosts. It may have even masqueraded as another virus, though we have no way to corroborate that."

"We may never know," Mark said, frowning as he watched the living corpse. "Too much was lost in the chaos after the CME."

"Sir, what do you want me to do with it?" Benson asked.

"Have you learned everything you can from it?" Mark asked, glancing at her.

"There's a chance we might learn more, but I think it's unlikely," she replied, giving a slight shrug.

"Then I want you to put together a research team. Have them continue to document the subject. If needed we'll obtain others. I want a full profile prepared," Mark ordered. Benson merely nodded. "Once your team is operational, appoint an interim commander and come see me."

"May I ask why, sir?" she said, pursing her lips.

"I have something special I want you to look into, and I need you to handle it personally. Discretion is critical," Mark explained, watching her reaction closely. If she proved trustworthy she could be an enormous asset, one he was going to need in the days to come.

If not, she'd need to be eliminated.

15

MY NAME

The corpse still lacked a name, but at least he knew that he was a *he* and not a she or an it. It wasn't much, but it anchored him. It meant that he could learn, could become more than he was. It gave him hope that he wouldn't always be a shambling monstrosity devouring the flesh of every victim he could lay hands to.

His shuffling body moved more quickly than it had, taking sure steps up the dirt track leading down the mountain towards the jungle below. A cluster of structures sat on the edge of the massive trees and while there were no lights, there was at least some possibility that he could find food there.

The hunger gnawed at his insides, demanding more fuel. Even if it hadn't he would have sought food. Food made him smarter. Faster. Food made him greater than he had been.

A strange sensation built, beginning at the base of his spine and tingling up to his brain. The pulse carried a command to rival the hunger. *Come to me*, it demanded. His body obeyed without thought, hurrying towards the strange sensation. It pulsed from the village below like some bright beacon. He must reach the voice. It was his sole purpose.

All around him other zombies appeared. A ragged collection of butchered locals sprinkled with tourists. The shuffling horde flowed towards the same squat building, which was already surrounded by a throng of moaning corpses.

He pushed forward, reaching the back of the throng. There, on top of that building. There was a black man clad in white with violent eyes of the most putrid green he could imagine, the kind lurking in children's nightmares. This man wore an impossibly white smile, each tooth ending in a gleaming point as if filed. His head shone under the moonlight, shaven bare like an egg.

How could the nameless corpse reach this man? He watched the throng. They beat upon the walls of the building to no avail. They lacked the strength to enter or climb. He would fare no better even if he could forge a path through their ranks.

He must be stronger. Strength came from feeding. There were no humans around, no source of fresh meat. But there were zombies. So many zombies. He leaned forward, snatching a young man with a scraggly beard and vacant eyes. The man hissed, extending a black tongue like a twisted snake.

He seized the young man's head in both hands, snapping the neck with a sharp crack. The body slid to the ground, the thud muted by the moaning zombies. He knelt, grabbing the head with both hands. He slammed it into the ground in three brutal blows, the last splitting the skull. Then he pried away bits of bone to fish out the grey matter within.

He devoured it, wolfing down chunks as quickly as he could extract them. The hunger abated. He fed more quickly, slurping up the remains. More. He must have more. The next to fall was an old woman, short and round in a pale dress stained with dirt and blood.

"Stop," the voice commanded. A voice that *must* be obeyed. He froze, gazing up at the figure atop the building. The nameless corpse's hands were coated in gore, his face smeared with the same. That was bad. Wrong. People didn't do that. He remembered a word. Decorum.

The figure hopped from the roof, landing lightly next to the nameless zombie. He needed a way to refer to himself. Thinking in the third person was wrong somehow. Awkward. So much pronoun confusion.

"You were feeding on these fodder," the black man said, smile becoming a wicked grin as he stared down at the nameless corpse. "Can you understand me?"

"Yes," the corpse rasped from a throat no longer suited to speech. It was the first word he could remember attempting.

"You possess speech," the man gasped, giving a delighted clap and a still wider grin. "I can't believe it. You're far more advanced than anything I could have hoped to encounter. Give you a few weeks of feeding and you'll be decent conversation. What's your name?"

"I—I can't remember," he said, voice still rough but marginally more understandable.

"Nonsense," The man replied, waving a dismissive hand. "It's in there somewhere. You just need to reactivate that part of your brain, to recover those neural pathways. That will take time and food. Feed on these zombies. Feast on their brains and their spines. Go ahead, that one. The short man with the weasily face."

He turned to scan the zombies. There, that was the short man with the face like a weasel. He shoved a middle aged woman out of the way, seizing the short man by the neck. He threw him to the ground, dashing his head against a rock. Perfect. He knelt and began to scrape the contents from the skull.

"Excellent," the sharp-toothed man said. He seemed extremely pleased. The nameless corpse continued to feed, scraping until nothing remained. "Now then, what is your name?"

"I—" he said, struggling to find a name. A face flashed. Red hair. Freckles. A goatee. He was shaving. That was *his* face. "I don't know."

"Another then. Pick one," the voice commanded. Sharp Teeth's voice nearly thrummed with excitement.

The nameless corpse turned to the throng, grabbing the nearest person. It was one of the tourists, a woman in a sundress. He slammed her head into one of the thick wooden posts supporting the house's awning. Then he fed again, gobbling the sticky mass as quickly as he could get it into his mouth.

"What is your name?" the voice thundered.

He considered the question. Something danced just out of reach. A woman with red hair yelling his name. Liz. His sister. What was the name she yelled? "Trevor. My name is Trevor."

"Wonderful," the sharp-toothed man laughed, throwing his arms skyward. "You may pick three more. I must send the rest south to delay our pursuers. Come. Feed quickly. Then follow me. I have so much to teach you."

16

YUKON

The Mother blurred down the narrow alley, severing the spine of a nascent deathless with a wicked slash. This one was an old woman, feeble before death but all too deadly now. The corpse toppled to the rubbish-strewn ground joining the bodies of the other dozen she'd just dispatched. Grim work, but necessary.

She leapt three stories straight up, grabbing the lip of the neighboring roof and pulling herself atop it. From her vantage she could see most of downtown Cajamarca, a sprawling city by her standards. The strange buildings sat at the top of a series of rolling hills, stands of unfamiliar trees scattered throughout wide streets. It had probably been a pleasant place before the sun's recent change had woken the deathless. Moon willing, it would be again.

The clash of combat came from two streets over. She couldn't see Bridget, but had no doubt the growls and metallic clattering came from her. It was joined by the harsh crack of gunfire, something she was still growing accustomed to. The weapons were so impersonal. Even the smell they emitted when fired was horrible.

Yet they were potent, as Jordan had proved. He'd adopted few of the powers that made Ka-Dun so deadly, yet he was nearly Blair's equal in ferocity. It demonstrated just how potent the weapons could be, though his reticence to embrace the powers gifted by his blood limited him greatly. Blair's command of shaping grew daily, making him the strongest Ka-Dun still living. Perhaps she should ask Jordan to teach him, and in the process have Blair teach Jordan to accept what he'd become.

Bridget required no such supervision. She was still too timid, but took to her powers with nearly the same ease as Liz. It was too early to tell which would be the dominant Ka-Ken, though she suspected Liz's determination would eventually overshadow Bridget. The smaller woman spent too much time batting eyelashes at men and not enough honing her ability to kill.

A yipping from somewhere below drew her attention, the cry of a panicked creature. The Mother scanned the street, gaze roaming between motorcars and toppled waste bins as she sought the source. There. Several deathless were converging on an overturned boat next to a path leading into a park. A canoe, that was the word. Odd with no visible source of water around. What had the owner used it for?

She dropped silently to the ground, blurring to the top of a blue metal vehicle not far from the canoe. Something moved under it, scooting as far from the grasping claws as it could. The poor creature's heartbeat thundered.

The Mother leapt to the ground amidst the deathless, snapping bones and shattering skulls as she blazed through their ranks. She grabbed what had once been a child by its feet, slamming the corpse's head into a middle aged woman who'd shoved her arm under the canoe in search of the frightened animal. Both skulls exploded, showering her with putrid gore. She ignored it, tossing the canoe aside and snatching up the animal in one arm.

It had golden fur and was the size of a large coyote or small wolf. Like those animals, it possessed four paws, a tail, and a long muzzle. The similarities ended there. This was one of the twisted creatures that mankind had made from the noble wolf, the mongrels they called dogs. She nearly dropped the beast in revulsion, but it gave a timid whelp of pain.

She examined it for the source of the pain. It bore a gash along its side, perhaps caused by scooting under the canoe. Perhaps inflicted by the claw of a deathless. If the latter was true the animal was doomed, but if not it might be saved. She stood in the road, twisted with indecision.

The animal looked up at her with wide brown eyes. They stared adoringly at her, then the beast leaned forward and licked her wrist. The Mother cursed her own weak heart, but she couldn't leave the animal to die scared and alone. It wasn't the beast's fault that it had been twisted by man.

She blurred up the street, cradling the animal to her chest. It was so thin. Not quite starving, but only a day or two away from that plight. It had grown dependent upon human masters and couldn't feed itself. Such a thing enraged her, but she reserved that for the people who'd created the animal. Not the animal itself.

The Mother leapt onto the roof of a stone building venerating some imagined god. She sank into a comfortable crouch, cradling the poor beast as it gazed adoringly up at her.

I am Yukon. My pack is dead. You saved me.

The thoughts were simple, more so than a wolf's. Yet they were earnest. This creature had a kindness and compassion that a wolf lacked, though she couldn't decide if that would be advantageous in this new world.

I am the Mother. Rest, Yukon. I will bring you to a place of safety.

Then she blurred back to the temple where they'd gathered those they had already saved.

17

PURSUIT

Liz leapt from her rocky perch, bounding thirty feet up the ridge. She seized an outcrop in one furry hand, flinging herself skyward again. This time she landed on top of a granite spur that jutted over the edge of the ridge's crest. They'd made it to the top, and in record time. Well, record time for a female. Blair could have just blurred to the top in a matter of seconds, but they couldn't afford to send him ahead. It would take both of them to bring down this deathless.

She could simply have ridden his shadow, but it was still a new power and she wasn't sure how quickly she could emerge or what potential counter attacks that might expose her to. Given how little they new about this Irakesh, playing it safe was the only sensible move. It still sucked. Even if that weren't true, blurring took a lot out of Blair. What good would catching this guy do if they were too weak to take him down when they got there? She wasn't positive he'd healed entirely from his earlier confrontation with the deathless, in any case.

Blair landed on a neighboring outcrop, dropping into a crouch to stabilize himself. He was majestic somehow, with his silver fur and amber eyes. He glanced in her direction. "I never dreamed we'd be able to do something like this. We just scaled an entire cliff face in less than a minute. Sometimes it still catches me off guard."

She couldn't help but smile. Despite everything they'd been through he'd somehow retained his enthusiasm, something she needed desperately right now. Everything was going wrong, but there he was in the middle of it keeping despair at bay.

"It still blows me away," Liz admitted, turning to the moonlit trail threading its way north. She started loping in that direction at a ground-eating pace. Blair fell into step beside her. She glanced at him. "I think what gets me most is not knowing everything we can do. I feel like there are so many surprises still ahead of us. Especially if we're really going to live for thousands of years."

"I know what you mean," he replied, leaping over a fallen tree. "When we first saw Ahiga he'd transformed into a wolf. What else could he do? I feel like we haven't even scratched the surface. I was hoping the Mother would teach us, but..."

"But she's too focused on saving the world to give two shits about us?" Liz finished, a deep, rumbling laugh welling up from her chest. It felt good.

"Unfortunately," Blair conceded, shaking his head. "I get the sense that she expected Ahiga to prepare me and with him gone, she doesn't have a contingency plan. Which leaves me on my own. At least she treats your opinion with something approaching respect. A little less for Bridget and Cyntia, but still more than she gives Jordan or me."

"Her whole culture centered around the divide between the sexes," Liz replied, bounding over a rise. A wide valley stretched below her. The trail led that direction, toward a ramshackle town nestled in the valley's farthest corner. "I have to admit I do like that they were a matriarchy, and it's kind of nice being the stronger sex for once. But it's also interesting seeing her casually dismiss you as useless. I half expect her to tell you to get in the kitchen and make her a sandwich."

"You know I'd get in there and make it," Blair replied, grinning wolfishly as he started down the trail into the valley. The wind surged for a moment, then faded to a low keen as they descended the ridge. "I'm actually okay with the way she treats us. I'm sure our culture must baffle her just as much as hers confuses us. Besides, shaping is pretty amazing and I never really cared about being bigger and stronger. I think men made out all right in this deal."

"Yeah, I'm pretty happy with my end of it, too. Makes you wonder where the deathless come down on split powers. From the little the Mother's told us, they came first," Liz said, sending up a cloud of dust as she slid down the trail. "If that's true, then they were the prototype for this virus. She may have modified it based on what she'd learned with the deathless. The culture she built here must have come later, along with the werewolves."

"That would make sense," Blair allowed, dropping thirty feet to the next switchback. She leapt after, landing in a crouch next to him. He still seemed to be chewing on his ideas. "We need to know more about the deathless. The beast says their shaping is different. How? What exactly can they do? The green bolt Irakesh hit me with was agonizing, and the wound was difficult to heal. I'm wondering if there's a theme to their powers, just like there is to ours."

"Theme?" Liz asked. The possibility that their powers had one hadn't even occurred to her.

"Shaping seems to focus on two primary areas. Mental powers, like fooling and controlling the minds of others," Blair explained, sliding down the hillside to the next switchback. "The second is altering DNA. Changing my physical appearance, becoming a wolf. Possibly even altering the DNA of others."

"Whereas females focus on ferocity and stealth," she added, landing next to him in a crouch. "I guess there are themes."

Conversation dwindled as they picked their way from switchback to switchback. Blair seemed focused on the village below, though she couldn't say why. He seemed apprehensive, as if he expected to find something bad there.

"Do you see that?" he asked, pausing on a switchback near the valley floor. He stabbed a finger towards the edge of the village.

Something moved in the darkness. A lot of somethings. Dozens upon dozens of zombies shambled in their direction. A horde of ravenous corpses, all moving with the same driving purpose.

"They haven't acted like this before," Liz said, flexing her claws.

"They're coordinated, like a swarm," Blair growled, pacing restlessly as their foes approached. "This isn't accidental. I can control minds, so it stands to reason that Irakesh might be able to do something similar. He left them to stop us. Doesn't make a lot of sense, though. We can just go around them."

"We can't, actually. If we circle around, they'll head back to the Ark and trash it," Liz said, suppressing a sigh. "He outmaneuvered us like children. They're a threat and he knows it. This is a way for him to get ahead of us."

"So I guess we deal with them," Blair said, leaping to the next switchback.

There were perhaps two hundred zombies. Not insurmountable, but a definite drain on their energy. Exactly what this Irakesh had intended, no doubt. Damn the cunning bastard.

"We're going to be too weak to pursue him if we cut them all down," Blair said, with a frustrated sigh. "We'll need to retreat to the Ark and tell the Mother what happened. Maybe she'll have an idea."

"How far away is he?" she asked, grinding her teeth. The last thing she wanted to do was face the Mother and tell her how badly she'd failed.

"He's farther north by at least a couple miles and moving quickly. We could probably match his pace if we followed, but I don't know if we could narrow the gap," Blair said, clearly as annoyed as she was. "How do you want to handle this?"

Liz dove into the approaching zombies, rending and crushing a path. She vented her frustration, ripping off limbs and crushing skulls with powerful blows. Blair followed, cutting down any that got behind her as she tore a path through their ranks.

18

SUSPICIOUS BEHAVIOR

Director Phillips clasped his hands behind his back, watching dispassionately as the room echoed with amplified gunfire. The wall screen showed the perspective of a helmet cam, its occupant manning the side mounted gun in a DC-16 Mohn chopper. The weapon streamed death at a young tourist in a floral-print dress. Her auburn hair was matted with blood, and her pale shoulder bore long jagged scratches.

The woman took a half dozen fifty caliber rounds to the midsection, which tossed her body back like a toy flung about by a retriever. Yet she rose to her feet, giving a screech of rage despite the hideous wounds. She began limping towards the camera. The gun fired one more time, this time obliterating everything from the neck up. The body toppled to the ground and lay sill.

Then the camera tilted crazily, turning until it was focused on a soldier with a thin black goatee and haggard brown eyes. Yuri Filipov, Commander Jordan's favorite subordinate. "Is shit, command. Cut them down, but zombies just keep coming. Don't have many rounds left."

The Director was silent as he considered. So many unanswered questions, but the man was in a firefight.

"Corporal Filipov, I know you're in the thick of it, but we need a status. Where are you?" The Director said, arms falling to his sides. His fists clenched as he suppressed the urge to take a step closer to the screen.

"Is Panama," the Russian replied, glancing over his shoulder then back at the camera. "Peru status unknown, but bad when left. Werewolf tore off Yuri's leg."

"Acknowledged. Yuri, is the package secure?" It was amazing that the man was still conscious, much less manning a heavy weapon with that kind of injury.

"No. Is still in hangar," Yuri replied. His head turned and the camera spun wildly. There were a flurry of gunshots, then his face returned. "Cannot breach perimeter. Is impossible. Have enough fuel to make Houston, but need extraction from there."

"Acknowledged. Get back in the air and get as much footage as you can in Panama. We'll dispatch another team to secure the package," the Director ordered, face dispassionate despite his roiling emotions. It was all going to shit so very quickly.

Yuri gave a tight nod. Then the screen went black. The Director spun to face the room. "Get me viable extraction options. I want that package back in our hands and I don't want to lose anyone doing it. Estimates and full brief in two hours."

Mark turned on his heel and strode up the center aisle, not pausing as he stepped through the automatic doors. He knew their timing to the millisecond and had made every motion as efficiently as possible. Many people would have laughed had they known it. Such a small thing, passing through a door at the optimum speed.

Yet it was from the simplest actions that one's core self arose. The standards you set. If you held yourself to excellence in the little things, you quickly realized that big things were just an accumulation of all those little things. So Mark made the little things count.

He ducked into an elevator moments before it closed, eyes widening as he identified the car's other occupant.

"Heading to your quarters?" the Old Man asked. That nickname was most definitely at odds with Leif Mohn himself. He wasn't an old man so much as he was eternal. His platinum hair and stern face hadn't aged in the entire time Mark had known him. The bastard was even more timeless than Patrick Stewart.

"Yours actually. We just received a live combat report from Panama," he said. The Old Man always liked knowing as soon as data was obtained. "Peru sounds bad. The package was never delivered."

Mohn stabbed the button labeled 24 for Mark, then 26 for his own quarters. Mark had always wondered why he kept an entire level between himself and the senior staff, but he'd never asked. He wondered what the Old Man would say if he did. The man clearly valued privacy, but when the world ended, that kind of paranoia was just too expensive.

"Where is it now?"

"We have confirmation that the package is still in Panama. An extraction team landed, but faced heavy resistance from these walking corpses," the Director replied, eyeing the Old Man sidelong as the car began to descend. "We haven't created an official term for the creatures, though Z, zombie and zed have been suggested repeatedly."

"Draugr, Mark. They're called draugr. I don't care about the package. What I do care about are the Arks. I want a bird assigned to every one and I want hourly reports detailing everyone coming or going. That includes the one in Peru," the Old Man ordered. The car slid smoothly to a halt and the doors opened. Mark made no move to exit.

"What about the package? That's a live nuke, sir," he protested, surprising himself.

"It's in hostile territory. Recovery will cost us and we have twenty-one more." Mohn gestured for Mark to exit the elevator car. "Focus on the Arks. We need to know everything."

"Arks?" Mark asked, stepping into the doorway, but not quite exiting. "You're talking about the pyramids, right?"

Surprise flitted across the Old Man's face, the sudden realization that he'd made a verbal slip. Mark had seen it hundreds of times on just as many faces, the mark of a man who'd revealed information he'd intended to keep secret.

"Yes, Mark, the pyramids. They're the pinnacle of an entire civilization. If they're all occupied like the one in Peru, we're dealing with some very dangerous people. So focus our resources there and forget about the package," Mohn ordered. His gaze hardened, but not before Mark caught something else there. Deception. The Old Man was throwing him off the scent about something. But why?

He stepped from the elevator and turned to face the Old Man. "Of course, sir."

The doors slid closed.

"Benson, this is the Director," Mark said, the sound picked up by the sub-dermal microphone inserted into his throat. "Get two researchers, one on the word 'Draugr'. The other on the word Ark, with a capital A."

"Yes, sir," she answered instantly. "I'll have reports compiled within the hour."

Mark didn't bother replying. He headed up the corridor towards his quarters with slow, deliberate steps as he contemplated the unthinkable.

19

TRACKER

Cyntia raised her muzzle, tasting the night air as she sought Trevor's elusive scent. She'd found it three times now, but each time it had vanished as quickly as she'd discovered it. Brief hints that the man himself was close, just out of reach. Each time a more conventional search had shown two sets of tracks making their way north.

The familiar musk of sweat reminded her of leaning against Trevor back before the final assault in Cajamarca, one of the last times she'd seen him alive.

Do you taste that, Ka-Ken? His scent is sickly. Tainted. He has become one of the deathless. Your quest is futile. Your He cannot be reclaimed, cannot be redeemed. He has become the ancient enemy, terrible and cunning.

Cyntia ignored the voice, as she often did. It rarely told her anything useful, though it had taught her to track by scent. It had claimed that she was a tracker, one of the Ka-Ken gifted with supernaturally enhanced senses. That was proving useful, as she'd have otherwise lost Trevor's trail long ago. Even still, the quest seemed futile and she understood why the others thought her foolish to pursue it.

Their opinions of her ranged from ambivalence to disdain, perhaps because she was the weakest of the females. The omega of their little pack. She was comfortable with that role, or she would have been if she cared for any of them. Yet she did not. She'd joined their number because she and Liz had once been friends. The fact that Liz refused to join a search for her own brother showed just how divergent their priorities had grown.

Trevor was a good man. Strong and intelligent. Capable. The sort who faced the end of the world on his feet, shielding those weaker than himself despite the sacrifice it might call for. It didn't hurt that he had the kind of shoulders you couldn't keep your hands off of. He didn't deserve the fate that had befallen him, one she simply couldn't accept.

But was that a reason to go haring off searching for him? Not really. Cyntia understood her need for him was irrational, but it was all she had. So she searched.

Cyntia knelt next to a boot print. The tread matched those she'd followed from the site of the motorcar where they'd found Sheila's corpse. It might not be Trevor, but it was the best lead she had. She loped along the dirt track, following the bootprints.

The moon rose, the slender crescent providing more than enough light to see as she continued her search. Hours passed as she fell into a steady rhythm, pounding along in the direction she hoped Trevor had gone.

What would she do if she found him? What if he was a zombie, like the others? It was possible that there might be a cure, but she didn't know of one. The Mother might, but Cyntia didn't trust her. She'd probably kill Trevor on sight if he was one of the undead. So what could she do? Put him out of his misery? She just didn't know. It was a special brand of agony, the uncertainty. So she put it from her mind. First she had to locate him, and then she would deal with what came next.

Her journey took her over ridges and switchbacks, but the elevation gradually decreased as she neared the jungle. Was that their destination? She quickened her pace, fear spiking as she realized that she might not be able to track them through the dense foliage. There would be a million competing scents, and the jungle would swallow their footprints.

There. Up ahead a small fire flickered between the trees. Someone had set up a camp and the tracks led in that exact direction. She crept through the trees, suppressing the wave of hope that surged within her. If it *was* Trevor, then the fact that he could light a camp-fire suggested that something of who he had been had survived. Mindless zombies didn't need fire.

She neared the camp, slipping from tree to tree with the shadows cloaking her approach. Only one figure sat in the firelight, a familiar green baseball cap and shock of reddish-orange hair poking out from under it. Elation filled her. She dropped the shadows, stepping into the firelight.

"Trevor?" she asked, tentatively. Would he be happy to see her? She knew he'd been attracted to her, but he'd also acted as if she were a distraction most of the time. She'd hoped it was merely an act concealing affection similar to her own.

The figure stirred, turning to face her. His eyes were glassy, but they focused on her. Trevor had no visible wound, but he was far too pale to be living. Yet there he stood, next to a fire it seemed he'd created. How could that be if he was a zombie?

Cyntia felt a sharp pain as something grabbed her arm and twisted it behind her back. Claws settled around her throat, just barely pricking the skin.

"Shift back to your human form, or I will slash out your throat. By the time you recover I'll have severed your head, and trust me when I say there's no recovering from that. Not even for a Ka-Ken." The voice was male, cultured and friendly with an almost British accent. Incongruous when set next to the man's actions.

"All right," she agreed, willing herself to shift back. She shrank, but the man's grip didn't slacken as her body changed. A few moments later she stood there naked. Her eyes pleaded with Trevor for help, but his glassy gaze returned to the fire. What had she stumbled into?

"I will release you now, but know that if you struggle or attempt to attack me I will destroy you," the voice said, releasing her as promised. She stumbled forward, turning to face her assailant.

The stranger's ivory clothing shone under the moonlight, his features shadowed. Only his eyes stood out, pools of sickly green that studied her dispassionately.

"You are following me. Why? Are you one of those Isis has recruited? Be truthful and I may spare you," the man commanded, his eyes narrowing as he awaited her response.

"I was with them, yes. I left to find him," she said, nodding towards Trevor. "He was one of our companions before the world ended. I...I care for him." The admission was difficult.

"You've found him. Let us assume I allow you to live. What then?" the man asked, raising a single eyebrow. His stance relaxed, though she had the feeling that he could still kill her before she could cross the distance between them.

"I don't know. I was hoping he was still alive, but he's...is there anything left of the man who used to exist?" she asked, her gaze shifting to Trevor. He stood placidly, seemingly unaware of their presence.

"He is very nearly intact, a rarity even in my time. It can only happen when the individual accepts the change," the man explained. He gestured at the fire. "Be seated. Let us discuss this like civilized people. I will answer your questions and you will answer mine. If those answers please me, I will allow you to live."

Cyntia did as she was bid, sitting on a sloped rock near the fire. The warmth of it was welcome. She gathered her knees to her chest, conscious of her nakedness, though the stranger seemed oblivious. Trevor sat as well, just a few feet away. His posture was wrong, and his head moved with jerky little twitches.

"He gave his name as Trevor. In time he will recover more of his former self if he feeds often and well. Eventually he will remember nearly everything from his former life. He will closely resemble me, once he has fully awakened as a deathless," the man explained, razored teeth flashing in the firelight as he spoke. He sat on a fallen log on the far side of the fire. "I hope that answer suffices. I am Irakesh of the Cradle. And you are?"

"Cyntia," she gave simply.

"Well Cyntia, you have found this man you care for. You know that in time he will become much as he was before," Irakesh explained, steepling his fingers as he studied her with that horrible green gaze. "Yet he will be deathless, the sworn enemy of your kind. We are on opposite sides of a war. What will you do if he attempts to kill you? Will you allow it, or seek to slay your mate?"

"War?" Cyntia scoffed, waving a dismissive hand. "I fight no war. I seek only to live my life as I choose. If Trevor becomes the man he was, then I will help him remember."

"He will become so much more than he ever was," Irakesh explained, gaze still weighing her. "In time he will grow powerful, a deathless of incredible strength. He will fight at my side, helping extend my rule through the northern continent. Standing at his side means standing at mine. Is this something you can accept?"

"If you will help Trevor become the man he was, then I will follow you," Cyntia said.

20

DON'T POKE THE GODDESS

Jordan fell back as the Mother swept into the Ark like a force of nature. He trailed in her wake, while Bridget hung back just a bit further. The last time he'd seen that expression on her face, the Mother had ripped off his arms right before tearing out his throat. She'd worn it since the night before, when she'd told them they were leaving the newly fortified church where the refugees were holing up. She hadn't spoken since and Jordan was smart enough not to be the one to break that silence.

"What do you think happened?" Bridget asked, voice pitched low. They waited as the Mother's form retreated down the corridor. It seemed wise to give her whatever space she needed right now.

"I don't know," Jordan said, cinching the strap across his chest. The weight of the guns in his pack kept pulling it loose. It was possible he'd been over prepared, but what was the point of being so strong if you didn't use it? "She just stopped mid-sentence while she was giving that 'accept the gift' speech. She must have felt something. Blair is pretty good with that shaping crap. Maybe he sent her a message?"

"If he did contact her, she didn't much like hearing it," Bridget replied. She peered after the Mother, apparently not in any more of a hurry to follow than Jordan was.

"We should warn the others about her mood," Jordan suggested. This corridor was the fastest way to reach the mess, but he didn't want to brave it yet. "No sense poking the antediluvian goddess when she's upset. We should head to the mess and see what we can find out, then maybe we'll send Liz down to talk to her."

Bridget gave a tight nod, but her attention was still on the Mother's retreating form. She'd gone pale and he couldn't blame her. The way the Mother acted, the power she displayed. She *was* a goddess in every way that mattered.

After a few tense minutes Jordan steeled himself and started up the corridor. Bridget followed, breathing more relaxed now. They wound silently through the halls, relieved that they could no longer hear the Mother.

"Jordan?" Bridget asked, shattering the silence. She touched his shoulder, giving a quick squeeze before releasing him. "I enjoyed this trip. You're easy to travel with. Thanks for showing me how to shoot."

"I never envisioned gun-toting werewolves, but with our strength it makes sense to carry some real firepower," he replied, happy to focus on something else. He grew more relaxed as they neared the relative safety of the mess. "I'd like to train everyone to shoot and see if we can't get you to carry rifles at the very least. Handguns don't make a lot of sense. If something is that close, we can just eat it."

They entered the mess, which was lit by a series of softly glowing diamonds set into the walls at regular intervals. Blair and Liz were hunched over the marble table, poring over what looked like a map. They didn't so much as glance up when he and Bridget entered.

Bridget sidled over to the table, slipping into the seat next to Blair. Her interest there was clear, though she'd flirted with Jordan more than once already. He liked Bridget, but he'd been around enough women like her to spot trouble before he got embroiled in it.

"What are you studying?" Bridget asked, peering at the map. Jordan dropped down across from her, his bulk filling the space next to Liz. The map was local, a printout that they'd liberated from Mohn Ops.

"You want to tell them?" Blair asked, setting down a black Sharpie he'd been using to draw with. He'd added a circle around a village to the north. There didn't seem to be anything remarkable about it.

"You have a better understanding of Irakesh. Besides, if I tell the story I'll probably end up breaking something again," Liz countered, scrubbing a hand through her long copper hair. She was more agitated than Jordan had ever seen her.

"All right," Blair said, turning to face Jordan. Bridget sat close enough that her shoulder touched his, but if he noticed, he didn't show it. "While you were gone we found a deathless in the Ark. He gave his name as Irakesh, and he demonstrated powers we can't even begin to understand. I don't know what he was after or how he even got inside, but he escaped up the ravine to the north."

"We followed him," Liz broke in, eyes narrowing. "He sent a couple hundred zombies to slow us down and by the time we'd dealt with them, he'd gotten away."

"Please tell me you guys have some good news to report," Blair added, setting the marker down and massaging his temples. "We really need something to hold onto at this point. Trevor's gone. Power's out across the globe, so far as we can tell, and zombies are everywhere."

"We do have a spot of good news," Jordan interjected. He reached for a bowl of peanuts that someone had left, picking up a handful. "We're up to fourteen refugees and the church is secure now. The faster zombies have probed the defenses a few times, but two of the refugees are werewolves and have kept them at bay."

"There's bad news too," Bridget said, looking up at Blair from under her long lashes. He seemed to eat it up. "The Mother sensed something happening, I think she felt Irakesh leaving the Ark. I've never seen her that angry. I wouldn't recommend talking to her any time soon. I think she might seriously hurt someone."

"I'm going to go get packed," Jordan said, tossing the handful of

nuts into his mouth. He savored the saltiness as he picked up his
backpack.

"Packed?" Blair asked, raising a quizzical eyebrow.

"An enemy operative invaded the Ark, got whatever it was he was
after, then fled north. The Mother's reaction suggests whatever he
took is of vital importance." He paused to chew before continuing.
"She won't be able to pursue him because she has to stay here and
consolidate her power base. More cities need to be cleared and she
has to contact every werewolf that she can find. But at the same time
she can't let this Irakesh get away. Someone has to go after him. Us.
So I'll be in my room packing."

They looked thoughtful as they digested his words, but no one
said anything as he left the room and headed up the tunnel towards
the quarters they'd taken for themselves. He took long deliberate
strides, carefully considering the situation as he wound through
corridors.

Who was this Irakesh? What abilities did he possess? More
importantly, what had he stolen? They'd need those answers before
they began their pursuit, which meant someone would have to question the Mother. Hopefully one of the trio in the mess would be bold
enough to take that on. He certainly wasn't going to. He'd already
been killed by her once and if it happened again it would be a lot
more permanent.

Jordan rounded the corner to the row of rooms where his quarters
lay. He'd deliberately chosen one far from the others. It gave him soli-
tude, and time to think was something he needed in abundance these
days. His entire life had done a violent 180 and he didn't know who he
was anymore. A soldier, certainly, but what cause did he fight for?
The lack of an answer bothered him more than he cared to admit.

He dropped his pack next to the strange foam bed. The deep blue
substance molded itself to his body, which was comfortable but also a
little unnerving. He sat heavily, allowing the bed to form around his
legs. Perhaps a nap was a good next step. He was exhausted from the
trip to Cajamarca and he'd need to be sharp if they were dispatched
to pursue this Irakesh.

Beep beep, beep beep. The insistent chiming came from a bulky black box sitting on his makeshift desk. He had no idea what purpose the clear platform jutting from the wall had served, but it filled its new role adequately. He stood up, hand dropping instinctively to the .460 holstered at his side even though there was no real cause.

It was his sat-link, a device Mohn provided all senior officers. It allowed them to send and receive messages from just about anywhere in the world, regardless of cell coverage. He'd assumed the device had burned out in the second wave, but clearly he'd been mistaken. It was very much active.

He picked up the black plastic box, flipping the tiny screen open. It flickered to life, displaying a single mail icon. He touched the screen with his finger, heartbeat accelerating as he waited for the contents to be displayed. The message was succinct and demanding in typical Mohn fashion.

Report situation immediately.

21

NOT TOO BRIGHT

Blair just wasn't very bright. He had to accept that. What other possible reason could he have for invading the sanctum of a twenty-five-millennia-old werewolf goddess furious enough to shred him into very tiny Blair pieces? Yet he didn't have a choice. Someone had to talk to the Mother, to explain both what had happened and what the team hoped to do about it. Since he'd been the one to let Irakesh get away, that responsibility fell to him.

He took a deep breath as he walked down the ramp and into the Ark's central chamber. He expected the Mother to react instantly to his presence, blurring across the chamber to thunder her rage. The last thing he'd ever have guessed was to find her kneeling before the central obelisk, tiny hands gathered in her lap. Silver hair hung down her shoulders, head bowed. Her entire body shook, agonized sobs rolling from her.

To his surprise a golden retriever lay curled up at her feet, his wet nose pressed against her knee in a canine show of support. The Mother didn't acknowledge the animal, but neither did she push it away. The dog looked up at Blair's approach, thumping his tail against the marble in greeting before turning back to the Mother.

It was the most vulnerable he'd ever seen her. The implacable goddess was gone, replaced by a woman overwhelmed by all that happened. It called to the compassionate side of Blair and while he knew she might kill him for witnessing such weakness, he couldn't help what he did next.

He padded slowly across the warm marble, removing his fleece windbreaker and settling the garment around her shoulders. Then he sank down next to her and gathered her into a hug. To his shock she sobbed into his shoulder, loud wails continuing as she released her grief. It was long minutes before she finally stopped, looking up with those emerald eyes.

"I've failed. Every preparation foiled, every plan in ruins. All my work undone. The world lays naked before the deathless," she said, her voice a bare whisper. She pulled the fleece tighter, shoulders slumped.

"Mother, I don't understand. Who is Irakesh and why was he in the Ark? It sounds like he's done something terrible," Blair asked, choosing each word with deliberate care. He'd seen her shifts in mood and didn't want to risk her flying into a sudden rage. Not that she could be blamed at this point.

"He is a deathless from my time, the son of my best friend and greatest adversary," she explained, regaining a shadow of her composure. Tears had carved paths through the dust coating her face. That and her diminutive size made her seem so young. "Irakesh must have smuggled his way into the Ark before I placed it in stasis. He was in a rejuvenator in my very sanctum, yet I was unaware of his presence. When he woke, I'm sure he lurked in the shadows until he was certain I was away. Then he emerged to steal the most precious thing he could. The access key to the Ark of the Redwood."

"Like the one I gained when I touched the Mother's hand?" Blair asked, the confirmation of his suspicions like a physical blow. It confirmed the existence of other Arks, and it meant that their enemy was about to claim one.

"Just so," she replied, with a shallow nod. She wiped a tear from her cheek and rose gracefully to her feet. "It allows the bearer complete control over the Ark they are linked to. It also allows them to draw on the strength of the Ark, regardless of distance. Your own strength will grow, once this Ark is repaired and you've had time to master it. Irakesh already knows how to accomplish such a feat. Even now he races for the Ark of the Redwood. If he reaches it he will have a tool of incredible power, one that will allow him to reshape the northern continent into his own empire. An empire that serves his mother, Sekhmet."

"So I have this kind of power over your Ark?" Blair asked. The prospect was dizzying.

"You would have, had the control rods not been so severely damaged," the Mother corrected. The mask was returning, but at least she didn't seem angry. "Until the Ark is repaired your control is limited and you will not be able to draw on the strength it contains."

"Irakesh will have to get to this Ark of the Redwood. I've spoken to the others and we're prepared to pursue him. We can stop him, Mother. We won't allow him to take an Ark, but if we are going to succeed we have to know what he's capable of," Blair said, pushing the conversation towards its true intent. The Mother's gaze weighed him, then she delivered a rare smile.

"Very well, I will allow you whelps to test yourselves against Irakesh. He is clever and his bloodline potent, but he is young and you may be able to defeat him if you demonstrate the same resourcefulness that allowed you to wake me," she explained. The fleece jacket tumbled forgotten to the floor, revealing the same white skirt and blouse she usually wore. "I will tell you of the deathless, of their powers and how you might counter them.

"I designed the champions to have their power divided by sex. Men are able to shape both their own DNA and that of others. As an extension they can touch the minds of others," she explained, more forthcoming than he'd ever seen her. "Women are larger and stronger. I removed their ability to shape but gifted them with a powerful resistance to such forces. This will be vital to overcoming Irakesh, for his powers are also blunted by this resistance."

"It would be helpful to understand the nature of those powers," Blair offered, encouraged by the half smile she wore. He wasn't sure what he'd said or done to improve her mood, but he wasn't about to question his luck. "What can the deathless do? Irakesh both walked the shadows and blurred. Then he hit me with a burst of light. It was the worst pain I've ever experienced."

"Deathless absorb the light of the sun in the same way we use the moon. They channel this energy directly," the Mother replied. "This manifests in a variety of ways. They can remove light entirely, allowing them to shadow dance. This is accomplished differently than a female champion, but the end result is nearly identical. They can also use it to alter their appearance, but it is an illusion, whereas you can actually shape DNA. This light can be released in radioactive bursts, which is what Irakesh did to disable you. He cooked every part of your body at once and it took time to repair your muscles and blood vessels."

"How does he blur?" Blair asked. The rest made sense, but it didn't explain that power.

"The energy suffuses every part of his body, allowing it to accelerate. In this one way they are very similar to males," the Mother answered, smearing the dust across her cheek with the back of her hand. "However, it is more taxing for a deathless to blur and they typically use it only as a last resort."

"Are they more powerful than we are?" Blair asked, afraid he wasn't going to like the answer.

"In some ways, yes. Their ability to shape is more versatile and better defined, and none of their powers are determined by their sex. However, they are physically weaker than champions. The average deathless is weaker than you and would be completely outmatched by a female," she said, raising a single finger. "There is a caveat, however. Deathless gain strength by consuming the flesh of the fallen. If they consume enough they can become enormously strong. Irakesh has not lived long enough to achieve such massive strength, but other deathless you encounter may."

"There are other deathless? How many are out there?" Blair asked.

"Only those who took shelter in a Great Ark could have survived.

My own Ark was damaged, so I was unable to bring a retinue. Other Arks have two banks of rejuvenators."

"How many great Arks are there?"

"We don't know. Osiris, Sekhmet and I discovered one on every continent. To my knowledge the one in the land you call Antarctica was abandoned, but the other six are all functional," she said, face growing pained. "The Ark of the Redwood holds my daughter Jes'Ka and her servant Lucas, but many of the others may possess a full pantheon. There are also lesser places of power that may have allowed their lords to survive."

"You speak of the Arks as though you discovered them alongside the deathless," Blair said.

Her eyes flashed, face hardening.

"That is a conversation for another time, a mistake I'd rather not revisit. For now you must concern yourself with Irakesh," she said, good humor evaporating. "You must race him to the Ark of the Redwood and you must wrest the key from him before he can use it."

"You've seen inside my memories, so you have access to global maps. Do you know where this Ark is?" Blair asked, happy to steer the conversation in another direction.

"Much has changed, including the sea level, but it is on the western coast of the northern continent. The Ark was on the shore in my time, but now rests at the bottom of a bay, one that could correspond to the city you call San Francisco," the Mother explained, cocking her head as she considered. "It is imperative that you find Irakesh before he reaches the Ark."

"How do we take the key from him?" he asked.

"Kill him."

"When we pursued him just after the theft he sent a swarm of zombies to slow us down. He's bound to try something similar. Is there anything we can do to counteract that advantage?" Blair asked.

"Had your kind not shaped the mighty wolf into compliant little servants that might have been possible," she said, though she reached down to stroke the golden retriever at her feet in spite of her words. Perhaps her opinion was changing. "There isn't time for you to create a pack in any case. The animals you bond must be willing and the bond takes weeks or even months to be complete. Yet the sooner you start the sooner you will have allies."

"Bond?" Blair asked, intrigued.

"There is much Ahiga should have taught you. You can assume the form of a wolf and can strengthen wolves in your presence, making them faster, stronger and more resilient to damage. Whether this same feat will work on the twisted canine bodies your kind have created I do not know."

"How can we track him?" Blair asked, sidestepping to a less sensitive subject.

"Because you both possess a key, you are linked, in a way. You can feel his presence and he yours. You have probably already experienced this. The closer he is, the stronger the feeling," she answered, striding towards the chamber that held her rejuvenator. "Tell the others they are to accompany you. Leave immediately. If you fail here, it will be the final failure. The world will belong to the deathless and the champions will be extinguished."

22

WELCOME TO THE JUNGLE

I rakesh swatted his neck, crushing the tiny insect that had alighted there. He searched the memories he'd gained from consuming brain matter. Mosquitos they were now known as. They'd been called blood drinkers in his own time, reviled by everyone. Most insects avoided the deathless, but mosquitos were more than happy to drain his blood. They were quite capable of accidentally spreading the deathless virus.

"Master," Trevor called, voice pitched low enough that the buzz of the cicadas and rushing water nearly drowned it out. He crouched low along the bank of the Amazon, pointing through the brush towards a small group of figures moving in their direction. His expression was vacant, a sure sign that it was his Risen speaking and not the man's true consciousness. That was likely still trapped, still trying to wrest control of his own body.

Irakesh turned to study the figures, which were difficult to spot in the odd green and brown clothing. Camouflage, that's what it was called. There were a half dozen, each carrying one of the wonderful guns he'd learned about from the officer in the House of Mohn.

Cyntia prowled the jungle behind Trevor, hair bound into a simple ponytail. The Ka-Ken wore some of the clothing they'd liberated from the last group they'd encountered. Irakesh was still digesting that lot, but it was wise to take opportunity whenever it was found. Consuming more victims would not only increase his strength, but also afford more knowledge of this new world.

He didn't like relying on Trevor and still didn't trust Cyntia. She was timid, but also calculating. The way she watched him was exactly the same as he might have reserved for a more powerful deathless, always searching for an advantage but playing the dutiful servant until the right moment. He'd considered killing her, but had not for two reasons. It might upset Trevor, and he was just beginning to make progress with his new vassal. Also, she could have enormous potential if he could turn her fully.

Such a thing had been exceedingly rare in his own time. Even Ra had only turned a few champions, and that had required all of her considerable charms to accomplish. If he could do such a thing, it would win him much prestige in addition to a powerful ally.

"Cyntia, circle around behind them. Trevor and I will approach. When they are focused on us attack from behind. I know you find the act distasteful, but you should feed on any you kill. It will increase your strength and help you protect Trevor," Irakesh ordered, as reasonably as possible. The first step was getting her to feed indiscriminately. It would increase her power dramatically and would teach her to love feeding. He could use that eventually.

Cyntia gave a nod, disappearing into the shadows. It bothered him that she could use something so similar to his own power, almost as much as her near immunity to his shaping. It made her dangerous, though that would be true of Trevor eventually as well. He'd already shown more independence than he should have been capable of, but also an ability to troubleshoot problems that would make him an invaluable advisor once he was properly trained. Such a dangerous dichotomy.

Irakesh marched through the jungle, stepping over ferns and around the trunks of unfamiliar trees. He made no effort to disguise his progress, allowing the nearby soldiers to see him. Trevor trailed after, slipping through the jungle with the skill of a lifelong hunter.

Where had he come by that? Irakesh would need to ask when the opportunity arose.

"Hello," Irakesh called, raising his hand in a friendly wave. The soldiers fanned out, shooting each other glances when they realized they'd been spotted. "You're the first people we've seen in days. Thank god. We could use your help."

He drew up short in a small clearing, waiting as four men and two women lined up along the edge. They looked ready to flee back into the jungle, each cradling a rifle. Most had pistols at their sides as well. Those weapons would be exceedingly useful.

"Who are you?" a beefy man asked, stepping fully into the clearing. He was bald, with a bandana tied around his forehead to block the sweat. His bearing screamed soldier, but he was too relaxed. Too sure that Irakesh was no threat because he wasn't armed.

"My name is Irakesh. The man behind me is Trevor," he offered, taking a step closer. It had the desired effect; all six soldiers brought their weapons to bear, ready to gun him down if he did something that displeased them. He ignored the weapons, plastering a smile on his face. "We are deathless and we are hungry. Your group will satiate that hunger. When you are dead we will take your memories and your weapons. If there are others you hold dear, we will pry their location from you and visit death upon them as well."

It was a bit dramatic, but he'd always enjoyed such flourishes. What was the point of being deathless if you couldn't terrify the unblooded?

The man's jaw sagged open, eyes widening. Irakesh grinned as Cyntia materialized behind one of the soldiers, a stocky woman with a pump-action shotgun. The woman shrieked, drawing the attention of most of the others.

The man who'd spoken and the other woman both had the presence of mind to fire at Irakesh. Unfortunately for them he was no longer there. He split his focus, triggering two powers at the same time. First, he blurred behind the leader so quickly that his passage kicked up a wind that swirled some of the large green leaves littering the jungle floor.

The second was more difficult, but also more fun. Irakesh left a perfect illusion of himself standing where he'd been before blurring. Rifles cracked as the fools desperately tried to bring him down. The bullets passed right through his illusion, giving the impression that he was completely immune to their weapons.

Irakesh extended wicked black claws, like a werewolf's but smaller and more precise. He reached around to slash the leader's throat, seizing the man's rifle as he fell. The memories he'd ingested didn't tell him what type of gun it was, but he understood that if he pulled the trigger it would belch a hail of small metal balls. So he aimed the gun at the next soldier and did exactly that. The man went down in a spray of blood, body jerking from multiple impacts as the gun roared.

Trevor sprinted low across the clearing, slamming the woman on the far right into the bole of a tree. Her spine cracked, spilling her limply to the ground. Her shotgun tumbled away, caught by Trevor before it could hit the ground. He brought the stock smoothly to his shoulder, aiming at the next soldier. The man spun to face him but it was far too late.

Trevor stroked the trigger and the gun roared. The force of the blow picked the man up, hurling him back several paces. He didn't rise. The move impressed Irakesh and not just because it demonstrated that Trevor had the skills of a warrior. Most new deathless would have fed on their first target, unable to pull themselves away to focus on the rest of combat. Trevor had done so without hesitation, quelling his instincts in favor of tactical sense. He was strong willed, perhaps too strong.

"Excellent work," Irakesh called, surveying the bodies littering the clearing. A few still moaned, but none were any threat. "Now it is time to feed. We will need our strength for what is to come."

23

PURSUIT

"Which direction?" Liz asked, turning to face Blair. He wore a set of camouflage fatigues complete with a matching cap. They were a little too baggy, but choices had been limited. His eyes were hidden behind sunglasses, just like her own. They cut the sun to a manageable glare, though she still found herself squinting. Part of that was dealing with the cacophony of jungle sounds, so overpowering to her new senses despite being nearly a hundred yards away.

"That way," he said, nodding in the direction of the jungle stretching down the hill behind the village. It was the same one where Irakesh had left the horde of zombies to slow them. "The feeling is faint. I'm guessing he's at least a day or two ahead of us. Maybe more. I was hoping we'd be able to pick up a trail too, but there are just too many competing scents."

"Yeah, all I can make out is monkey pee and flowers. Jordan, you're a soldier. Any suggestions on how we can catch this guy?" she asked, turning her attention to the blond giant. He wore a very similar uniform, but it was tailored to fit his well defined frame. Where Blair was merely muscular, Jordan was a wall in clothes.

"I've never been a jungle guerrilla, but I know warfare. You want to catch this guy? We need to figure out where he's going and get there first. Following him allows him to set all sorts of fun traps and to lead us wherever he wants us to go," Jordan explained, resting the barrel of his automatic rifle against his shoulder. Liz still had no idea what kind of gun it was, but she knew from her brother that it was a high caliber just based on the size.

"So how do we catch him, then?" Bridget asked, peering around the village nervously. It was littered with the carnage from their battle. Liz didn't blame the petite woman for being nervous. She was nervous herself.

"We need a vehicle, but that will come later," Blair interjected, already starting towards the jungle. "If he's in there, then he'll have to move at the same pace we do. Once we're on the other side, somewhere in Columbia, we can find a jeep or a boat or something. We know this world better than he does, so that gives us a small advantage."

"Agreed," Jordan said, striding after Blair. Liz trotted after, and Bridget brought up the rear. "There's an airport in Panama where Mohn keeps some of its aircraft. There's no way they had time to change security, so if we can get there I can probably find us a helicopter. Maybe even a jet. Assuming any of it survived the CME."

"That might work. If the Mother's memory is correct, we're looking at San Francisco, so if Irakesh goes by land he'll have to pass through Panama. We can follow him that far, then fly north if we haven't caught up to him by then," Blair said as Jordan fell into step beside him. It surprised Liz how friendly the two had grown since Jordan had risen as a werewolf. He'd dogged their steps for months, even destroying Trevor's house back in San Diego.

Liz fell back a few paces to allow Bridget to catch up. She eyed the other woman sidelong, part of her irked by the woman's perfect hair and creamy skin despite the humidity. It made her feel so, well, ginger. "Walk the shadows. Try to stay a little ways behind us. Paranoid maybe, but Irakesh might have left some surprises and if he did I want to be ready."

"All right," Bridget agreed, giving a tight nod. The shadows enveloped the tiny brunette, covering not only the sight of her but also her scent. Liz jogged along the road, taking a sharp right into the jungle after Jordan and Blair. They were a good forty or fifty feet ahead, moving swiftly as they passed beneath the thick canopy. None of them knew the jungle well, but she hoped their new senses would alert them to danger.

They moved north for several hours, marking the sun's passage as it occasionally broke through the jungle to illuminate a patch of dim undergrowth. Blair moved unerringly forward, clearly focused on some distant goal none of the rest of them could see. Sometimes they travelled along a path; at others they wound through the thick undergrowth.

Blair finally paused in a clearing, kneeling next to something. Jordan dropped back next to a tree, rifle cradled in both massive arms as he scanned the area. Ever the perpetual soldier. Liz glided into the clearing, crouching next to Blair.

"What did you find?" she asked, pitching her voice low. It was swallowed by the cacophony of the jungle, monkeys chattering, water dripping, and a hundred other sounds.

"There's blood on these leaves," Blair replied, holding up a scarlet-stained leaf for her perusal. "Someone was killed here. Maybe several someones. I think it happened as recently as yesterday, but I'm not a forensic scientist or anything. Just my gut call based on how it smells."

"What do you think—" Liz began, but the jungle exploded around them. Bullets ripped through the clearing, catching Blair in the chest. He was blasted backwards, rolling through undergrowth as the barrage continued. Liz dove for cover, huddling behind a tree. A bullet punched through the bark near her head, setting her ears ringing.

"Liz, see if you can get behind them," Jordan bellowed, popping out from behind the tree where he'd taken cover. He sighted down the barrel of his rifle, squeezing off a noisy trio of shots. Then he dropped back into cover. A woman screamed in the distance and a shape plummeted from a tree. The next time Jordan fired it came from the opposite side of the tree.

Liz closed her eyes and took a deep breath. She summoned the shadows, feeling their cool embrace wrap around her. She glided silently through the jungle towards the gunfire. It came from at least four different places she could identify. There were probably more that she couldn't. What the hell had they stumbled into?

She leapt into the air, seizing a thick branch. She used it to swing herself atop a perch in a neighboring tree. It afforded her a great vantage. There were five opponents, each carrying an old carbine rifle. Those she recognized. They were .308s, the kind her brother used for hunting. Although they were incredibly accurate they didn't hold many rounds and sucked at close range. They were also slow to reload.

Their opponents were spread out along the jungle floor, which meant she now had the high ground. They seemed unaware of her. Perfect.

Don't kill them. A voice rang through her mind, powerful and clear. She recognized it as Blair, though the voice was much stronger than it had been even a few weeks ago. *I will handle this.*

He must have sent the message to all of them. Bridget hadn't attacked despite having time to get into position, and Jordan huddled behind his tree waiting. Liz relaxed, deciding to wait and see what Blair would do.

He rose to his feet striding towards his assailants. His wounds had already healed. Another burst of gunfire lit the clearing, but Blair blurred to the right as the bullets ripped apart the foliage where he'd been standing. He blurred again, landing next to the root of a tree so thick that it blocked his body below the neck. What was he doing?

Blair extended a palm as he gazed up into the trees, then closed it into a fist. Tendrils of blue light shot from his hands, very similar to the ability Ahiga had used on her back in Acapulco. All five assailants went limp, weapons tumbling to the jungle floor as their bodies followed. Blair walked forward, stopping in their midst. None rose, though she could still hear their frantic heartbeats. Bridget appeared near Blair a moment later, already having shifted into a terrifying silver beast. Great, she'd be naked later. Again.

Liz leapt into the air, keeping her human form as she landed nimbly near Blair. It was getting easier to perform superhuman feats without needing to shift. That was advantageous. If nothing else it saved her from losing yet another set of clothing.

"They're Peruvian national police," Blair said, staring fixedly at one of the men they'd captured. The man's bearded face had landed in the mud, coating it in sticky brown goop. "This one is their leader. They were patrolling this area because someone wiped out one of their hunting parties here."

The man's eyes widened and he began to quiver. The scent of terror was overpowering. Blair turned to face her as Jordan moved cautiously to their position. "The bodies were eaten. All they found were bones, and they looked like they'd been gnawed. They assume we're deathless like Irakesh. Better to shoot first and I can't say I blame them. It's been bad from what little I glimpsed."

"You pulled all that from his mind?" Bridget asked. Liz didn't think the awe was feigned.

"I'm used to having to deal with you ladies when using my powers," Blair explained, offering a genuine smile. Why did it bother Liz so much that it was directed at Bridget? "These guys have no defenses. None. I can just sort of take what I want. Speaking of which, they have jeeps. Six of them. Back at their camp. There are about thirty-five of them and they're terrified. They don't know what to do other than hide in the jungle."

"This one is the leader?" Jordan asked, slinging his rifle strap over his shoulder as he knelt next to the terrified man. "Can he understand English?"

"He doesn't speak it well, but that shouldn't matter to you. You can learn Spanish just by pulling it from his mind," Blair explained. His tone was dispassionate, as if he were talking about reading data from a computer.

"You can't do that," Liz said, recoiling from Blair. "That's rape, just in a different way. They're not your playthings. Let them go."

"Liz, if I let them go, they'll try to kill us and we'll end up killing them," Blair protested, turning his full attention on her. "If you ask me to I will, but I think it's a bad idea."

"They aren't going to kill us," Jordan said, squatting next to the leader and withdrawing the hand cannon holstered on his thigh. "Just tell them we want to borrow a ride. They saw Blair do that Jedi magic shit. Bridget is a nine foot werewolf. They're going to quietly do whatever we ask and hope we go away without killing anyone."

"We'll cooperate. Just do not kill us," the man protested in ragged English. It sounded as if he could barely move his face. He looked pathetic in the mud there. Liz felt horrible for inflicting this on the man, even indirectly. "You can take one of our jeeps. We'll even give you a little food. Just go away and do not hurt us. That's all we ask."

"All right," Blair said. He gave a shrug and opened his fist. Their captives relaxed as one, suddenly in control of their bodies again. They scrambled away from Bridget as fast as they could, huddling near the giant gnarled roots of a capirona tree. "I do think Bridget should remain as she is for now. It might 'incentivize' them to follow through, and maybe it will mean I don't need to poke around in anyone else's head."

I'm letting this go because you're the leader and I don't want to undermine you. Blair's voice echoed through Liz's mind. *But you cannot allow this sort of moral quandary to keep you from making hard decisions. Remember when we ran from what we'd become? What if we'd stuck around and woken the Mother immediately? How many more champions could we have created?*

This is different, she thought back, struggling to suppress her anger. *These are people, Blair. The people we're supposed to protect. I know we're fighting a war, but that doesn't mean we use the same methods the enemy does. If we make that choice, what do we become? There are some lines I'm not willing to cross. You need to accept that.*

All right, he agreed, though she could sense his reluctance. *We'll play this your way, but there's a reason the good guy usually loses, Liz. It's because the bad guy fights smart and isn't hindered by arbitrary rules.*

24

HIDDEN REBEL BASE

Blair stifled his frustration as he followed the Peruvian police into their hidden rebel base, a series of crude tree houses built at the top of the mighty capirona trees common in this part of the jungle. Each had a trunk wider than his dining room table, some rising more than a hundred feet into the jungle's thick canopy.

Ropes had been strung over some of the wider branches, allowing people to flit safely between houses. It was ingenious, really. Staying off the jungle floor meant avoiding deathless, just as mankind's ancestors had once avoided predators back when they'd roamed the plains of the Serengeti. It also provided a vantage over the surrounding jungle, allowing them to spot intruders before they arrived.

That's exactly what had happened when their group had approached. The camp had erupted into activity, every member taking to the trees and arming themselves with a rifle. Each and every soldier glared down at them, ready to rain death if Blair and his friends proved a threat. More than a few shot terrified looks at Bridget's lupine form.

The center of the camp was a fire pit surrounded by logs set far enough back to serve as comfortable seating. It was ringed by the six jeeps he'd seen in the leader's mind, each battered vehicle painted with the same olive so many militaries seemed to favor. He wasn't sure how they'd even gotten them into the jungle, but the jeeps must be nimble if they'd made it this far. That would prove useful, though he wondered if fuel would be an issue.

"They are scared," Rodrigo said, glancing up at his compatriots before turning back to Liz. His face was covered in mud but still noble somehow. Blair noticed that his hand never strayed too close to the pistol at his side. The rifle was slung over his shoulder, as non-threatening as he could make it. Having just been inside of the man's mind, none of this surprised him. "I will not ask them to come down unless you insist. If all you wish is a vehicle, the sooner you take it the better for all."

"We'll be away shortly," Liz said, pointedly ignoring Blair as she walked next to the dark-haired leader. That irked him, though he understood her reasoning. Maybe she was even right about him being too callous. It was a fine line to walk, one he knew he struggled with. "We don't have time to waste. We're chasing the thing that killed your people."

"What did this?" Rodrigo asked, flinching when Liz reached up to comb her fingers through her hair. "We have run afoul of zombies, but there has been nothing else like the strangers who devoured our people. We heard the gunshots, but when we arrived they were all dead. They should have been able to reach the trees. Or at least run away, yet all of them were killed within just a few feet of each other. Their bodies were just...gone. It makes no sense."

"Blair?" Liz asked, pausing at the circle of jeeps to face him.

"This was done by one of the deathless," Blair explained, stepping forward to join them. He pointed up at the trees. "These defenses will work for now, because the deathless are still stupid and slow. That will change as they feed. They'll get stronger and smarter. The thing that killed and ate your people was more advanced than the zombies you've seen. Much more. If we don't stop him he'll help his kind take over everything. Even if he doesn't you're still going to face things you can't deal with here."

Bridget's silver form joined their little group, but Rodrigo refused to look at her. He'd gone even more pale.

"How do we defend ourselves then? If we cannot hide here, we have nowhere else to go," he explained, shoulders slumping. "Our people haven't given up, but many are beginning to despair."

"You're not going go be able to do it here," Jordan rumbled as he joined their little group. He gave an expansive gesture toward the southern wall of foliage. "You can escape quickly, but since it's so open your enemies can come at you from all directions. You need somewhere with choke points so you can manage the flow of enemies. I don't know that you're going to find it in a jungle."

"Even if we can, food is an issue," Rodrigo admitted with a sigh. He leaned against one of the jeeps. "The jungle has enough of a bounty to sustain us, but many of our hunting parties do not return. Most went by themselves or as a pair. Yesterday we sent a larger party for the first time. As you know, they were killed by this—what did you call it? Deathless."

"There is an option, but it's dangerous," Blair offered. It was crazy, but it was the only option he could think of. "There is a mine up in the mountains, about two days from here. Yanacocha. If you go there you will find a pyramid. Inside is a woman of incredible power, one we call the Mother. If you approach her and ask for aid, she can protect you from the deathless and see that you have food."

"He's right," Liz agreed with a quick nod. Blair was genuinely surprised after their disagreement. "Getting there will be challenging, but if you treat her with respect, she'll probably help you."

"I'm guessing she'll take you to Cajamarca," he added. Blair removed his hat, squeezing it like a rag to ring out the sweat. "We've started gathering refugees there and they could use the protection you can offer. If some of you are willing to take a chance, you may even accept the gift from her. You could become like Bridget over there, strong enough to protect your people."

"Whatever you choose is your decision," Liz said, walking over to the jeep. "We won't interfere, so long as you give us one of these. You offered food, but since it sounds like you're struggling we don't want to burden you further. We can fend for ourselves as long as you give us enough gas to get out of Columbia."

"You can take this one. It has a full tank, which will get you as far as Columbia," Rodrigo explained, opening the door and gesturing to Liz.

"How do we get out of the Jungle?" Liz asked, moving past Rodrigo and sliding into the driver's seat.

"Follow that trail to the north. It winds down a steep road, but if you are careful you will be fine until it levels out. You will emerge along the bank of the Amazon, just across the border into Columbia. It's not an easy journey, perhaps five or six days if you drive all day," he explained, visibly relieved when Liz slammed the door behind her.

Blair removed his pack, moving to the far side of the jeep. He opened the rear door and slid inside. The pack fit neatly between his legs. Jordan jumped in the front passenger seat ahead of him, rolling down the window and positioning his rifle so he could fire if needed.

Bridget picked up her pack in a massive clawed hand, reaching inside for a camouflaged shirt. She began to shift, pulling it over her head as she did so. By the time she was human, she'd slid into the back seat next to Blair, her bare legs tantalizing. She gave him a knowing smile as she caught what he'd been staring at.

He stared at the back of Liz's head, conflicting emotions raging between them. What the hell did he want out of all this? It was going to be a long trip.

25

WAKING UP

T revor stared at himself in the small shaving mirror he'd taken from one of the corpses he'd devoured back in the jungle. Parts of it were familiar. He was still a freckled ginger, even if his face was more pale than it had been. His goatee was *exactly* the same. The hair had stopped growing when he'd died, so at least there was no more shaving.

He'd even retained the battered green baseball cap he'd brought when he, Blair and Liz had flown to Peru to wake the Mother. If someone didn't look too closely, they might think he was the same man. That illusion was shattered the second he opened his mouth, especially if he smiled.

Every last tooth now ended in a sharp point, a mouthful of fangs sharks would envy. The scientist in him knew why of course. They were the most efficient way to rend flesh. Human teeth were largely flat because they were omnivores. He'd become a carnivore and subsisted purely on flesh. The tastiest kind was living human.

It amazed him how gratifying the simple act of staring at the mirror could be. For weeks now he'd been a prisoner trapped in his own body, unable to exert even rudimentary control. That had changed over the last two days, as he'd fed over and over. Each brutal act had horrified him, but the worst part was that feeding was already becoming normal. It revolted him less than it had yesterday. How long until he began to enjoy it?

He glanced at the camp, sizing up his companions. Irakesh sat on a wide rock near their little fire, leafing through a pocket-sized copy of the *King James Bible* liberated from one of their victims. He turned each page with deliberate care, treating the battered thing with a reverence Trevor found surprising.

Cyntia was curled up in a sleeping bag on the opposite side of the fire. Her heartbeat was slow and strong, breathing even and deep. She was asleep, thank god. He liked her and had things been different they might have become romantically involved. That was no longer possible, given what he'd become. Even if it were he didn't like what was happening to her. Irakesh had encouraged Cyntia to feed often, and Trevor could already see it having an effect. Her gaze had grown wild, and she was more prone to violence. He wished he could tell her to flee, to get away from Irakesh.

"Your world is a very strange place," Irakesh began, closing the tattered black bible. It was the sort a soldier might carry into combat. Irakesh set it on top of the backpack he'd recently salvaged. "This tome contains such strange mythology. Do your people really believe this?"

"A lot of them do," Trevor admitted, unsure how to answer. Speaking still felt strange, but part of him was pleased that he could manage it now. "Or if not that book, then another book they claim is holy. I imagine you'd find them equally strange."

"Genesis in particular amused me. The idea that earth was created in a single day by some sky god in robes? It's preposterous," Irakesh scoffed, rolling his eyes. The gesture seemed too normal somehow, out of place on his master's monstrous face. "The world is far, far older than your people can conceive."

"You might be surprised," Trevor shot back, setting down the shaving mirror and taking off his hat. It was reflexive. He wasn't sweating. He couldn't sweat. "Our scientists estimate the world is about four and half billion years old. It will live another four to five billion before the sun goes out." He squinted up at the brilliant orb, shading his eyes.

"Why do you scrunch your eyes like that?" Irakesh said, shaking his head with an amused smile. "We are deathless, not humans. The sun is our ally. Staring into the sun for at least three minutes a day is actually good for you."

"Fuck," Cyntia growled. Trevor glanced over to see her recoiling from the sun as she sat up in her sleeping bag. Had she just stared into it?

"I guess the same isn't true for werewolves?" he said.

"Her kind rely on the moon," Irakesh raised an eyebrow at Cyntia, delivering a look that bled contempt. "But I was speaking of your holy tome. This Bible. Did you know there is a passage that says...let me see." He picked the book up and thumbed to a slim page. "Ah yes, Timothy 2:12. My favorite absurdity thus far." He cleared his throat, affecting a mocking pose. "'I do not permit a woman to teach nor to hold authority over a man; she must be quiet.' Do your people practice this? Isis will be *furious*." He grinned like a mischievous frat kid who knew that a professor was about to be pranked.

"Yeah, that part only flies with a very small part of the world," Trevor argued, a bit floored by the passage. He'd never really studied the bible, but he'd never heard *that* part. "Women are equal to men where I come from, at least legally. There's still a wage gap, but it's a lot better than it used to be."

"You treated women as lesser beings?" Irakesh asked, looking at Trevor as if he'd sprouted a third eye. "They did not have all the legal rights of a man? I don't understand how your society functioned."

"Not well. So your society was matriarchal?" Trevor asked.

"Mine was, as were those Isis founded on this backward continent and the one to the north," Irakesh said, shaking his head. "Not all were. Osiris ruled the sprawling continent north of the Cradle. There were others, though I had no dealings with them."

"Is there nothing of our world you like?" Cyntia asked, hovering at the edge of the conversation. Trevor hadn't heard her get up, but then he rarely did unless she wanted to be heard. She settled on a stump not far from Trevor as she rubbed sleep from her eyes.

"Oh, yes, many things fascinate me," Irakesh admitted, setting the book on a rock next to him. "It amazes me that nearly everyone possesses the ability to write. Very few learned in my own time, and most of those recorded religious texts or important history. We wrote on stone so our words would last. The idea of using this paper your kind discovered never occurred to us. For all of our advancements it seems your world has done things ours could not."

"Were you there to see the creation of the deathless? What are we exactly?" Trevor asked, picking up his rifle and checking the slide for the fourth time in the last hour. The question had been bothering him, but he'd been reluctant to ask as he was still feeling his way with Irakesh.

"Ahh, I've been wondering when you'd find the courage to ask," Irakesh said, a toothy smile slipping into place. He rose, moving to a tree stump near Trevor. "The deathless arose from the desperation of Isis. The woman you know as the Mother. In our time her lover Osiris lay dying. She sought a way to preserve his life, and after many trials and with the aid of *my* mother, she finally found or created the secret to eternal life."

"The Mother was responsible for making the deathless? I thought she created the werewolves," Trevor asked. The two seemed contradictory.

"She created both," Irakesh explained. He picked up a stick and sketched a shape that might have been Europe. "Isis, her mate Osiris, and my own mother Ra were born in this place." He tapped an area near the northeast edge of the continent. Trevor wasn't great at geography, but he guessed it was meant to be England. "They discovered the First Ark, the one with the greatest strength and largest store of knowledge. They were pursued by Set, a cruel and sadistic tyrant even I feared.

"She pioneered a science you might call genetic manipulation, the shaping of human DNA. She created a virus that would allow one to live forever, but with the unfortunate side effect of killing you first."

"The zombie plague," Trevor said, suddenly understanding.

"Just so," Irakesh replied with a nod. He seemed to really enjoy the tale, each part punctuated by grand flourishes. "Initially Ra was adamantly opposed to the creation of the virus, but in time Set's strength grew. In order to stop him, she accepted the virus and became one of the most powerful deathless.

"Isis tried to stop her, but the virus was potent," Irakesh said, grin growing predatory. "It dramatically improved Ra's ability to shape. She was much, much more powerful than she'd been before. Where Isis had once been the undisputed master, now she was little more than an irritation. Ra could have killed her, but in honor of their centuries of friendship, she banished her from the Cradle. Isis fled to these shores, leaving Ra to rule. My mother forged a powerful army of deathless, using them to create an empire that spanned continents."

"That's horrible," Trevor said, aghast at the slaughter.

"Is it?" Irakesh asked, raising an eyebrow. He seemed genuinely confused. "Why?"

"I can't speak for your time, but my world had seven billion people. Almost all of them are dead now because of what she did," he explained. Irakesh merely laughed.

"Seven billion people. I can see from the memories I've ingested that this world has been poisoned. The oceans are filled with your refuse and at the same time empty of fish. Thousands of species have been wiped out. Forests cut down. You've gutted this world, prying every resource you can from her dying body," Irakesh said. He shook his head sadly. "Our kind are violent. Brutal. Yet we exist in harmony with our environment. We keep the population in check, and it is a good thing. Only through the virus will this world have a chance to heal. Those you call innocents are choking the life from her. So tell me, Trevor Gregg, which is a better world? One poisoned and robbed of resources, or one where the deathless rule over a controlled society? One that exists in harmony with its surroundings."

Trevor didn't answer immediately. His heart said that the deathless were wrong. They were unnatural and shouldn't exist. Yet

Irakesh's words made sense. Humanity had raped the world and if something like the zombie plague hadn't come along, how long would it have been before they wiped out all life?

"What about the werewolves?" he asked, setting his rifle against the rock. "They're powerful enough to rule over mankind without spreading a plague to wipe out everyone."

"Ahh, you're wondering if Isis presents a better way," Irakesh said, giving a warm laugh. It seemed out of place coming from a mouth full of fangs. The scarlet eyes didn't help, either. "She set up a class-based society. Only a handful killed come back as werewolves, making her champions very rare. Ra's method gives anyone a chance to rise among the deathless. Take you, for example. In time you will learn shaping and become powerful and respected by your peers. If you'd been slaughtered by a werewolf, you'd probably be dead now."

"I guess," Trevor said, though he wasn't sure he agreed with that logic. He had many more questions about the ancient world, but needed time to digest what he'd learned. "So where are we going? I still haven't figured out what your plan is. I know we're heading north, but you haven't said why."

"You are simply full of questions," Irakesh replied, amused grin slipping back into place. "I must admit I am very pleased at how quickly you're learning. It's nice to have decent conversation. I wasn't expecting that. My plan? I'm going to found an empire. I'll use the Ark of the Redwood to control the northern continent."

"Ark of the Redwood?" Trevor asked. It sounded like the name of a bank.

"Isis and Ra spent centuries exploring the world. They discovered many Arks. The one to the north is called the Ark of the Redwood. I stole the key from Isis, and we're heading north to seize it," Irakesh said. He rose from the rock, peering down at the river. "I will use that as my power base and will forge every deathless for a thousand miles into an army the likes of which this world has never seen. By the time Isis can turn her attention to me I'll be too well entrenched to remove."

"So we're going to walk all the way to North America?" Trevor asked. "That will take months. Longer if we encounter resistance on the way."

"I do not plan to walk. There is a port for the craft you call planes in the kingdom of Panama. It is there that we will find transport," Irakesh said, arching an eyebrow. The grin was gone. Evidently he didn't like being questioned.

"How are we going to fly it?" Trevor asked. He'd never learned to fly, but he was willing to bet it wasn't that hard. Garland had done it. Of course the learning curve was likely to be both steep and fatal.

"We must find a corpse who possesses this knowledge. Surely there will be at least one between here and there. If not we will decide on another course of action," Irakesh said, giving a shrug. The grin was back. "Either way we will escape our pursuers."

"You've mentioned these pursuers a few times," Trevor said, scratching his goatee. "Who are they? Couldn't we just turn around and ambush them?"

"They've been sent by Isis to stop us. She has gathered a small pack of champions and sent them after us. It's possible we could overcome them, but until I am certain I see no reason for a confrontation," Irakesh explained. He turned back to face Trevor. "I fought a pair of them, a Ka-Dun and Ka-Ken. Both were powerful, though untrained. We will face them again, but before we do I must teach you the rudiments of shaping."

Trevor knew immediately who Irakesh must be referring to, but carefully schooled his features to neutrality. It was best Irakesh not understand his connection to Blair and Liz, or it might be used against him.

Cunning, my host, the voice whispered, slithering through his mind. *Keep such knowledge to yourself. Be a dutiful servant and diligent student. The day will come when you are able to best your master.*

"I can learn to shape?" Trevor asked. He remembered the fantastic powers Blair had demonstrated.

"Of course," Irakesh scoffed, waving dismissively at Trevor. "You will be one of the most powerful shapers of this age. Your ability to shape is dictated by three things. The strength of your bloodline, the strength of your will, and your imagination. Your bloodline is impeccable, only one step removed from the native virus. Your will is stronger than any I've ever seen, and you clearly possess the ability to think creatively. With training you will be an incredible force."

"Can we start now?" Trevor asked. So much had been taken from him, and he sensed that the key to his freedom lay in mastering shaping.

26

DISOBEYING ORDERS

The Director picked up the clipboard attached to the door. So odd that with the level of tech Mohn had they still used paper charts for patients. Of course the medical industry was always the last to adopt anything, so maybe that shouldn't surprise him. He scanned the contents, noting that the surgery had been a success and there were no complications. What's more the patient would be ready for active duty the following day. Excellent.

He pushed open the heavy door, closing it gently behind him. The white-walled room was dominated by a wide hospital bed in an elevated position. Its occupant was pale but awake and alert. His normally well-trimmed goatee had grown into a scraggly black beard, and there were dark circles under his eyes. Yuri Filipov, looking considerably better than he had in the firefight in Panama. His legs lay on top of the sheets, both the flesh and blood one and the newly installed chrome cyber leg.

"How are you feeling, Yuri?" Mark asked, pulling a metal chair to the side of the bed and sitting down.

"Is good," Yuri said, giving a wide grin through the beard. "Replaced Yuri's leg. Better than new. Yuri cannot believe."

"I'm glad to hear that. I've read your report on the incident. In your estimation the pyramid is lost then?" the Director asked. Satellite footage had already confirmed it, but he wanted to hear Yuri's assessment anyway.

"Werewolves everywhere," Yuri said, shaking his head. "Commander ordered extraction team to pull out after big red werewolf tear off leg. Commander's position very bad. Did not see what happened after, but if commander survived would contact Mohn."

Despite the man's brevity and incredibly thick accent he had a keen eye. It just took a little effort to tease out the details. In this case, it sounded as if he'd missed the end of the fight. "You said that the package was still in Peru?"

"Is there," Yuri replied, giving a tight nod. "Beacon still broadcasting. Could be retrieved with small team. Drop in hot, enter hangar, get back on runway. Give Yuri team of four and could be done."

"Can you do it quietly?" the Director asked, leaning in close to the bed. "Off the books."

Yuri gave him an unreadable look for a long moment before replying. "Is possible. Is cover story for return? Landing will be questioned."

This was one of many reasons the Director trusted Yuri. He didn't ask why it was off the books. He didn't even want to know. All he was interested in was accomplishing the mission he'd been assigned.

"Let me worry about the landing. I'll have a flight cleared for this evening. Head down to hangar six at 7 PM. Your team will already be assembled," Mark said, rising from the stool. He walked to the door, then turned back to face Yuri. "The mission is critical. If the package can't be retrieved, it must be destroyed. I don't care if you have to detonate Panama. No one gets that weapon."

He stepped through the door and closed it behind him. This kind of flagrant disobedience would likely be the end of his career. In the past he'd been able to examine things with a clinical detachment, to make tough choices and commit unthinkable acts when needed. So why was he struggling here?

Maybe because the whole god-damned world had ended. Mohn had a responsibility to protect the human race, and for the first time in Mark's life, morality was overriding self-preservation. Maybe there'd be a clever quote about that on his tombstone.

27

SALVAGE OPERATION

The Mother surveyed the wreckage in the central chamber, a fresh spike of despair piercing her breast. So many centuries of labor to modify this place to suit her needs. It had required the full might of her empire for the entirety of that time. Now it lay in ruins around her, perhaps damaged beyond repair.

A wet nose pressed into her leg. She looked down to find Yukon staring up at her adoringly. The strength of his loyalty pulsed from him. He was a simple creature, accepting that she was master and he just a companion. What surprised her was how content he found himself in such a role. It was something no self-respecting wolf would have accepted.

Wolves could acknowledge another as alpha, but that was just first among equals. Yukon accepted that she was superior in all things and that she would take care of him, in the same way a child viewed a parent. It baffled her.

"We're going to embark on a journey," she said, stroking his golden fur. He leaned into her leg, closing his eyes as she pet him. "We must head west to the ocean."

She *must* repair the Ark, not just to secure her power base but also to lend strength to Blair's cause. The closer Irakesh came to the

Ark of the Redwood the stronger he would become. If Blair was to have a chance he'd need to pull strength from her Ark, but to do that it must be repaired.

In her own time she could have simply ordered her vassals to mine the necessary stone, then have it brought to another Ark or a place of power for imbuing. That was no longer possible. She'd have to mine the stone herself, and it must be done at a place of power. There were only two such places that might contain a charge this early in the cycle. One lay half a world away, but through luck or happenstance the other could be found in the ocean a few days west.

All she need do is secure one of these mighty ships she'd plucked from Blair's memory. This could be found in the city men had named Lima, somewhere to the southwest.

The Mother turned from the chamber, extending her aura to encompass Yukon. They blurred through corridors until they reached the surface, bursting into bright sunlight in a swirl of dust.

So fast, Yukon sent, giddy like a small child. Far more playful than any wolf would allow. *I am strong near you.*

"Your strength will grow as we bond, little Yukon," she said, smiling in spite of herself. She hated what had been done to the noble wolves, yet Yukon had proven brave and loyal. Perhaps there was more to these dogs than she'd been willing to admit.

What was that? She shaded her eyes, studying a cloud of dust along the south ridge. A vehicle rumbled down the trail, approaching the valley. Who dared violate the sanctity of her Ark? She shifted, baring her fangs as she and Yukon blurred towards the interlopers.

She charged up the trail, covering two miles in mere heartbeats. She landed on top of the hood of the jeep, which slammed on its brakes. There were four passengers, all wearing uniforms similar to the Mohn soldiers she'd so recently slaughtered.

"Peace," the man in the driver's seat cried. He had scraggly black hair badly in need of a comb. "We've come in peace. We were sent by your, uh, Ka-Dun. He said we might find sanctuary here."

"Blair offered sanctuary?" she growled, flexing her claws.

"Yes," the man replied, nodding vigorously. "He said that the werewolves are champions. Please, we have little food and no place to go. The zombies are everywhere. We are willing to work to earn our keep, but we need help. Do not turn us away."

She considered. These men came as supplicants sent by her servant. If Blair had promised safety, then she was honor-bound to grant it. Was he wrong to do so? Very few had likely survived the deathless. They *did* need protection. He had done well, she decided.

"Very well, but you will serve as I bid. How many are you?" she demanded, dropping to the ground next to the jeep. She shifted back to her human form. The man's eyes widened as he stared at her through the jeep's driver-side window.

"There are about thirty of us. The rest of the vehicles are up the ridge, a mile or so back. I am Rodrigo," he said, pale underneath his tan.

"You may address me as Mother. Gather your people, Rodrigo. We journey west, first to Cajamarca and then on to Lima. You will aid me in my task," she said, allowing a smile.

Blair had done very well indeed.

28

MEDELLIN 12KM

M edellin 12km. Blair heaved a sigh of relief as they whizzed past the green sign. After days of slogging through jungles and backroads, they'd finally reached recognizable civilization. They were dirty, sweaty, tired, and more than a little irritable. Maybe they'd travel more quickly now that they'd reached real freeways.

Then again maybe not. He peered out the rear passenger window at the cracked asphalt stretching before them. It was clogged with a sea of cars, more familiar Toyotas and Fords replacing the generic motorcars he'd seen back in Peru. Figures shuffled between those vehicles, zombies in various stages of decay. Most looked up as they approached, shambling towards them with hungry eyes and low moans.

Jordan guided the jeep smoothly around them, his reflection in the rear-view mirror impassive. One of the zombies got a bit too close, a dark-haired woman in a white dress. Her face was bathed in blood, her eyes hollow and vacant as she lunged for the front of the jeep. Blair braced himself as Jordan romped on the gas. The vehicle jerked, bones snapping as they rolled over the woman. He focused on the horizon trying to ignore the stench of rotting flesh.

The road wound towards one of the largest skylines he'd ever seen, massive buildings clustered together in the center of a city that sprawled across the high valley and the hillsides surrounding it. It reminded him a little of Los Angeles, though many of the structures had a definite Spanish feel. He got the impression that some of the smaller churches were centuries old. They contrasted oddly with the more modern skyscrapers, a sea of steel and glass looming over their sleepy companions.

"This place was voted the most innovative city in the world just a few months ago," Liz said. Her voice seemed too loud in the oppressive silence.

No one wanted to speak or even look at each other. How could they? This had been a city with nearly four million people and now it was a tomb, a brutal reminder of the extent of their failure as the guardians of mankind.

"Maybe some of them survived," Bridget offered into the silence lingering after Liz's statement.

"I'm betting there are hundreds of survivors. Possibly thousands," Blair replied, facing Bridget across the mountain of gear littering the backseat. "The smart ones will hunker down, but that will only last until food becomes an issue. I'd expect more than a few are holed up in grocery stores or more defensible buildings around them. Just like Cajamarca."

"Cut the chatter," Jordan growled as the vehicle decelerated to a near crawl.

Blair leaned out the jeep's rear window into the hot wind to look for whatever Jordan must have seen. They'd entered a relatively clear part of the freeway, with only a few cars towards the edges. The center lanes were all empty, both of vehicles and zombies. It wasn't hard figuring out why. The corpses were all occupied.

A horde of zombies surrounded a pair of battered land rovers. They reminded Blair of Trevor's vehicle, though both were white instead of the deep green Trevor had favored. Each vehicle had a sort of crow's nest built on top, surrounded by sheets of metal that had been welded together. Each nest had three figures who held long chrome poles with machetes duct-taped to the end. They were dressed all in black with umpire's masks obscuring their features. It must have been murder in the heat.

All except one of them anyway. A white-furred werewolf towered over her companions. She was far too large to be male, corded muscles bunched under her fur. She wielded a spear much like the others, which she used on the gathering horde with impressive ferocity.

She scythed through them, slicing spinal cords and severing heads. Her companions jabbed at any zombie who made it onto the vehicle, but left the rest of the work to her. Evidently she'd been at it for a while, because a large pile of bodies now surrounded each vehicle. Not that it stemmed the tide of zombies. At least thirty still attempted to overwhelm the defenders, with more drifting towards them with each passing moment.

"They've seen us," Jordan announced, slamming on the brakes. He used his left foot to push the e-brake into place. "How are we handling this? We need to decide now."

One of the men on top of the rovers pointed in their direction. Another on the rover without the werewolf ducked out of sight, returning a moment later with an assault rifle of some kind. An M-16 maybe? Jordan probably knew.

"Blair, you're with me. I want to try talking but if they get hostile, immobilize the humans. I'll deal with the female," Liz announced, opening her door and dropping to the asphalt.

Blair opened his own door, back straight and shoulders square as he approached the rovers. A few zombies noticed them, but before they could pull away from the pack the man with the M-16 began picking them off with precise head shots.

"Stay where you are," the white-furred female roared. She leapt from the rover, landing behind the milling mass. She danced between them, claws sending up sprays of blood as she cut down most of the remaining horde.

A pair of corpses moved towards Blair. He waited for them to approach, then blurred for a fraction of an instant. Just long enough to snap both necks. They collapsed to the asphalt, clearing the path for Liz.

She waited patiently while the werewolf completed her grisly work. The white turned to face them, licking blood from her muzzle as she approached. She stopped just a few feet away, baring her teeth as she flexed her claws. "Who are you and why have you come to Medellin?"

"My name is Liz," she replied, stepping forward until she stood next to the towering werewolf. Her heart rate was steady, though Blair noted a sheen of sweat from the sweltering sun. "We're just passing through on our way to Panama. I'm willing to exchange news if you're interested, but then we're moving on."

"I'm afraid that's not possible," the werewolf rumbled. An apologetic rumble. She pointed back towards the city. "We have a gathering there and our leader meets all travelers. Medico Roberto will decide what to do with you."

"I wasn't asking," Liz growled, beginning to shift. The camo shirt tore from her shoulders, while the cargo pants all but exploded. In the blink of an eye, she went from two inches shorter than Blair to two inches taller than the strange werewolf. "My pack has been trained by the Mother and we outnumber you. Maybe you should rethink the whole detaining us thing."

Blair was already moving. He needed to do something to impress these people, to cow them before the guy with the assault rifle did something stupid. He extended his hand, concentrating on the dozen or so zombies moving towards the rover. Blair split his will into a dozen spikes, like the heads of some giant imaginary hydra. It came easily now.

He thrust at the zombies, pulling the milling mass away from the rovers. He forced them to gather into a tight knot about fifty feet away, making the gesture he used to control them as theatrical as possible. It seemed to work. The man with the rifle and his companions all gaped openly.

"The Mother?" the White asked.

"The one who created us. She's taught us to use our abilities.

Abilities that you can't even begin to imagine," Liz-wolf growled, looming over the white werewolf.

The report of the assault rifle rang out every few seconds, each shot downing a zombie who was closing in on them.

"I don't want to fight. I am Diana," she replied, giving a shallow bow. "Even if we could win, some of us would die and that benefits no one. Please, return with me to our compound. Meet Medico Roberto. If you seek to travel through our city he can help you. Surely it would be better to have us as allies. That is better than we few survivors fighting amongst each other."

What do you want to do? Blair thought at Liz.

We'll head back with them. She's right about us not fighting. It's foolish to fight amongst ourselves, Liz sent back. The subtext wasn't lost on him.

Stand down, he thought to the entire team. He could feel Jordan and Bridget relaxing from inside the jeep.

"All right, we'll go back with you, but if you betray us get ready for a lot of blood," Liz-wolf growled. She gestured at their jeep. "My team will follow your rovers if you want to lead the way."

"There will be no betrayal," Diana assured them. She walked back to her people, who'd already slid into their rovers and started the engines.

29

MEDICO ROBERTO

J ordan ignored his jagged thoughts, instead focusing on the two rovers they were following. They wove down a narrow corridor just wide enough for one car. It had been created along the main freeway by lining it with a row of SUVs and busses on either side, and must have taken hundreds of man-hours to move into place. A shrewd choice. It controlled the flow of zombies, channeling them into easily managed kill zones at the few intersections left open for people to enter the corridor.

Metal screeched as one of the rovers mashed a stray zombie into the door of a yellow Pathfinder. The move sent a shower of gore onto the jeep's windshield, cutting Jordan's visibility to shit. He flicked the windshield wipers, but only succeeded in coating the glass with a thick pink film.

"Fucking lovely," he growled, leaning out the window to see. The wind provided no relief from the stench, only adding exhaust to the mix. None of it kept his mind from the dilemma.

He'd been worrying at the same problem for days, ever since the sat-link had come online back in the Ark. Mohn Corp. was still out there. Despite the catastrophic damage that had crippled the world's electronics they still had satellites. Somehow that wasn't surprising.

It meant they'd been far more prepared than they'd indicated. They probably had a sizable military presence in Syracuse and were obviously still gathering intel. What sort of resources did they have? If it included aircraft, they'd almost certainly make a play for Panama. They might even be there already. Did he still have a place with Mohn? Would he want it if he did?

"There it is," Liz-wolf called over the wind. She was right. They were coming up on a stadium parking lot. The inside of the chain-link fence was lined with SUVs, just like the corridor they were driving through. Whoever was in charge knew what they were doing, at least when constructing defenses with limited resources.

The two rovers paused in front of a bus blocking their path. A figure appeared in the driver's window, aiming the business end of a .308 in their direction. Not the best choice of weapon. He might kill his first target, but he'd never have time to acquire another before they returned fire. Even if he could, the weapon was terrible at close range. He should be using a shotgun or even a heavier caliber pistol.

The man lowered the rifle, resting a hand on the wheel of the bus. It shuddered for a moment, then slid smoothly backwards with almost no sound. Was it powered by natural gas? There should have been more noise if it was diesel like most busses back in the states.

The first rover maneuvered through the gap, quickly followed by the second. Jordan depressed the gas, allowing the jeep to follow at an unthreatening pace. They were allowed into a stretch of asphalt bordered by a tent city. The part near the center looked like a market, while those tents closer to the edge were residential. He'd guess there were perhaps three hundred people here.

They looked ragged. Worn out. Most were dirty and avoided eye contact with each other. Children flinched when adults got too close. The unnatural quiet was painful. It was as if people were afraid of speaking, as if it might attract the same angry god that had visited the zombies and werewolves upon them.

They are in need of protection, Ka-Dun, a voice rumbled in the back of his mind. It didn't speak often, maybe because he almost always ignored it.

The brakes squealed as Jordan pulled into a spot next to one of the rovers. So odd that they still had those brightly painted lines for parking when the rest of the city had gone to shit. He threw the jeep in park, setting the e-brake with his left foot. Then he turned to Liz, spearing her with his gaze despite how intimidating he found her wolf form. "Listen, I know you don't trust me. I don't blame you. But we're about to walk into a potentially hostile situation and I need to know that we can count on each other. Can you and Blair shelve your squabble long enough for us to figure out what our play here is? We don't have the luxury of infighting."

"We're going to go see this Medico. If he's a doctor, hopefully he'll be reasonable. I'm sure he'll send us on our way," Liz rumbled, seemingly unimpressed by his gaze. She did dart a guilty glance at Blair.

"And if he doesn't?" Blair asked, throwing his door open and hopping out. Liz followed, unfolding from where the jeep's passenger seat used to be. That poor seat was never going to be the same.

Neither picked up a weapon and he was tired of trying to convince them they needed to carry guns. He rolled his eyes behind his sunglasses and exited the jeep.

"Then we deal with the situation if it arises," Liz said. Blair didn't look happy with the answer, but gave a tight nod of agreement. It was more than he'd seemed capable of only a few days before. Whatever had gone down between them had left a scar. They were good fighters, but he missed the professionalism of Mohn's elite.

Jordan moved to the back of the jeep, swinging open the rear door and hefting the black duffle with the weapons. Bridget followed, so he handed her his holstered .460. "This is the most powerful handgun I've ever fired. Men have broken their nose from the recoil, but I'm betting you can handle it. You won't find a better compact weapon."

He picked up a 12 gauge for himself, stuffing four boxes of shells into his cargo pants. If this came to combat it would be close quarters.

"Thanks," Bridget said, strapping the .460's neoprene holster to her thigh. It was impressive how quickly she'd adapted to carrying a gun, especially compared to the others who were unwilling to even pick one up.

The conversation died as the snowy werewolf approached. She was flanked by two of the men in their ridiculous umpire's masks. The cost to their peripheral vision far outweighed any protection it might grant. It was a security blanket and a bad tactical one at that.

"This way," Diana rumbled. She gave Liz a deferential nod, gesturing for her to follow. Liz fell in beside her, smelling of wet dog and sweat. Jordan and the rest fell in behind her. The umpires kept a respectful distance, watching them warily but with the obvious terror of those who know they're seriously outmatched.

They were led through several rows of tents, mostly occupied by families, though more than one held tables with jerky or canned food. Only one had water and it had two guards with M-16s flanking it. He felt their gazes, giving a grin when their postures straightened. They knew a manageable threat when they saw one. Liz would tear them apart, so they left her to Diana. But they could handle a normal man and as far as they were concerned that's exactly what Jordan was. They were the only non-amateurs in the plaza. Water must be in short supply for them to have been assigned guard duty.

They reached the final row of tents, which butted up against the wall of the stadium. Diana stopped in front of large green pavilion of the type he'd seen at U.N. installations in Africa. It was perfect for a mobile command center, again if resources were an issue. Four guards waited outside, two linebacker types and an odd pair. One was a short, skinny guy with dark skin and wire frame glasses, from South India most likely. The other was a blonde in her early twenties with hard brown eyes and the best bitch face he'd seen in a while. The classic hot-girl defense mechanism.

Neither was human. There wasn't anything obvious, but they were too aware of their surroundings. Too unalarmed by the pair of nine-foot werewolves that ducked into the pavilion. Besides, the only way they'd have been left as guards was if they were more than they appeared to be. He gave them a respectful nod as he followed Blair into the tent. Bridget trailed after, hand never leaving the .460's rubber grip. Jordan felt like a proud father.

A smattering of plastic chairs surrounded several folding tables that had been pushed together to form one large desk. It was cluttered with piles of paper, books, and a map of the city with little green army men scattered at different locations. A bear of a man with a bristly black beard that grew like an untended hedge stood at the tables, peering at his map. He wore glasses with a thick black frame and a battered fedora Jordan would have recognized anywhere.

"Dr. Roberts?" Jordan asked, stepping up between Liz and Diana. Both glowered down at him, but he ignored them.

"Commander Jordan?" Roberts raised an eyebrow. He rose from behind the desk, crossing his arms. His voice was frosty. "You're the last person I would have expected to see, though I shouldn't be surprised. The pyramid started this whole mess and I've long suspected that Mohn must be at the heart of everything."

"You're Medico Roberto? That's priceless," Blair said, grinning with some of the enthusiasm Jordan thought circumstances had stamped out of him. It was the closest Jordan had seen him drift to the man he'd been when he first arrived at the Ark, before this whole messy op had started.

"I can't believe you're alive," Blair continued. "How did you get here? Did Alejandro make it?"

"Smith?" Roberts blinked as he took in Blair. He stepped from behind the desk, offering a hand. "I guess it makes sense that you'd be alive. I've deduced that werewolves rise from the corpses of those they slay. Whatever killed you must have been the progenitor of the disease their bite contains. Fascinating. You're the very first werewolf."

"You know these men, Medico?" Diana rumbled, eyeing them with renewed curiosity. She licked her chops, probably a reflexive gesture, since she didn't seem hostile. It was damned unnerving, though.

"Yes, Diana, it's all right. Could you ask Daveed to bring us some water? We have a few things we need to discuss and it may take some time."

Diana gave a shallow bow, then ducked through the tent flap and back into the sweltering heat.

Roberts waited for her to go before speaking. "Now then, why don't you all explain exactly what brings you to my city, and why I shouldn't have you executed?"

30

TEAM CRAZY

Trevor threw the rusted-out Bronco into low gear, powering over the curb and onto the other side of the highway. Irakesh thumbed his way through a book written in Spanish about Christopher Columbus, seemingly oblivious to the rough ride. It was the third he'd devoured in as many days. His thirst for knowledge was insatiable and Trevor couldn't really blame him. He had thirteen thousand years to catch up on, after all.

"Did you catch that scent?" Cyntia purred into his ear, leaning forward and rubbing a hand along his shoulder. She reeked like a brothel, somehow managing to *smell* like sex. The fact that he was quite clearly dead didn't seem to phase her in the slightest.

That was just one of a number of signs that she was growing unstable. From the sly looks Irakesh shot her, Trevor was pretty sure the deathless knew why. If he had to guess, it had something to do with the either the frequency or the content of her feeding. She ate zombie and human alike, as often as possible. It had strengthened her. She'd gained at least two inches when in wolf form and was visibly stronger, but her once shiny blond fur had faded to a flat dun. Her eyes had changed to a terrifying scarlet when she shifted.

It might even make sense from a scientific standpoint. The werewolf virus altered DNA. Eating zombies meant she was ingesting a rival virus. If the changes were any indication, both viruses were mutating. Into what Trevor couldn't say, but he bet Irakesh could. What he wouldn't give for one of Erik's CellScopes and fifteen minutes of the Aussie's time. He could analyze the blood and answer the question definitively.

"No, what was it?" he finally answered, testing the air. His sense of smell had grown sharper, but it was his hearing that was truly amazing now. Yet there was nothing over the roar of the engine.

"A familiar scent. There's a female nearby, and a few humans," Cyntia explained, resting her head against his shoulder like some needy cat. He ignored her as best he could, pity warring with distaste.

"Which way?" he asked, scanning the roadway. The heat was oppressive, but since he no longer sweated it didn't bother him the way that it used to. He was simply aware of it.

"They are up ahead," Irakesh broke in, closing his book. His eyes narrowed as he peered through the windshield. "See that large white trailer? A semi, I believe it's called. They're on top of it, lying flat. It looks like they're clearing nascent deathless. There's a pile of bodies around their vehicle."

Irakesh was right. Trevor could see the werewolf now, her black fur a stark contrast against the blue sky. She held a spear of some kind and was jabbing at the zombies clustered around the truck. Her companions were all humans in camouflage fatigues. Each had a rifle, but none were firing. Made sense. Bullets were going to become very scarce in the near future. Let the werewolf do the work unless they got into trouble.

"Trevor, handle the men. Kill them and devour the bodies. Leave the Ka-Ken for Cyntia; she will gain great strength from consuming her," Irakesh instructed. He turned that awful gaze Trevor's way.

"We could just pass them by. If we're being pursued, confrontations like this could reveal our presence," Trevor suggested. More to save these people's lives than because he feared discovery. Hell, he welcomed discovery. The more time he spent with Irakesh the more certain he became that the deathless had to be stopped. If only he could do that himself.

"It was neither a request, nor a suggestion. You will enact my will, thrall," Irakesh growled, eyes flaring an evil shade of green. Trevor felt something hot wash over him, seeping into his nerves. The sensation was becoming all too familiar and it made him grind his teeth. Irakesh could yank him about like a puppet, working with the strange voice to keep Trevor a prisoner in his own body. "The strength we will gain here more than outweighs potential discovery. Besides, the time will soon come when you and Cyntia are powerful enough to help me destroy the Ka-Dun Isis sent after us."

For now he imposes his will on you through domination. In time your strength will grow and you will be able to resist his influence. He is well trained, but young. You will eclipse him, but you must be patient. He must not see you as a threat until it is too late.

Trevor didn't respond to the strange voice, instead nodding to Irakesh and focusing on the road ahead of him. He didn't know what the voice was and it confused the hell out of him. One moment it was working with Irakesh, the next offering advice on how he could backstab the bald monster.

He guided the Bronco to a stop near the semi. The people on top had noticed their arrival and were snatching up rifles. None made a threatening move. Cyntia gave a growl and began to shift. She planted both powerful legs against her door and kicked with all that incredible strength. The door popped off like a cork from a champagne bottle, slamming into a nearby Focus with a tremendous clatter.

Trevor massaged his temples. "Couldn't you have just opened it?"

Cyntia leapt out, charging towards the semi before Trevor could even open the door. Why was he the one who'd ended up on team crazy?

He flipped the latch and rolled out the door, coming up in a crouch. They hadn't seen him. He dove forward, rolling into the shadow cast by the semi. Then he was gone, form melting into the mass of zombies still milling about the semi. He needn't have bothered after Cyntia's showy entrance. The men's rifles vomited slugs in her direction, sharp cracks stinging his ears as they all fired. It was so different than when he had ear protection at the range. Especially with his dramatically enhanced hearing.

Then Cyntia was gone, melting into the shadows just as he had. The black-furred female spun around, scanning the area for her opponent. Neither she nor her three companions seemed sure what to do. Perhaps they hadn't encountered anyone who could shadow walk. Cyntia had received instruction from Liz and maybe the Mother herself. It afforded her an unfair edge against this poor werewolf. Pity. It all but guaranteed the midnight's death.

Your compassion is a weakness. Bury it. The Ka-Ken's death will bring your ally strength. If you wish to be free of your master, you will require her aid.

Trevor dropped a hand to his .45, flicking the catch on the holster with his thumb. He eased the weapon from the black leather as he waited for Cyntia to appear. A moment later she burst from the shadows behind the poor female, shredding her throat with razored claws even as she bit down on the spine. Cyntia's victim crumpled, drawing the eyes of all three men.

Now.

He leapt skyward, giving a slight forward spin to compensate for the recoil. Trevor sighted down the metal sights, aligning the barrel with the first man's forehead. Then he blurred, constricting the trigger like a boa. It coughed a round, which punched through the bridge of the surprised victim's nose. His weapon aligned with the second target and he constricted again. The second round took his target through the throat, exiting through the spine. The third target he cored through the heart, which beat loudly enough to make it an easy target.

Trevor landed on the edge of the semi as all three men collapsed, twitching involuntarily as their bodies realized the truth. They were already dead.

"Well done," Irakesh called, stepping from the vehicle. An alarmingly predatory grin spread across his face. "Look. Cyntia has already finished her meal. It will make her strong."

Trevor turned towards her. There weren't even bones left, at least not that he could see. Cyntia licked a piece of gore from her muzzle, giving him the single most alarming smile he'd ever seen. She was drenched in gore, eyes wild and bestial. Then she dropped to her haunches and began to feed on the first human. He wanted to be sick, but instead felt the most awful hunger.

Trevor dropped to his knees and began to feed on the first man, face mercifully obscured by the bullet's entry wound. He started with the brain, always the most important part. The man would have memories that could prove useful, and devouring his mind would strengthen Trevor.

The rush came. Countless fragments stormed through him, bits of memory. A wife and child, brutally killed during the initial outbreak. A new friend, dead beside him. Wait, what was that? He chased down a distant image, an old thought. Expertly guiding a Cessna into an S-turn.

"Irakesh," Trevor called, wiping gore from his chin. "This is it. The man was a highly experienced pilot. I think I can fly us once we reach Panama."

"Excellent," Irakesh said, a wide grin splitting his too-handsome face. "All we need do is ensure we are uninterrupted long enough to find this nuclear device and one of these wonderful aircraft I see in my new memories. You shall be rewarded, thrall. Watch with care. I would have you master this ability. It will serve us well in the days to come."

Irakesh blurred, suddenly standing next to Trevor on top of the semi. He closed his eyes, extending both arms, fingers splayed into the breeze. Trevor felt something. A gathering energy crackling just past the edge of sight, something electric he couldn't quite see. It gathered around Irakesh and then pulsed outwards, a finger's breadth beyond hearing or sight.

Every shambling corpse stopped. They slowly turned to face Irakesh, then took a step towards him in unison. They shuffled towards the semi with single-minded purpose. Just the way *he* had on the day Irakesh had ensnared him. What was it that his master had just done?

He sent out an energy pulse. The mindless will do anything to feast on such pure energy, so they seek it at all costs. Once they are close they will be within range of his blood and he will dominate them.

I can do this, too? Trevor thought. The scientist in him was fascinated. It had to be signal based. Even light was a wave, which was just a form of signal. Irakesh was somehow broadcasting a powerful signal.

It is a simple thing, easily mastered. One of the pillars of deathless power, the ability to gather an army. All deathless of note have many such thralls. With so many nascent deathless this power will be even more vital in this age. Learn it well, for once you have freed yourself you will need it to establish your own power base.

At least twenty zombies had already gathered. More appeared from the thick trees on the side of the road. Still others down both sides of the road. They were coming from all directions. Hundreds. Maybe thousands.

"What are you going to do with them?" Trevor asked. He was positive that he didn't want to know, but he couldn't bear not knowing, either.

"I can feel the Ka-Dun in that direction, perhaps two or three miles away. I will send every deathless we encounter to stop him."

31

STEVE

Jordan eyed Bridget and Blair chatting in low tones in the corner of the pavilion. Bridget was giving one of those coy smiles, letting her hair screen her face. Four feet to their right a very agitated Liz-wolf tried to pretend she wasn't watching them.

Yup, Jordan definitely missed Mohn professionalism. He shifted his attention back to Dr. Roberts, who thumped the table with each point in his tirade.

"Mohn orchestrated the entire incident at the pyramid. They led us there like lambs to a slaughter; that cannot be denied. They allowed scientists and artists to explore a site that they knew to be dangerous. I watched Alejandro get torn apart. *I* was torn apart," Roberts barked, eyes searing everyone. He leaned forward, looking right at Jordan. "You were the head honcho. The guy at the top. You knew what was going on there, knew about the werewolves and the radiation. All of it. You let our team get slaughtered for your personal crusade. Now you expect me to simply allow you to walk out of here as if nothing had transpired? I'm not going to do that, Mr. Jordan. I'm going to have you executed."

Jordan was still considering a response when Blair spoke.

"No, you're not," Blair said, turning from Bridget to face the doctor. The words were quiet. So quiet Jordan might not have heard them without his enhanced hearing. He watched as Blair took three very deliberate steps towards the desk, eyes locked on Roberts. "If you try, we'll have to resist and that will end very, very badly for your people."

"What the hell happened to you, Smith? You should be on my side. He betrayed us all. They murdered the world, man. How can you not see that? You, of all people," Roberts asked, rising to meet Blair's advance. This was going south. Quickly. Still, Jordan's interference would solve nothing. Roberts might listen to Blair. Maybe.

"I *am* on your side, Roberts," Blair said, planting both hands on the table. Only a foot separated the two men now. "Mohn has a lot to answer for, more than you can possibly know. Jordan here hunted me all the way to San Diego and blew up the house of a very good friend. He fought to the end to keep us from waking the Mother and trust me when I say we very much need her if we're going to save anything of humanity."

"You're not helping his case," Roberts snarled, jerking his head towards Jordan. "Hell, you're admitting he's the problem."

"Was," Blair shot back, gaze unflinching. Jordan was pleased to see him showing some steel. "When the Mother woke she slaughtered three hundred Mohn personnel in a matter of minutes. Jordan was one of the first casualties. He rose from the dead just like we did. He's one of us now, for better or worse. The fact is he's been invaluable. His military expertise has saved our asses more than once and it's very much needed if we're going to stop the thing we're chasing."

The angry-looking blonde ducked through the tent flap, looking directly at Roberts. "Medico, we've got a problem. Team four didn't report back, so we sent out a team to investigate. They found traces of a fight. Shots fired. There was blood everywhere, but they said they couldn't find any bodies."

"Did they have any other details?" Roberts asked, shooting Jordan a look that promised this wasn't over. "Send the scout in. Now."

"Sure, I'll grab him. One sec," she said, ducking back out. She returned a moment later with a skinny teen in tow, baggy shorts stained black from use. "This is Fiero. He was the lead scout. Fiero, tell the Medico what you saw."

"It was awful, sir," the boy said, ducking his head to avoid meeting anyone's gaze. "There was blood all over the top of the semi. And these scratches, sir, like from claws. But there weren't any bodies. I think they were eaten, sir. Maybe by zombies, but that doesn't make a lot of sense. They'd have gotten away. Yselda can kill a whole pack of zombies. She would have gotten away. She'd have gotten them out."

"Did this happen a little ways north?" Blair interrupted, looking directly at the boy. "Maybe four or five kilometers?"

"Yes, about four, I think. Out there on the freeway. It's the farthest north we patrol, towards the border with Panama," he explained, darting quick glances at Blair as he spoke.

"Did you find any shell casings?" Jordan broke in, leaning forward in his chair. He hoped the gesture made him slightly less intimidating.

"Yes, sir," the boy said, darting a single look Jordan's way and then dropping his gaze. "We found three bullets."

"Did you find the rounds, or just the shell casings?" Jordan asked, steepling his fingers and resting his elbows on the table in front of him.

"Both, sir. I've got them right here," he reached into his pocket and extended a dirty hand. "Here you go, sir. I wasn't sure what to make of them."

"Three bullets from a .45 caliber pistol," Jordan said, examining one of the shells. He held it up so they could all see that the entire front had flattened. "This one probably fired into the skull, judging by the round. It punched through the bone and into the brain, killing him instantly. This second one might have been fired into the heart. See how it's only flat on one side? Probably hit a rib on the way in. The third one looks just like the first, so probably another head shot. Someone executed those people with extreme precision at close range. Then they ate the bodies, because otherwise these bullets would still be lodged in their victims."

"That would account for the team with Yselda," Roberts said, shifting his gaze to Jordan. He still wore his skepticism. "But how did they take her out? What could beat a female werewolf? She was one of our best. You know what did this, don't you?"

"Yeah, we do," Jordan said. He turned to face Blair. "You should probably field this one, Professor Smith. I'm not sure he'd believe anything I said and even if he did I don't know that I can explain exactly what it is we're chasing."

"All right," Blair said, giving a short nod. He removed his hat, dropping the sweaty thing on the desk. His hair was all askew, but somehow it didn't detract from his air of seriousness. He'd changed so much since arriving at the dig site just a couple months back. In another couple, he'd be a damned good soldier. "I'm sure you remember the woman sleeping in the sarcophagus."

"Of course I do. All we did was wonder who she was, for weeks," Roberts said, face tightening.

"The woman you saw was the Mother, the progenitor of the were-wolf species," Blair explained. He used both hands in an unconscious attempt to tame his wild hair. It failed. "She created them to battle what you and I call zombies, something she referred to as deathless. I'm sure you're well aware of what a threat the zombies pose, and since you're still alive you know firsthand about werewolves. You've probably even spoken to the beast in your head. That was very deliberately created by the Mother to help guide us."

"Okay, let's assume I'm willing to accept this narrative," Dr. Roberts replied, expression anything but accepting. This was going to be a tough sell. "What does this have to do with my missing team? I'll take a history lesson later, but right now I need answers."

"I'm getting there. Something else was asleep in the pyramid, what the Mother calls an Ark. This thing stowed away when The Mother put the Ark into stasis just over thirteen thousand years ago. He woke up and stole something very important," Blair explained, sinking back into his chair. "His name is Irakesh and he's a deathless. Not the typical mindless zombie, but something more akin to a vampire. He's smart and powerful, with abilities we're just beginning to understand. We've been chasing him all the way from Cajamarca."

"Chasing him where?" Roberts asked. He'd relaxed slightly, but was still scowling.

"To Panama. This is the part that's really going to piss you off," Jordan interrupted, a bead of sweat trickling down his cheek like a stray tear. He had to own up to this, like it or not. "This is news to everyone, something that wasn't relevant until now. Mohn was terrified of the werewolves. They were sending a nuke to blow up the Ark, but it never made it. I believe it's at the Mohn airfield in Panama. It's possible Irakesh is after that nuke and we have no idea what he'll use it for. What we do know is his final destination. He's heading for an Ark in North America, probably somewhere near San Francisco. If he reaches it before we do he'll control every zombie for thousands of miles. He'll wipe out the few survivors and set up his own little empire."

Everyone stared at Jordan.

"So you were going to nuke the pyramid and wipe out Cajamarca. Millions of souls. Yep, sounds like Mohn. So let me guess: this Irakesh is who you believe took out my team?" Roberts asked, straightening. His gaze was unreadable.

"We haven't seen anything else that could do it, not with that level of precision," Jordan continued. His posture was as slumped as he ever allowed it to get, almost ramrod straight. "We need to keep him from getting that nuke."

"All right, you've got my attention. I want to run this by my advisor before I make a decision," he said, rising from his chair and crossing to the tent's entryway. "Wait here. I'll return in a moment."

He left before anyone could give an answer, leaving them sitting in silence. Jordan refused to make eye contact with anyone, fearing the condemnation he'd find there.

He eyed Liz-wolf sidelong as she touched Blair on the shoulder. "Can you feel him?"

"He's close," Blair said, staring up at her. "Just a few miles from here. This is the closest we've been."

The tent flap stirred, admitting Roberts and a man who must have been lurking just outside the tent somewhere. He was tall and handsome, with a neatly trimmed black beard and grey eyes. He wore loose black pants of something that might have been silk, and a tight-fitting black tank top that showed off impressively muscled shoulders. He screamed douche.

"Steve?" Bridget cried, surging to her feet. She'd been so quiet Jordan had almost forgotten she'd been in the room. "My god, you're alive." She flung her arms around him, burying her face in his chest.

Steve looked down at her distastefully, gently disengaging himself from her. "Hello, Bridget. Blair. Commander Jordan."

"How the fuck are you alive?" Jordan roared, slack-jawed. His .45 appeared in his hand, and he broke out in a cold sweat. "I killed you. We all saw it."

32

AMBUSHED

Blair gaped at Steve. Bridget had told him how Mohn had executed him, though Blair had never heard that Jordan had been the one to do the executing. Steve pushed Bridget away, walking straight over to him. Blair rose, tensing as the man who'd once been his best friend approached. The last time he'd seen Steve the man had been in the throes of radiation sickness. His mind had deteriorated into madness to the point that he'd attacked Blair.

The stranger before him couldn't have been more different. He stood taller and wore a familiar confidence Blair had come to expect. Steve had always been cocky, yet this was more pronounced and less in your face. The quiet air of a man who knows how dangerous he is, but takes no pleasure from the fact.

"Hello, Blair, it's been a long time. I don't really count the Ark, since I wasn't in my right mind," Steve said. He extended a hand. Blair stared at it. Steve had betrayed him, had taken Bridget and any chance he'd had at making it in the archeology world. It had knocked Blair all the way to the bottom of a wine bottle for the better part of three years. He'd spent a lot of evenings wallowing there, hating his old friend. Blaming him for the wretch he'd become.

"Hello, Steve," Blair finally replied, seizing Steve's hand just as he was starting to drop it back to his side. It was time to let go, to get over all the bullshit. To try, anyway. Steve had fucked him, but hadn't he made mistakes, too? He was too tired to hold on to the anger anymore. "I'm glad to see rumors of your death were greatly exaggerated. How the hell did you end up in Columbia?"

"And how are you still alive?" Jordan interjected, .45 still cradled in his hand as if he were considering whether or not to use it.

"You believed me dead because that's what I wished you to believe," Steve said, giving Jordan a predatory smile. Then he turned back to Blair. Steve's grip was just a bit too firm, not quite enough to hurt but enough to show it could. Yup, same old Steve. "I shaped the Commander's mind and those of the others gathered there. They believed I was dead, a necessary fiction if I was going to escape."

"There were several dozen of us watching. You shaped all of us?" Jordan interrupted. He raised an eyebrow, obviously skeptical.

"Just the few of you close enough to see what had really happened," Steve admitted, looking a trifle less smug. He walked over to one of the chairs and settled into it with the grace of a jungle cat, something he'd never possessed before. "Everyone else assumed I died in the blast and I blurred away before they could figure out otherwise. From there I made my way north. I was trying to make it back to the states when the world ended. I've never seen anything like the fireworks in the sky. After that I started looking for survivors and ran into Dr. Roberts and his group."

Blair was conscious of Bridget sinking into a chair on the far side of the room. He glanced at her, but she was staring at her feet. Her hair screened her face, the defensive mechanism he'd seen so often over the years. It still affected him, but much less powerfully than it once had. It had ripped the scab off his old wound when she'd run to Steve, though ironically he'd also felt a stab of pity. She'd been rejected and he knew exactly what that was like. He shouldn't be involved with Bridget, shouldn't open up his heart to her. Yet all he wanted to do was offer comfort.

"I'm glad that we're all acquainted," Roberts broke in, sarcasm lathered all over the statement. He leaned against one of the poles holding up the pavilion. "The question remains: what are we going to do about this Irakesh. If he's as big a threat as—"

Someone screamed in the distance. Then someone else. A third. A chorus. People were panicking, somewhere to the northeast. Blair looked to Liz for instruction.

"Let's get out there and find out what the problem is. Maybe Irakesh has come to us," she said, turning away from Blair.

Blair stripped as quickly as he could. Everyone else had started to do the same, even Dr. Roberts. The only exception was Steve, who gave a sympathetic shake of his head as if they were all cretins. He shifted, clothing disappearing as he did. In his place stood a seven-foot black werewolf. There was no trace of the clothing. It seemed he knew the same trick the Mother used, but how had he learned it?

Liz-wolf ducked through the tent flap, followed by Bridget. Jordan came next, his shotgun comically small in the meaty werewolf fist. Roberts had shifted into a grey werewolf, fur the color of ash the morning after a campfire.

"After you," Steve-wolf said, his lupine grin disconcerting despite the fact that Blair had grown used to such grins. He slipped into the moonlit evening that had descended while they were in the tent. It was still ungodly hot, but that was quickly forgotten when he saw the level of chaos. Cracks of sporadic gunfire came from all directions, as did the screams. They were under attack, but by what?

Blair leapt atop a one of the tall markers at the end of each row of parking spaces. This one read B6 in faded red lettering, a reminder of a more sane world when this place would have been used for soccer games. He scanned the rows of tents, immediately spotting the threat.

Zombies streamed through two holes in the row of SUVs blocking the northwest part of the parking lot. It looked as though they'd pushed through by sheer numbers. There were hundreds of them, most shambling but more than one sprinting towards targets. People were tackled to the ground where clusters of zombies began feeding on their still living victims.

Helpless refugees stampeded away from the threat, pushing frantically towards the southern exit. A woman was shoved to the ground, her short scream terminated as person after person trampled over her. She wasn't the only casualty. Children were separated from parents, some crushed under the weight of the crowd, while others were left sobbing in forgotten corners.

"Blair," Liz-wolf bellowed from the next row of tents. "We have to stop them. Bridget and I are going to drive a wedge in their ranks. Back us up."

She didn't wait for a response, bounding down the row towards the zombies. The crowd parted before her, streaming around her as they continued their mad flight. There was no sign of Bridget, but Blair guessed she'd already taken to the shadows.

"Steve, with me," Roberts yelled from a spot not far below Blair's perch. "We need to get to the southern gate. This might be a trap and if it is I don't want those people to rush right into a bunch of zombies."

"Of course," Steve said, unruffled by the chaos. He loped after Roberts as the pair headed for the southern gate.

Blair blurred after Liz, rolling under a small pavilion and into the next row. Out of the corner of his eye he caught Jordan blurring down the next row. It was good to see him embracing some of his abilities.

Then Blair was amidst the zombies. He tore and gouged, ripping through spines and tearing out throats. The thing that had once been a young woman loomed in front of him, dress torn down the front to expose a milky white breast splotchy with blood. Blair grabbed the side of her head, slamming it into the pavement with a sickening crunch and a spray of gore. Again and again he fought, struggling to stay near Liz and Bridget as they fought their way towards the breach.

Zombies still flowed inside, a seemingly endless stream. They'd been joined by those unfortunates caught by the initial horde, and now there were more zombies in the parking lot than humans. The werewolves were making a dent, but it just wasn't enough.

He had to do something. But what? What would Ahiga have done? He'd have had some bullshit Yoda-like advice that would have amounted to 'figure it out your fucking self, whelp'. Ahiga's mental abilities had been more powerful, more developed than his own. Yet surely that strength had come from practice, from pushing his abilities. Blair had already proven he could stop a handful of zombies. He had to find a way to do more.

He leapt into the air, grabbing a sign emblazoned with L2 and using his momentum to swing onto the top of the crossbeam, landing in a crouch. He surveyed the sea of zombies before him. How many could he stop?

Blair shaped his will into a mass of spikes that surrounded him like a sea urchin. They wavered and then burst in a flash of pain. He shook his head to clear it. This time he shaped the spikes more slowly, concentrating on making each one a perfect stiletto. Only after he'd finished one did he attempt another. He built one after another in quick succession, but it wasn't fast enough.

Be calm, Ka-Dun. Power comes through deliberate, focused attention, the beast rumbled in the back of his mind. *You possess the power to save these people, but you must block out the world and give yourself wholly to your task.*

People screamed below even as Liz and Bridget did their best to stem the tide. Jordan had entered the fray, dropping zombies with well placed shots from his shotgun or cutting down those who came too close with his wickedly sharp claws. Their effort seemed so pitiful in the face of that much carnage.

Blair shaped more quickly, adding dozens of spikes. It tore at his brain, flashes of agony rippling through him as he struggled to sustain them all. Then at last he'd reached his limit. He knew if he tried just one more, the rest would unravel. So he closed his eyes, flinging the spikes in every direction. They sank into the zombies, gathering hundreds of disparate wills under his control.

It was like trying to swim upstream against a waterfall, so many wills buffeting him. A cacophony of half-formed consciousnesses, each driven by the singular need to feed. Even though each was a weak-willed zombie, the sheer number made the task nearly impossible. Yet he persevered. He would *not* give up, not abandon the survivors below.

Blair opened his eyes. Every zombie within a hundred yards had frozen, each turning their ruined faces at him. They glared hatefully, straining to reach the freedom he denied them.

"Liz," he roared, his voice echoing over the chaotic din. "I can't hold them for long."

Liz and Bridget blazed through the captive zombies, cutting them down in a flurry of carnage. Nor were they the only ones. Jordan led nearly a dozen men and women into the fray. Most had knives or machetes, though a few emptied rounds into the helpless zombies. They joined the grisly work, mowing through the enemy with an intensity that made him proud.

Each death made his work easier, the strain less. Eventually it became effortless, with only a dozen or so zombies remaining. Then those too were cut down, leaving Blair sweating and tired on top of his perch. He dropped to the ground, leaning heavily against the pole he'd been standing on.

"Blair, that was amazing," Liz cried, flinging furry arms around him. Bridget wasn't far behind, joining the group hug. "I can't believe you held them all."

"Always full of surprises, aren't you Blair?" Bridget added. They disengaged as Jordan approached, leading the men and women who'd helped him defend.

"Casualties are bad. At least a hundred were killed, maybe as many as twice that. We'll have to see how things ended up with Dr. Roberts and Dr. Galk," he said, voice revealing more emotion than Blair would have thought the man capable of.

His joy turned to ashes when he turned to see the sea of corpses littering the parking lot.

33

CONSEQUENCES

Mark woke up with a start, the tablet tumbling from his chest to thud on the thick grey carpet. He rubbed sleep from his eyes as another knock came at the door. The digital clock's numbers read 2:38 AM. Who the hell would bother him at this hour? An emergency might prompt a phone call, but someone knocking at his door? He'd have their ass scrubbing air ducts for the next month. He lurched to the door and tapped the lights before opening it. The door slid open to reveal the Old Man's platinum hair.

"Hello, Mark. I'm sorry for waking you. Can I come in?" he asked, plunging past Mark and dropping into the tiny room's single chair without awaiting an answer.

"What can I do for you?" was all he could muster. Mark sat heavily on the bed, the only other place to sit. Even being the Director only afforded him so much space in a facility like this.

"You can explain your actions. I wanted to hear it for myself rather than call a formal inquiry," the Old Man said matter-of-factly. He crossed his arms, gaze boring into Mark.

There was only one thing he could be talking about. Mark had known the instant he'd ordered the extraction in Panama that it would come to this. The Old Man was far too paranoid not to have him watched, and he kept himself apprised of everything that happened in the facility. He'd probably learned about the mission moments after the bird had launched, though clearly he'd waited until Mark was off balance to broach the subject.

"We've worked together fifteen years, Leif," he replied, taking a chance with the Old Man's name. No one was on a first name basis with Mohn. Not even Mark. "In that time I've done everything you've asked. I haven't questioned off-the-books activities you refused to explain, not even Project Solaris or your work with Object 3. I never once asked you for the whole picture even though I was well aware you knew things you had no right to know, things about some sort of ancient civilization and about the impending end of the world. I haven't questioned you, because up until now I haven't had reason to."

"You feel that's changed?" the Old Man asked, brows furrowing as he studied Mark. His gaze held a dangerous intensity.

"We can't leave a nuke sitting in Panama. I don't care if we have twenty-one others. Besides, we need to know what's happening in South America. You and I both know that's the green zone. If we can reclaim Panama we have a chance at an outpost there. Even if we can't, it's irresponsible to leave a weapon like that lying around."

"So you disobeyed a direct order. You had to know I'd find out. What did you think would happen after that?" the Old Man asked. He leaned back in the chair, though Mark knew the apparent relaxation was a ruse. The Old Man never relaxed.

"I guess that depends. If the mission is a success I expect I'll be reprimanded," Mark replied. He forced himself not to break eye contact. "If it fails I expect you'll remove me and put someone else in charge. Higgins maybe. He's the most experienced section chief."

"He's nothing but a sycophant and we both know it," the Old Man shot back, fire in his eyes. Here came the anger. "I need you, Mark. I need you because I have no one else. You're the glue holding this place together and I can't have you questioning me, not this late in the game. We're close to the realization of everything this company was founded to do. You have to trust me, Mark. Can you do that?"

Mark considered for a long moment before answering. The pragmatic move would be to play the dutiful soldier and say yes. "You know I'm just as connected in the systems as you are. You had to know I'd find out about the phone calls to London. There's nothing there that matters, not that you've told me about. Yet you seem to be orchestrating a massive operation, one you haven't bothered to tell me about."

"I knew this would come up sooner or later," the Old Man said, heaving a sigh as the fire died. He withdrew a ruby pendant on a gold chain, fingering the stone as he spoke. The same eye of Horus he'd used during his demonstration back in Panama when he'd announced the end of the world. "I can't tell you what's going on in Europe yet, not until I'm certain we're secure. I see how my actions could have caused you to question my authority, but that has to stop now. You need to trust that I'm doing what's best, both for this company and for humanity. If you can't do that, you become a liability and as huge a loss as that will be, I'll have to deal with you. I know you know that."

"I know," Mark said. The room was a constant 67 degrees, but it felt like a sauna. "So where do we go from here?"

"I overlook your lapse in judgement with Panama and you ignore my phone calls to London," the Old Man said, rising from the chair. "I know you don't like being kept in the dark. Neither do I. Let's not let this become a habit."

"Understood, sir," Mark said. "I'll keep you apprised of the situation in Panama. In the meantime you might want to study the reports from the vault."

"I read the first one. The objects we brought up top absorbed radiation from the CME as expected. What else is there?"

"The lesser objects in the vault also picked up traces of energy. Even the ones we thought completely inert," Mark explained. The Old Man was smart enough to see the significance in that.

"You were right to bring it to my attention. I'll go over the reports." He walked to the door and it slid open. The Old Man turned, already half outside the room. "Get some sleep, Mark. The next few weeks are going to be even worse than the last few."

34

SUNSTEEL

Irakesh was pleased. The dead ruled the tarmac below, thousands of zombies. Nascent deathless he would soon turn to his will, roaming about in little packs as they sought sustenance. He stepped away from the roof's edge, still baffled by the strange black substance they stood on top of. It bubbled and sloped, uneven from years of rain no doubt. It was a flimsy material, ill suited to the task. The black substance clearly kept the rain from leaking into the building below, but it would have to be reapplied every decade or so. It lacked the permanence of stone.

Metallic craft littered the runway, most lined up near several other large buildings. Terminals, that was the word. His new memories supplied many such things, though the words still tasted strange.

Irakesh glanced to his right where Cyntia and Trevor stood. The champion was falling fast, much to his delight. She fed indiscriminately now. Deathless, human, or even her own kind. It had made her strong, perhaps the equal to the powerful Ka-Ken who'd so very nearly slain him back in the Ark. That would be critical when the confrontation came. It *would* come, of course. He could feel the Ka-Dun somewhere behind him along the road leading to the metropolis they'd so recently passed. So much metal, so little stone.

He faced Trevor, his unwitting ally and very first thrall. The man was more promising than Irakesh could have dreamed, but that fact also made him exceedingly dangerous. For now Irakesh could dominate him, but in time his thrall would gain strength enough to resist.

You risk much, my host. Perhaps he should be sacrificed during the confrontation with the Ka-Dun. There will be other thralls, more pliable and less troublesome.

Irakesh ignored his Risen, studying Trevor instead. The man knelt next to the narrow lip at the roof's edge, rifle cradled in one hand while he shaded his eyes from the midday glare. The gesture was reflexive, muscle memory left from his time among the living. That would fade in time, as both mind and body accepted his new abilities. Trevor bit his lip, eyes narrowing as he scanned the terminals.

"Something has disturbed your Ka. Out with it. What do you wish to know?" Irakesh demanded. It happened often, this brooding. The change had preserved much of Trevor's old identity, and that man had been burdened with a great many morals. Those would take time to break down.

"You've driven us relentlessly to reach this place. What's so important? You have to be after something," Trevor asked, direct as usual. That part of his demeanor was quite refreshing. There was no subterfuge to the man, a near impossibility in his own age. Direct men died.

"The first of the cattle I devoured knew a great many interesting things," Irakesh replied. He decided to be magnanimous. Perhaps it would increase Trevor's loyalty and if not, it cost nothing. "There is a device here that I desire. A bomb of incredible power that will discharge a fantastic amount of energy."

"Why?" Trevor demanded.

Irakesh's hands balled into fists, but he resisted the urge to chastise the man. If he wished Trevor's cooperation, he needed to treat the man closer to an equal, no matter how much it galled him.

"Unlike many of my contemporaries, I will allow you to ask such impertinent questions. Your curiosity is natural. Yet if I must explain my motivation behind every action I will have no time to act," Irakesh said, forcing honey into the words. "You must trust me. If you prove yourself, as I have no doubt you will, then you will earn my trust. Until then I must ask your patience."

"I get that you don't want me questioning every decision, but this has to be an exception. That bomb could annihilate a city. That concerns me. Humor me. Why do you want it?" Trevor asked, voice as dispassionate as ever.

Cyntia loomed behind him, eyes burning with feverish intensity. A subtle reminder of where her loyalties lay.

"I cannot. That knowledge could be used against me, should a Ka-Dun pluck it from your mind. In time I will teach you the proper mental defenses to prevent such an act, but for now it is enough to know my will. We have come for the bomb. Then we will find a craft to take us north. One you will fly," Irakesh said, moderating his tone as much as he was able. "However, I do not wish you to feel you are being ignored. You may ask another question and I will answer it. Surely there are things you must be curious about."

"All right. How about an easier question, then. Why is your sword gold during the day but silver at night?" Trevor asked, stroking his goatee with a free hand. Such a casual gesture but it penned volumes about the man.

"A clever question. Very few recognize the true nature of Sunsteel. I will give you a worthy answer," Irakesh said, impressed again by his pupil. He eased his sword from its sheath, offering the na-kopesh to Trevor. "See how the blade is curved? That makes it excellent for decapitating an opponent. Or, if you wish to prolong their agony, you may disembowel them just as easily. A singular weapon, even during my age."

"Yes, but why does the blade change color?" Trevor asked, hefting the weapon experimentally. He gave a tentative slash, the air humming as he sliced it.

"It reacts to the sun or the moon, absorbing energy from whichever light it basks in," Irakesh explained, extending a hand. Trevor handed the weapon back, a bit reluctantly.

"It absorbs light?" Trevor said, gawking at the blade. "How? Can you tap into that as a power source?"

"Yes," Irakesh replied, considering how much he dared reveal. All in this case. "The blade can draw on energy wherever it is found. Including the energy you or I possess. If you stab a foe with Sunsteel you can feast upon their life force, growing stronger through the act."

Be wary, my host. Imparting such knowledge will cause him to covet the blade.

"If you wish, I will teach you to wield it," Irakesh offered, slamming the blade home in its sheath. "Once we are in the air I will give you your first lesson. We will practice every day afterwards. Someday these skills may save your life."

"I...don't really know what to say. I'd love to learn to do what you do with that thing," Trevor said, a glimmer of eagerness leaking into his tone. He feigned a disinterested expression, of course. Trevor was eager for this knowledge, enough that he might even cooperate in the short term. "If we're going to get this bomb, let's do it. You said that Ka-Dun is behind us. I'd rather be out of here before his pack arrives."

"I know who it is," Cyntia said, hackles rising as she bared her fangs. The fear was sharp. Pungent. She backed a step away from Trevor. "Liz. Liz and Blair are coming. They'll bring Bridget and Jordan."

Irakesh covered his smile with a tiny cough. It was rare for Trevor to show emotion, and in this case it revealed much that he guessed the man would regret.

"Jordan? As in Commander Jordan? The guy from Mohn?" Trevor asked, turning a sharp eye on Cyntia.

"Yes, he was a soldier with Mohn. Do you know him?" she asked, pursing her lips.

"He tried to kill us. Repeatedly. He chased us from San Diego to Peru and the last thing standing in our way when we were trying to wake the Mother," Trevor said. His eyes narrowed, flaring green as he placed his hand on the barrel of his gun. "I owe that son of a bitch. He gutted my house with fucking missiles. He blew up my Mustang. I spent three years restoring that thing."

"Then I will gut him and feast on his innards," she hissed, eyes narrowing in unconscious imitation of Trevor. The fear was rivaled by anger, sharp and acrid. "But Liz is strong. Bridget less so, but still more potent than I."

"Than you *were*," Trevor gave, shaking his head. "You're stronger now. A lot stronger."

"Trevor is correct, but the Ka-Ken is not the real threat. The Ka-Dun, this Blair. *He* is the threat. You must kill him before all others," Irakesh demanded. They must not allow the Ka-Dun to get too close. He'd proven resourceful with his shaping, and that made him a threat.

"There's no way I'm doing that. That, you cannot force me to do," Trevor said. He turned to face Irakesh, crossing his arms and glaring defiantly. Yet there were cracks in that defiance. Uncertainty. Fear that Irakesh could force him to do this act he so despised. "I won't kill Liz, either. She's my fucking sister, Irakesh. He's a friend. Don't make me do this."

"I *can* compel you, you realize that?" Irakesh asked, removing his hand from the hilt of his blade so he could cross his arms in imitation of his thrall. He felt *less* as his hand left the warm metal.

"Maybe, but I'll fight you," Trevor said. A low growl came from Cynthia's chest as she stepped next to him. The meaning was clear.

"You will lose, both of you," Irakesh said, matter-of-factly. "But if I force you to do this, you will never trust me, never work with me as a proper thrall should. Tell me. If I spare your sister and the Ka-Dun, will you agree to serve me without question? I'll have your loyalty or I'll have your sister's pelt for a cloak."

Trevor's eyes grew thoughtful.

Give him a moment; let him mull this. If he assents, this one will likely keep his word, so long as you take care not to push him too far past the demands of his conscience.

"If you leave them alone then I'll serve you, but the moment that changes I will plant that sword in your fucking back," Trevor growled, eyes flaring again. Cyntia coiled like a spring beside him, claws flexing.

Should he strike now? Irakesh retained the advantage, but that would eventually change. No, he had time yet. He would use Trevor, then find a clever way to dispose of him, if need be. Cyntia would have nowhere to go, and her loyalty would almost certainly transfer to him. Assuming she retained some part of her sanity.

"A bargain, then," Irakesh said, extending his hand. It was the gesture of trust used by most cultures in this new age. Trevor hesitated. "We will get what we came for and be away from this place. If we do encounter the Ka-Dun and his pack we'll delay them and then flee. There will be no killing unless we are forced to it. In fact, I have an idea. I will show you how to shape an Anakim. This creature will be powerful enough to delay your friends, but not so strong that they cannot overcome it. I will include a small horde to further delay them, so that we might avoid a direct confrontation. Does that suffice?"

If he detects the lie, you must stand ready.

Irakesh tensed as Trevor raised a hand, but it was merely to take his. His grip was firm and powerful, a shadow of Irakesh's own.

35

CAPTAIN DOUCHE

Jordan trusted Steve even less than he liked the smug bastard. The man in question lounged in a blue canvas camp chair, leg up over one side and a plastic water bottle in one hand. A douchey smile ran counterpoint to the unquestioned superiority in his gaze. This despite the sea of carnage around them, hundreds of bodies that had recently been friends and family to the people who called this little sanctuary home. Or had called it home. All that had changed in a matter of minutes, but this guy was above it all. He was alive, so clearly that was all that mattered.

"We'll have to rebuild, but I don't think we can do it here," Dr. Roberts said, shoulders slumped and voice impossibly weary. A marked contrast to Steve. "The survivors won't trust this place. Besides, with fewer of us we'll need a smaller location to defend." He removed his battered fedora, wiping the sweat from his brow before replacing it.

"I'm afraid I have some bad news on that count," Steve said, pausing dramatically to sip from his water bottle. This one liked being the center of attention, just like he had when he'd first shown up at the Ark with the original science team. The famous Dr. Galk. "I've decided I must accompany Blair. I hate to desert you, Dr.

Roberts, but this Irakesh is a serious threat and must be stopped. As Blair and his friends have had trouble thus far, it seems clear that they're in need of my help."

"We're doing just fine on our own, thanks," Liz said, tone dry and eye roll implied behind her oversized sunglasses.

"We can use the help," Bridget said, though there was a certain reluctance to the admission. She sat in the chair next to Captain Douche, though she hadn't made an attempt to touch him since he'd rebuffed her advance earlier. Must be tough on her seeing the guy again, especially knowing that her newfound pack harbored such an intense dislike for him. "He's been a werewolf as long as anyone except Blair and he has more knowledge of the Ark than any of us."

"Bridget's right. He could definitely be an asset. You're welcome to come if you'd like, Steve," Blair allowed, donning his sunglasses as he left the relative shelter of the pavilion. If it could be called that. It was really just a tarp and some poles.

Jordan frowned. Blair looked at this guy like a friend, but Steve's body language was all wrong for that.

"I'd be happy to join you. Maybe I can teach you a few things about shaping," Steve offered, magnanimous and smug all at once. Jordan wanted to pound that smugness out of him. He'd be damned if he'd allow Steve to undermine Blair.

"I'd guess that's the other way around," Jordan rumbled, taking a step closer to loom over Steve. At 6'4" most people were immediately intimidated, but Steve stared up at him with an amused smile. "You saw how Blair handled that last fight. He caught and held over a hundred zombies. Can you do that, Steve? Because I didn't see you do much of anything."

The man's demeanor wavered, as uncertainty flitted across his face. It was gone in a moment. "I suspect I could if I had to. That's far from my only trick, though. You've already seen that I shift with my clothes. Can any of you do the same?"

Jordan fumed silently, not answering. He looked to Blair for support, but the man just shrugged.

Steve's smile grew still more smug. "I thought not. There's much I can teach you if you can put aside your animosity and listen. Blair did the same for you, unless I am mistaken, Commander. Weren't you an enemy not so long ago? I seem to remember you doing your damnedest to kill me and I suspect the same is true of Blair."

"I had orders," Jordan growled, eyes narrowing. "I freely admit Mohn was in the wrong on this one, but can you blame us? We were trying to stop the spread of werewolves. We had no idea the zombies were coming. What the hell else did you expect us to do?"

He looked to Liz for support, expecting her to break up the squabble. Instead, she stood there with arms crossed, watching.

"I've heard about enough of this," Blair said, rising to his feet. The fire had returned to his eyes. "We don't have time for a pissing contest. Liz, do you have a problem with Steve coming with us?"

"I'll take all the help we can get," Liz said, slinging her pack and heading for the jeep parked next to the pavilion. She did take a moment to shoot a distasteful stare at Steve over the rim of her sunglasses.

Blair rounded on Steve, eyes challenging. "Jordan has been invaluable. Whatever beef you have with him, put it aside. He's had my back through some rough shit and odds are good he'll save your ass before the day is out."

"Blair? Is that you?" Steve said, uncoiling from his chair. He gave a sly smile, the sort you wanted to punch repeatedly until the guy doing it was unconscious. "I didn't recognize you with a backbone. Have they put you in charge? Because you're certainly acting like it."

"Quit being such an asshole," Bridget interrupted, surging from her chair and shoving a finger in Steve's face. "You're jealous. It's all over you. Blair did what you couldn't. He woke the Mother. He controlled those zombies today. All of them. So what if you can transform with your clothes? You're trying to act all mysterious and wise, but you don't know shit. Just a few dribbles you stole from the Mother's mind while she was sleeping."

Jordan couldn't help but smile when he saw the effect the words had. Bridget had just called him out, and his expression said her assessment was spot on.

"You're taking Blair's side?" Steve barked. He struggled for words, face going splotchy as his eyebrows drew together like thunderclouds. "Seriously? Bridget, you flirted with him for weeks while I was *dying*. You think I didn't know? I was dead to you, but the second we were both captured you suddenly wanted me again. Because Blair wasn't around. You'll take whichever one is available, you unfaithful bitch."

Blair blurred. Jordan couldn't track him, not even close. One instant he was standing near the edge of the pavilion, the next his fist was connecting with Steve's jaw. The force of the blow flung Captain Douche tumbling across the pavement. It was the sweetest thing Jordan had tasted in weeks.

Before Steve could rise, Blair was there, kneeling on his back. He leaned close, hands gripping Steve's shoulders so the man couldn't rise. "You're right. She *was* unfaithful, but she's also my friend. More than that, she's an ally, Steve. A member of my pack. *You* are not. You? You're the unfaithful bastard who cheated with my girlfriend right under my nose, despite claiming to be my best friend. So don't go aiming for any sort of moral high ground here. You're both in the wrong.

"To answer your question earlier, no, I'm not in charge," Blair continued, releasing Steve and standing up. "Liz is. But that doesn't mean I'm going to sit around and tolerate your bullshit. You want to help? Great. Fall in fucking line or you aren't welcome here. We clear?"

"Crystal," Steve said, rising gracefully to his feet. Blair turned on his heel and headed for the jeep. He missed the way Steve glared hatefully after him.

Suddenly, Liz's silence made sense. She'd made Blair step up and defend the pack, strengthening his own position. Clever.

Jordan tensed at the sudden vibration in his pocket. The geolocator. It was the first time it had done anything in days. Had Mohn sent another broadcast? He turned and bent next to one of the crates in the corner. He opened it, pretending to survey the array of pistols laid out on the thick grey foam. Then he deftly plucked the geolocator from his pocket. He bent low over the screen, scanning the notification.

It was a transponder ping, sent from members of his unit at timed intervals. The little green arrow was pointing north. Someone was out there, but there was no way to know how far. The thing had over a thousand-mile range, so they could be in the next village or somewhere in the Gulf of Mexico. Whoever it was, they were coming closer, though. That much he did know.

36

ANAKIM

"Observe carefully, Trevor," Irakesh instructed, turning to face the throng of nascent deathless before him. They crowded the inside of the hangar, packing the area between the odd metal conveyances that these moderns referred to as airplanes. "I am going to create an Anakim, one of the most potent servants the deathless possess."

"A giant?" Cyntia rumbled, her blond fur barely visible in the near darkness.

Irakesh was genuinely surprised. It should have been impossible for any memory of the Anakim to survive. "Just so. How do you know of them?"

"From the Bible," Cyntia explained, giving a furry shrug. "The Anakim were giants. My mother used to scare me with stories when I was little."

"You're going to make a biblical giant?" Trevor asked, raising an eyebrow. He rested the barrel of a rifle against his shoulder, the weapon cradled with the same casual familiarity Irakesh exhibited with his na-kopesh.

"A giant, yes. But I seriously doubt it will resemble anything from your silly book," Irakesh said, turning back to the horde of nascent deathless. He scanned the crowd, looking for the best candidate to begin his work. "There. Do you see that one with the bristly hair? The tall one."

The deathless he'd indicated stood at least seven feet tall, an extreme rarity in his time. He was heavily muscled, probably a combatant in one of the games the moderns called sports.

"I see him," Trevor allowed, taking a step closer as his gaze landed on the deathless Irakesh had indicated. "What are you going to do?"

Irakesh didn't answer, instead raising a hand and aiming three fingers at the deathless. He concentrated for a long moment, gathering the energy until his hand began to glow. Emerald light banished the shadows as his hand grew brighter, the sudden illumination drawing every eye in the hangar. Each deathless stared hungrily at his hand, all sensing the power there and understanding on some dim level that it would make them stronger.

A bolt of light shot from Irakesh's hand, streaking into the large deathless's chest. It played across his entire body, crackling like lightning as the change began. The deathless's eyes flared green, and his teeth began to lengthen. Then he lunged suddenly, seizing the corpse of a slight woman like a wolf might a hare. He began to feed, as urgently as Cyntia in the throws of her most berserk fury.

"What did you do?" Trevor asked. His eyebrows drew together as he studied Irakesh's creation.

"I have accelerated his metabolism," Irakesh explained, using words that would be familiar in this age. He allowed himself a slight smile as the change continued. "For the next few hours the Anakim's hunger will be even more insatiable than usual. He will devour every nascent deathless he can reach. Each one will make him larger and stronger. In an hour he will be taller than Cyntia."

Irakesh needn't have bothered explaining, for the change was clear enough for any to see. The Anakim's shoulders and chest began to expand, tearing apart the shirt that it wore as they grew larger. The creature took a step towards another victim, gaining several inches of height even as it did so.

"If we had weeks I could make it strong enough to crush the Ka-

Dun following us, but even this pitiful creature will be a threat," Irakesh said, giving a low laugh. He turned to face the largest plane in the hangar, one near the wide doors leading to the runway. "Come, we have work to be about."

He strode deeper into the hangar, dimly aware of the Anakim growing larger behind him. Bones cracked and popped as it fed, low grunts growing deeper as the creature's strength increased.

37

SATISFACTION

Blair couldn't help but grin as he wallowed in childish delight. He leaned back against the jeep's cracked leather seat, throwing an arm over the back of Steve's uncomfortable spot in the middle. A glower descended, clearly making Steve's displeasure known. It warmed Blair.

For so many years he'd trailed after Steve in college and then later grad school. It had always galled him how easily things came to Steve back then. Steve had the grades. He had the body. He had the women. So many women. He was notorious at parties from Stanford to Berkeley.

Blair had struggled for his grades while gorging on too many late night cafeteria pastries. Steve's dorky friend. It was embarrassing to think about, but at the same time liberating. He'd just proven to himself that he wasn't that guy anymore. He'd grown and changed in so many ways. He was Steve's equal. Hell, maybe his better if he hadn't just gotten lucky back there.

"Bridget," Jordan called over his shoulder from the passenger's seat. "I brought an extra couple clips for that .460 I gave you earlier. Might save your ass if we get into an extended firefight." He offered a pair of heavy black clips over his shoulder.

"Thanks," Bridget called back, shifting in her place on the other side of Steve. She took the ammo, tucking the clips into her pants pockets. Blair was impressed by how naturally it seemed to come, the ammo and the weapon belted to her thigh. She'd been spending a lot of time with Jordan and it looked as though it had paid off.

Blair's hand lay tantalizingly close to the soft curve of her shoulder. He remembered her leaning into him while they stared out across Lake Sonoma or in front of the fire in their first apartment. He smiled, withdrawing his arm and dropping it into his lap to give Steve a little more room. It wasn't smart treading over those memories, but for the first time in a while they didn't hurt. Did that mean he'd moved on? To what?

"Eyes front," Jordan boomed. He unbuckled his seatbelt and leaned out the window, anchoring himself to the chair with his legs. Blair leaned out his own window and shaded his eyes as he scanned the road ahead. What had Jordan spotted?

A vast airport equal to anything back in the States sprawled before them, curiously devoid of zombies. Not a single figure moved between the planes on the tarmac, or anywhere inside the wide windows on both floors of the terminal. That shouldn't be possible.

"This place should be crawling," Blair said, ducking back into the car. Bridget and Steve were looking in his direction, but Liz was focused on driving. "Where the hell are all the zombies?"

"We saw Irakesh control them before," Liz said over her shoulder. The jeep rumbled down a steep hill maneuvering around a battered Volkswagen. She reached out and tugged Jordan back into his seat. The ease of it made Blair shudder. "Jordan, what would you do if you could control a horde of zombies and knew we were coming?"

The taller man pursed his lips as he scanned the tarmac, wheels clearly turning as he assessed.

"I'd concentrate most of them around my objective, as tightly as possible. I might send a significant force to delay the enemy, but only if I could do it without giving away my position. I'm guessing his objective is a hangar here, so that means if we go tarmac to tarmac we'll find him eventually," Jordan replied, turning to eye Blair over his sunglasses. "Can you give us a hint? I know you can feel him."

"Give me a sec," Blair said, closing his eyes. He reached out, allowing his senses to roam the area. He sought a certain resonance, half feeling half intuition. There. A strong pulsing, like a heartbeat. It was stronger than it had been before and he'd picked it up much more quickly. Did that mean Irakesh was closer?

It does, Ka-Dun. He is near. Be wary. That one is exceedingly dangerous.

The beast's voice was a welcome presence. It was truly a part of him now. He opened his eyes. "Over there, to the left. It's one of those warehouse-looking buildings on the far side of the airport."

"Those are private hangars," Jordan replied. He removed his glasses, delivering a sobering look as he turned to face the back seat. "One of them is the Mohn facility I told you about. Where the nuke was stored. I've only been inside once and I didn't see much, but the building houses a full Mohn facility."

Blair supposed even a man with a rank like commander wasn't privy to everything. It was still odd seeing a gap in Jordan's knowledge, though.

"You think Irakesh is heading for it? How could he possibly know it even exists?" Liz asked, glancing at Jordan as she guided the jeep onto the road paralleling the airport. It led directly to the private hangars.

"I can steal memories. What if he can, too?" Blair said, chilled by the thought. How old was Irakesh? If the deathless could plunder memories, how much did he know about the world? How many lives had he lived?

"It's possible," Jordan allowed, turning to face the road. "There were three people at the Ark who knew about this place. Both were extracted when you attacked. Corporal Yuri Filipov and Major Sanders. Both left by helicopter. If either went down in the CME, I guess Irakesh might have found the wreckage. Maybe he captured one of them or has some other way of learning this location. Either way it seems unlikely he'd show up at the exact spot Mohn was storing a nuke unless he knew about it."

"So we assume he's there and that the nuke is his objective," Liz said. She romped on the gas, sending the jeep jolting forward. The hot wind whipped Blair's hair about as he scanned the buildings ahead. "Whether it is or not, we go to the one Blair says. I'll just keep driving until you give us a target."

Blair stared hard out the window, watching the eight-foot chain fence roll by as they passed the first of the hangars. There were roughly a dozen, lining both sides of the cracked asphalt. A few cars dotted the road, but the place was eerily empty. A tomb to mark the passing of an entire civilization.

The sun hung low in the sky, threatening to sink into the vast Pacific that swallowed the western and southern horizons. It cast a bloody hue over the buildings, a fitting mood for the work they were about to engage in. What would Irakesh do if they finally caught him? What hidden powers did he possess?

"There," Blair called, stabbing a finger out the window. He could feel the pulse now, strong and clear. "That building on the right. Three down. He's in there. I'm sure of it."

Liz gunned it, tires squealing as she jerked the wheel left. They shot through an opening in the fence, the jeep bouncing as a tire hit the curb. The air reeked of burnt rubber and exhaust as they rocketed towards the building Blair had indicated. There wasn't a single plane, bus, or car in the vicinity.

The wide chrome hangar grew larger as Liz gave the vehicle still more gas. Was she going to slow down? It didn't matter, not to him. He was still thinking like a human, but he'd become far more than that. Blair blurred.

Liz's copper hair writhed in the wind like a mass of tiny snakes, fanning backwards on either side of the headrest to his place in the back of the car. Steve was just beginning to turn his head, mouth slowly opening. His chest expanded as he sucked in a breath to say something. Then Blair was gone.

He opened the door, rolling onto the hot asphalt. The jeep lumbered next to him, a snail creeping along. It would take an eternity for it to reach the hangar. He blazed forward, wind ripping at his clothing as he crossed the distance to the small door set into the center of the hangar. Forty-six was emblazoned above it in crisp red letters, as if painted onto the blinding metal surface just the day before.

Blair rolled into a crouch before the door, slowly standing until his face was even with the little window. It too was mirrored. That made sense, of course. Mohn wouldn't leave an obvious way to see into one of their facilities, especially not one where a nuke was being held. No matter. He cocked his arm back, balling his hand into a tight fist. He blurred forward, punching it through glass in a spray of tiny shards.

A cyclone of dust burst next to him as Steve's black-clad form appeared in a crouch. "We should wait for the others. They can't move as swiftly as we can and we don't want to get overrun."

"Jordan can. Besides, the thing I've been chasing for weeks is right behind that door. He could be boarding an aircraft as we speak. You and I need to delay him until the others arrive," Blair growled, planting his foot against the door. He shifted, kicking with all his might. The door was flung inward, rattling an erratic path across smooth concrete. The tattered remains of his t-shirt still clung to his furry shoulders.

"All right," Steve agreed, giving a tight nod. "But we're telling the others this was your idea."

Blair grinned back, striding into the hangar's dim silence. His eyes adjusted, revealing several massive shapes. Planes, all of different sorts. There were four of them. The closest was a Cessna about the same size as Garland's. He paused, straining his senses. He heard nothing, but what did he smell? The cloyingly sweet stench of rotting meat.

Shapes moved in the darkness, shambling towards them in a mindless mass. So many. A wave of low moans broke over them.

"What's your plan, Blair?" Steve asked, more than a little smug.

He shifted, his clothing vanishing into his midnight fur. How the hell did he do that?

"I can feel him that way," Blair said, pointing towards the farthest of the bulky shapes. It was a massive cargo plane of the kind used in every military movie from the past two decades. Large and squat with four engines and a long ramp extending down the back. "He's inside that plane. Right now. We just have to get there."

"That's going to be a problem," Steve said, grabbing Blair's shoulder. He pointed into the darkness. "A big problem."

The ground shook as a massive figure pounded a path towards them. It towered over the other zombies, a good ten or eleven feet tall and wider than any linebacker he'd ever seen. The thing made Lizwolf look like a puppy. The giant resembled the other zombies, pale flaccid skin and too-white, razored teeth. Yet where they wore dull, vacant expressions its eyes shone green with cunning. Where they shambled it thundered, massive muscles bunching as it surged towards them. It moved so swiftly, knocking shorter zombies aside like kindling as it approached.

"Move," Blair roared, rolling out of the thing's path. It thundered past, leaving the stench of death in its wake. He shot to his feet, turning to Steve. "Get something sharp and stab it in the spine. I'll distract it."

"Got it," Steve shot back, blurring to the door of the Cessna. He yanked it open and disappeared inside.

Blair turned his attention back to the huge deathless just in time to receive a meaty fist to the face. It shattered his jaw, sending bone fragments rattling through his skull. He blanked, coming to in a heap against a wall. There were gaps. Pieces missing. So many things danced out of reach. How badly hurt was he? The ground shook as something large approached. Damn him for a fool. Why hadn't he waited for everyone?

Give over to me, Ka-Dun. Your mind is damaged. This battle you cannot win.

Blair let go, falling into darkness.

38

PRE-FLIGHT

T revor flipped each of the four switches in rapid succession, enhanced hearing picking up answering clinks from within the bowels of the plane. They were followed by a rush of liquid flowing down what he assumed must be fuel lines. He turned back to the manual in his left hand, scanning the next paragraph.

"I do not understand," Cyntia complained from the co-pilot's chair next to him. Her arms were crossed, but left just low enough to frame a generous expanse of cleavage. He was supposed to look, both because of male instincts and because she wanted him to. He didn't. "Why do you need the book? You said you'd learned how to pilot from the corpse you ate two days ago."

"He knew how to fly a Cessna," Trevor answered, only giving her half his attention. He needed to concentrate, but if he ignored her she'd find increasingly annoying methods of getting his attention. That was a growing irritation as the feeding affected her mind. "This is a much larger aircraft and the startup sequence is radically different. I can figure it out, but I need a little time."

"You've run out of time, I'm afraid," Irakesh said, slipping into the cockpit through the thick steel doorway behind the pilot's chair. Trevor was willing to bet the door could stop heavy-caliber bullets or maybe even a rampaging werewolf, though he wasn't eager to find out. Irakesh pointed through the canopy towards a sliver of light coming from the far wall. "The door has been opened and two Ka-Dun have entered. One possesses the access key, this Blair you've named him. The other is unfamiliar to me, perhaps an ally acquired during his journey. Either we leave now or prepare ourselves for combat. The thralls I've left will not delay them for long, not once his Ka-Ken arrives. Even the Anakim will be little more than a distraction."

"This thing's been mothballed. I need at least a few minutes for the self-fueling to complete. I can't rush this," Trevor protested, eyeing a long blue cylinder that reminded him of a thermometer. The level slowly rose, indicating the active fuel level to the propellers.

"We don't have that time," Irakesh growled, eyes flaring a sickly green. He turned to Cyntia. "Get out there and prowl the shadows. If they make for this plane harry them, but do not let yourself be drawn into a prolonged engagement. The goal is not to win, but to delay."

"And don't hurt Liz or Blair," Trevor added firmly. He swiveled the leather pilot's chair to face Irakesh.

"Trevor, do you need to be present to oversee this process?" Irakesh asked, nodding toward the array of gauges along the cockpit.

"No, the fueling will take care of itself. It's all automated," Trevor replied, eyes narrowing. He didn't like where this was going.

"Then you will also delay our pursuers," Irakesh ordered, gesturing towards the open door on the other side of the cockpit.

"No, I won't," Trevor replied, meeting the deathless's gaze. "Our deal is that I won't fight Blair or Liz."

"Nor will you," Irakesh growled. "You will fight their companions. They are sure to have brought them. I will deal with Blair. Cyntia can delay Liz."

"That's not our bargain. You said you wouldn't hurt them," Trevor shot back, anger rising. He felt heat rising from Irakesh, pressing down on his will, a blatant reminder that he was the master.

"The deal was that I would not ask you to hurt Liz or Blair, nor hurt them myself. You said nothing about asking Cyntia to do it,"

Irakesh said, hand shooting out in a blur. He seized Trevor by the neck, hefting him from his seat. "You also said nothing about attacking your sister's companions. We made a deal, you and I, and you *will* abide by it. The fact that you no longer care for this deal is immaterial. Either you cooperate or I will force you to kill your sister then feast upon your meager mind myself. Am I making my will understood, *thrall*?"

"I will kill you for this someday," Trevor growled. Today the deathless could jerk him about like a puppet, and all he could do was dance. Tomorrow would be a different story.

"No, you will kill me for *this*," Irakesh said, caressing the words as an ominous smile bloomed. He extended a hand, tips touching Trevor's chest. Agony flooded him. His limbs were on fire, throat constricting. Trevor collapsed to his knees, hugging the chair for support. He was dimly aware of Irakesh's smug voice as the deathless continued. "Calm yourself, Cyntia. I haven't harmed him."

Trevor was aware of the dirty-blond form that had sprung into existence next to him. He hadn't even seen her shift. She stood protectively over him, ready to attack Irakesh, though he could smell her fear.

"What did you do to me?" Trevor asked, wobbling alarmingly as he struggled to his feet.

"It will pass in a moment. Let's just say I've assumed a more direct form of control," Irakesh's grin grew wider. He gestured to the cockpit door. "Don't let me stop you. You both have tasks to accomplish, do you not?"

What did he do? Trevor asked. He waited for a response from the voice. Nothing. *Can you hear me?*

The voice was just...gone. Trevor's gaze locked on Irakesh. The deathless gave a knowing smile.

39

BAD TO WORSE

L iz flung open the jeep's door, kicking off the seat with enough force to send the vehicle skidding across the pavement. She landed in a crouch near the doorway her two companions had just disappeared through. Damn Blair and damn Steve for following him. If he wasn't already dead she was going to kill him. They should have attacked as a group, but those two school kids had rushed blindly ahead.

"Bridget, through the door to the right. I'll go left. Jordan, follow and watch our backs," Liz commanded, low voice rumbling like a semi.

Bridget's silver form leapt through the door, managing majestic if not beautiful. In contrast, Liz probably resembled a very large pit bull whose territory had just been invaded, ungainly but undeniable.

She sprinted through the door, gathering the shadows close about her as she entered the dim. A chorus of familiar low moans echoed through the hangar, obscuring most other noise. The exception was the din of combat coming from somewhere near the center, the area obscured by two bulky planes. She heard the low grunts that were probably Blair and Steve, followed by a hollow boom as something empty was struck with massive force.

It was too dark to see, too crowded to pick out individual noises in the cacophony. A haze of putrid death shrouded everything, making it impossible to track by scent. How the hell was she supposed to find targets in this?

She was aware of Jordan's shorter blond form entering quietly behind her, the butt of his rifle set against a furry shoulder as the thick barrel scanned the darkness. Sensing sudden movement a couple dozen feet to her left, Bridget lunged from the shadows tearing into a trio of zombies. They went down in a spray of gore, extinguished like candles as more of their brethren surged forward. They seemed endless.

"Bridget," Liz roared, pointing towards the direction she'd last heard combat. "Carve a path in that direction. Jordan, cut down anything that gets behind us. Let's move." She surged forward, unlimbering her claws. A corpulent zombie stood before her with a mop of curly hair and a cracked pair of glasses that had somehow clung to his face. She brought an elbow down to crush his skull, already moving to the next target.

The trio flowed with incredible synergy despite having only worked together for a few weeks. Jordan mercilessly cut down the zombies trying to close ranks behind them, while she and Bridget mowed a wide path through the hangar. They rounded one of the planes, this one a mid-sized Cessna like the one Garland had flown. As she rounded the plane's white nose she finally saw Blair, his silver body shattered and broken against the wheel of another plane.

A huge zombie loomed over Blair, taller than her by at least a couple feet. The thing seemed consternated by the plane in the way, leaning back and forth as if unsure how to reach him. Its limbs were too long, chest too broad. The ungainly creature finally dropped to its knees and extended an arm under the plane. It patted the ground a few feet to Blair's left, searching. It wouldn't be long until it found him.

Blam.

A gunshot cracked behind her. Right behind her. She jerked around, expecting to see Jordan killing a zombie. What she found turned her innards to ice and constricted her throat with death's black hands. Jordan lay in a pool of his own blood, both fanged face and furry chest an unrecognizable mess. That she might have been able to process, but it was the attacker that untied her like a pair of shoelaces. It was Trevor.

For one tiny shaving of a moment she caught his gaze, eyes horribly green just like Irakesh. His teeth, too white and razor-sharp. Trevor was her brother, but everything in her cried that he needed to be destroyed. Then he vanished, slipping into the shadows just as she would have.

She did the same, more instinct than conscious thought. There *was* no conscious thought, only reeling from what she'd just witnessed.

"Liz, help me," Bridget-wolf bellowed. Liz spun in time to see her silver form roll between the giant zombie's legs.

Bridget leapt onto its back, tearing at its throat in the same way a lion might tackle a bear. The creature was unimpressed, seizing Bridget by the arm and slamming her into the side of the plane with a horrible boom that thundered through the silence left in the wake of the gunfire. Metal buckled and glass shattered as her body sank into the plane.

Liz glanced back at Jordan, scanning the darkness for Trevor. Dammit, why did she have to make choices like this? She spun to face Bridget again, bounding around zombies until she had a clear line of attack. Then she charged, aiming for the zombie's knee. She caught it with her shoulder, spilling the thing onto its side with the sharp crack of bone. She rolled away, feeling the wind as one of its meaty arms slammed the ground where she'd just been.

The giant zombie crawled towards her, face a twisted mask of rage. Hopefully it couldn't heal that leg as quickly as she could, which might give her time to wear it down. She danced backwards, glancing around to make sure no zombies had gotten too close. Perhaps if she landed on its back she could—

A fist emerged from her gut, furry fingers slick and red with her intestines still clutched between clawed fingers. She was shoved forward, into the reach of the giant zombie. It seized her leg, shattering her kneecap in a parody of the wound she'd given it. She shrieked, beating at the meaty fist that clutched her leg. She risked a glance behind her, but there was no sign of her assailant. It had been a werewolf; she was sure of that.

Taste the air, Ka-Ken. What do you smell?

It was a familiar scent. Cyntia. That fucking bitch. Liz roared, knifing both hands into her own leg just above the zombie's hands. It sent a spear of hot flame up her leg as she severed it, but she was free. She scrambled backwards, gathering the shadows about her in a protective cloak.

There was no sign of Cyntia. She lurked somewhere in the shadows, patiently waiting to strike. Why hadn't she struck when Liz was vulnerable? She glanced at the dented plane. There was no sign of Bridget. She too had escaped to the shadows. That was why Cyntia hadn't attacked. Her cowardice didn't surprise Liz; hell, it was welcome. It meant she was predictable, and that might give Liz the advantage in their game of wolf and mouse.

Searing heat surged down her leg as she flopped around like a fish. Being so vulnerable terrified her and a panicked part of her mind wondered if there was some way for either Cyntia or the massive zombie to find her in the shadows. She had to get control. Liz seized the knee just above the bloody stump, pinning it in place as a new tibia suddenly extended from the gaping wound. It was joined by a fibula, then a mass of muscles that writhed into place like a sea of scarlet snakes. The tide of agony threatened to pull her under, but she wouldn't allow it. Couldn't allow it.

When the pain finally ceased she looked to the spot where Blair had lain. There was no sign of him, just a pool of blood. Good, he'd healed and probably found his way back into the fight. She needed to do the same. Liz scanned the darkness, assessing the combat to see where she might be of most use. There was still no sign of Bridget, but somewhere on the far side of the hangar she heard the ring of metal on metal. It sounded like someone fighting with a sword, at least if her memory of Lord of the Rings was any indication.

A scuffle came from the far side of the plane, two large bodies grappling. She caught a flash of fur as the pair spilled to the ground, one of them the blond fur she recognized as belonging to Jordan. The other was a sickly version of the same color. Cyntia. Liz dropped prone and rolled under the plane, springing to her feet on the far side near the combatants. Jordan was getting the worst of it.

He lay on his stomach pinned by Cyntia's much larger form. His left arm was bent at the wrong angle and there was no sign of any of his ever-present guns. Cyntia bit down, savaging the back of his neck as she began to feed. She ripped loose a mouthful of fur and flesh, gulping it down greedily. She seemed unaware of the gore coating her face, already bending for another bite.

"Get off him, you fucking bitch," Liz roared, stepping forward and kicking with all her considerable might. The blow caught Cyntia in the chin, splintering her jaw and flinging her backwards with a sharp crack. Cynthia tumbled backwards, rolling into the shadows as she regained her footing and glared at Liz with hateful eyes, now the deep scarlet of a heart wound. When had they changed?

Those eyes winked out as Cyntia fled back into the shadows. Liz looked about warily as she knelt next to Jordan and felt for a pulse. She'd never seen him so badly wounded, but knew that Blair had recovered from worse. Hopefully he was okay. She pushed through the fur until her fingers found the carotid artery. The pulse was thready, but at least there was one.

Movement behind her. She began to spin, but too late. Cyntia lunged from the shadows, fangs painted red from Jordan's blood. She seized Liz, yanking her throat forward even as her fangs descended. Fresh agony ripped through her as Cyntia bit into her throat. She couldn't breathe. Everything was fire. She tumbled backwards, Cyntia's once smaller form crashing down on top of her.

40

TURNING POINT

Blair came to with a gasp atop the wing of the Cessna. He was coated in something hot and sticky. Blood. His blood. Deafening peals of combat echoed over him like a gigantic church bell. Gunshots and crates smashing and metal bending. He rolled to his feet, taking in his immediate surroundings. The giant zombie lay twitching on the ground nearby, seemingly unable to rise. Its hand still clutched a furry leg. Auburn fur. Liz. Where was she?

Rage surged through him as he surveyed the hangar, but she was nowhere to be found.

Something tugged at him. Blair turned towards the far side of the hangar where he'd seen the biggest plane earlier. The one Irakesh was presumably inside, or perhaps had just emerged from since the link had grown stronger. He was in the darkness somewhere, waiting. There was movement near the plane, though he doubted it could be Irakesh. The deathless was too crafty to be spotted. So who was it?

Blair blurred across the tarmac, leaping into the air and landing on top of the cargo plane with a hollow thud. It was much bigger up close, wide enough to hold a tank or a whole lot of troops and long enough to play volleyball inside. Something was clicking from the interior below, something that sounded an awful lot like a larger version of the fuel pump he'd had on his rusted out Pontiac back in high school. Were they getting this thing ready to fly? Of course they were.

The figure Blair had spotted was Steve, prowling the darkness with that midnight fur. He crouched near the far wall, beneath two gigantic doors they would have to open to taxi the aircraft out. Blair needed to leave Steve out there as bait. It was callous, but also smart. Steve would probably approve.

"Complacent," a smug voice whispered from directly behind him, even as something hot spiked into his back. A glittering golden blade burst from his chest, slick with his own blood. "You perch up here watching the darkness as if you are the predator, but you've always been the prey, Ka-Dun. I led you here. I feel you even as you feel me."

Irakesh. Blair rolled forward, the blade making a wet pop as it slipped from his chest. The wound was excruciating, but he'd grown used to pain like that. What shocked him was the icy chill that passed through him, an almost living thing that stole the warmth from his blood.

Be wary of the weapon, Ka-Dun. It is an ancient thing and very dangerous. Sunsteel leeches your strength, delivering it to your foe.

Blair blurred, leaping from the plane and catching one of the ribbed supports lining the top of the hangar some thirty feet above. It was farther than he'd tried leaping before, but the blur gave him the momentum. He caught the cool metal in one hand, swinging himself on top of it as he scanned the darkness below.

Irakesh was right. The deathless had the advantage here. He'd led Blair all the way from Peru and seemed to hold all the cards. Yet Blair's allies still fought below. A shape materialized from the darkness behind Steve, but it wasn't Irakesh. He'd recognize that close-cropped red hair and freckled face anywhere, even with the horribly sharp fangs. Trevor was working for Irakesh.

The deathless planted the barrel of a massive-looking revolver at the base of Steve's skull and pulled the trigger. It roared, barrel bucking as a short gout of flame erupted. Blood spurted as the wound exited Steve's face in a shower of bone fragments and gore. Steve collapsed, rolling to the ground bonelessly. It would take long moments to recover. Moments Blair knew Trevor wouldn't give him.

Blair dropped soundlessly from his perch, swinging just a bit to angle towards Trevor as he fell. One former friend about to murder another. Life certainly had a black sense of irony.

He landed heavily on Trevor's back, bearing the deathless to the ground in a crunch of bone. Trevor's revolver skittered away across the hangar's concrete floor, but that didn't mean he was unarmed. Each finger now ended in a thick black fingernail, sharp enough to carve flesh. His fangs were just as lethal, designed to rend just like a shark.

Trevor struggled to dislodge Blair from his back, but Blair drove a knee hard into his spine even as he reached around to tear out the deathless's throat. It helped to think of him that way and not as the man who'd so recently saved his life, who'd opened his home and risked everything to protect Liz.

"Predictable," Irakesh's voice hissed behind his ear. The breath was cold and lifeless. "This is why my kind will always win."

Blair thought he was ready, already beginning to blur. It wasn't enough. Irakesh's golden blade punched through his chest, delivering a wound twin to the one he'd scored moments earlier. That one had mostly healed, though Blair could still feel it. Not good.

The wound around the blade was ice and Blair could feel his life slipping into the silvery metal. It horrified him, but he couldn't pull away. Moving took effort. Blurring seemed impossible. He was going to die.

"Get off of him," Bridget roared, materializing from the shadows and barreling into Irakesh. She knocked him off Blair, wrenching the awful sword from his back and spilling him to the concrete in a spreading pool of his own blood.

Blair flopped onto his side, struggling weakly to his knees. Trevor disappeared back into the shadows but hopefully was too wounded to attack immediately. Blair focused his attention on Irakesh, smiling despite the agony. Bridget had an arm wrapped around his shoulder and was digging out his entrails with her other hand, ripping the stringy organs out as she bit down on his face.

Irakesh struggled to free himself, but Bridget was far stronger. His sword was still clutched weakly in one hand, while the other clawed ineffectually at her wrist. Then Trevor appeared again, apparently having recovered his revolver. He unloaded three quick shots, each belching a round into Bridget's head from close range. The stench of gunpowder battled the rich tang of blood, the blend overpowering in his weakened state.

Bridget shrieked, releasing Irakesh and leaping away. She left a trail of blood behind her, but there was no sign of her as she vanished into the shadow's waiting embrace. Irakesh did the same, as did Trevor. Only he and Steve were still there, struggling to rise.

You must feed, Ka-Dun, and soon. Your strength wanes.

I don't have time, he thought back, staggering to his feet. He couldn't recall having felt this weak even before he'd become a werewolf.

He didn't dare waste energy blurring, choosing instead to lope towards the plane he knew Irakesh would have to leave in. At least he knew his nemesis's destination, though stopping him from taking what he wanted was another matter.

The press of zombies had receded; so many had been cut down during the early fighting. There were still dozens remaining, though Blair paid them no mind. He could easily avoid them. They all could, assuming they weren't so wounded they couldn't move.

Blair skidded to a halt next to Steve, sliding an arm under his shoulders and hoisting him to his feet, "Hang in there, Steve. I've got you. You're damn hard to kill. I thought for sure you'd gone down for the last time when Trevor shot you in the head."

"You know him?" Steve looked shocked and more than a bit groggy. He held his hand to his forehead, which still leaked blood. He must be weak if his wounds were no longer fully healing.

"Yeah, long story. He's Liz's brother. We have no idea how he ended up with Irakesh, but that's bad for us. He was lethal before.

Now? I'm not sure we can stop him," Blair admitted, scanning the darkness. There was no sign of anyone near them.

He did hear fighting on the far side of the hangar, a knock-down, drag-out brawl from the sound of it. It was probably Liz, though who or what she was fighting remained a mystery. He couldn't focus on that right now.

"We're being hunted. Trevor and Irakesh can both hide in the shadows; that's the bad news," Blair said, helping Steve towards the aircraft. If they were on board Irakesh would have to kill them before taking off.

"You're implying there's good news," Steve said, pushing Blair gently away. "I can manage, I think. My head is starting to clear."

"There is good news, at least a little," Blair said, scanning the darkness as they approached the long metal ramp leading into the cargo area of the plane. "Bridget is still out there, too. That's the only thing keeping Irakesh and Trevor from killing us."

"Lovely," Steve growled, eyes a bit more focused now. He too scanned the darkness. "So we're out here as bait, basically. They attack us. She attacks them."

"Something like that. Irakesh will have to make a move soon. He can't let us get into the pla—" Blair began. He was interrupted as Trevor materialized from the darkness, barrel aimed at Blair's face. Blair blurred, ducking even as his friend's finger stroked the trigger.

It boomed, a round whizzing through the space his head had just occupied. Then a much larger shape burst from the darkness. Bridget. She tackled Trevor, the pair rolling through the darkness like feral dogs. They snapped and clawed at each other, nothing human in either face.

Blair had a split second to consider. He knew Irakesh would appear any second now that Bridget was occupied. *Use your mind, Ka-Dun. He cannot shape as you do. He can fool the eye, but you can fool the mind.*

That was it. Blair had invaded Liz's mind. He'd plucked thoughts from other people. Ahiga had even invaded *his* mind. So why couldn't he invade Irakesh's? If he understood the deathless, they lacked the ability to either attack or defend on that front. It might be the one advantage he possessed.

"So stupid," Irakesh roared, appearing in front of Blair. He rammed his blade through Blair's throat in a shower of hot pain and wet, sticky blood. Blair sagged to his knees, clutching weakly at the sword lodged in his neck. The pain was a living thing, eating at his vision like a cancer. "You should never have come, Ka-Dun. I'd have preferred not to kill you. I'd have preferred a truce. Yet you are forcing my hand. I cannot have you dogging my every step. I have work to do, so if you are so determined to harry me you must be put down like a rabid animal."

Blair glanced at Steve. Or rather at where Steve had been. Evidently he'd blurred away, because there was no sign of him now. Blair wanted to be angry, but he couldn't force himself. He didn't blame Steve for fleeing. There was nothing he could have done to help, only get himself killed. If Blair was to survive he'd have to save himself. He had one chance. If it worked he'd get the drop on Irakesh for once. If not, he'd be dead and it wouldn't matter.

"Why are you smiling?" Irakesh demanded, eyes smoldering as he yanked his weapon from Blair's throat.

Blair honed his will into a spike. It came easily now, even with the agony and exhaustion. He had almost no strength left, but Mother willing it would be enough.

"Because," Blair rasped through his ruined throat, gaze locking with Irakesh. "I'm in your head."

Then he struck, sliding past the deathless's defenses with surprising ease.

41

DECEIVED

Irakesh was escorted into the throne room, a cavernous chamber in the very heart of the Ark. A narrow red carpet stretched the length of the chamber, four massive glow bulbs hovering above. Each blazed like a miniature sun, though their soft ivory light left shadows in the corners. None of the brightly clothed sycophants lining either side of the carpet were careless enough to let their booted feet touch the plush velvet. Doing so would have been a gross breach of etiquette, one they may not survive.

He strode boldly up that carpet, knowing he stood far above them all in position if not experience or age. It was a crowning moment, yet a disquieted part of his mind whispered that this was all somehow wrong. How was that possible? He was where he'd always been meant to be, the Ark of the Cradle. His mother, the goddess Ra herself, was resplendent in a bejeweled headdress and a shimmering white robe that plunged at the neckline. She lounged in opulence atop her golden throne on the raised dais. One bronzed leg was thrown carelessly over the side as she swirled the contents of her goblet. She surveyed the small army of cloaked sycophants, every last one scheming for a coveted rejuvenator when the Age of the Lion ended in a handful of weeks. She didn't appear to have noticed Irakesh, though he knew that was an act. She'd sensed his approach hours ago, the moment he first reached her city.

"What merit could such a strike possibly possess?" Ra asked, her melodic voice sweet but eyes glittering hard like diamonds. They promised a swift but merciful death, should the answer displease her.

"What merit? We could overwhelm Isis *now*, right at the end. If nothing else, damage her Ark so that she cannot slumber away the millennia and live to fight us in the next age," a bold-faced deathless explained, as if to a doddering idiot. His ill-chosen tone had likely signed his death warrant, though he seemed oblivious to his own mounting peril.

Unsurprising. Irakesh thought it a minor miracle that Khonsu had lived this long. Even his fashion sense was lacking. A tightly bound side-lock of black hair dangled down the side of his face. His silver robes had gone out of fashion when Isis had departed centuries ago, yet he'd stubbornly clung to them because of his love for the moon.

Khonsu plunged boldly ahead, hands clasped before him in something that was probably meant to be supplication. "You could assail her with lightning and death as a prelude to an assault, providing a distraction. The rest of your warriors could storm the central chamber and destroy the obelisks."

"Galu, how old are you?" Ra called as if Khonsu hadn't spoken. She turned towards the diminutive figure perched in a high backed chair a mere two steps below the throne. Irakesh almost never noticed the child, as was intended. She so cleverly faded into the background unless Ra brought attention to her as she had today.

"I have seen five cycles, most holy," Galu said, voice so soft only their enhanced senses allowed them to perceive it. She gave a reverent nod, screening her face with dark curls that had no doubt taken her thralls hours to perfect. Her ivory robe was twin to Ra's.

"Why do I keep you in my company at all times, Galu?" Ra asked, placidly. Irakesh stopped, not yet wanting to be the subject of his mother's attention. Khonsu was doomed and he didn't want even a passing association with such an event.

"To ensure that any flaw a child could spot will be corrected before a plan is implemented," the child answered, eyes low. She looked so tiny in that monster of a chair.

"Tell me, Galu, what flaws do you detect in Minister Khonsu's plan?" she asked, eyes growing a malevolent green as her attention settled on the subject of her wrath.

"Such a strike has little chance of success," Galu said, watching the minister as his long face purpled. Were it not for Ra's protection Irakesh was certain the fool would have attacked. It underscored how truly foolish the man was. "We have no knowledge regarding Isis's defenses. Even if we did, such a strike would deplete our Ark, draining precious power. This power will be needed to preserve those of us who accompany Ra to the next age. If we use it now, we risk running out before we have arrived."

"Such a gamble is unlikely to use a significant amount of—" Khonsu began, face twisted in rage.

"Silence," Ra roared, rising from her throne and taking a step towards Khonsu. Gold flowed from her palm, coalescing into a long staff with a scarab head. A giant sapphire set in the middle of the beetle's thorax pulsed with power. The sight of the legendary weapon invoked even more fear than Ra's thunderous expression. Khonsu quailed before her, shrinking into his voluminous black cloak as if its shadowy folds could offer protection.

"I could burn you to ash in a heartbeat and none would so much as note your absence. Yet such is my disgust that I will not soil my hands with your filthy flesh. Instead, I name you anathema. You are no longer welcome at this court, Khonsu. In fact, any who participate in your death will be named a friend of the gods," she said, robe swishing as she swayed forward. She swept down the stairs, past the frenzied mob that formed around poor Khonsu. The man's screams were quickly choked off as they began to feed. Her gaze fell on Irakesh, turning his bowels to water. "Attend me, my son. I would walk the gardens."

A silver shape lingered in the corner of his vision, but when Irakesh spun to face it directly, whatever he'd seen was gone. His eyes narrowed. Had it been a Ka-Ken spy? It wasn't like their ancient enemies to make such a mistake. A Ka-Ken was never seen unless she wanted to be. So what had he just witnessed? Should he mention it to his mother? Surely if something were there, she'd have already detected it. She was the undisputed master of this place.

"Irakesh, did you not hear me?" Ra called, the faintest note of disapproval creeping into her voice. Irakesh hurried after, following her down a wide marble corridor that led to the terraced gardens along the outer edge of the Ark.

She glanced at him over a bare shoulder exposed by her robe. By design, of course. Ra had lost none of the allure that had led to her being declared the most beautiful woman in the world, her auburn locks flowing down perfect shoulders like a waterfall. Her face a pristine oval, eyes like glittering emeralds. Many deathless still harbored a very human lust for her, despite supposedly being removed from such mortal passions. She wielded that lust with the potent skill of one bred to manipulate. A skill he very much envied.

"My apologies, mother. I thought I saw something. I'm sure I must have been mistaken," he said, inclining his head respectfully. He avoided looking directly at her. It was safer that way.

They strode down the corridor for several moments, a pair of seekers hanging respectfully back, but ready to spring into combat should a threat present itself. They were the very best death merchants in the entire Cradle and their reputation for lethality was well earned.

"Tell me what you saw, my son. You are my direct progeny and must learn to assert yourself, even with me," Ra said, the rebuke delivered with a rare smile. She paused to face him. Now he had no choice but to meet her gaze. She arched a delicate auburn eyebrow. "Show me."

"Very well," Irakesh said, scanning his own memory for what he'd seen. "It was quite curious. It looked like a Ka-Dun, but vanished so suddenly it must have been a Ka-Ken." He gestured to the hall ahead of them, concentrating as he drew the energy necessary to shape.

A wavering illusion appeared, a silver-furred werewolf with amber eyes. It was majestic and powerful, but not nearly so powerful as a female. The Ka-Dun's face was maddeningly familiar, but Irakesh had no idea why. Where could he possibly know it from? He'd never even met a real Ka-Dun, though he'd been in a battle and seen one die. At a distance.

"You saw this one? A moment ago while we were speaking?" his mother asked, more surprised than he'd ever seen her.

Something was dreadfully wrong. His mother would never show such a lack of composure, not even if Isis herself invaded. That *wasn't* his mother. This might not even be the Ark of the Cradle. He could be a prisoner in his own mind, shepherded about by a clever Ka-Dun. But who? Or why? He would have answers.

Risen, aid me, Irakesh commanded. *Are my senses being fooled?*

There was no answer. That cinched it. His mind had been invaded. He could trust nothing. Not his senses, nor even his thoughts. He understood in that moment that he was being assaulted, but if he let it the Ka-Dun could redirect his attention and he'd once again be lost in the memory the bastard had conjured. He must act both swiftly and decisively.

"Show yourself, Ka-Dun. I am not your plaything and I will not be taken in by your games," he roared, drawing his na-kopesh. Had that been at his side a moment ago? It hadn't. The memory the Ka-Dun had chosen had occurred before his mother had awarded him the weapon.

"How does it feel to be the prey for once, Irakesh?" a voice said from behind him. He spun to face the intruder. Recognition brought a flood of memory. Blair. He'd been about to kill the Ka-Dun just before the clever fool had broken into his mind to prevent his own death.

"You're more resourceful than I ever would have imagined. I have never faced a more worthy opponent and I will not underestimate you again," Irakesh said, sheathing his weapon. It would do him no good here. "You've managed to stave off your own death, but don't think you've won. I have training, Ka-Dun. I can push you from my mind."

"Maybe, but I've already rifled through your memories," Blair said, lopsided grin spreading across that smug face. "I can see where you're going. I even know how you intend to get there. That and so many other things. You think you're so superior, but your world is gone. Mine is still here and I know it better than you ever will."

"Perhaps, but your friend Trevor knows it just as well," Irakesh gave back. He smiled when pain entered Blair's gaze. "Yes, you begin to understand. Your friend is my thrall now. He does my bidding. Even while we wrestle within my mind he is killing your friend Steve. He will kill Jordan and Bridget as well before he is finished. You may have learned a few scraps of memory, but they will avail you *nothing*."

"We'll see about that," Blair said, coy smile emerging. He stepped towards Irakesh. "You took something that didn't belong to you and I intend to get it back. That key belongs to the Mother. I'm not going to allow you to set up your own little empire. Seeing your memories, I'm not sure *your* mother will look too kindly on it either. Sounds like you might be doomed no matter what you do."

Rage thundered through Irakesh, largely because Blair was right. If Irakesh pulled this off, he'd be a rival and his mother would treat him as such. If he failed, she would do nothing to help him. At best she'd be indifferent, at worst an implacable enemy. For the first time since waking he doubted his choices.

"You've overstayed your welcome, Ka-Dun. Let me show you what a disciplined mind can do," he growled, closing his eyes. He envisioned his mother's garden, where he'd spent countless hours as a child. Then he envisioned the wall around it, impossibly tall to his young eyes. He focused everything on that wall, leveraging the years of training as he strengthened his defenses.

This was the first step, pushing Blair out of his innermost thoughts. It seemed to have worked, unless the Ka-Dun was far more powerful than he'd assumed. Now he must awaken to his current surroundings. When he did so time would be critical. He'd wasted too much time here. It was time to flee, time to take the others and go. He'd send a whisperer to each of them, then they'd be on their way.

It would mean creating an illusion far more complex, far larger than any he'd ever done. Yet he must. He would. Irakesh opened his eyes, suddenly back in the hangar bay. He melted into the shadows even as Blair gave a half-hearted swipe in his direction.

42

FEAR & LOATHING IN PANAMA

Jordan clawed his way back to consciousness, staggering to his feet as he took in his surroundings. He'd never had a migraine, but he imagined the blinding agony must be something like this. He raised a hand to his temple, unsure how it might help but desperately needing the pain to stop. A bright corona surrounded his vision. He staggered to his feet, peering groggily around.

The dead cluttered the dimly lit room. It reeked of gunpowder, blood, and the sickly rot of a thousand zombies left to ferment in this hangar. Underlying it all was the sharp smell of gasoline and the plasticky smell he'd always associated with large office buildings. Nothing moved near him, either through luck or the intervention of the others. Most of the zombies were down, though clusters still prowled the spaces between the planes in search of food. They hadn't noticed him as of yet. The ones nearest him were shuffling towards a very loud fight taking place forty or fifty yards away.

Two massive werewolves brawled, growling and snapping as they circled each other. He recognized Liz quickly enough, but the blond werewolf she grappled with was new. It reminded him of Cyntia, but she was larger than Liz, whereas Cyntia had been noticeably smaller.

So who was it, how had she gotten here, and why the hell was she fighting *against* them?

He compartmentalized the question. Priorities must be dealt with. He'd been incapacitated for an indeterminate amount of time. Someone had used the shadows to perform a close-range execution-style headshot. That meant either a female werewolf or a deathless. He seriously doubted Irakesh would stoop to using a gun, but that was probably more likely than yon female werewolf having used a gun instead of her perfectly lethal claws. A third possibility existed. There might be another deathless or another werewolf. He just didn't have enough data to know.

Jordan scanned the ground around him, eventually locating his weapon. He picked the rifle up, checking the scope and dropping the slide back to ensure a round was chambered. He dropped to one knee, sighting down the scope at the werewolves. Neither seemed aware of him as he tried to align the crosshairs over the blond female.

It was incredibly difficult with them rolling around. The blonde seized Liz, slamming her face into the concrete in a spray of blood and broken teeth. He used the split second to align the crosshairs with the blonde's face, then squeezed the trigger. The rifle bucked, kicking against his shoulder with incredible force as a deafening boom tore through the hangar. A gout of flame left the muzzle, hurling the bullet towards his intended target.

It never hit. A figure blurred into view about midway between him and his target, a familiar man with red—almost orange—hair and a sea of freckles. As ginger as they came. His eyes were horrible pools of green and his teeth razored fangs, every bit a deathless. He ripped a hunk of metal from the wing of a neighboring aircraft, somehow managing to interpose it between the bullet and the blond werewolf. It impacted with a hollow ringing like some giant gong, knocking Trevor back a step.

"I haven't enjoyed anything since I was turned," Trevor said, casually tossing the improvised shield to the concrete with a clatter. He took several unhurried steps towards Jordan, hand falling to a holstered weapon at his side. Jordan wasn't sure what caliber it was, but he'd guess .45. A heavy round used for taking a man off his feet, perfect for a deathless as it could slow prey. "Not until now, anyway. I'm glad you didn't die when I shot you in the head. I want you to see my face when I kill you. To know my name. You blew up my fucking house in San Diego; do you remember that? You tried to kill my sister. It's time for some payback."

His grin was unnerving, but Jordan refused to be cowed. He considered what he knew about his opponent. Trevor Gregg, Liz's brother and the man who'd accurately predicated the solar event that had forever changed the world. The man who'd held open the jaws of Mohn's ambush back in San Diego, then led his friends all the way to the Ark where they'd stopped his team and woken the Mother. In a way Trevor was his antithesis, more so now that he was deathless.

"When I came after you before, I was doing the wrong thing for the right reasons," Jordan said, tossing his rifle to the concrete as he unlimbered his claws. "Now I'm doing the right thing for the right reasons. You've become a goddamn monster, Trevor, and I'm going to put you down like one."

"You're going to try," Trevor hissed, eyes flaring even as he faded from sight. Damn but Jordan hated the whole shadow walking thing everyone but him seemed capable of doing. It put him on the defensive, allowing Trevor to make the first move. To strike on his terms. That almost guaranteed he'd lose. So what could he do about it? Jordan blurred, zipping across the concrete and weaving between the few straggling zombies still on their feet. He rolled under an aircraft, coming up in a crouch on the far side. Nothing he'd just done would shake Trevor, but keeping on the move would make it harder for his opponent until he could come up with a way to even the odds.

In the distance Liz continued her fight with the blond female, apparently getting the worst of the exchange. One of her eyes was swollen shut and she was missing teeth on her right side. Her chest heaved from exertion, each swing coming a bit slower than the one before. He wasn't going to find help in that quarter. Hell, she was the one who needed help.

He felt rather than saw a shape materialize behind him. Jordan rolled to his right, a sharp crack sounding as a bullet hummed through the space he'd just occupied. It punched into the concrete, sending up a spray of fragments that drew a line of pain down his cheek. That wasn't a .45. It was too deep, too powerful. What the hell kind of rounds was he using? No wonder he'd gone down so hard when Trevor had first shot him.

Trevor was gone again, melting into the shadows with that awful grin plastered on a too-white face. Jordan moved again, this time rolling to the left and coming up in a crouch. He sprinted low across the hangar floor towards a Cessna on the far side. This wasn't going at all well and he wasn't sure how to turn it around. Normally his response in a tactical cluster fuck like this would be to flee. If only that were an option.

Jordan skidded to a halt next to the Cessna, spinning so his back faced it. Trevor would have to come at him from the front, but would that knowledge help? He might be able to dodge again, but sooner or later he'd be too slow and Trevor would pick him off. He needed some way to even the odds, and he needed to do it quickly. He scanned the hangar, hoping to find something of use.

Zombies shuffled around most of the planes, but their numbers had been thinned by the beleaguered werewolves. Corpses littered the hangar, some in piles. There was even a massive zombie corpse, perhaps fifteen feet tall. It was sprawled near a far Boeing cargo plane, still clutching a severed leg with auburn fur.

None of it helped. None of it provided an advantage against Trevor. He was outclassed and he knew it.

Jordan tensed as something materialized before him, but it was far too late. Trevor's fist blurred towards his chest, shattering his ribcage directly over the heart. Fragments of bone burst through his aorta, tearing his heart into useless slag. He tried to roll backwards, but Trevor had apparently anticipated such a move. The deathless leapt backwards, jerking the massive black pistol from its holster and gripping it with both hands as he sighted down the barrel. He squeezed the trigger three times in rapid succession, each belching a round into Jordan's already damaged chest.

Jordan collapsed in a heap, strength deserting him as he struggled to rise. This was it. Trevor had proven the stronger combatant, using his deathless powers with expert skill. Perhaps if Jordan had embraced his with the same zeal he might have had a chance, but instead he'd relied on his training and his weapons. It had been a mistake. A fatal one. He stared defiantly up at his opponent as he waited for death.

Something black and shiny swooped into view, landing on Trevor's shoulder. It was a raven. A big one. The bird croaked something that might have been words into Trevor's ear. Trevor turned a hateful gaze on Jordan as he holstered his weapon. "I'm going to let you live with this, Jordan. The knowledge that all your training and fancy military hardware didn't mean shit in the end. That you lost to a redneck scientist who never spent a day in the military. Have fun with your new playmates."

Just like that he was gone, swallowed by the shadows like some horrible nightmare. Why hadn't Trevor finished him off? It made no sense. Unless he knew something Jordan didn't. New playmates? He struggled into a sitting position, planting his back against the Boeing's large wheel. He was growing lightheaded, which made sense if his heart was no longer pumping blood.

He could feel it knitting together inside his chest, excruciating as bits of bone were ejected from his tissue. They burst from his skin, coated in thick, sticky blood. Then his heart began to beat again. The lightheadedness faded and he was able to focus on his surroundings. He struggled to his feet, turning towards Liz and her strange blond opponent. Or rather where her strange opponent had been.

Liz was alone, kneeling on the ground with shoulders slumped. She was a mass of blood and both eyes were closed, though even from this distance he could hear her shallow heartbeat. She'd clearly lost her fight, yet her opponent had vanished just as Trevor had. They'd been beaten, yet left to live. Why?

Jordan used some of his dwindling energy to blur to Liz, wrapping an arm under her shoulder. He hauled her to her feet, conscious of the dozen or so zombies closing on them. Where were Blair, Steve, and Bridget?

He was about to carry Liz to a corner when something roared by above the hangar. He knew the sound intimately. It was the thundering engines belonging to a B114 cargo plane, used exclusively by Mohn to deliver troops into combat zones. Several thumps sounded above as the roar faded.

His augmented hearing picked up the squeal of rubber on pavement as the plane touched down outside. They were landing, but had probably dropped two squads on the roof to begin securing the hangar. Reinforcements would follow quickly, and they were in no shape to fight back.

"What's going on?" Liz croaked, raising her one good eye to look at him. He'd never seen her so exhausted, so battered.

"We're in a whole lot of trouble. Irakesh just pulled back," Jordan explained, helping Liz towards the far wall.

"Why? We're losing," she slurred, not healing nearly as quickly as he'd have expected.

"Mohn is here," he replied grimly.

43

DESPERATE GAMBLE

B lair raised a hand to his forehead, squinting beneath the weight of the pain. The throbbing left in the wake of his forcible ejection from Irakesh's mind staggered him, pitching him into the side of a plane's huge rubber wheel. He blinked away tears, scanning the wreckage littering the hangar. Most of the zombies were down, minus the odd straggler. There was no sign of Bridget, though he could see Steve's glittering eyes from where he crouched in the far corner of the room. Unmolested. Had he participated in the battle, or stood by to protect himself?

It didn't matter. There was still a battle to fight. Blair turned his attention back to the hangar, scanning for survivors. His breath caught, eyes tearing when he finally located Liz. Her broken body sagged into Jordan's smaller form, threatening to collapse without his assistance. At least she was alive. Powerful relief flooded him, his body uncoiling as the tension ebbed.

Cyntia had retreated for some reason. So had Trevor apparently. He knew Irakesh was gone. What were they planning? He turned his attention to the fat cargo plane. It hadn't moved, though he could still hear the audible clicking as it fueled. They must be inside. If he was going to launch an attack he needed help. Who was still standing on their side?

Jordan's hulking form limped as he helped Liz towards the far wall. He wasn't in much better shape than she was. Blair heard a grunt of pain from across the hangar, a rare show of emotion from the normally stoic ex-Mohn officer.

Irakesh *was* going to flee; he was sure of it. But to where? Blair had no idea how the deathless knew what a nuke was, much less what the bastard had planned for it. Cities had become deathtraps full of potential new soldiers he could use. Why blow one up? If that wasn't the purpose, then what was? Maybe he could use it on the Mother, though how he intended to deliver the weapon was a mystery. Pilot the plane all the way back? No, that wasn't his style. Irakesh wouldn't risk the Mother's wrath. He knew he was outmatched, or why flee in the first place?

Blair lurched forward, catching himself against the cool metal of a wing. He barely saw the aircraft, his attention focused on Jordan and Liz. The former Mohn soldier had picked Liz up, but seemed unsure where to move her. He glanced around the hangar, finally catching sight of Blair. Jordan started in his direction, then abruptly froze. His gaze went skyward.

An engine screamed in the distance. A plane engine, one approaching very rapidly. It was the first aircraft Blair had heard since the world had ended. Who was it? Who had both the technology and knowledge to find this hangar, of all places in the world? Boots thumped on the roof above. There was only one group it could be, one thorn always in their side. Did Mohn know they were inside, or were they here for their nuke?

The far side of the hangar erupted inward, launching zombies into the air like toys. Two smaller explosions sounded above as bits of metal rained down. Soldiers rappelled through the holes, even as a massive form appeared in the gaping rent now dominating the hangar's south wall. It lumbered forward with a metallic pumping of pistons, a chrome behemoth even taller than the giant zombie Liz had slain.

Familiar suits of power armor flooded in behind it, fanning out around the mech like foxes around a wolf. Lines of red shone from above, the laser sights attached to rifles. They were surrounded and in no shape to fight. Blast it. They were too beat up to take on both sides.

"Blair, we have to go," Bridget hissed from the shadows behind him. "We can't fight them."

She was right and he knew it. He gave Jordan and Liz an agonizing glance. They stood in the pool of light cast by one of the holes in the ceiling. The mech was already making for them as a dozen barrels swung in their direction.

"She's right," Steve whispered, appearing in a crouch next to Bridget. "We have to get out of here, Blair. We can't help them, only die ourselves. If we're lucky they'll take care of Irakesh, but if we want to live we move. Now."

"Fine," Blair growled, anger surging through him. There weren't any other options, but he hated having to run. Again. "We'll fall back through that rent. Bridget, stick to the shadows and meet us outside."

He blurred without waiting for an answer, following the shadowed wall of the hangar until he reached the hole left by the massive machine Mohn had brought. Two suits of power armor guarded it, but the hole was a good twelve feet high. He leapt, twisting in midair even as the pair spun to face him.

Steve barreled into the back of the suit on the right, seizing the helmet in both hands and twisting with incredible strength. The armor's arms shot up to stop him, but too late. Steve's furred muscles tensed, and the armored helmet twisted. The man's neck and skull were crushed, sending the armor toppling to the ground.

Bridget materialized in midair above the second armored suit, landing heavily on its back and driving it into the pavement with incredible force. She brought both fists down onto its shoulders, crushing the armor like tinfoil. It was truly terrifying to witness, reminding him of just how much stronger females were. At least she was on his side.

Something whined from behind him and to the right. Blair spun to see the aircraft Mohn had no doubt arrived in. It was twin to the cargo plane Irakesh planned to steal, save that it bore a pair of massive mini guns under each wing. Those guns had begun to spin, and were aimed in his direction.

Blair blurred, rolling away as rounds streaked around him. Some bit into the pavement, others into the wall of the hangar. Only his speed saved him, as he flipped backwards away from the deadly weapons. The plane began to track his movements, but too slowly to keep up.

"Circle the building," he roared, already sprinting around the right of the domed building. Bridget and Steve followed, and within moments their retreat was mercifully obscured by the building. He dropped into a crouch, chest heaving as he caught his breath. Steve blurred into place next to him.

"What now?" he asked, glancing at Bridget as she loped to a stop near them.

"We—" Blair began, trailing off at the sight before him. "It can't be."

A second plane taxied onto the runway, the same one he knew to still be inside the hangar. It moved through the still-closed doors, which rippled around it as if they were water. The plane picked up speed, already moving away from them. He could see Trevor's form in the cockpit, his shock of orange hair unmistakable.

"It can and is," Steve answered, rising to his feet and taking a step towards the plane. "You said that deathless could manipulate light, that they used illusions. Irakesh fooled us all."

"That means Mohn isn't aware they're leaving," Bridget said, resting a furry hand on Blair's shoulder. "We're the only ones who can stop them, and we have to do it now."

"What about Liz?" Blair asked, aware of the quaver in his voice. The high whine of jet engines and the stench of gasoline hung thick around him. He knew the answer, but someone else had to give it voice.

"There isn't any choice, Blair," Bridget said, gathering him into a furry hug. He was a child enveloped by a parent. "We have to let her go. Maybe they won't kill her. Maybe..."

"If we're going to do something, we do it now or not at all," Steve interrupted, grabbing Blair's shoulder and yanking him from Bridget's embrace. "You said you came here to stop Irakesh. You know what's at stake. Would Liz want you to give that monster a nuclear weapon? Control of the Ark you said lies somewhere north? Because if you go back for her, you're handing him victory. Can you live with that?"

Blair met Steve's gaze, the same dispassionate gaze he'd known for almost a decade nested in that wolfish visage. The same visage he wore. He was a warrior now, a champion. Steve was right. If he didn't stop Irakesh, no one would.

"Bridget, see if you can catch the rear of the plane. Steve and I will blur to the front and punch through the cockpit. If we shatter that glass, they won't be able to take off," he said, voice firming even as he started towards the plane.

It had reached the main runway and was accelerating. Act. Don't think. He blurred forward without waiting for an answer, streaking across the tarmac.

His fur whipped around him as he closed the gap to the cargo plane, or bomber or whatever it was. The plane accelerated, the space between it and the end of the runway quickly shrinking. How long until it was airborne and he could no longer reach it? He risked a glance behind him. Bridget loped along the runway, barely matching the plane's pace. There was no way she'd catch it in time. Steve was closer, a midnight streak several meters behind Blair.

He turned back to the plane, redoubling his speed. Even blurring, it was a near thing. The plane's front wheel had already left the ground when he leapt, grabbing the back of the right wing. The roar of the engine was both powerful and deafening, its pull threatening to yank him inside. He dug his claws into the clean chrome wing, vaulting atop it. Blair slipped, tumbling backwards towards the inexorable pull of the engine.

Then Steve was there, seizing his shoulder and heaving him

towards the main body of the plane. Blair seized the edge of the wing, steadying himself as the plane left the ground and took the air. Now what? Steve was yelling something, but it was lost in the roar of the engines. He had to bring the plane down, even if it cost his life.

The plane abruptly tilted, the wing dropping suddenly. Blair's grip held, but he saw Steve tumble off. His midnight form tumbled towards the trees below, dropping nearly a hundred feet into the unbroken canopy. Fuck. Hopefully Steve had survived, but whether he did or not Blair had a job to do.

He stared at the cockpit, a few dozen feet ahead. How could he reach it?

Blur. If you hurl yourself with all your strength you can reach it, Ka-Dun.

The beast was right. It was his only chance. Blair gathered his legs, focusing his energy. Then he blurred, pouring more into the power than he ever had before. He leapt, somehow moving faster than the plane. His body hurled through the air, as close to true flight as he'd ever know. His claws caught the lip of the cockpit, the point where glass and metal met. He found purchase, somehow clinging to the metal despite the insistent tugging of the wind.

He could see into the cockpit, see Trevor just two feet away. His friend looked the same, until he turned and met Blair's gaze. Trevor's eyes were the same putrid green as Irakesh's. His mouth opened in shock, exposing jagged rows of fangs used to rend flesh. Blair couldn't bring the plane down, but Trevor could.

Blair plunged into Trevor's mind, forcing his way past the death-less's defenses.

44

MOUNTAIN CAMP

"Where are we?" Blair asked, turning in a slow circle. Thick flakes of snow obscured the looming pines surrounding the spacious cabin. He and Trevor stood on the back deck, fenced on two sides with a path leading up the hillside behind them.

Trevor turned to face him, but didn't immediately answer. His eyes were normal, the same hazel he'd gotten to know during their mad flight from San Diego back to the Ark in Peru. His teeth were mercifully normal. There was nothing to reflect the monster he'd become. Even his coat was a battered mess, warm and worn from years of faithful service. This was Trevor, not the monster he'd just seen. Or so it appeared, at least. Irakesh had already proven how deathless could alter appearances.

"Mountain Camp," Trevor said, crunching through thick snow to the railing near a large silver grill. He picked up the tongs dangling from the side, cocking his head to the side as he studied them. "It's the nickname one of Liz's friends gave the place. She grew up rich down in Monterey and this place seemed so rustic to her. To us it was just home. We grew up here, in Tuolumne. You ever been to Yosemite?"

Blair glanced down at himself. He wore the same dark brown coat he'd worn to class every night, complete with the black stain on the right sleeve from his mishap with some soy sauce. It was glaringly normal, just like everything else around them.

"Yeah, I've been. I only live a few hours away, a little north of San Francisco. I've never heard of Tuolumne though," he replied, taking a cautious step towards the railing near the grill. Blair swept off an armful of snow, settling against the perch he'd created.

"We're about an hour north of Yosemite. Up in the foothills. Gold country once upon a time," Trevor explained. He replaced the tongs, turning to study the house. They stood outside an office, a dusty old computer on a makeshift table that had been converted to a desk. A buffalo hide hung against one wall. The others held a variety of notes and pictures that must have accumulated over years. A sliding glass door led onto the deck where they stood. "It's so odd seeing it empty. My mom and dad still live up here. It's never this quiet. They've always had dogs, sometimes a cat or two. That's missing, like the world is empty somehow. Maybe this is the best you can conjure up with whatever it is you're doing to me. I'm curious to see just how detailed this fantasy is."

Trevor crossed the deck to the sliding glass door, tugging it open and stepping inside. He removed his boots, gesturing for Blair to follow. Then he turned and exited through a door on the far side of the office, entering a wide linoleum hallway. It was flanked by a bathroom on one side and a faded brown door on the other. Trevor stopped in front of it, clearly waiting. Blair hesitated only a moment before entering the office. He slid the door closed behind him, crossing the worn carpet and joining Trevor in the hallway. A light from the far end illuminated Trevor's face. It looked like it came from a kitchen.

"This is Liz's room. I wonder, do you consciously know what it looks like? Or would you have to enter it to have my mind reveal the memory to you?" Trevor asked, resting a hand on the door knob. Something burned in Blair's throat, a palpable reaction to the vivid reminder of the friend he'd lost.

"Trevor, we need to talk," Blair said, crossing his arms to ward off the cold. He could see his breath now. Had that happened outside as well?

"About what I've become," Trevor said, giving a quick nod. He opened the door and stepped into the bedroom. "About why I'm with Irakesh. Why I'm working with your enemy and may have to kill you."

Blair followed him in, taking a moment to study the place where Liz had grown up. A queen-sized bed under a plain white comforter dominated the corner, with a plain oak dresser that had been recently varnished standing next to it. A small lamp and a dog-eared copy of a book entitled *Ishmael* sat on the table. He glanced up, noting an array of florescent stars dotting the ceiling. Each sticker was placed into familiar constellations. Orion's belt. The big dipper. Others he didn't know. The walls were covered in huge maps, mostly of South America and Australia. There were pins in Costa Rica, Belize, Peru, and a few other countries.

"She'd kill you if she knew you were in here," Trevor said, delivering one of those boyish grins that they'd shared just before the world had gone to shit. "I think she really likes you, which is odd. She has a thing for tall dark men from exotic places. Did you know that's why she was in Peru in the first place? She was running from the last guy, Ernesto. She does that you know. Runs, sometimes."

"Trevor, we don't have long," Blair said, sitting lightly on the edge of the bed. It creaked under his weight. He glanced around the room again, crinkling his nose at the musty smell. That door must not be opened very often. "I know it has to be hard to face everything that's happened, the horrors you must have endured. But I need you to. I need you to tell me what Irakesh is planning."

"That's not why you invaded my mind," Trevor said, crossing his arms and plopping into an old chair in the corner. A hint of neon green entered his gaze. "You want me to crash the plane, to stop Irakesh."

"How did you know?" Blair asked, conscious of the surprise he'd just betrayed. Could deathless read minds, too?

"It's all over your face. Besides, that's what I'd do in your place," Trevor explained, giving a slight shrug. He ran his fingers through his goatee, the gesture an instinctual habit Blair remembered well. "I would if I could, Blair. I'd do it in a second, kill us all to stop Irakesh. I don't know exactly what he's planning, but I can tell you it isn't good. He's ruthless and driven, the worst combination. He has powers I can't even begin to comprehend and trust me when I say I don't want to live in a world he has control over. I'm not even sure he's the biggest risk. You remember Cyntia? She's been corrupted. Irakesh has had her feed on everything. Humans. Zombies. Even another werewolf. The virus has mutated and it's made her powerful, but unstable. She hates Liz, you know. She'll kill her if she gets the chance."

"If you know all that why are you working with Irakesh? Trevor, this isn't you. I know you've changed. Hell, I know that better than anyone," Blair said, leaning forward. He studied his friend intently, searching for signs of the man he used to be. "The virus changed me in ways I still don't understand. You must have undergone something similar, but whatever happened you can fight it. The fact that we're talking is proof that you're still you."

"You don't understand the problem," Trevor said, removing his glasses and cleaning them with his shirt. He avoided looking at Blair. "The deathless aren't like werewolves. Werewolves are independent, but deathless can impose their will on those weaker than them. That's how Irakesh can control a horde of zombies. It's how he's forcing me to help him. He can use me like a puppet and there isn't a damn thing I can do about it. Trust me Blair, I've tried to resist. Do you think I want to help him steal a nuke? Help him kill you and Liz? I've tried to fight, but there's this thing inside of me. It's like the beast you described, but Irakesh calls it a Risen."

"If it's like the beast, then you can fight it," Blair suggested. Cautiously. He stood up, crossing to the window and staring outside. Snow continued to fall, blanketing a steep driveway that disappeared into the trees down the hill. "It took both Liz and me a while to get control. You must be able to do the same thing. Fight it, Trevor. The world could be riding on your shoulders right now. You're the only one who can stop Irakesh."

"Then the world is doomed," Trevor said. Blair turned to face him, jaw dropping at the sudden transformation.

Trevor's eyes were the bright green of toxic waste, twin to Irakesh's. The jagged teeth were back. He was very much the deathless now, though his voice was the same. Still, there was a sadness to his gaze, a hint of the man who had once existed. Then he lunged, blurring towards Blair with a speed nearly as great as his own. Blair toppled backwards onto the bed, rolling away from Trevor even as claws raked the comforter in the spot he'd just occupied.

Blair released his friend's mind, suddenly landing back in his own. The wind howled around him, and his arms ached from the effort of maintaining his grip on the edge of the cockpit. Trevor stared out at him, a pilot's headset covering his ears. His gaze bore the same sadness as he raised a hand. Then sickly green light burst from his palm, washing over Blair in the familiar agony he'd felt when Irakesh had paralyzed him back in the Ark.

The wind ripped him away from the cockpit, sending him tumbling through the air towards the jungle's thick canopy hundreds of feet below.

45

PRESENT FOR THE MOTHER

Yukon trotted down the dock, largely ignored by the Mother's new pack. They moved a variety of strange-smelling boxes and loud guns onto the very large boat where the Mother waited. Yukon knew he should be at her side, but she'd been preparing the boat for days and it was dreadfully boring just standing there.

He hadn't gone far, of course. The memory of the strange not-deads was still large and frightening. They'd tried to eat him, would have eaten him if the Mother hadn't saved him. She protected him, just as he protected her in his own small way. She kept him alive and he went places that she could not, watched her growing pack to make sure none of them were dangerous. He guarded the door while she used the poop-stealing water chair, always watching. You could never be sure. Even if they smelled right, humans could sometimes surprise you in a nasty way.

Yukon ducked between a pair of men hefting a wide wooden crate that looked heavy. He couldn't smell any food, but he recognized the odd tangy scent of cans. Tasty things came in cans. He hurried past them, up a long walkway that led to the railing circling the huge boat.

A cargo ship, Rodrigo had called it. He was the Mother's new beta, a pleasant enough man who liked to scratch behind Yukon's ears as though he were some mangy cat. Yukon tolerated it, of course, because he knew it was meant as a friendly gesture.

"Ugg, wet dog," one of the men said, crinkling his nose as Yukon slipped past. Yukon ignored him, though he knew the comment was meant as an insult. Was it his fault the rain continued to fall for the third straight day? Besides, he didn't smell nearly so bad as that man had. He reeked of beer and sweat, with something less pleasant lurking underneath. Yukon didn't even want to know what the last part was.

He trotted up to the railing, pausing for a thorough shake to remove most of the rain, once he was under the shelter of the boat's lowest level. It was covered by the floor above, which was covered by the floor above that. It continued like that all the way to the top, which was a long, flat surface now covered in stacks of big metal crates. Yukon had enjoyed running between them for a while, but it had grown boring with no one to play with.

Yukon adjusted his grip on the purple dodo, an amusing little stuffed animal he'd found near the dock. The Mother was very tense and he hoped the present might make her smile, something he'd very rarely seen since she'd saved him. How long ago had that been? He didn't know. He wanted to understand the human concept of time, but it was lost on him. It was day, or it was night. What did yesterday matter? It was gone and it wouldn't come back. Tomorrow would get here soon enough. Why worry about it?

He padded around the edge of the lowest level until he came to the steep metal stairs leading to the next level. They'd scared him at first. They had holes in them, not quite large enough for a paw to go through but enough that he still felt as though he might. Yukon ran up the stairs, almost tripping as he finally made it to the top. His heart was beating faster, but he moved on quickly and did not look back at the stairs. At least going up was easier than going down.

He repeated the process several more times, finally making it to the level just below the top. It was the last with any shelter and some of the rain pelted him over the railing. It wasn't bad though, just a little cold. He didn't understand why humans were so offended by the idea of getting wet. Rain fell, you got wet. It was natural and you dried off if you lay down by a fire or with the rest of your pack.

Yukon wandered through the narrow door, stepping over the strange lip and onto the cold metal sheet inside. Was the lip meant to keep water out? Only humans would bother. Of course, only humans were smart enough to build a giant house that floated on water. They were very handy in their own way and they took care of dogs, so he probably shouldn't be so critical.

Critical. Such a strange word for a dog. The Mother had warned him that he would begin to change if he spent time near her. Awakening, she called it. He wasn't sure exactly what that entailed, but he thought it meant he was getting smarter. He was also a little faster and a little larger. That could be handy if he needed to protect his pack.

"Yukon," the Mother called warmly from her place next to Rodrigo. They stood in front of a strange wall full of dials and controls, like a car only more complicated. Above the wall sat a wide window, which showed the harbor in front of the boat. Yukon couldn't see much of it unless he got up on his hind legs. The Mother had called it undignified, so he avoided doing that in her presence.

The Mother patted her thigh, summoning him closer. It was a subtle acknowledgment, but enough to fill him with joy. She was his world and he would do everything in his power to keep her happy and safe. Yukon trotted forward, pushing the purple dodo at the Mother's tiny hand once he reached her. She glanced down, surprise evident on her radiant face. Then her eyes twinkled and she delivered a rare smile. It was brilliant. Like the sun.

"Thank you, Yukon," she said, resting a delicate hand on his head. She never pet him like most humans. They saw him as a pet, a lesser animal to be praised like one of their pups. Not the Mother. She treated him with respect, as an equal. "You remind me of the gentleness that this world still possesses. Once again, you have humbled me."

You don't smile enough. I wanted you to smile. He thought at her. Yukon was aware of a very confused Rodrigo standing a few feet from the Mother. He watched her uncomfortably, the way Yukon had once eyed the vacuum cleaner.

"You're right. I have been consumed by all that has gone wrong, but I must not lose sight of the reason I fight. To preserve the gentle parts of the world," the Mother said, placing the dodo on top of the console. That was the word for the strange wall with all the dials.

The Mother gave him another smile, then turned back to Rodrigo. If another human had done that he'd have known he was dismissed, but Yukon could feel the Mother's mind. Gratitude swept over him even as she spoke with Rodrigo.

"How soon can we depart?" she asked, absently stroking the tuft of crazy fur on top of the dodo's head.

"The men will be done loading supplies within the hour," Rodrigo answered, giving a slight bow of his head. The man smelled of oil and wariness. "Alfonso used to run construction sites. Big hotels and stuff. He knows about the equipment we'll need to break up the rock once we reach the island. He says we can use jackhammers and we've loaded up a small truck to carry loads back to the ship."

"Well done, Rodrigo. Your efforts don't go unnoticed," she said, crossing her arms over the strange white garments she always wore. They weren't like other people's. They shimmered and moved like living things. "Have you given any more thought to my offer?"

"I have, but Mother, I am afraid," he said, scrubbing his fingers through the wispy beard he'd let grow on their way here. Yukon approved. It wasn't quite fur, but it was the closest humans could get. "You say that I probably will not rise, but if I do I'll be a great champion. I want to help you, but I don't want to die."

"I understand. It is a difficult sacrifice to make, one very few are willing to attempt," she said, reaching up to place a hand on Rodrigo's shoulder. Yukon felt a little stab of jealousy. "There is no shame in serving as you are. I value your counsel. Please, make the crew ready. I will await your return."

Rodrigo gave a grateful nod, all but scurrying from the room.

After his departure the Mother turned to the console, staring out the window at the open ocean. Yukon couldn't see much, save the steel-grey sky blanketing the horizon. What was she staring at? He wanted to put his paws up on the console, but knew she'd disapprove. So he lay down at her feet and waited.

46

AWAKEN, KA-KEN

*A*waken, *Ka-Ken. You are in danger.*

Liz came to with a gasp, blinking away the grogginess. She sat up, or tried to, anyway. The movement was halted as she reached the edge of the motion allowed by the restraining straps. They were black and metallic, but woven somehow. Bands looped around her chest, arms, and legs, neatly pinning every limb against the metal bench. It was cold even through her clothes.

She gave up struggling, choosing to study the inside of her cell rather than listen to the bubbling rage that accompanied the voice. It was a small room, perhaps six by eight. The narrow bench was molded from the same chrome as the rest of the room. It didn't even have a cushion. Not exactly the Plaza back in Acapulco.

The wall opposite her was clear like plexiglass, revealing a hallway that stretched in either direction and an identical cell across from her. The thin lighting came from twin tracks set into the hallway ceiling. The same type she was used to in places like airplanes that were trying to conserve power.

Wait a minute. What was the deep thrumming? It reverberated through the walls, through her entire body. Powerful and deep, like a jet engine. Oh god.

Had Irakesh captured her? Why would he have let her live instead of killing her immediately? Was he that much of a storybook villain, predictably stupid? Perhaps he'd captured the others too. She scooted up as far as the straps would allow, peering at the cell across from her. There was a dark shape on the bench in the other cell. Another prisoner. Liz tested the air, but there was nothing beyond her own scent. The room was completely sealed.

The figure leaned forward, resting tree-trunk arms on top of his knees. Jordan was bare chested, with a pair of camouflage pants and familiar black boots. The light glittered in his hazel eyes, unmoved by their current circumstances. He opened his mouth to speak, then shook his head with a half smile. He must have just realized what she had; if the rooms were sealed, no sound would travel between them.

Why wasn't Jordan bound? Liz glanced at the bench next to him, finding a familiar trio of straps piled there. They weren't frayed or broken. How had he gotten them off?

Males are notoriously difficult to imprison, Ka-Ken. They have many such tricks.

She latched on to the voice, hoping it could keep her afloat. She wasn't alone. Not truly.

Do you know where we are? she thought back.

Yes, Ka-Ken. We are in the slipsail that the soldiers brought. They were not allied with the deathless, but have no love for us either.

Not allied with Irakesh. A third party had intervened. At a Mohn facility. After the world had ended. Her eyes rose to meet Jordan's, a satisfied smile growing across that chiseled jaw as he nodded at her. It was the sort that a proud father gave a child who'd just done something impressive. Or figured something out. But how could he know, unless...

Can you hear me, Jordan? she thought at him, praying for an answer.

None came. Jordan's expression tightened and he began to pace back and forth behind the glass. Was he trying to reach her and failing? He'd shown neither the interest nor aptitude for the abilities

Blair had taken and run with. Maybe he wasn't strong enough to reach her.

To her surprise he stopped pacing and began nodding vigorously. He pointed to his head, then back at her.

If you can hear me hold up three fingers. She thought at him. Her back had begun to ache from the awkward position, so she settled back against the bench. She could still see Jordan. His hand shot up, three fingers extended.

This was going to be tricky. She'd never been very good at charades. Hmm. If she stuck to yes or no questions she could at least get some answers.

"Did Mohn capture us?" she asked, voice hoarse from disuse. She knew he couldn't hear her, but hearing a voice helped. Even her own.

Jordan nodded. So the beast had been right about that much, at least.

"Were any of the others captured?" she asked, shifting again. Her neck ached.

He shook his head, then his face grew uncertain. He gave an apologetic shrug. So maybe Mohn had more of them, maybe not. They could be in the neighboring cells. Or they could be dead.

The Ka-Dun lived upon our capture. He and the spiteful one ran. I believe the other Ka-Ken may have accompanied them.

Blair, Bridget, and Steve had escaped then. They could have been captured or killed after they'd fled, but she wouldn't accept that. She needed to know they were out there, still trying to stop Irakesh or maybe coming to rescue her. She quieted the voice telling her they weren't coming, that Blair would do his duty and stop Irakesh even if it meant sacrificing her.

Her face blazed. Jordan could hear her.

"How do I get out of my straps?" she asked, turning her gaze back to Jordan. She felt a tear slide free but ignored it. She had to be strong. There wasn't any other choice.

Jordan began pacing again, glancing at her occasionally. Clearly the answer was too complicated to be explained through mime. He paused, turning to face her. Jordan planted both hands against the glass, eyes boring into her. His face curled into a snarl, sweat beading his forehead.

Liz!

The voice crashed down around her like a rolling wave of thunder. Overpowering and more than a little frightening.

"Can you think more quietly?" she asked, wincing at the ringing in her head.

I'm sorry. His voice was still loud, but tolerable. *I told you I'm not good at this shaping crap. The beast showed me how to escape. I just looked at the latches and wanted them undone. I could feel the locks, feel the mechanism inside. Then they popped open. The beast calls it telekinesis. Probably won't work for you. Guess you'll have to rely on brute strength.*

"What do you think they're going to do to us? I mean, why are we alive?" Liz asked. Maybe Irakesh was the classic villain and prone to villainous mistakes, but Mohn certainly wasn't. Everything they did was with a cold, methodical purpose.

Study, Jordan thought back, finally retreating to his bench. *I don't think they had any forewarning about the zombies. They knew an enemy was coming somehow, but the Director assumed it was the werewolves. The sudden appearance of zombies threw everything they knew out the window. If it were me I'd bring us back and try to convert us into weapons. They can use us to make more werewolves, then use those werewolves as shock troops against the zombies.*

"So how do we escape? Do you have any allies we can turn to?" she asked, hoping he had a solution. She certainly didn't. Liz shrank a bit within the confines of the straps. She so badly wanted to break into a hysterical crying fit. Horror bloomed as she realized again that he could probably hear her thoughts. She resisted slamming her defenses into place. She needed him in her head right now.

I'm sorry, Liz. I don't have a lot of good news on that front. I delved into their commander's mind sort of accidentally and it turns out it's someone I know. A guy named Yuri. So do you, actually. You tore his leg off back at the Ark, though he doesn't seem too broken up about it, since Mohn has apparently given him a cybernetic replacement, Jordan explained, leaning forward into the light again. *They're probably taking us to the White*

Tower, the Mohn R&D facility in Syracuse, New York. We'll be brought to the Director and he'll decide what to do with us. Odds are good we'll be interrogated, tested, and then either disposed of or converted into weapons for Mohn. Escape is...unlikely."

Liz closed her eyes and stopped trying to hold back the tears.

47

EARLY BRITISH TRACKWAYS

B ridget pushed open the door to the bedroom with her back, balancing the napkin-covered tray in one hand and a dog-eared copy of *Early British Trackways* in the other. The book had survived the end of the world, survived the battle with Irakesh. Somehow that gave her hope that they might as well.

The room was dim and musty, but she resisted the impulse to draw back the hideous yellow curtains. Blair's face lay directly in their path, mouth open atop the fluffy pillow with its moth-eaten pillow case. Her new senses gave her more about his health than seeing his complexion would have, in any case.

She deposited the tray on the nightstand next to the bed, careful not to make any noise as she retreated to the high-backed rocking chair in the corner. She was becoming quite familiar with it, even a little fond of the rasping sound it made as she rocked. It was blessedly normal after everything they'd faced, a tiny reminder of their old life that she could hold onto while waiting for Blair to convalesce. How long would that take?

Not long, Ka-Ken, the voice rumbled, her truest friend in many ways. One that didn't judge her for past mistakes. *His reserves were depleted, but the moon has hung high these past nights and his strength returns quickly. He will wake this day, or perhaps the next.*

The days were long in Panama and it was still a good hour before dark. Did that mean she had at least that long before he woke? She rose from her chair, bending next to Blair. His hair was as wild as ever, dirty-blond curls plastered to his forehead. She brushed them aside, an electric thrill passing through her as she did so.

"How touching," a sardonic voice said. She spun to find Steve looming in the doorway. Why hadn't she detected his approach? He gave her a smug smile. "Thought you might have a bit of alone time before I returned? It's all right. If you need a few minutes, I'll excuse myself. I wouldn't want to interrupt you with your new man. Or is it old? I can't keep track."

"You're a real asshole, Steve," Bridget said, bile rising in her throat. Surprisingly, it wasn't guilt that caused it. It was anger. How could she ever have loved that man, betrayed Blair to be with him? "Yes, I care about Blair. I never stopped caring, unlike you. You were all too willing to shatter his heart and cast him aside."

"Whereas you felt bad for sleeping with his best friend behind his back?" Steve countered, crossing his arms over the black tank top he'd found somewhere. She'd found those muscled arms so attractive once. "That makes you so much more compassionate than me. I'm sure it's a real comfort to Blair that you feel bad about betraying him."

Bridget rose from the chair, ready to lash into him. Then Blair's breathing changed. It accelerated from long, deep breaths to shorter shallow ones. He was waking up. The last thing he needed was the two of them fighting about his most painful memory. "Why don't you go prepare the plane? You've been smug for two days about learning to fly. It's wonderful you can steal memories from corpses. Why don't you put it to use so we can follow Irakesh?"

"Sure, why don't I do that?" Steve said, with a predatory grin. He glanced at Blair, then back at her. "We wouldn't want to disturb our patient with such an uncomfortable topic, would we? I'll head back to the airport. If he's able to walk, bring him. If you two haven't shown up by morning, I'll come back and carry him."

Fear stabbed into her as she considered the subtext to his words. He knew she and Blair had become friends, and also that she wanted more than that. This was a warning, not because he wanted her back. Because he wanted to demonstrate power. Classic Steve. Don't fuck with him or he'd ruin any chance she'd ever have to mend the rift with Blair. He knew he had her, and he was right. A few choice reminders was all it would take to drive her and Blair apart again. He got off on having that kind of control over people.

"Thank you," she said, dropping her gaze and sliding it across the floor to Blair. "There's stew on the stove if you're hungry."

He stared at her for a long moment, either gloating or because he wanted to be sure she was properly cowed. Then he was gone, the house's ancient floor still as death. How did he do that? He'd intimidated her before; now he was positively terrifying. He'd learned so much delving into the Mother's memories as she slept.

"Bridget?" Blair asked, scooting into a sitting position and rubbing the sleep from his eyes. "How long have I been out? And where the hell are we?" He peered blearily around the room before his gaze settled back on her.

"We're in a small villa north of the airport. Someone's private little castle, though there's no sign of whoever owned the place. It's not far from where we found you," she explained, sinking back into the rocking chair. She clutched the book in her lap like a talisman. "How much do you remember?"

"I remember attacking the plane," Blair said, tossing the blankets back and crossing to the window. His boxers clung to well muscled thighs, a marked contrast to the bit of fat he'd had when they'd been together. She didn't necessarily find it any more attractive, but the new body suited him. He yanked open the curtains, wincing at the setting sun. "Trevor was piloting it. I entered his mind and tried to get him to crash it, but I failed. He used that green light to knock me off the plane. I don't think he wanted to, but Irakesh is controlling him."

"I gathered that much talking to Steve," she said, hugging the book to her chest. "He said that your friend almost killed Jordan and tried to kill him. I know you were close, but it looks like he's an enemy now, Blair."

"Maybe," Blair said, turning to the tray of food. He twitched aside the napkin, picking up the thick bowl and the bent silver spoon. He kept talking between shoveled bites. "Thank you for the stew. It's good. Anyway, I think Trevor is battling the thing in his head the same way we do. Eventually he'll master it, just as we did. I just hope he does it in time to stop Irakesh."

"You have a lot of faith in a guy who almost killed you," Bridget said, probably more harshly than she should have. This Trevor was Blair's friend and no doubt he was wrestling with the grief. "He dropped you almost a mile. Every bone was broken when we found you. I don't know how you're still alive. You've been out for three days."

"Three days?" Blair said, choking on the stew. He set the nearly empty bowl back on the tray. "Irakesh could be there by now. I can barely feel him."

"Maybe he is," Bridget said, rising from the chair. She put a comforting hand on Blair's shoulder. "We can't change how things happened; all we can do is decide what's next. Steve is at the airport preparing a plane for us. Apparently he found a zombie that used to be a pilot. Steve's learned how to pluck memories from their minds and believes he can get us to San Francisco."

"That's good news, I guess," Blair said, shrugging. "I don't know what we'll find when we get there, but we have to pursue him. Even if he's reached his destination, there's still a chance that we can find a way to get the key back. Did you see what happened to Liz and Jordan?"

"Mohn took them," Bridget said, releasing his shoulder and sitting on the corner of the rumpled bed. "I went looking for them while Steve searched for you in the jungle. I watched them take off and I could smell their trail leading into the plane."

"So Mohn has Liz and Irakesh got away. It's good that we're so far away from the Mother. She'd probably burn me to death with her laser eye beams," Blair said, eyes twinkling. He plopped down next to her, picking up the papaya she'd cut for him. "I know I should be depressed, but you know what? I'm not going to let this get to me. We're alive. Steve has found an amazing way to help us track Irakesh. I still have the Mother's access key and we've got you to deal with Cyntia. Three of them versus three of us."

"You've changed a lot, you know that?" Bridget said, giving him a playful punch on the arm. "The old Blair would be brooding in the corner and cursing our misfortune. I like the new you."

Blair gave a dazzling smile and then looked down uncomfortably as if he'd just remembered something. It wasn't much of a stretch to guess what. He cleared his throat, taking the book from her hands. "*Early British Trackways*? This is the first book written about ley-lines, isn't it? I remember you reading this back at Stanford. You wanted to go to England to measure electromagnetic sites."

"You called me a starry-eyed pagan," Bridget said, laughing. She tapped the cover of the book with her index finger. "Looks like I was right. The Arks store energy. Why couldn't old ruins and sites do the same thing? The Mother said that she believed the Ark was built there because it harnesses the power flowing through the area. What if that's where the greatest number of ley-lines intersect? Their whole society seems to have been built on the power of the sun and the moon. What if the ley-lines channel that energy?"

"Maybe you're right," Blair conceded, flipping through the book. He looked up at her, grinning again. "You look shocked. I know I'm the diehard scientist, but it's hard to argue with evidence. We're using the power of the moon. Irakesh uses the power of the sun. The Ark itself absorbs energy. What if ancient cultures were aping their forebears, building pyramids and stone monuments to capture magical energy? If that power had stopped flowing from the sun, some of it would still be present on earth. What if all those monuments were trying to capture the last little bit of that energy, fueling dying cultures across the globe?"

"That could account for a lot of ancient myth," Bridget said, smiling now as well. She missed this side of him and it touched her that he was willing to share it again. "It could also explain why there's no magic today, or at least there wasn't any. If it gathered at places like the Great Pyramids or Tikal, then the people there would have used it until it was gone. Once that happened, those civilizations would have lost their power source and fallen apart."

"Maybe that's why Irakesh so badly wants the Ark. If it's situated right in a middle of a bunch of them, that would give him a whole lot of power," Blair theorized, handing her the book.

His fingers brushed hers. Her heart was beating so quickly. She met his gaze for an instant, shocked to find a hunger smoldering there that she'd thought extinguished forever. Bridget leaned forward and kissed him for all she was worth. It was warm and salty and right.

Then he pushed her back onto the bed and there were no more words.

48

SKYHAMMER

T he Director marched down the corridor, flashing his badge at the in-wall scanner he'd ordered level seventeen be outfitted with. It shot a brief red line over the card, then the entire panel turned green and the twenty-four-inch titanium doors slid open. During that fraction of a second, the card had checked his DNA, his security clearance, and any dangerous pathogens he might be carrying. It was a miracle of modern medicine, one that would never again be found anywhere else. The factory that had manufactured them had gone dark, along with the rest of China.

"Your stated business, sir," the soldier standing beyond the door said, his ML-44 submachine gun leveled at the Director's gut. The weapon could belch a dozen rounds in under a second, each smart bullet homing in on a different vital organ. This too was a precaution he'd instated.

"I'm heading to cell F-4 on this block for a documented prisoner interaction," he explained, choosing his words deliberately. The guard raised a quizzical eye at the last one.

If he'd said interrogation that would have made sense, since that was how Mohn dealt with enemy combatants. But Mark had said interaction, which was voluntary on the part of the subject. It was more of a visit, and less an interrogation.

"Yes, sir," the guard said, snapping the weapon into a ready position and stepping out of his way. The beefy man's Kevlar covered vital organs, while molded pads did the same for knees and elbows. Protecting the joints was vital. They were an easily exploited weakness.

"The estimated duration of the interaction is eight to ten minutes," the Director said, pausing to stare directly into the guard's eyes. The man had missed a question. That sort of thing led to incomplete data and that too could be exploited. "We don't break protocol this far down, Corporal. Ever. I don't care if Leif Mohn himself comes down here. You *always* ask every question. Is that clear?"

"Yes, sir. It won't happen again," the man said. Was he actually blushing? Who'd assigned this fool?

Mark swept past the guard, passing the first two cells. Each sat behind two-inch plexiplate glass, a fun substance a subsidiary in Berlin had invented. It redirected kinetic and thermic energy throughout the entire pane, so long as it received a constant low-level charge. It made them almost unbreakable, something that was coming in very handy since the end of the world.

The Director paused at the next set of cells, both of which were occupied. He began with F-3, studying the woman who'd wreaked so much havoc in San Diego. She was an unassuming 5'8" with copper hair and a smattering of freckles on pale skin. Pretty. The type of girl who didn't usually get her nails done.

The straps on the bench bound her, further reinforcing the image of the helpless woman and the mercy of the evil corporation. Oh, how the media would have a field day with it, if they'd survived the apocalypse and then somehow pierced Mohn's security.

She was a problem, but one he couldn't deal with just yet. He turned to face F-4, the reason why he'd come all the way down here. The Director wasn't surprised to find that Jordan had somehow found a way out of his restraints. He'd been a formidable operative before he'd become what R&D were now calling Homo Lupinus.

The Director placed his hand against the plexiplate. It flared red, then an opening roughly the size of a dinner plate melted into the center. "Hello, Jordan. I'm glad to see you're still alive. We feared the worst when you didn't report in. For weeks."

"There were extenuating circumstances," Jordan said, flipping a leg up on the bench and leaning back against the wall. "You already know what I am. I wasn't sure I'd be welcomed back into the fold after what you did to Steve back in Peru. He's still alive, by the way. Used shaping to make us think he was dead."

"You're well aware that what happened with Dr. Galk was a necessary field test," Mark shot back, ignoring the bit about Steve being alive. He wouldn't be distracted. The Director leaned in, spearing Jordan with his gaze. "You could have contacted us at any time using your sat link. It was found in your pack when you were captured. You defected, Jordan, and that's exactly how the Old Man will see it. How do you suggest I explain that? If you can't be trusted the only use you serve is in the lab."

"Don't," Jordan said. Mark watched the man's gaze move over his left shoulder, where he knew the camera sat. "We're being recorded. Let this serve as an explanation. There's a lot to fill you in on. Take an informal report and let the Old Man see it. If he's going to damn me, let him damn me. I have nothing to hide."

"It's your funeral," Mark said, eyeing the camera before turning back to Jordan. "We know what happened up to the moment Yuri left the pyramid. I presume you allowed subject alpha to successfully infiltrate the structure and wake his target?"

"I failed to anticipate their avenue of attack, because they demonstrated abilities we hadn't seen. Blair altered his appearance to mimic our personnel. By the time we realized what was happening, they were already inside," Jordan explained, not trying to hide from the blame but simply explaining circumstances. It was interesting that he'd called subject alpha by name. "They cut down our guards. We pursued in the X-11s, but they held us off long enough for Blair to get inside. He woke the Mother. She tore me apart and slaughtered every last man under my command. It was violence on a scale I've never seen. The carnage was...impressive."

"So you woke up as one of these things and the other werewolves just accepted you as one of their own?" the Director asked, genuinely interested now. He was about to have one of the most troubling gaps in his data filled, and if the Old Man accepted those answers he might just get his best operative back.

The latter was critical, especially given that Jordan was much more powerful now. The more Mark learned about the Old Man the less he trusted him. If a battle was coming, Jordan could be the game piece that delivered the checkmate.

"More or less. They didn't entirely trust me, but the whole zombie apocalypse thing caught us all off guard. It made sense to work with them to try to save who and what we could," Jordan explained with a shrug. "I joined and we started clearing zombies. Werewolves— champions, we call ourselves—are very good at it."

"So that's why the werewolf plague was released? To combat the zombies?" the Director asked, already deeply troubled by the prob- able answers. He'd had plenty of time to consider the situation and already suspected what Jordan was now confirming. They'd been blind to the facts and had seriously curtailed the spread of the were- wolves, thereby ceding most of the world to the zombies.

"Yes, sir. The woman who woke helped design both. She wasn't very forthcoming, but I gather that she was atoning for what she felt was a mistake," Jordan explained, toying absently with one of the straps. "A bad mistake. The zombies aren't the worst of it, sir. They evolve into some pretty nasty varieties, but even they can be contained."

"There's something worse?" the Director asked, bracing himself for yet another hammer blow.

"Yes, sir. The zombies evolve as they eat. Some eventually gain intelligence and their own type of abilities to go along with them," Jordan explained. He rose from the bench and approached the gap in the glass. "The Mother wasn't the only thing we woke up. The evolved zombies are called deathless. They're very much like vampires, but not the sparkly kind from shitty movies. The brutality and ferocity is like nothing I've ever seen. One of those deathless was asleep inside the Ark. I believe he's the single biggest threat the world has ever faced."

The Director considered Jordan's words. Ark. The Mother. Deathless. It was a whole new lexicon, one Jordan was obviously very comfortable with. He'd changed more than just physically. Was he still capable of being a part of Mohn, or had he gone native?

"Explain," he demanded.

"His name is Irakesh. He has abilities even the werewolves had a hard time dealing with. He's ancient, cunning, and a canny strategist. He's got military training, though no military we'd know," Jordan answered, expression hard. The Director sensed a lot more anger there than he expected. "We fought him at the Panama air base. Yuri's unit arrived just as Irakesh left with one of our planes. The one holding the package you sent to Peru."

"You're telling me that this deathless has one of our nukes?"

"Yes, sir," Jordan replied, breaking eye contact. Another anomaly. He was embarrassed. That took Mark aback.

The Director fished his smartphone from his pocket, swiping to wake it. He opened a call to Ops, "Benson, are we still tracking the rogue bird heading north from Panama?"

"Yes, sir," she answered. He was quickly coming to rely on her. She too would play an important role if he needed to take a stand against the Old Man. "It's over southern California. East of Los Angeles."

"Do we have a lock?" he asked, meeting Jordan's gaze.

"Yes, sir, target is locked," the tech answered. He could tell she wanted to add more. She knew the cargo the plane was carrying.

"Use the Skyhammer. Take it out," he ordered.

49

GOTCHA

T revor engaged the autopilot, releasing his death grip on the controls as he waited to see what the plane would do. It continued a steady course, the yoke unmoving as it roared through the sky. "It worked. The plane will fly itself on the course I've locked in. It can't land or take any sort of evasive action, but we should be safe at this altitude. It's not like there are any other planes to run into."

"You continue to impress," Cyntia purred, running a finger along his shoulder from her place in the co-pilot's seat. She'd returned to her human form, but the corruption was visible even there. Her once shiny blond hair was dull and limp, her dark skin cracked and peeling.

Trevor's emotions had been muted since the change, but even now his heart went out to her. This was a woman he could have fallen for, were he still alive and she not falling deeper under Irakesh's influence. He turned to face her, aiming his tone at neutral.

"I'm going to go speak with Irakesh. Would you mind keeping an eye on things? I'd feel better having someone up here. I don't trust the autopilot just yet," Trevor asked, unbuckling his harness and rising to his feet. It was a lie, but one he hoped she'd accept. She seemed to like it when he asked her to do things, and he found it increasingly difficult to be around her.

"Of course," she said, shifting to provide a view of more than ample cleavage in her blood-spattered tube top. "If anything happens, I will come for you. Do not be long. I worry when you are alone with Irakesh. I do not trust him."

"Uh, sure. I'll try to make it quick," he said, pulling the heavy metal handle and popping the door open. He stepped through and closed the hatch behind him, heaving a mental sigh of relief.

The hum of the engines was muted as he strode through the belly of the plane. It was domed with a cargo net above and wide rubberized tiles lining the floor. A huge chrome box sat in the center, covered in bold red warning labels. A nuclear weapon. Something that belonged in a bad Bruce Willis flick. Of course given what he'd become that shiny box was the most normal thing he'd seen all day.

"Yes, Trevor?" Irakesh said. Trevor scanned the room, but there was no sign of the deathless. He must be cloaked in shadows. Perhaps near the back of the room? That's where most of the books his unwelcome master had accumulated.

"Our fuel is down to twenty percent, about three more hours. We're going to have to set down soon. I need a destination," he explained, walking towards the rear of the plane. He kept his tone even and his back straight. He'd be damned if he showed Irakesh how nervous he was.

"Head north and stay near the coast," Irakesh demanded, finally emerging from the shadows. He was in the corner where Trevor had assumed, still wearing the pristine white garments so out of place on such a monster. They contrasted sharply with his dark skin. "I don't know where exactly, but I will feel it when we get close."

"How do you not know where it is?" Trevor asked, glancing at the nuke. Irakesh was a planner. It seemed so odd for him to leave something like this to chance.

"The land has changed much since my time," Irakesh admitted, running a clawed hand along his ebony scalp, utterly hairless save for thick, dark eyebrows. "Back then the oceans were much lower. The world was colder. The entire coastline I knew is underwater and I have never been to the Ark of the Redwood. I only have rough maps from my mother's Ark. Not much use, I'm afraid."

Trevor was stunned. It was as straightforward an answer as Irakesh had ever given, and it revealed more about his past than anything else he'd said.

The door behind Trevor groaned open. He turned to see Cyntia stepping through, lips pursed. "Trevor, there is a strange light blinking on the console. It seems urgent. What should I do?"

"Deal with it," Irakesh ordered, waving a hand casually towards the cockpit. "I have much to think on. Let me know when we are nearing the end of our fuel. I will tell you when—"

A klaxon sounded from the cockpit, one reminiscent of the air raid sirens from the '50s. The dim lights running along twin tracks suddenly flashed red. Trevor spun, blurring into the cockpit and back into his seat. He studied the readout beneath the red button. Proximity alert.

"Something's locked onto us. It's coming from above and it's dropping fast," he yelled over his shoulder to the belly of the plane. "Grab onto something."

He toggled off the autopilot, jerking the yoke to the right. The plane veered, but changing the direction of that much mass took time. Time they didn't have. From above, he could see something twinkle, then it streaked into view like a wrathful star. It was a huge chunk of metal, glowing red from re-entry. A detached part of his mind identified it as something he'd read about in sci-fi books. All you had to do was position a huge chunk of metal in orbit. Release it over your target and gravity did the rest, obliterating it with the force of a many-kiloton bomb. Your own personal meteor.

Trevor yanked harder, but he could see the inevitable. The streaking hunk of metal was ahead and above them and falling to match their course. The only reason he could perceive it was because he'd blurred, slowing time around him. It streaked towards them and he watched in horror as it sheered off the plane's right wing in a hail of fiery shrapnel and screeching metal.

His blur provided all the time in the world to study the explosion of fragments advancing on the cockpit. They'd puncture it, instantly equalizing pressure. Their forward momentum would war with the changing pressure to see if they were ejected, but no matter the outcome the plane was doomed.

"Grab onto something," he roared, releasing his blur.

The cockpit shattered, peppering all of them with molten debris. Cyntia cried out in pain, but Irakesh endured it, face twisted into a rictus of rage. The deathless's arm shook against the force of the wind as he forced it forward, seizing the back of Trevor's chair. "We must secure the bomb."

"This plane is going down. You can die with the bomb, but that won't save it," Trevor roared back over the howling wind. It pressed him back into his restraints, tossing him about as the plane fell end over end. They'd be very, very lucky to survive this and that wasn't going to happen if they wasted precious seconds trying to recover the bomb. "You want to try for it? Go ahead. I'm saving my own ass."

He waited for Irakesh to exert some sort of control, but the deathless merely hissed at him and darted back through the doorway into the belly of the plane. Now that was interesting. Why hadn't he ordered Trevor to accompany him? Maybe it meant his control wasn't as ironclad as the deathless pretended.

Trevor undid his restraints and blurred again, seizing the lip of the shattered canopy. Shards of glass cut into his palm as he swung outwards, fighting the plane's spin and the wind to get free of the dying aircraft. Then he was tumbling loose in the air, the plane's wake hurling him into a frigid bank of clouds.

He lost sight of the plane until a rush of hot wind boiled away the cloud. It was accompanied by a sound louder than god's name, heralding the inevitable destruction Trevor had just predicted. Wreckage stormed through the sky around him, a two-foot fragment of wing humming past his head. The plane had dissolved into thousands of fiery streaks, radiating in all directions like some macabre firework.

It covered hundreds of yards, probably a half mile or more. Trevor blurred again, feeling the drag as he reached deep into the well of power he'd accumulated from the sun. He scanned the sky, shrapnel slowing to a crawl with his enhances senses. There was Cyntia, incandescent and screaming as her fur and flesh burned. The howl hadn't reached him yet, but he knew she was in utter agony. He wouldn't wish that on any one, least of all her. Would she live? It might be better for her if she did not.

A flash of movement caught his attention. Nothing should be moving that fast during the blur. A patch of pulsing green energy undulated beneath him, little motes of red and black dancing within the cloud. What the hell was that? It must have been something Irakesh had done. The green energy was identical to the light they used, and it *felt* familiar.

Time sped up again as the blur sputtered out. Trevor had nothing left to give. He plummeted towards the dry brown landscape, Riverside's chrome-dotted desert stretching out before him. He'd die less than two hundred miles from San Diego. That was fitting somehow, coming home at last. At least there'd finally be an end to it.

Trevor gave in to the free fall, closing his eyes and stretching his arms and legs as the wind ripped at his clothing. It was an enormous relief. He'd feared the worst after Blair and Liz had failed, thought Irakesh was certain to win. He didn't know what that would mean for the world, but he was certain it wouldn't be good. Somehow a force powerful enough to nuke them from orbit had pinpointed their position.

How had Mohn known where to find them? That would have required satellites and there was no way they could have survived the CME. It would have fried every satellite in orbit, and if it was as large as the data suggested it would have fried anything on the moon as well. So how had Mohn just fired something from orbit? It made no sense, unless they'd somehow created a satellite with some very potent magnetic shielding.

"Trevor," a jagged voice thundered over the roar of the wind. He opened his eyes, shifting his flight to turn towards the speaker. The cloud of energy had matched his trajectory and speed exactly, pulsing just a few feet away. He could feel the power there, the enormous energy.

The ghostly outline of a face appeared, jagged fangs and neon eyes set into a mask of determination. "Trevor, you can save yourself, but you must listen very closely."

He strained to listen, the words very nearly lost to the wind. Trevor sucked in a breath and roared back. "What do I do?"

"Turn over control to your Risen. I will show it how to do as I am doing, to become energy rather than matter," he shouted back, moving closer to envelope Trevor. His skin tingled, but he ignored it. He reeled from the sudden knowledge. Irakesh would survive the fall. Should he let himself die, denying Irakesh one of his strongest tools? Or should he survive and try to break free?

Irakesh was so powerful and Trevor's every attempt to resist had failed. Yet the logical part of him said that that would change eventually. Sooner or later he must be able to break free, as Irakesh had no doubt broken free from his former master. He closed his eyes, relaxing despite the rushing wind and the ground he knew was surging up at him.

I will tend to this, the voice hissed in its oily drawl, back from wherever Irakesh had banished it. *Surrender and we will both survive and grow in knowledge. The power he offers will serve us well.*

Trevor shuddered, though not from the frigid air around him. The devil within or the devil without. He made his decision, releasing conscious control over the situation. Something large shoved him down a deep well, black water pulling him under as the world disappeared.

50

EXCALIBUR

Liz now had a pretty good idea what a caged lion must feel like. She sat up on her bench, giving a small smile of satisfaction at the pile of torn straps on the ground next to the cool metal. It had taken her hours of struggling, but she'd had nothing else to vent her rage on and eventually the straps had torn loose. It was a small victory, but an important one. It meant she wasn't powerless.

She glanced across the hall to the other cell, but Jordan hadn't returned. They'd taken him last night, though where or why was a mystery. He'd given her a reassuring look and a shrug as the three soldiers had led him off. Had he been executed? Or was he being tortured? Liz rose to her feet, pacing back and forth in the narrow confines of her cell.

There was movement down the hall. Liz pressed her face to the far corner of the glass, peering down as best she could. Two figures approached, one in a pressed black suit and starched white shirt. The other wore the black t-shirt and camo pants she was coming to know well. Jordan and the man he'd called the Director.

The Director's hair was jet black streaked with white. Lines creased his weathered face, yet there was a solidity to him as he approached her cell. This was a man not easily deterred, one who pursued a goal no matter the odds or cost. One who'd orchestrated the occupation of the Ark and had destroyed Trevor's home and possibly his life when he'd come after her and Blair back in San Diego.

He paused in front of her cell, cold eyes sizing her up as he rested a palm against the glass. She took a step back, trying not to look threatening. They'd never open the glass if they thought she was a threat. The area around his hand pulsed red and a narrow window oozed open somehow in the center of the glass. Not enough to escape through, but enough to get her arm around his neck if he was foolish enough to approach.

"Good morning, Ms. Gregg. My name is Mark Phillips and I'm the director of this facility," he explained, his expression unreadable. He turned slightly and gestured at Jordan. "I'm given to understand that you've spent some time with the commander. I've brought him as a show of good faith. Hopefully, that will engender at least a little trust."

"That's asking a lot," Liz said, wishing that she could take the words back. She wasn't very good at playing meek. She moderated her tone. "You've been trying to kill us for months. Because of you, the world is burning and the champions who should be protecting it were never created."

"That's hardly fair, Ms. Gregg," the Director gave back, clasping his hands behind him. His calm was infuriating. "We caused neither the zombie nor werewolf virus. Those were set in motion in a distant past we're struggling to understand. We did try to contain the spread of the werewolves, but much to our embarrassment we failed utterly. That said, you have every right to your animosity. But you have to ask yourself, what's best for the world right now? We can't change the past."

"So you're what's best for the world? The benevolent corporation helping to restore humanity," Liz replied, her tone laced with venom. She took a step closer to the glass. "What is it you get from all this? A chance to rule the new world?"

"You've seen entirely too many movies, Ms. Gregg," the Director said, smiling for the first time. He took a step closer, within easy reach if she wanted to seize him through the tiny window. He had to know that. "No corporation is benevolent. A corporate entity exists for one reason, to look after the interests of its shareholders. But that doesn't mean we're all soulless suits who dump oil in the gulf and rig elections. Mohn isn't perfect, but we do have humanity's best interest in mind. We want to help the world recover from the greatest calamity in living memory."

"Let's say I buy your bullshit," Liz said, glancing at Jordan. His face betrayed the barest hint of concern, but she had no idea why. "What is it you want from me? I'm not interested in being your lab rat."

"I'd like you to stop Irakesh," the Director said, breaking eye contact as he glanced at the camera above him. He turned back to her. "My superior isn't convinced that can be done, so I want to show him it's possible. I need your help to do that."

"Liz, he's on the up and up. About this anyway," Jordan broke in, joining the Director next to the window. "This would just be a simple training exercise. We're not asking you to do anything that would compromise your safety or that of the team's."

The Director shot him a sharp glance after that last part, and she wasn't surprised. The way he said 'the team' meant he still considered himself part of their pack.

"All right. I'll play along for now," she said, taking a step back from the glass. At the very least, the cooperation would get her out of this cell and might give her a chance to escape.

The Director placed his hand against the glass again. It flared red, then flowed into the ground like a curtain of ice melting. The Director gestured down the hallway. "Right this way, Ms. Gregg."

"Where are we going?" she asked, resisting the urge to bolt as she stepped into the hallway. Jordan fell in behind them as she and the Director made their way past another pair of cells.

"Up two levels to a training room. I've got something special to show you, something that might provide an edge against Irakesh," he answered, nodding at the guard who waited next to a thick steel door. The guard made no obvious move, but the door slid open. He eyed Liz warily, clutching his rifle as she passed. What had they been told?

They entered a wide hallway that led to an elevator. The walls were featureless grey, no decor beyond signs leading to a spiderweb of smaller hallways. The Director waved his hand in front of the panel next to the elevator, then turned to her as they waited. "What I'm about to tell you is known to only six people in the world. Well, six surviving people, anyway. Not even the commander had any inkling."

The doors slid open with a hiss and the Director stepped into the elevator. He waited for her and Jordan to enter. Then he stabbed a button marked 19. The door slid shut and the elevator moved smoothly upward. "Mohn knew a catastrophe was coming on or around December 21, 2012. You're familiar with that date?"

"Sure," Jordan broke in, his scalp gleaming with sweat under his freshly shaved stubble. "Every crackpot X-Files fan knows that date. The world was supposed to end. We all thought it was horse shit, just like Y2k."

"It marked the end of the Mayan calendar, didn't it?" Liz asked.

"Yes, the end of their long count," the Director affirmed. The elevator slid to a smooth stop and the doors opened. He stepped into a cavernous room lined with training mats. The walls were covered with an array of wicked-looking swords, axes, and spears. Many were crudely shaped obsidian, though a few were more modern blades. "Nor were they the only culture to come to that conclusion. The Egyptians knew it, too. So did the ancient Chinese and the aborigines of Australia. They all predicted the same approximate date.

"It represents the beginning of the next age," the Director explained, striding towards a raised dais at the far end of the room. Something golden glittered on top of it. He paused, waiting for them to follow. "The age that just began is called the Age of Aquarius. Your friend in the pyramid back in Peru went to sleep in the Age of Leo, so far as we can tell."

"That doesn't explain how you knew all this was coming. Blair says our earliest recorded history comes from about four or five thousand BC," she said, following him towards the dais. Jordan lagged a bit behind, staring curiously at the weapons on the walls.

"Professor Smith is mostly right," the Director admitted, stopping next to the dais. The glittering object was a wide-bladed sword. A broadsword, if her memories of Trevor's D&D games were accurate. The Director picked it up by the hilt, holding the glittering blade aloft. "The history we know is recent compared to what must have existed, but there were many artifacts and quite a few ruins to suggest an older culture. There was Plato's legend of Atlantis, given to his mentor Socrates by an Egyptian Pharaoh. There were tales of magic, tales of strange beings and of gods."

"So you believed all those old legends enough to prepare for the end of the world?" Liz asked, aware of the skepticism leaking into her tone. She didn't care. Her gaze fixed on the blade. There was something familiar about it, like a half-remembered melody she wanted to hum.

"We'd never have accepted them without proof," the Director admitted. He offered the weapon hilt first to Liz. "This is part of that proof, one of three objects with inexplicable properties we've gathered. Each is incredibly powerful, but beyond that fact they are each unique. We also gathered a number of lesser objects, but using them drained their energy until they went inert. Each of those is on the walls around you. This one is different. Our scientists tell us it's charged with the same energy as the other two objects, but the one man who attempted to harness it was burned to a cinder in the blink of an eye."

Liz took the proffered weapon, testing the weight as she gave an experimental swing. It felt right in her hands, as if it had been crafted for her and her alone. It was just the sort of cheesy magic sword she'd have expected in one of the fantasy novels Trevor loved so much.

Ka-Ken, this is a weapon without peer. It is forged from Sunsteel, just as the na-kopesh wielded by your enemy. Through it you can gather energy, even from the sun. Even the Mother lacked the secret of their forging. This one may well be unique, and its lineage goes back to mighty Osiris and even before.

"Where did you get it?" she asked, forcing her gaze back to the Director.

"It was recovered from the bottom of a lake in England, one at the center of a great deal of mythology," he explained, gesturing at the blade. "The runes you see carved there are no script we've ever seen, though they appear more Egyptian than European. More than one of our scientists have theorized this might be the weapon that gave rise to the legends of Excalibur, though that is mere speculation."

"It was designed for my kind," Liz said, certain it was true, even as she spoke the words. "I could use this to take down Irakesh and that treacherous bitch Cyntia. I'm sure of it."

"Excellent. That's exactly what I was hoping to learn," the Director said, giving what appeared to be a genuine smile. "Now all I have to do is convince my superior to give you the most priceless weapon we've ever recovered."

51

WILD-CAT TOM

I rakesh drifted to the ground, green and black wisps crackling as he solidified. A large silver box coalesced next to him, prompting a sigh of relief as he saw his prize was intact. That more than anything would give him an edge over the other Ark Lords who had no doubt appeared in recent days.

He gazed up at the steely grey sky, small black veins of smoke the only reminder of the wreckage that had so recently rained down from the heavens. It had been scattered all over the strange rocky landscape. The mountains around him were jagged and austere, the granite bones of the earth laid bare. It was unlike any place he'd ever been, brown and desolate. Only a few scrubby bushes dotted the surrounding area.

The only other feature was a thick black road leading to a smattering of structures to the north. He searched his memories, but found nothing about this place. Yet another reason he must rely upon Trevor. It irked him, but he had little choice. Irakesh gazed skyward again, searching a moment before he found another crackling green and black cloud.

It was smaller than his had been, but not by much. That alarmed him. Trevor shouldn't have been able to pick up such advanced shaping so quickly. Yet he had. It presaged the powerful deathless he'd become.

Trevor's friends were still in pursuit; of that Irakesh was certain. The Ka-Dun hadn't come any closer, but neither was he growing more distant. Odds were good he was marshaling his forces for another strike. By the time the Ka-Dun caught up, Irakesh would be at the Ark. Ra willing, he'd have time to detonate the bomb, as well.

Trevor's cloud approached rapidly, drifting landward as Irakesh had done only moments before. Trevor's Risen was still in control, though that would change as soon as the danger had passed. It was an interesting failsafe, the addition of a second consciousness for all deathless. He wasn't sure he'd have made the same choice if he were crafting the virus today. The Risen was potent, but sometimes did as it willed rather than as the bearer wished.

Hot wind swirled around Irakesh as Trevor's cloud enveloped a shrub a few feet away. The green tendrils pulsed weakly, gathering into a tighter and tighter pattern until they coalesced into the man himself. Trevor blinked rapidly, sagging to his knees and bracing himself on a neighboring boulder. He looked both disoriented and a little ill. Unsurprising. Shifting your entire body to energy took much from the best shapers, and Trevor was still struggling to master the trick.

"What happened?" he gasped, staggering back to his feet. His strange copper hair played in the wind, a reminder of how much the world had changed since Irakesh had begun his ageless slumber. His contemporaries had been dark skinned with dark hair and eyes.

"I gifted your Risen with the knowledge of form shaping. You became pure energy, a taxing but potent ability," Irakesh explained, studying the road stretching in both directions. The sun's warm embrace trickled power into his depleted reserves, but more slowly than he'd like. He had to remind himself that it was early in the cycle and as such, it would be years before he had anything approaching his former power. "You should be able to draw on that knowledge now that you've used it, but I'd caution you not to use it too freely.

More than one deathless has transformed back midair, plummeting to their untimely demise."

"Thank you," Trevor said, rolling his neck with an alarming series of cracks. He eyed the silver box next to Irakesh. "You saved the bomb? That's impossible. How did you get it to the ground safely?"

"A great many things are possible for a shaper," Irakesh replied, unable to suppress his grin. Saving the bomb had been extremely taxing. He'd very nearly failed. "Now we need to find a way to transport it. If Cyntia survived the fall, she'd be ideal for carrying the box. Neither of us is strong enough to move it quickly."

"If she didn't survive we can find a four-wheel-drive vehicle of some kind," Trevor suggested, squinting in the sunlight as he studied the road. Irakesh was quietly pleased; his thrall still seemed cooperative. Perhaps it was the man's relief at Cyntia's possible death. That didn't surprise Irakesh, as Trevor's growing distaste for the fallen Ka-Ken was obvious.

The unmistakable cocking of a shotgun sounded from behind them. Irakesh turned to see a trio of men rise from the surrounding desert like a mirage made flesh. Each wore mottled tans and grays designed to fade into the landscape, with odd-looking goggles he was unfamiliar with. All three had rifles at the ready, the black barrels and dark wood unlike the previous guns Irakesh had seen. Their leader had a bushy white mustache and leathery skin, with a thick belly that suggested he enjoyed beer.

He gestured at his companions to remain behind him, and then stepped forward with his rifle aimed at Irakesh's face. "Just what the hell are you poor fuckers? Ain't never seen anything like what you just did, and that makes me want to fill your pointy asses with lead. You got a reason why I shouldn't?"

"I can offer three," Irakesh said, taking a step closer and raising a calming hand to Trevor. He didn't want his thrall killing these men, not just yet. "Firstly, your pathetic little weapons cannot kill me. Try if you wish. But know that when you fail, tales of your death will echo through this new age."

"You got balls redder than a brick built shit house, so maybe you're the fucking devil hisself in this new hell. Don't mean I'm afraid of you," the man shot back. He called back over his shoulder, careful not to look away from Irakesh. Smart. The speaker turned to a companion. "Roberto, either one of them so much as moves I want you to give 'em one of your special presents." The man he indicated was almost as wide as he was short, but he moved well despite his girth. He gave a tight nod, reaching into a satchel hanging from his belt.

"You said three reasons," the leader said, turning his full attention back to Irakesh. "It's dryer than a goddamn popcorn fart out here and I ain't that patient to begin with. My finger's starting to itch, so why don't you finish your blustering so we can kill you and get back to something more interesting?"

"Assuredly," Irakesh said, grinning at the unnatural patch of darkness he spotted along the side of a boulder behind the men. "The second reason is that we can protect you from the things you call zombies."

"Don't need protection. We've been taking care of ourselves pretty damn well, thank you," the man said, finger tightening imperceptibly. Irakesh found his misplaced confidence endearing. He'd make an amusing thrall if he could learn obedience.

"Very well. I believe you'll find the last reason the most compelling. Cyntia, would you eat the man's companions? Start with the fat one," Irakesh called, hoping he was right in his assumption. If not he'd deal with the matter himself.

The patch of darkness detached from the rock, shifting into an eleven-foot-tall werewolf. She lunged with all the ferocity of a female, massive maw engulfing Roberto's head, even as her meaty hands wrapped around his midsection. He gave a muted shriek that ended abruptly as Cyntia ripped his head and most of his neck free. Blood fountained to the dry dirt as she wolfed down flesh and bone.

The second man, a tall, lanky fellow, turned to run. Cyntia didn't even set down her meal, dragging Roberto's remains by one fat arm as she leapt. She came down on the man's back, driving him to the ground with a sickening crunch of bone. His rifle tumbled away, forgotten as she began savaging his shrieking form.

The remaining man's jaw fell open as he eyed his companions' corpses.

"Yup, third reason was definitely the best. You got me fucked in the ass like a prison yard bitch," the mustached man said. He set his rifle slowly on the ground. "Name's Wild-Cat Tom. Kill me if you're gonna, but if not can we get out of this heat? I got a little ranch a ways north. Boys and I hunt pigs up there. Used to do it with tourists, but works just as well now that the world's gone to shit."

"Very well, take us to this camp. Is there some form of transport there we can use to journey north? Oh, and Tom, from now on you will address me as master," Irakesh said, grinning broadly. If Tom was disconcerted he hid it well.

"Yeah, I've got a big Toyota Tundra. Uh, master," Tom said, bending slowly to pick up his rifle. "It guzzles gas like a pig eatin' shit, but the roads are a mess and it will get us around the worst of it. Where is it we're going?"

"North," Irakesh answered, turning to Cyntia. "When you are done feasting would you be so kind as to carry the bomb? At least until our new friend can load it onto his transport."

Cyntia glanced up at Irakesh, face coated in gore as she worried a piece of grizzled fat. She gave a low growl, eyes feral. Excellent. Her beast truly ruled now.

52

WATER LANDING

Blair peered out the right side of the cockpit as the plane soared over the moonlit bay glittering beneath them. It was a sight he knew well. He'd seen the Golden Gate Bridge often enough, because he lived a bare forty miles north. Yet even from this altitude he could tell that something was wrong. A myriad of dim blocky shapes were spread across the bridge, straddling lanes or pressed against the guard rail as if trying to escape, just as their human owners had no doubt attempted.

Dozens of figures picked their way between the vehicles, their shambling gait all too familiar by now. Blair heaved a sigh, turning to Steve, "I didn't really expect it to be any different than the other cities we flew over, but this is home. I guess I still held out hope that somehow it hadn't spread this far north."

Steve turned in his chair, peering over a pair of black sunglasses he'd liberated from the corpse of the captain who'd once sat in that spot. His stubble could almost be called a beard, but had been cut fashionably short. "Being a pragmatic bastard sucks. I expected as much, but it does sting. The bay was home for both of us once upon a time."

For all three of us, Blair thought. Bridget was still in the back of the plane. She'd made herself scarce for the entirety of the eleven-hour flight. He knew her well enough to know that something was wrong, something that had to do with Steve. Was it guilt over what they'd done back in Panama? Maybe she felt like she'd betrayed Steve in the same way she'd once betrayed Blair. What did that make him?

"Can you feel him?" Steve asked.

Blair pointed out the co-pilot's window to the area just south of the Richmond Bridge. He could feel something there, pulsing in a deep rhythm that might have been a heartbeat. "Oakland, maybe. Or Berkeley. Irakesh could be farther out than that, but probably not too far. He's getting close. We should find a spot to set down."

"Yeah, that's going to be a problem," Steve replied, banking in a long, slow turn that carried them towards the ocean near the Golden Gate Bridge.

"Why do I get the feeling I'm not going to like what you're about to suggest?" Blair asked, scanning the bay for an answer. It was cluttered with boats of all sizes, from the massive ferry he used to take into the city to smaller sailboats.

"The bridge isn't an option and I doubt we'll find a stretch of highway that will work. We don't need the plane any more, either. If we survive this, we can get another one. It has to be a water landing. It's the only way," Steve gave back in that detached calm that Blair so envied. "I can take us north along the coast, maybe dump this thing somewhere near Stinson beach. We can hike up Mount Tam and into Mill Valley. That will put us just north of the bridge."

Blair thought hard, scanning the shadowed skyscrapers without much hope. He unbuckled his seatbelt and stood. "All right. I can't think of a better idea. We'll do a water landing. I'll go let Bridget know. How long?"

"Maybe ten minutes? Might be less. This thing moves almost six hundred miles an hour," he said, glancing at Blair as the plane righted its course. "Grab what you think we need from the back. We're going to have to get out the second we hit the water, or risk getting pulled under when this thing floods. I know we're werewolves and all but I still don't think we'd enjoy that."

Blair nodded, ducking through the door into first class. Bridget had organized the place, moving the green duffles Steve had loaded into neat stacks near the door. She looked up as Blair entered, her gaze darting towards the cockpit. There was fear there. He wasn't imagining it. She perked up a bit when her attention moved to him, but he could tell she was still laboring under the weight of something she couldn't share.

"Are we there yet?" she asked, delivering a weak smile. Chestnut curls dusted the shoulders of a tight blouse she'd been wearing for the last couple of days. He let his eyes linger for a moment.

"Nearly. But 'there' isn't the airport. There isn't any place to set down, especially without power. There are no runway lights and we don't have enough fuel to wait until dawn," Blair explained, dropping into the plush leather seat next to hers.

"Oh, god. We're setting down in the bay, aren't we?" Bridget asked, hand resting on the edge of his chair. She wasn't tall enough to actually reach his arm, so he leaned into her. It felt good.

"Yup, water landing. Steve's going to dump us right off the coast. He wants us to grab what we can. We're going to make for shore and hike in," Blair explained. A detached part of his mind realized just how crazy that plan sounded, but there wasn't the slightest doubt in his mind they could pull it off. This was the easy part.

"Okay. The three bags on the left of the door are probably the most important. Food, water, and weapons mostly," she said, gesturing at the bags with a delicate hand. She wore the beginnings of a smile, shy enough that it might run back into hiding at any moment. "Blair, listen, I've been meaning to talk to you. I mean, I know this isn't the best time, but I just want you to know..." She trailed off, words seeming to elude her. Her gaze shone with feeling. It said all the things she seemed incapable of.

This is your She, Ka-Dun. Feel the strength of her bond.

Blair's mind went immediately to Liz. Was she okay?

"Listen, I know things went south a long time ago. We both remember what happened," he said, leaning over and taking her hand. He paused, staring into her eyes for long moments before continuing. "We've all made mistakes. I know you regret what happened, and looking back I think I can see why you did what you did. I'm not excusing it. It was horrible. But I've stopped hating you for it and you need to stop hating yourself. Let it go, all right?"

The smile burst to life and she buried her face in his chest. Blair encircled her in his arms, stroking her hair. Hot wet tears soaked through his shirt. His chest grew warm, and he whispered into her ear, "We're going to get through this. I don't know what's going on between you and Steve, but that's not my business. What is my business is us. When this is over, we'll sit down and have a long talk. I don't really know where we stand. There's a lot to sort out, but we'll do it together, okay?"

She pulled back, wiping her eyes as she smiled up at him. The gesture left streaks of black in their wake. He hadn't realized she was still wearing makeup. She'd always been skilled enough in its application that he could rarely tell. Her posture straightened and her chin took on that set that told him she was about to do something she found terrifying.

"Blair, you have to watch out for Steve," she said, gaze more sober than it had ever been. She paused, glancing at the cockpit before those deep brown eyes found him again. "I don't know what he's planning, but it isn't good. It's the same way he acted just before he and I...well, before we did what we did to you. Only this time it's worse. Blair, he hates you now, no matter what you might think."

"I won't argue with that. I embarrassed him. He'll never forgive that. Ever. But I don't see what he'd stand to gain in screwing me over," Blair said, leaning back against the leather. He'd expected a lot of things from Bridget, but this wasn't one of them. How long had she been carrying this around, worrying about telling him?

Your She speaks with wisdom. This rival Ka-Dun cannot be trusted.

"Just watch yourself around him, okay?" she asked, resting an arm on his bicep as she rose to her feet. "Promise me you'll be careful?"

"I promise, but you'll look out for me, right? Bridget, you're a female. I'm not worried about Steve," he said, giving her as warm a smile as he could muster. She was clearly worried and that suggested

Steve had given her cause. Just what was the bastard up to? It didn't matter. Blair needed him right now.

"You two almost finished back there?" Steve yelled from the cockpit. The perfect timing suggested he'd been listening to their conversation and wanted them to know. Or wanted Bridget to know, anyway. What was he holding over her?

"Yeah," Blair called back, rising to join Bridget. "We'll get the emergency door ready to open as soon as we hit the water."

"Might want to buckle in," Steve yelled back, leaning over his chair so they could see his face through the cockpit's open door. "This is going to be a rough landing. Surf's pretty choppy from what I can see."

"You ready for this?" Blair asked, turning to Bridget.

"Yeah, I'm ready. Just remember what I said," she replied, rising to her tiptoes to kiss him. She broke it a moment later, giving an embarrassed smile as she knelt to retrieve one of the bulky canvas duffles. "This bag's the most important, but those two would be nice to have as well. I'll grab another one after we hit the water. You can pick up the last one."

"One last thing before we go. Steve showed it to me while we were in the cockpit earlier," Blair said, resting his hands on her shoulder. He stared deep into her eyes.

I've got a gift for you. As much as I might enjoy it, I'm sure you're tired of shredding your clothes when you change, Blair thought, extending his mind towards Bridget. He pushed the same memory Steve had shared, impressing it upon her mind.

Bridget gasped, then gave one of the delighted smiles he'd so loved in their previous life. In the blink of an eye she shifted to a full nine feet of silver ferocity, her clothes disappearing into her skin as she did so. She gave a wolfish grin, "Thank you, Blair. This is an incredible gift. I can't believe he shared it with you."

There was a loud whirring and a sudden clunk as the plane's landing gear extended. Was that useful over water? Steve must think so. The plane descended sharply. Blair glanced at the windows, which revealed a shadowed expanse of green on a low squat mountain. Mount Tam, a place he'd hiked dozens of times over the years. Clusters of coastal redwoods dotted the top shoulder, leading down familiar trails into Muir Woods.

The plane dipped to the side, revealing a thin strip of dark, dark blue. The unmistakably cold waters of the northern California coast. It bordered a thin strip of sand lined with clusters of buildings. Stinson Beach, the overpriced mecca so much of San Francisco fled to on the weekends. It was beautiful under the darkening sky, but growing closer at an alarming rate.

The plane dropped sharply, angled downward. The roar of the engines softened as they slowed, the coast still whipping by but much less quickly now.

"This is it," Steve bellowed from the cockpit. Blair braced himself against the seat closest to the emergency exit.

The plane shook as it impacted, tossing him forward as water sprayed up over the windows. He kept his footing, just barely. Bridget-wolf seemed unfazed, already shouldering the second duffle as she yanked on the long red bar labeled emergency. The plane had already begun listing to the rear, the sea visible through the windows in the back rows.

Then the door opened. Blair expected water to rush in right away, but found they were several feet over the soft swells lapping at the side of the plane. For just a moment it looked like a large boat, but steam rose from the engines, dispelling the illusion. Steve rushed towards them from the cockpit, sunglasses still affixed to his nose.

"Let's get the hell out of here before this thing goes down," he yelled.

Bridget didn't hesitate, diving into the water in an impressive arc of fur and muscle. The duffels didn't slow her at all. Blair hoisted his own, diving after her into the frigid Pacific. The shock of it washed over him as he went under, but he kicked powerfully muscled legs. The motion carried him into the moonlight, and he began to swim for shore.

53

SOBEK

The Mother leapt to the prow of the strange vessel, a truly massive craft shaped from forged steel. She landed on the rusted metal, balancing on the balls of her feet as she enjoyed the salty wind.

Such a marvel would have been impossible in her day. They'd never thought to construct things from so much metal. It seemed an incredible waste of a material that had been deemed precious in her time. Yet the people of this world used it everywhere, in buildings, conveyances, even toys.

The ship cut through the waves under a sky that boiled with harsh grey clouds. It had rained the last seven days and would rain again before the sun left the sky. The thickest patch of clouds had gathered above an expanse of black rock that loomed out of the ocean. She recognized it, of course. The place these moderns called Easter Island had been holy during her age, the wide cliffs encircling a deep crater hidden from view. It was there that she'd find the rock she needed.

They rounded the immense volcanic stone, which brought a beach into view. Stark blue waves crashed along the shore, but that wasn't what drew her eye. Eleven rocks stood all in a row. They were too tall and thin to be natural, and though they'd been worn by wind and time they still resembled people.

"Rodrigo," she called, turning back toward the bridge of the vessel behind her. The tall windows were obscured by a salty film, but she could see his form within. Could smell his apprehension. It was always there around her, that lingering fear. "What are those things along the cliff?"

"Those are the Moai statues, Mother," he explained, bobbing his head. "The natives erected them centuries ago. They claimed they were full of mana and that they could use the energy to smite their enemies."

"So something of this place's significance has survived the gulf of time," she mused, directing her attention back to the tall man. "Make port. This is the place I have long sought. I would sup on the holy shore, winds willing."

Yukon trotted to the rail she perched on, placing his hind paws on the edge so he could peer over the side. Such a simple, trusting creature. So unlike the mighty wolf, yet the dog was loyal and trusting, compassionate and forgiving. These qualities had no place in her world, but perhaps they were needed in this one. Yukon had much to teach her.

"Mother," Rodrigo called back, moving from the massive wheel that guided the ship. His dark form passed behind the glass until he emerged into the sunlight, the bill of his strange black cap shading his eyes. "Lorenzo spotted something on the northwestern side of the island. He's not sure what to make of it."

She whirled, scanning the cliffs. A bit of energy flowed into her eyes, sharpening the frothy waves dashing themselves against the porous black rock. Between a pair of outcroppings a small ship perhaps half the size of her vessel was moored to the base of the cliff. Several dark figures scurried down a rope dangling from the side with incredible speed, faster than any unblooded could track. They were blurring. The Mother did the same, expending more energy as she accelerated to many times their speed. Now the figures moved like falling feathers, while everything else around her appeared frozen.

A trio of green scaly creatures with menacing snouts, each with blood-red eyes. It couldn't be. Only one god used such minions, but he was in the Cradle. How could he have arrived so soon? She'd not delayed for more than a few days and had much less distance to travel.

She dropped the blur, spinning to face Rodrigo. "Drop anchor, then get the other unblooded below decks. My foes have arrived before us. I may be able to barter with them, but your presence will inflame their hunger and they may not be able to control themselves. For your own safety you must flee."

In her own time her servants would have died rather than leave her side, but Rodrigo had no such compunctions. He ducked back into the cabin, diving for the lever that released the anchor. Then he seized the microphone, his voice booming across every deck. "Attention, everyone, this is Captain Rodrigo. All personnel report to the fuel storage room on deck six immediately. Go now. Drop anything you are doing and run."

Then he was following his own advice, dropping the microphone in his haste to scramble through the oddly shaped door at the rear of the cabin. Some might call the action cowardice, but the Mother was pleased by his obedience. He'd been an excellent servant, one worthy of the sacrifice.

A warm nose nudged her thigh. Yukon's liquid brown eyes peered up at her. He sent no thoughts, despite his newly awakened intelligence. He merely waited expectantly for her will. She smiled, stroking his soft golden fur. "Yukon, you may wait here. They will sense our connection and shall not harm you. But do not attack, no matter what happens."

Yukon laid down at her feet, licking an errant patch of fur on his hindquarters. Then he froze, hackles rising as he leapt to his feet.

"Calm, Yukon," she said, gripping the fur at the back of his neck so tightly she nearly pulled him from the deck.

Her fears were justified a moment later when a figure blurred into place on the rail directly in front of her. A second appeared to starboard and another to port, but it was the one before her that she focused on.

"Hello, Sobek," she said, slowly releasing her grip on Yukon. She straightened and took a slow step towards the reptilian god. "You're a very long way from the Cradle."

She was still horrified by his appearance, even all these millennia later. His once handsome visage had been twisted beyond recognition. He'd always been fascinated by the crocodiles that prowled the mouth of the River of Life where it spilled into the sea. They were patient, powerful killers that men had long feared. Even the occasional deathless had fallen to their jaws. Sobek had been so obsessed that he'd begged her and Ptah to shape him into their likeness, more reptile than man now.

"Yes," he thrummed, voice low and deep. His mottled green snout split into a toothy grin. "I did not seek refuge there. I slumbered elsewhere, somewhere far closer to the Pole. You are not the only deity to understand the significance of this place, nor to seek position in this age." His long tail swished across the deck, a languid reminder that he could strike at any moment.

"Do you really expect me to allow you to establish control over the Lesser Pole, a site so close to my own stronghold you could come upon me within days?" she asked, shifting as she spoke. By the time she'd finished, the words were low and deep, possessed of a violence to match his own. It was time to remind him who he'd accosted.

"You mistake me, Isis," he replied, chest rumbling out a low laugh. He dropped into a crouch. "I neither seek nor desire your approval. My master will have this island and it will aid him in dominating this new world. That does not mean I will attack you, but it does mean I will deny you this place."

The Mother's mind raced, thoughts and connections forming as she considered all she knew from her millennia with the man Sobek had once been. He valued no one outside himself, save in that they could help serve his agenda. They were nothing but tools. But in that she found her answer.

She blurred, far faster than even Sobek could track. A direct strike at him would avail her nothing, as even her mighty claws would find difficult purchase on that scaly hide. So she took one of his two thralls, grabbing the vassal around its wide neck. The other arm encircled its chest, pinning the beast's arms.

"Will you, now?" she asked, grip tightening still further on the beast's neck. Bones popped. "How many such servants do you possess, Sobek? I see only two. You're a cautious god. If there were more they'd be with you. I can kill this one and be on the other before you take a step."

"Isis," Sobek said, extending his hands in a placating gesture. The long gray claws ruined the effect, but she paused to hear his words. "Surely we can come to some accord. This island is only valuable for its stone. I will quarry and deliver some of it to you. You must need it, or why journey here so soon after waking?"

"Do you think me a fool, Sobek?" she hissed, claws drawing pinpricks of black blood upon the servant's scaly neck. "You would betray me in the first century. The first decade, even. You'd be a dagger to my throat, one thirsting for my blood. To say nothing of this master you serve."

"Not so," Sobek said. He licked the lips running the edge of his snout, reeking of apprehension. She'd chosen a wise tactic. He extended an arm, his hand beginning to vibrate as light flared in the palm. The Mother's eyes widened as gold pooled there, flowing into a gleaming golden staff that she recognized instantly. It was tipped with a winged scarab, a large sapphire set in its belly.

"Where did you get that? Sekhmet would never have given it up willingly," she said, grip slackening slightly.

"Who says she gave it up? I took it while she wasted time picking her pantheon, then fled for distant shores to secure my passage to this age. I know how strongly you desire it, for you better than any know the true worth of a Primary Access Key. Hear my offer, mighty Isis," he said, bowing his head in supplication. His gaze shifted back and forth between his minions, as he seemed to weigh their relative value. "I will give it to you as a sign of goodwill, a proof that I intend no animosity between us. Surely parting with such a magnificent weapon shows I intend no confrontation. You would flay the flesh from my bones with such a weapon."

"Why part with it?" the Mother asked, eyes narrowing. Then it occurred to her. There was only one way Sobek would part with such a treasure. Self-preservation. "You know Sekhmet will come for it. You want to rid yourself of it rather than risk her wrath."

"She hates that name, you know. Any who use it are flayed alive. I'd rather Ra focus on you, and you can make use of such a potent artifact. Besides, my master would not take kindly to Ra visiting war upon these lands. I would suffer mightily for such a slight. We both gain, Isis," he rumbled, as close to embarrassed as a reptile could be. "I need time to build my strength, to recruit new followers. My master will rule the land this world calls Australia, across the great sea. Away from you. I require this place only that I may build weapons with which to secure his new empire."

"Very well, I will give you a decade. Ten years to mine and build," she said, cocking her head to the side. She hurled the reptile from her, the beast tumbling into its companion against the bulkhead with a hollow boom. Both rolled into a crouch, ready to attack if called upon to do so.

A low growl came from Yukon. She reached down to stroke his muzzle, turning back to Sobek. "In exchange, you will fill this vessel with stone. You will give me the Primary Access Key. You will send no vessels to my continent, or to the continent to the north. Have we an accord?"

"I'd also have a mutual pledge that we will not attack each other during that time," Sobek rumbled. He gave throaty growl as he extended the staff. "Do you agree, Isis?"

"We have an accord," she said, nodding resolutely. Then she took a step closer to Sobek. "If your mind should turn to betrayal, I would counsel otherwise. I sense an unseen hand jerking us about like puppets. A threat to both of us, to your master as well."

"What do you mean?" Sobek said, eyes narrowing as a troubled rumble burbled up.

"Study this world's history. Look especially to the land they call Egypt," Isis replied, finally giving voice to thoughts that had troubled her for some time. "For thirteen thousand years we slumbered. The world should know almost nothing of us, just vague scraps and myths…"

"Yet our names survive," Sobek finished after she trailed off. He'd never been the smartest of their band, but that didn't make him stupid. "They survive *exactly* as they were. Even genetic memory couldn't do that. Someone woke early, and their hand guided this culture. Perhaps others."

"Or that someone never slumbered at all," Isis countered. She raised a hand to forestall his protest. "I know, such a feat would have required an incredible store of energy, one we assumed could only be found in an Ark. What if we were wrong? None of us knew Set's whereabouts when we entered the Arks."

"Set died in another age. There must be some other explanation," Sobek replied, giving an agitated rumble. Still, she had placed the seeds of doubt. Enough that his attention would be divided in the coming years.

Isis had chosen a dangerous course, but Sobek's eventual betrayal was nothing beside the power of the staff. Now she could meet Sekhmet in battle on equal footing, could control any Ark in the world. She was once again a true Ark Lord.

54

PERMISSION DENIED

J ordan tensed as the elevator doors slid open to reveal a wide auditorium with three rings of seats facing a massive screen. Every figure was focused on that screen, which showed a man of indeterminate age with blond hair and the beginnings of crow's feet. He had a hard jaw and even harder eyes, the kind of eyes that broke anything lingering too long under their oppressive stare. That stare shifted to Jordan, giant eyes narrowing.

"Commander Jordan. The prodigal son returns to the fold," the Old Man said. It was Panama all over again. Could he never escape this guy? The Old Man smiled, and it chilled Jordan to his very core. "Please, have a seat. You're relevant to this discussion and I want your input. Director Phillips seems to think I should give you a squad and send you after a creature that's the closest thing we know of to a god. He's demanded I give you Object Two; what's more, that I should put it in the hands of Ms. Gregg, a woman who hates us with an intensity we cannot possibly fathom. Tell me, what do you think?"

Jordan swallowed, sifting through the different approaches he could take here. Fuck it. It was time for honesty. He strode boldly down the stairs and past the first two rings, the heads of the most powerful organization left in the wake of the apocalypse swiveling in his direction. Section chiefs and their top aides whispered quietly, clearly surprised by his arrival. Interesting. The Director must have kept his return quiet.

"The Director is right. If we don't stop Irakesh, he'll seize control of a pyramid just like the one in Peru. It's designed to harness the power of the sun and will amplify his powers," Jordan explained, jaw set. He kept his posture rigid and looked the bastard right in his digital eye. If he was going to be crucified, he'd do it with dignity. "His powers are already immense. If we let him get a base of operations, he *will* become our primary competition on this continent. It will lead to war and that's a war we aren't equipped to win. Our infrastructure is critically damaged. Our communications with survivors near nonexistent. That isn't the case for Irakesh. He can control the dead and hurl them against us in near limitless numbers while we struggle to save survivors. His army is endless. We have a chance to stop him..." The Old Man met his gaze, expression unreadable. "If we take the hit and succeed, we'll have eliminated our primary competition. If we fail, we'll have risked nothing."

"Nothing?" Mohn snapped, eyes smoldering. Then he struck, spittle flying at the screen as his face twisted. "You want us to deliver one of our most potent artifacts into his hands. To alert him to the fact that humanity still has a technologically advanced stronghold. Are you insane or just reckless? He *cannot* know about us, Commander, not until we are strong enough to defend ourselves. Right now we have the power of anonymity, a power you'd casually discard. We saw how things turned out on your watch down in Peru. What makes you think you'll have any more success now?"

"Because," Jordan roared, beginning the shift. It came swiftly, his clothing shredded in the blink of an eye as blond fur exploded around his expanding body. His voice boomed through the room now, bestial and immense. "We have the forces capable of taking him down. Werewolves were created to fight his kind, the deathless. You have two of them. Give us a plane, a squad, and Object Two. We'll take Irakesh down and end this. It's worth whatever risk that might mean."

"*If* you're successful," the Old Man shot back, apparently unfazed by Jordan's new form. The fury was still there, but the Old Man had reigned it in. A smart move, as it made him appear more reasonable in front of his underlings. "I will not trust the weight of the world on your shoulders, Commander. Not a second time. Not after the monumental disaster in Peru. That was our chance to hold onto South America. Do you know where that is, Jordan? In the middle of the green belt least affected by this disaster. The place where power grids weren't utterly destroyed. The place where we could have re-established civilization.

"*You* cost us that. If I trust you a second time it will jeopardize the little we've been able to save," the Old Man continued, tone scathing. Jordan remained unbowed. The Mother represented a powerful ally, one with a knowledge of their enemies gathered over millennia. Waking her had been the right thing to do, though admitting that here would mean a swift trip to the lab. He wasn't sure how he'd avoided it thus far.

The Old Man weighed him for a long moment before continuing. "Commander, your new friends view us as an evil corporation. One hell bent on world domination. You know better. You know the truth. Am I a tyrant? You're damned right. But my duty is to safeguard as many human lives as I can. I built this company to prepare for this day. We have to find survivors and get them back on their feet. We have to save what can be saved.

"Even if Irakesh becomes a major threat, it will take him months or possibly years to solidify his hold on the west coast," the Old Man argued, his gaze now taking in the whole room. All eyes were once again focused on him. "By that time we will have restored order to the east. We'll save everything that can be saved and we'll get humanity back on its feet. If I let you risk a strike and you fail he may come for us much sooner."

"He already knows about us," Jordan growled, taking strength from his lupine form. That got their attention. All eyes settled back on him. "He stole one of our planes, the plane with a nuclear asset you meant for Peru. Deathless can ingest memories when they consume brain matter. There was only one way he could have known about Panama. He killed and ate one of our officers. He's coming for us. The only question is: do we do something about it while we've got the upper hand, or let him become a threat we can't stop?"

"We used one of our Skyhammers to knock his bird out of the sky. He got up and walked away from that with the asset intact. It's still broadcasting," the Old Man replied, unmoved. The rest of the room was shaken, whispers rippling through their ranks.

"That's why we have to stop him," the Director's clear voice rang through the room, silencing everyone as he rose to his feet. He allowed the silence to stretch before speaking again, ever the master showman. "Leif, I've served you loyally for fifteen years. During that time I've backed every play, done everything to advance your agenda. I've done that because you've always been twelve steps ahead of me. Because you're the finest strategist I've ever seen. But you know what? Even you make mistakes once in a while and it's my job to call you on them. You're wrong. If we take a swipe at the bastard and miss, at least we'll have tried. If you don't want to risk Object Two, don't send it. But give the Commander a team and send him on his way."

"I'm sorry, Mark," Mohn said, though his eyes said the words were a lie. They smoldered. He was clearly incensed at having been contradicted in front of so many, but was careful not to let his composure slip. "Ingesting brain matter? Even if it's true, all this monstrosity knows is that Mohn existed and has installations all over the globe. He has no intel on which ones survived, because whoever he 'ate' in Peru didn't know. I can't risk that changing, not without a guarantee of success. You can't give me that and you know it. This Irakesh is an unknown quantity. We don't know what he can do and we do *not* want to be his top priority. Permission denied."

Jordan's eyes narrowed as he studied the Old Man's gaze. This wasn't over. He would exact retribution on both Jordan and the Director. The question wasn't if. It was when and how.

55

A PLAN

Blair picked his way up the last few feet of the trail, wiping sweat from his brow as he leaned against the damp bark of a coastal redwood. Being a werewolf gave him a lot more strength and endurance, but the duffel had to weigh at least a hundred pounds and he'd carried it all the way up Mount Tam, down into Muir Woods, and back up into Mill Valley. It was exhausting.

Highway 101 stretched below him, running north to south under the steel grey sky. It was flanked by hills to the west and a view of the Richmond Bridge to the east. He'd driven it often coming home from the city. For just a moment he pretended the cars clogging it indicated normal rush hour traffic, but only for a moment. Every last one was eerily still.

"Can you feel him?" Steve asked, pausing on the bike trail next to Blair. He carried a smaller duffel and didn't seem the worse for wear, despite their trek from the coast. His eyes were sharp, calculating. As always.

Blair turned to glance up the trail, about fifty feet down the hillside where it met a bike path paralleling 101. Bridget sat on a large rock, both duffels tossed absently beside her. She'd been avoiding Steve even more than she had on the flight, despite the fact that she'd found the courage to tell Blair he was plotting something. If only they didn't need Steve for what was about to come.

"Yeah," Blair replied, staring up at the low wall of clouds dominating the bay just beyond the freeway. "He's east of us, probably somewhere in Oakland. Coming closer from the feel of it. The Ark has got to be close, though honestly I haven't the faintest idea where. Could be underwater, for all we know. The coastline was three hundred feet lower thirteen thousand years ago."

"Blair, listen," Steve said, setting his duffel on the ground next to him. He shuffled back and forth, wrestling with whatever he was about to say. Blair stared hard at him. This wasn't at all like Steve. He didn't dither. He said what he meant. Steve looked up at him, eyes searching. "I have to ask you a hard question. I don't want you to think of it as an attack, okay?"

"Whatever you're going to say, just say it," Blair snapped, eyes narrowing. Bridget's warning lurked in the back of his mind.

"You've fought Irakesh twice now. Both times he's handed you your ass. You've also said our only chance against him is the access key, because that puts you on even footing with him, right?" Steve asked. The words thrummed in Blair's ears somehow. It was the oddest feeling, like standing too close to the speakers at a concert where you felt the sound more than heard it.

Somewhere in the back of his mind the beast gave a low growl, then a whine.

"Yeah, I haven't fared so well, thus far. I'm still learning," he shot back. It came out more defensive than he'd intended.

"So why not let me do it? I've got more experience with shaping. I was able to draw on the Mother's memories. I have the best chance of beating him," Steve said, resting a hand against a neighboring redwood. Blair felt lightheaded, more than the hike should have justified. It was difficult to think. "Besides, he won't be expecting it."

"Steve, I'm genuinely glad we found you and that you decided to help us against Irakesh," he said, resting his weight against the same tree. God but he needed some sleep. "I'm not giving you the key, though. To be blunt, I don't trust you. Even if I did, the Mother entrusted me with it. This is my responsibility."

Brief irritation flashed across Steve's features, then his face was all compassion again. The expression looked so out of place.

"Blair," Bridget called from down the trail. He glanced down at her. She was pointing towards the bay. He couldn't make out what she was indicating.

"Let's find out what she wants," Blair said, shouldering his duffel and starting down the trail. He still felt lightheaded, but the feeling was receding. What was wrong with him?

He reached Bridget quickly. She looked more excited than she had in days.

"I can smell Cyntia. I'd recognize that scent anywhere," Bridget said, pointing at the bay. Her finger indicated a spur of land just beyond the wide arc of the Richmond Bridge. Somewhere on the edge of Berkeley, from the look of it. "They're coming closer. I'm betting they're going to cross the bridge."

"That would put them on the other side of Larkspur, somewhere right around San Quentin," Blair replied, nodding towards the prison perched on the far edge of the bay. He'd passed by it many times when taking the ferry into the city. "Fastest way for us to get there is to hike down 101 to Larkspur, then head east up 580."

"I don't like it," Steve said, shaking his head slowly. He frowned at Bridget just as she was about to speak and she subsided. Blair wondered what she'd been about to say. "Not during the day, at least. They've got all the advantages. We should wait for nightfall."

"I agree," Blair said, nodding towards the dock in the distance. Several massive ferries were tied there, but also an array of smaller boats. Beyond it lay a small shopping center next to a stop light. "They'll have to come up Sir Francis Drake Boulevard if they come this way and we've got a perfect vantage. I say we find a good hiding spot and wait."

"What if they stop before they get here?" Bridget asked.

"I can feel him getting closer. If that feeling stops it means he has, too. When that happens, we go to them," Blair said, clenching his fist as he gazed at the Richmond Bridge.

"Won't he feel you coming too?" Steve asked, eyeing Blair sidelong.

"Yes, but I've got a plan about that."

56

24 HOUR FITNESS

T revor had been to the bay area a few times, but he'd never been to Larkspur before. The place reeked of money. The machines lining the gym could have arrived from the factory the day before. The TVs in front of the ellipticals were massive. There was even an olympic-sized pool. He stared out through glass at the luxury cars in the parking lot. There wasn't a used truck or a beat up Toyota anywhere.

"Why'd you pick this place, Trevor?" Tom rumbled. The tall redneck leaned against a squat rack next to a mirrored wall. He was a bit more dusty than when they'd first met. Dark circles marred his eyes. Yet he was still alert, his right hand inches from the .45 holstered at his side. This man was a killer, whatever he looked like. "I don't get it. This place is opener than a squaw's asshole."

"That's why I chose it," Trevor answered, gesturing at the wall of glass covering the entirety of the south wall. "See those boats and that big blue and white structure? That's the ferry building. We've also got the 580 and the 101, so we can run in any direction if we have to. That might save our lives."

"Okay, I git that," Tom admitted, stroking a grey mustache that drooped over his mouth. "But why this place? There's a Starbucks around the corner. We could've had coffee and been a hell of a lot safer. This place has got two full walls of glass. Someone with a weapon comes up and it's gone. We're pissing right into that cock-shrinking breeze. We're gonna get wet."

"You have no idea what we're dealing with," Trevor said, turning the full weight of his gaze on Tom. He gestured through the glass on the western side. "Somewhere out there is a group of killers every bit as nasty as us. You see how Irakesh is pacing over by those dumb-bells? He knows what's coming, and when it gets here, we're going to want that commanding view. Brick walls wouldn't even slow down what's coming."

Trevor patted his rifle, a brand new .308 he'd pilfered from some redneck who hadn't quite escaped the zombies chasing him. That could have been him. Hell, it *was* him, even if he was also a scientist. Fitting that he should take the guy's rifle. It wasn't as high caliber as he'd like, but not even a werewolf would enjoy being shot in the head.

"I'm gonna get fucked like a one-legged girl at prom," Tom said, giving a snort that might have been a laugh. He withdrew the ragged end of a cigar from his flannel jacket, rolling it around between his fingers.

"You know Cyntia hates that smell," Trevor cautioned, glancing to the corner of the room where the massive female was lounging. She'd accumulated a pile of perhaps two dozen spandex-clad corpses. She was slick with gore, about halfway through the stack. A ragged popping made him wince as she tore loose an arm. "I'd strongly suggest you not light that."

"Bitch doesn't scare me," Tom protested under his breath, hastily stowing it back in his pocket.

Cyntia's ears twitched. Then her muzzle swung in Tom's direction. "Bitch, is it?"

She gave a low growl as she barreled through the room, knocking an exercise bike out of the way with a casual swat as she came down on top of Tom. Trevor winced, expecting her to terrify the man.

Instead she lunged, tearing out his throat and wolfing down a large mouthful of bloody flesh.

Trevor took a slow step backwards, then another. Putting distance between them seemed wise, no matter what her feelings for him might be.

Movement from outside the windows drew his gaze, along the path paralleling the 101 maybe a mile distant. It was only for a moment, but there'd been silver fur. He only knew one werewolf with silver fur. His face became a stone, as devoid of emotion as he could make it.

You must convey this to the master, his Risen whispered, deep and low and powerful. It had been absent since he'd fallen from the plane.

You've been silent for days. Why are you suddenly talking to me again? Besides, in the past you've encouraged me to screw him over. Why are you suddenly on his side?

He must be told. You are all in danger, the voice continued, as if it couldn't hear his thoughts. Or didn't care. *The Ka-Dun will kill you. In this your purpose should be united with the deathless you serve.*

An incredible pressure built in the back of his skull, heavier than any migraine he'd ever dealt with. Spots danced in his vision and he sagged against the rack, catching himself against the cold metal. An urge to reveal Blair's presence spread like fire on a hillside, raging through him. It demanded obedience, demanded he confess.

"Trevor?" Irakesh called. He ceased his pacing, apparently oblivious to the fact that Cyntia had slaughtered a servant mere feet from him. His gaze was even more calculating than usual. "Are you all right? You seem to be in pain."

Tell him. The pressure intensified, curling his toes inside his boots. Cramps shot through his limbs.

"I probably just need to eat," he said, through gritted teeth. He forced himself to relax, forced back the pain. "Seems like I'm always hungry, no matter how much I consume."

"Feed then, and quickly. I feel the Ka-Dun in those hills," Irakesh said, nodding towards Corte Madera, the equally rich town directly south of Larkspur. "He was approaching, but has stopped. He can feel me, as I him. He knows we are awaiting his arrival and no doubt suspects a trap. It won't take long for him to send one of his females to scout this place. Then he will attack."

A low growl rumbled from Cyntia and she bared her fangs at Irakesh's approach. Irakesh merely raised a dark eyebrow. Trevor still couldn't believe how large she'd become. She had to be twelve feet tall now, perhaps even larger. She looked like an adult sitting in a child's treehouse. "I am loathe to interrupt your feast, but our enemies approach. There will be females of the purest blood for you to feast upon. Your strength will continue to grow, if you are able to slay them."

A deep booming howl rolled from her, surging through the room and thrumming through Trevor's chest. The windows began to vibrate. The howl continued, still lower. Glass exploded outward, showering the sidewalk like lethal caltrops. Maybe they'd annoy their attackers.

Cyntia rolled to her feet, rising into a crouch. Her back brushed the ceiling and she was nowhere near her full height. "I will feast on her while she still lives. I want to see the light in her eyes go out."

Trevor's eyes widened as he realized who she meant. Trevor loved Liz. Cyntia didn't want him to love anyone or anything but her, so Liz had to die. Something smoldered in his gut, begging to be released.

Kill her. Feast on her corpse. Gain in strength and remove the threat.

This time the voice was making a suggestion. It was insidious, slithering through his mind. Yet it had none of the demanding pressure that had come when he'd tried to hide information from Irakesh.

"Ra's breath, you crazy beast," Irakesh roared, glaring up at Cyntia. "Anything within twenty miles heard your challenge. There is more than just the Ka-Dun and his pack in these lands."

"Let them come," Cyntia sneered, leaning closer to Irakesh. She licked a piece of gore from the fur around her mouth. "I will kill them all. I'll kill you too, if you get in my way."

Irakesh was shaking, his face splotchy. Trevor had never seen the deathless exhibit such a reaction before. "Be ready to carry the bomb,

Cyntia. We may have to flee. You're welcome to gamble with your own life, but will you risk Trevor's? Can you protect him from a dozen champions? Or free-willed deathless?"

Cyntia's ears lay flat against her head and she turned a worried glance at Trevor. It made him sick to his stomach. She loomed over the silver case in the back of the room, as if protecting it meant protecting him.

"Good, you can see reason. The Ka-Dun has not come any closer, but—" Something huge and silver flashed through the west window, vaulting over a nautilus machine and barreling into Cyntia's even larger form with a meaty thunk. The two bodies rolled into the wall, shattering mirrors and knocking weights flying. Trevor was still reaching for his pistol when a set of claws slipped around his throat, shredding flesh and sending a gout of black blood down his chest. A foot was planted against his back and he went sailing into a curl machine, his left arm snapping with the brutality of the impact.

By the time he rolled to his feet, his black-furred assailant was gone. Where the hell had he gone? Trevor knew it was a male, knew it was one of the men who'd accompanied Blair back in Panama. But there was no sign of him.

"How?" Irakesh roared, dropping into a crouch next to Trevor. "The Ka-Dun is still distant. I should have sensed his approach."

"Blair's smarter than you gave him credit for," Trevor replied, snapping his forearm back into alignment. It hurt like hell, but pain didn't affect him as it had in life.

A 45-pound plate took Irakesh in the back, shattering his spine and knocking him on top of a treadmill several feet away. The black-furred werewolf had made a mistake, showing himself again so soon. Trevor ripped his pistol from its holster, leaping into the air as he took aim. A part of him rebelled at attacking Blair's friends, but the larger voice forced him into action. He squeezed the trigger, the round punching through the werewolf's shoulder.

Trevor twisted midair, landing in a crouch behind the werewolf. It spun to face him, but Trevor dropped his gun and extended his claws in a knife edge. They punched into the werewolf's tender midsection.

He seized something wet and squishy, tearing out a fistful of intestines as the beast gave a cry of pain and rage. It roared, spittle bathing Trevor as he dropped backwards towards the wall.

Trevor's jaw shattered as something hit him with incredible force. It took him a moment to realize a new assailant had entered the fray. The fist was silver. Trevor flipped backwards, rolling behind a bank of exercise bikes as he sized up the new assailant. His eyes widened. Blair looked more intimidating than ever, seven feet of fur-covered muscle and scornful amber eyes.

"Last chance, Trevor," Blair growled, eyes narrowing. He took a threatening step forward as the black werewolf behind him stuffed his guts back into his body. "Shake off his control, or I'll do what I have to. I'm done holding back."

57

PARTING THE SEA

Trevor vanished. Blair knew reasoning with him had been a mistake, but he couldn't kill his friend without one last try. He spun around, surveying the chaos in the gym in an attempt to locate Trevor. He found Irakesh instead, the deathless striding confidently towards him.

"You're too late, Ka-Dun," the deathless said, exposing a mouthful of fangs in a hideous parody of a grin.

Blair blurred, slashing at his ugly face. He stumbled forward, encountering none of the resistance he'd expected. His arm passed through the illusion. Dammit. Slippery bastard. He turned back to Steve. "Deal with Trevor. I'll find Irakesh."

He just needed to get into the deathless's mind, but to do that he had to find him first.

A deafening crash sounded as Bridget's form went sailing through the ceiling in a shower of plaster and metal. He tracked her flight through the hole, wincing as she landed on top of a black BMW in the parking lot several seconds later. The alarm began to blare, slicing the twilight. The heads of a hundred roaming zombies swiveled in their direction, slowly ambling towards the noise.

Blair spun to face Cyntia. Bridget would need a moment to

recover, so he was going to have to keep her occupied. The pale blonde didn't seem interested in following up on the fight though. She'd already snatched the silver case containing the stolen nuke. The massive werewolf barreled straight through the wall, bounding across the parking lot towards the waterline to the south where the ferries lay. Blair blurred after Cyntia. She had the nuke, which meant that Irakesh wouldn't be far behind. He couldn't go after them alone, though. He leapt over a pickup truck, landing on the pavement near the BMW Bridget's landing had destroyed. She was rising from the wreckage of the car, her silver fur marred by blood and debris. She moved more slowly than he'd have expected, shaking her head to clear it.

"Cyntia hits hard," Bridget growled, resting an arm on Blair's shoulder as she pulled herself free. "How did she get so strong so quickly?"

"My guess? Feeding. She's eating zombies, werewolves, and, from the look of that gym, people." Blair scanned the parking lot and the road on the far side. The ferry building lay a hundred yards past it, both huge boats still moored there.

It carries a terrifying price, Ka-Dun. The She's mind is already fragmented. The corruption will grow worse until she is a mindless, ravenous beast. She will attack anyone or anything around her, always seeking to sate her endless hunger.

"Let's get moving," Bridget said, taking a step on her own. Bones popped and cracked as they flowed back into place. In a few moments there was no trace of the injuries, save the sticky black blood drenching her fur.

"Retreat might be the wisest option," Steve said, blurring into existence next to them. His right arm hung limply at his side. "Cyntia kicked Bridget's ass and I didn't do much better against Trevor. Blair, even if we can hold them off can you really deal with Irakesh?"

Blair paused for a long moment, delivering a hard look. "I can and I will."

"Stay here, if you're afraid," Bridget growled, eyes flashing as she loomed over Steve. "Selfish prick."

Privately Blair agreed with her, but this wasn't the way to win Steve's aid. If they wanted his help, they needed to appeal to his ego. Blair rested his hand on Steve's shoulder, his silver fur contrasting sharply with Steve's black. "Steve, we need you for this. We've got no chance without you. You know that."

"You don't have a chance *with* me," Steve said, shaking his head slowly. He shrugged off Blair's hand, taking a step towards the ferry building. "I'll help, but we're going to fail. If we survive the attempt, I want you to reconsider giving me the key. Will you do that?"

"Okay, if we fail here, we can discuss my relinquishing the key," Blair agreed with a shrug. There wasn't a lot of harm. If they failed here, they'd almost certainly be dead. "Steve, hang back and engage Trevor when he shows himself. Bridget, do your best to contain Cyntia. Hit her and fall back into the shadows, if you need to."

"Okay," Steve said, half facing away from them. He was already ready to run, but at least he'd agreed.

"I'll do my best, Blair, but she's strong," Bridget said, gaze searching. She seemed to expect his disapproval. He reached up to rest a hand on her shoulder. The fact that he was so much shorter in werewolf form still felt odd. He'd probably never get used to that.

"We have to stop him," Blair replied, squeezing her shoulder. It was like squeezing furry granite. "I know you'll find a way, Bridget. Just keep her off balance until I can deal with Irakesh."

"If we're going to do this, then let's do this," she said, clenching a fist and baring her fangs. She took a step towards the dock, silver fur ruffled by the wind. She looked majestic despite the matted blood.

She leapt forward, crushing the hood of a black Mercedes as she bounded deeper into the parking lot. Blair loped after her, circling to the right. If he hugged the edge of the parking lot he could come to the shore neighboring the ferry building from the east side. That might let him catch Irakesh out in the open, and all he needed was a single glance to get inside his mind.

He resisted the temptation to blur, knowing he'd need every bit of his strength for the coming conflict. He glanced at the sun, low and heavy along the western horizon. Maybe a half hour before it passed behind the mountains and another two until the moon was up. He'd have preferred to face Irakesh during the night, but they were out of time.

Steve's midnight form ducked between cars, perhaps a dozen paces behind Bridget. No doubt he'd let her engage, then decide whether the fight was winnable. If it wasn't he would leave Bridget on her own, so Blair had to be quick with Irakesh. Take him down fast and hard. If only Ahiga had taught him more about his abilities, then he'd be more confident.

Blair leapt over the chain-link fence, avoiding a pale zombie that had once been a middle-aged housewife, if the glittering diamond on her rotting finger were any indication. He went low, sprinting between SUVs towards the grassy patch that sloped down towards the water. The ferry building perched over the water to his right, both massive boats still moored to a metal contraption that allowed passengers to board. Was that Irakesh's destination? Or was he after something else?

He skidded to a halt, claws digging furrows in the grass as he came up short. Blair had no words. Irakesh stood on the shore, arms raised like an Egyptian god accepting the worship of his people. Trevor crouched next to him, rifle aimed in Bridget's direction. Cynthia loomed protectively behind him, like a bitch watching over her pup. She had the silver box cradled under one arm, absently, as though it were no burden at all.

The bay had begun to froth and churn. It began near the shore, then worked outwards in a wide line. Then the waters began to part, a thin gap forming between them as if some giant pane of invisible glass had been dropped into the San Francisco bay. Irakesh widened his arms and the gap between the walls of water widened.

The ground quaked, tossing Blair to the ground. Something massive rumbled in the center of the bay, sending rings of waves racing towards the shore. A black structure glittered at the end of the gap in the water, massive and alien. A structure he'd seen before. The pyramid burst from the bay, sloughing water off as it rose into the sky.

He didn't know how much of the structure was above water, but it had to be seven or eight hundred feet at least.

The crack of a gunshot brought him back to the present. Trevor was already cocking the rifle for another shot. Blair glanced towards Bridget, but she'd already disappeared into the shadows. Trevor must be firing at Steve, who was hidden behind a red SUV. That wasn't going to stop Trevor's rifle, but it might buy him time to think.

Blair dropped to one knee, crouching behind a shrub as he studied Irakesh. This was his shot. The deathless was engaged in shaping Blair couldn't begin to understand. He focused his will, gathering the strength within him. It was as much resolving to succeed as it was drawing on any energy the virus may have provided. He *would* do this.

He thrust a spike at Irakesh's mind, hurling it with more strength than any he'd been capable of before. The blow struck something, a potent shield that rebounded his attack back through his own mind like a towering wave in a disaster movie. He collapsed, fire searing every nerve. Blair lay there, panting as he waited for the agony to subside. Sweat poured from him, drenching his fur.

Blair forced himself to his feet, legs trembling at the idea of supporting his weight. What the hell had Irakesh done?

He has fully linked with the Ark, Ka-Dun. It shields his mind. Were you near the Mother's Ark, you would gain the same protection.

"You couldn't have mentioned that *before* I made the attempt? How can I get through it?" he growled through gritted teeth. The pain was less, but still fiery.

Only the strongest shapers could pierce a mind block. You could seek to test your strength again, but if you fail it could kill us.

There had to be another way. But what could he do? If he couldn't attack Irakesh mentally, that left only one option: overwhelming force.

Blair rose to his feet and howled, a throaty note that echoed over the water.

Irakesh spun to face him, eyes alight with mischief. He met Blair's gaze and smiled.

58

SACRIFICE

Bridget slid into the shadow left by one of the wide blue poles holding up the white awning over the ferry building. A hundred and twenty yards separated her from the shore where Irakesh stood, putting her in the very last place they'd expect. Two ferries rocked slowly back and forth in the harbor before her, empty save for a few gulls that occasionally darted in to snatch a piece of flesh from one of the shambling corpses.

She'd originally planned to use those to leapfrog over to Irakesh, but thanks to whatever old world shaping he'd managed she no longer needed to. He'd literally parted the sea, and the gap that he'd created passed a mere forty feet in front of her. Bridget gazed over the railing into the resulting gap, jaw slack from the power Irakesh had displayed. The muddy path he'd exposed was littered with puddles, debris and all the other crap you'd expect to find at the bottom of a bay that saw thousands of commuters a day, everything from the cracked case of a Blackberry phone to faded Coke cans. Only one fish flopped around, a long silver thing she'd never be able to identify.

Irakesh spun suddenly, drawing her attention. He faced the hill where Blair crouched, half hidden behind a shrub. Blair shot to his feet, arms splayed out and shaking as if he were being electrocuted.

Then he fell bonelessly to the grass, flopping about as helplessly as the fish. She leaned over the railing, extending an arm.

No. Blair had been very specific in his instructions. More than that he'd been right. They had to stop Irakesh. If she went to Blair now she'd reveal her position and squander her only chance to get the drop on Cyntia. That was the only way she'd come out on top in a fight with the hulking bitch. Cyntia crouched on shore next to Trevor like a loyal dog, the glittering box a toy given by her master.

Ka-Ken, I must warn you. This one is beyond our strength. She has feasted upon the flesh of her own, the flesh of nascent deathless. The madness festers within her, but it affords her a fevered strength.

"Can she be killed?" Bridget asked, hopping atop the railing and gathering her legs under her.

Such a feat is possible, but exceedingly difficult.

"Then I'm going to kill her," Bridget said, leaping into the gap. The wind whipped around her as she fell, cool and damp and smelling of salt.

She fell between twin walls of water, which grew darker as she plummeted. Shapes moved within them, the occasional fish and things she couldn't so easily identify. Sharks maybe. Bridget turned her attention to the ground, which was rapidly approaching. She bent her knees, rolling with the impact. A tremendous geyser of mud fountained around her as she sank several feel into the sticky silt.

She disengaged herself from a tangled piece of seaweed, shifting into the shadows afforded by the towering walls of water. Irakesh had begun moving down the path, walking boldly through the mud as if it were a plush carpet. Behind him lumbered Cyntia, her gore-coated snout elevated as she whiffed for a scent. Bridget's stealth was complete though. Cyntia would find nothing, not until Bridget was ready to strike.

Trevor remained on the beach, back facing the gap. He must be covering their retreat to slow Blair or Steve, if the latter was actually brave enough to enter the fight.

Irakesh approached, with Cyntia just a few feet behind. Bridget melted deeper into shadow, pressing her back into the frigid water. It hit her like—well, like a bucket of ice water. She refused to move, to even breathe. Irakesh passed by, moving at a fast walk. His shimmering white clothing remained pristine, and the sword at his hip rode there as if an extension of his body.

Then Cyntia was even with her.

Bridget leapt, gliding into the air behind Cyntia. She extended her claws, dashing down in a quick set of blows that sprayed blood from the artery she had severed in Cyntia's ruined throat. It wouldn't stop her, but hopefully it would slow her. Bridget planted her feet on Cyntia's shoulders, flipping backwards with a powerful kick that sent the larger female face first into the muddy ocean floor. Cyntia slid forward, the silver box slipping from her arms and sliding into the wall of water where it fell on its side.

Bridget was tossed forward, staggered by a blow from behind. Something flared in her shoulder, and she raised a hand to probe the wound. It came back bloody. An instant later the crack of a gunshot followed the bullet, echoing through the strange corridor created by Irakesh. Trevor had entered the fight. That had to mean Steve was either dead or had retreated. Fucking coward. How could she ever have chosen him over Blair? As mistakes went she couldn't think of a more legendary one.

Bridget rolled with the blow, coming to her feet to the left of Cyntia. The larger werewolf was also rising to her feet, scarlet eyes blazing as she bared her fangs. Her blond fur was covered in a mix of blood and mud, painting her into an even more gruesome caricature of the noble creature she'd been just a few weeks ago.

"I'm going to feast on your heart, you little bitch," Cyntia roared, launching a swipe that very nearly took Bridget's throat. She fell backwards, allowing the blow to pass over her. It saved her, but left her open for her opponent's next attack.

Cyntia fell on top of her, jaw snapping near her face as her tremendous weight pushed Bridget deep into the mud. Bridget seized Cyntia's shoulders, forcing her back. The putrid breath nearly made her gag, and she could see bits of rotting flesh still stuck between teeth. Cyntia snapped again, nipping her cheek. It burned like acid.

Bridget roared, flipping backwards as panic flooded her. The slippery mud negated Cyntia's weight advantage, and she tossed the larger werewolf into the mud again. She didn't hesitate, flowing into the shadows as Cyntia regained her footing.

"Come out, you tiny little bitch," Cyntia roared, dropping into a crouch and scanning the darkness. "You can't hide forever. I *will* find you."

Then Trevor was there, the first time she'd gotten a good look at him. If you didn't look too closely he looked like a redneck ginger, with a freckled face and a dirty ball cap. His eyes gave lie to that illusion though, deep putrid green just like Irakesh. He cradled a rifle loosely in his arms, joining the deathless bastard in his shimmering white garments that somehow remained untouched by travel or even the mud.

"The black werewolf didn't engage, but Blair is recovering. He'll be here shortly. We should keep moving," Trevor said, slowly panning his gaze over the dark water. He must know she was there, but didn't seem alarmed. She couldn't detect panic or fear in his scent, but then the same was true for Irakesh. Maybe they didn't have emotions, or if they did maybe they weren't detectable in the same way that human emotions were.

"I agree. The Ka-Dun is no longer a threat, but I do not take chances," Irakesh said, approaching the box. His garments flowed in the frigid breeze now winding through the corridor. "Trevor, carry the box. Cyntia will need her hands free."

"What about Bridget? I want to eat her heart," Cyntia roared, taking a hostile step towards the deathless. Madness lurked in that awful gaze.

"Follow Trevor," Irakesh ordered, waving a hand dismissively as he started deeper up the corridor threading through the sea. "The Ka-Ken will come to you. I assure you this is so."

Cyntia roared again, slashing at a dark shape that flitted along the edge of the wall, just inside the water. She came back with a small white shark, ripping its throat out with the savage intensity she'd no doubt prefer to use on Bridget.

Bridget peered back up the corridor towards the shore, still not too distant. Nothing moved. If Blair were able to come, he'd already be here. He might be wounded or even dying. That was the only thing that would have kept him away. He cared about her. She knew it. Maybe it wasn't the love they'd once shared, but he was at least— what? Maybe fond of her? How stupid to even worry about such things right now. But there didn't seem to be any other time. Everything was always a crisis.

Bridget shook her head, turning back to Cyntia. Blair wasn't coming. Steve certainly wasn't. He'd leave her to die without a second thought. It had always been that way, though she'd been naive in the beginning. He had kept her because she was pretty and because she had a little clout in the anthropology community. Not because he loved her. Steve was too narcissistic for love. Fondness maybe. That fondness had evaporated over time, a little each day like a puddle drying up.

She was alone. Should she run? Blair would tell her that it was okay if she did. He'd assure her she'd had no other choice, that she had to flee. There was nothing she could do. But somewhere in his gaze she knew what she'd find. Disappointment. She'd faced it once, the night she'd finally confessed her sins and told him she was leaving him. She didn't have the strength to see that gaze again, not ever.

Bridget dropped into a crouch, eyes narrowing as she stalked her prey. Irakesh moved at a fast walk, the water parting thirty or forty yards ahead of him as he advanced across the floor of the bay. Trevor trotted beside him, rifle now slung over his shoulder on a strap so his arms were free to carry the box. She recognized the weapon, a .308. Jordan had shown her how to use one.

Cyntia lagged behind the pair, prowling back and forth a few feet away from Bridget. She let the gap widen, eyes sliding past Bridget as she whiffed the air for a scent. "Come out, Bridget. I'll give you a quick death. You won't feel anything, I promise."

Bridget's heart thudded. She tried to remind herself that she was a nine-foot monster with sharp fangs and even sharper claws. It didn't help. Cyntia turned her bowels to water. She towered over Bridget, her blond shoulders wider than the Civic Bridget had driven back in college. She healed so damned fast and she seemed flush with energy, as if she'd bathed in moonlight for weeks without expending anything.

Bridget slid a foot backwards, gripping the mud. Her legs tensed as the crouch deepened, then she leapt. Her hands seized the side of Cyntia's head, burying themselves in the thick blond fur. Her claws had already proven ineffectual. She had to try something else. Bridget wrapped her legs around Cyntia's shoulders, then twisted with all her might.

A sharp crack echoed through the corridor and Cyntia dropped to her knees. Bridget didn't hesitate. She dug the claws into Cyntia's eyes, gouging as deeply as she could reach. Maybe if she destroyed the brain she'd stop the body.

Cyntia's arms shot up, seizing her by the forearms. Claws tore into Bridget's flesh, wrenching a scream loose. The pain was white, blotting out everything. Yet Bridget forced the claws deeper, drawing a low wail from Cyntia. Then the pressure began to mount. The muscles in her forearms were liquid fire as Cyntia shredded them. Bridget's grip slackened.

Cyntia's grip tightened. Then she yanked Bridget's arms apart, pulling her taut in the air above her. Bridget shrieked as bones popped and broke. Time seemed to slow as her mind fought to understand. She saw, but couldn't comprehend. Her arms had torn loose, leaving jagged stumps in their place. Blood spurted from each, showering Cyntia. She was a cripple.

The larger werewolf spun, seizing Bridget's neck in one of her meaty hands. The other punched through Bridget's belly like a pile driver, blowing her spine out her back. The blow had hollowed out her middle and replaced it with agony.

"You have no idea how much I've been looking forward to this," Cyntia growled, with a ghastly grin. She brought Bridget's face closer until their eyes were only inches apart. "I'm going to eat you, Bridget. When I'm done, I'm going to find Blair and eat him too."

Then she lunged, tearing into Bridget's throat. She wanted to howl, to scream. To warn Blair somehow, tell him to run far away and never look back. Find a quiet place and just be safe, away from Irakesh. Away from Cyntia.

Blair, she thought, body going limp as she finally abandoned the struggle. *I'm so sorry. For everything. You deserved so much more.*

59

RAGE

Blair's mind fragmented with pain. Coherent thought eluded him, hiding behind stray memories and raw, animal pain. He was rocked by incoherent flashes as he fought for control. Bridget the first time he'd laid eyes on her, a wide-eyed freshman watching the awkward teacher's aide giving his first lecture. The way she'd looked at him had galvanized him in a way nothing ever had. Had spurred him to earn his master's, to pursue a doctorate, and to write a thesis that had earned him immediate acclaim in the scientific world.

Then he was in Santa Rosa, gazing through the kitchen window of his little two bedroom. Six empty wine bottles lined the counter next to him, all Ravenswood zin. It was the cheapest red he could stomach and also the guest every night for dinner. A single plate with a lonely fork sat on a clean dish rag. It ate at him, that memory. Brought him back to his lowest. Back to the man who'd given up and decided he wasn't worth a damn thing.

He heaved himself on his side, twisting to face the gap in the water. The pain was immense but he bore it. He had to make it down there, had to help Bridget and Steve deal with Irakesh. Failure wasn't an option. But it was happening anyway. He struggled to stand, collapsing to the turf. It smelled of salt and brine and misery.

Fight, Ka-Dun. Fight with the will the Mother gave you. Your body has been ravaged by deathless energy, but you are a shaper. You can undo the damage he has done. Fight, Ka-Dun. Fight, or all is lost.

Blair planted his palms against the grass, hair framing his face as he panted into the grass. Shaping wasn't magic. It was science. It was the application of will to manipulate energy. He could use that energy to heal himself. Repair the damaged cells, every last one. He envisioned his bloodstream, a bunch of red ovals flowing through myriad tunnels. His heart, thudding heavily in his chest. The very marrow in his bones. Blair reached deep within the well of power at his core, the place he'd saved for this very confrontation.

It built within him, a rolling wave of silver energy that burst through every pore. He screamed into the heavens, arms extended as his body went rigid. He sagged back, slouching to the grass as he fought for breath. He felt better. Tired, but the acidic pain had been banished. He could think again, unencumbered by whatever Irakesh had inflicted. Blair rose to his feet, taking a cautious step towards the beach.

He took another. Then another, staggering his way into the mouth of the watery corridor Irakesh had somehow created. He peered into the gloom, eyes adjusting to the near lack of sunlight in the distance. Shapes moved there, resolving into a pair of massive beasts. One was silver, noble. Majestic. The other a sickly blonde, twisted and feral. Cyntia crouched atop Bridget, who struggled weakly beneath her.

Something broke, tearing loose a sob that had been lodged in Blair's chest for nearly five years. He didn't need Liz's skill with medicine to know a fatal wound when he saw one. Bridget's arms had been torn off, her neck and shoulder savagely rent as Cyntia tore loose another hunk of flesh.

Blair. A quavering voice came to him, faint as if across a great distance. *I'm so sorry. For everything. You deserved so much more.*

It was more than mere words. So much more. The thought was so heavy with emotion it staggered Blair. There was a thick blanket of love, warm and golden. Yet underneath was a tide of sadness, of guilt so acidic it had eroded Bridget's very foundation.

Bridget, I'm with you, he thought back, filling the words with all the warmth he could muster. *I forgive you. For everything.*

He could almost feel her smile, feel the lightening of the pain. *I love you. So much, Blair.*

Cyntia lunged, severing Bridget's spine and burying her maw in Bridget's corpse. There was a moment of lessening, then Bridget was gone. She slipped through his fingers, leaving a faint fragrance of love and loss.

Blair sucked in a breath, trembling all over. He could only stare as the heat built within him, pure and righteous and total. He howled, low and deep. Cyntia looked up from her meal, ears pitched forward as she considered his challenge. He didn't give her time to think. Blair blurred as he never had, crossing the muddy gap in the space between heartbeats. He was on her in a fury, gouging and biting and rending. There was no strategy, no plan. He was one with the beast and all that mattered was killing his prey.

The vile one slew your She. She will not survive.

Blair dropped low, jabbing his claws into her right thigh over and over in a blurring hail of silvered claws. He gouged the muscle, severed the tendons. Then he seized the femur in both hands, wrenching with all his strength. Cyntia's leg tore loose in a shower of gore. He flung it into the water, already spinning for another blow.

"Kaaaa-Duuun," Irakesh shouted, his voice low and warbling like some ultra-slow recording. Blair looked up, catching sight of the deathless maybe a hundred yards down the ocean floor. He stood just outside of the tunnel leading into the Ark. "Iii hope yoouuu can swimmmm."

Blair knew a moment of absolute terror. He spun towards the shore, his worst fears confirmed. The walls of water were crashing together, accelerating in his direction despite the blur. He sucked in a breath, bracing himself as the rumbling wall crashed over him. The blow knocked him from his feet, dashing him against a rock and then up into the water. He lost sight of Bridget's body, but saw Cyntia kick off towards the Ark with her three remaining limbs.

That was the last thing he saw before his eyes succumbed to the enormous pressure, bursting with agonizing little pops he felt more than heard. Then his eardrums followed, leaving him in silent darkness. He released the blur, fire burning in his lungs as his body greedily sucked away the little oxygen he'd managed to grab. Not being able to save Bridget's body ate at him, but if he didn't get to the surface he was dead.

Blair kicked hard, swimming in the direction he hoped was up. The frigid water numbed his limbs, but maybe that was a blessing as it muted the agony. The physical agony, anyway. He looked away from the anguish like a child who'd stared at the sun a moment too long, but spots of Bridget still danced in his vision. He swam harder, the pressure in his lungs mounting. The pressure lessened, suggesting he was going the right direction. Blair blurred for a split second, using his entire body to propel himself upward.

The idea of diving had always seemed like a horribly suicidal idea. Especially when he lived in a place people referred to as the red triangle, due to the number of great whites. He was so numb he couldn't tell if the water was getting warmer, but that mattered so much less than the pressure.

Seconds passed as he pumped his limbs, clawing for the surface. Then he was free, bursting into the settling twilight. He sucked in for all he was worth, getting as much sea as he did air. He coughed and spluttered, scissoring his legs to keep himself afloat. Gentle waves rocked him back and forth. Without sight he had no idea where land was. Or did he? Blair sent out a ping, scanning the area. There, that direction. He sensed a familiar presence, perhaps a hundred yards distant.

Blair swam. He tried to ignore the pain, the anchor of emotional loss threatening to drag him under. Somewhere in the middle his eyes began to burn, something warm and liquid flowing into the sockets. He lacked the breath to scream, accepting the pain with the despair of futility. Then there was brightness everywhere. He squinted into the settling twilight, scanning the shoreline. Steve was crouched there in human form, eyes darting about as he sought signs of an enemy. He met Blair's gaze briefly, giving a simple nod before returning to his search.

Blair swam harder, jaw clenched and body quivering with sudden energy. He heaved himself from the water, charging across the shore towards Steve. The smug bastard just waited there, arms crossed as he rose to his feet. His black dress shirt wasn't even muddy. Blair seized him by the collar, lifting him with one hand. He brought Steve's face to his own, giving a low, deep growl. "Consider your next words very carefully, you fucking coward. Bridget fought and died down there. Where were you, Steve?"

"I know you're angry," Steve said, letting his arms fall limp. His whole posture slackened. No resistance at all. "Trevor had the beach covered. You were out of the fight. I didn't even see Bridget move down there. Didn't know she was there until I heard the fighting, just a few seconds before you. I'm sorry, Blair. I am. But there was no way I was going to rush in there unsupported. I saw what Irakesh did to you. What the hell chance did I have without the key? Maybe if you'd have given it up, I would have been down there. Did you think about that?"

Blair opened his mouth to retort, but something tingled at the base of his skull. Was Steve right? He'd gotten his ass handed to him by Irakesh. Again. As though he were a small punt-able dog barking at the mailman.

"You're still a fucking coward," he roared, spittle drenching Steve. He hurled Steve into a nearby Mercedes, shattering the windshield and shredding Steve's shirt. "We need to fall back and plan, that is, assuming you want some payback. I thought you loved Bridget. Isn't that what you told me when I confronted you for fucking her behind my back? That you loved her? Get up, you god-damned cockroach. Follow me or get the fuck out of my sight."

Blair spun, marching towards 101. He had no idea what to do now, but he was taking Irakesh down, no matter what it cost. Right after he snapped Cyntia's neck.

60

REVELATIONS

M ark dropped into the black vinyl chair, setting the glass down with a clink. The world was eating itself alive and he still had ice. The universe certainly had a strange sense of humor. He held his fingers against the trackpad until it vibrated and the iMac's screen came to life. He dragged a browser window onto the screen, navigating Mohn's intranet until he found the wiki. It still impressed him, the audacity of it. They'd tapped into the world's every communication for years, stockpiling data in facilities like this one. Each one took hourly backups of effectively the entire internet, which meant despite the sudden end of the world he could still use Google.

"What have you been up to, Old Man?" he murmured, pulling open a console and typing in his authorization. He executed a simple script until a series of phone calls appeared. Each included a time, destination and number of parties. Six had occurred in the last four hours, all to London. A Mohn facility was located there, so that had to be who he was talking to. Who else had a functioning phone after the CME?

Six phone calls in four hours. The Old Man hadn't done that since the first pyramid had appeared. Mark had been in the loop on that one. Mohn had told him before anyone else and the two had discussed options. They'd birthed the plan together. Yet he'd said not a word to Mark about whatever this new event was.

"Director, my ass. If you really trusted me, you'd have brought me in immediately," he said, picking up his glass and enjoying a swallow of the amber contents. Good whisky was going to become rare very quickly, but his gut said he wouldn't be alive long enough to enjoy it. A civil war was coming, one he'd likely instigate.

Mohn had always kept things back, but he'd brought Mark into every project except the mysterious Solaris. The Old Man had even called him his right hand a few times. If he was freezing Mark out now, that could only mean one thing. The Old Man was going to move against him, removing him as director and probably executing him. The only question was, how soon would the hammer fall?

There were people loyal to him, almost a third of the staff. Not enough to win, just enough to cripple what could be the last remaining bastion of human power in this crazy new world. If Mark fled though, it would mean abandoning the people who supported him. People like Benson. His people would be singled out, those most loyal purged. The rest would be under constant suspicion. The dilemma was maddening. He couldn't flee, but if he stayed he was as good as dead.

Then there was the matter of Irakesh. If they didn't stop the deathless, he'd likely succeed in setting up a power base on the west coast. He had at least one nuclear weapon and, if Jordan's reports were accurate, could control the tide of corpses sweeping the world. That made him the top threat to Mohn security. The Old Man saw that. It was inconceivable to think otherwise. At every juncture he'd outthought Mark. The Old Man's gift for understanding the context of a situation was unparalleled.

Mark leaned back in his chair, enjoying another sip as he chewed on the problem. If Mohn knew Irakesh had to be stopped yet was choosing not to, either the Old Man knew something about Irakesh's capabilities that he hadn't shared, or it meant that he was in league with him somehow. The first was quite likely, since Mohn had access to parts of the intelligence network even Mark hadn't been granted. The second sounded ludicrous, but Mark was too meticulous to dismiss it out of hand.

He withdrew his phone, swiping to his contacts and thumbing Ops. The red button flared twice, then shifted to bright green as he was connected.

"Yes, Director?" Benson answered. Her tone was facilitating, but not simpering. She'd been an excellent choice. She'd go far, if she survived the next week.

"Have viper six prepared for deployment. Send a team down to the brig and have detainees Jordan and Gregg brought to the tarmac," he ordered, setting his glass down and rising from his chair. He moved over to the mirror, studying his reflection. The pressed shirt was immaculate, but the tie was looser around the neck than he liked. His fingers itched to pull the slender silk until it too was immaculate. He denied the urge.

"Yes, sir," Benson replied. "Shall I notify you when they reach the tarmac?"

"Do that," he ordered, grabbing his coat from the bed as he moved for the door. "Also, have Object Two withdrawn from the vault and brought to the tarmac. Give custody to Commander Jordan."

"Acknowledged," she replied, then terminated the connection. That made him smile. He loved it when she took initiative.

Mark waved his hand in front of the door, stepping through before it finished sliding open with its accompanying hiss. The hall was empty, unsurprising since only the highest ranking officers were allowed housing in section seven. He walked up the corridor, shoes squeaking on the concrete as he rounded the corner.

He froze. A familiar figure stood before the elevators, a simple coincidence by all appearances. The Old Man's icy eyes glittered as they studied Mark, his fair hair so blond it was almost white. Not the kind of white you saw in the elderly, but the lustrous white of the Nordic. Just how old was he, anyway? He'd barely changed in the years that Mark had known him.

"Hello, Mark," the Old Man said, gesturing to the elevator. "Going down to Ops?"

"Yes, I was on my way there now," he said, striding down the corridor in his best attempt at appearing confident. Mohn knew.

The elevator chimed and the doors slid open, revealing a pair of black-clad security guards in full gear. Not his men. Mark stepped into the elevator, turning his back to the soldiers as Mohn joined him. The Old Man pressed the Ops button and the doors slid shut. He was silent until the car began moving.

"I'm told you had Object Two removed from the vault," he said, shifting to face Mark. His face revealed nothing. The tone was conversational.

"And?" Mark asked, staring back with all the intensity he could muster. If the Old Man was trying for a confession, he'd be sorely disappointed. Mark wasn't giving him anything.

The elevator came to a smooth halt. Mohn didn't answer, instead facing the soldiers. "Gentlemen, give us the room, please."

The doors slid open and both soldiers filed out. Mohn said nothing until the doors closed. "Mark, you withdrew an item of incredible power and put it in the hands of a god. How could you be that stupid? What if she hadn't just given it meekly back? She could have torn through this facility like a hurricane and I promise you, nothing we have could have stopped her."

Mark heaved an internal sigh of relief. The Old Man was talking about the training session he'd allowed Liz, not the order that would end Mark's career and possibly his life. He might not know that Jordan, Liz, and Object Two were on their way to the tarmac even now. "I believed she would cooperate. If she had resisted she may have done some damage, but we'd have contained her. Object Two might give her an edge, but it's just a sword."

Mohn scrubbed a hand through his hair, obvious irritation flashing across his features. Mark had never been on the receiving side of that irritation, but it looked as if that was about to change.

"I don't think you heard me," Mohn said, eyes skewering Mark. "A. God. As in a literal god, or something so close it doesn't matter.

What we're seeing is just the beginning. In a year that young woman could tear through this entire facility with ease. In ten we wouldn't even see her do it. We'd just die. Object Two fuels everything she is, Mark. You have no idea how powerful it is."

"If you do, then why haven't you told me? What is it you know that I don't? Because all the data we've collected on the sword say it's a repository for energy with a sharp edge. She can kill people with it, but her claws already worked fine. So why don't you enlighten me, Leif?"

"You checked my log records. You know I've been speaking to London," the Old Man replied, crossing his arms. He studied Mark for a long moment before speaking again. "You've never asked how I came by Object One, or how I know the things I do about the ancient world. Do you want to know how I know what one of them can do with an object like number two? Because I've met a god, Mark. Seen him in all his terrible fury. They are human if you want to get technical, but their lifespan is measured in millennia. They can modify their own DNA. Kill with a thought. Our ancestors worshipped them and they were right to."

"My god, you work for one of them," Mark said, eyes widening. He took a step back, but there was nowhere to go. "Is that why you founded this company? To help one of them control the world?"

"It's far more complex than that," Mohn replied, raising a hand to forestall Mark's protest. "Hear me out. It's past time I shared this with someone and I can't think of anyone better than you. You *are* my right hand, Mark. And I'm desperate enough to gamble everything, if it will ensure your continued loyalty. I need you, Mark."

"I'm listening."

"Do you remember when I revealed Object One to the board back in Panama?" the Old Man asked, touching his chest with two fingers.

"How could I forget? That was the moment you galvanized the board into coming here," Mark replied. He crossed his arms, still feeling trapped. "You said you'd received it from your grandfather, that it had some sort of powers."

"That last part was a lie. I didn't receive it from my grandfather. I *was* my grandfather, Mark," the Old Man explained, eyes searching. "I've faked my own death several times, so people didn't suspect that I never aged."

"Come again?" was all Mark could muster.

"I was born in 1838 in Helsinki. A woodsman by trade, if you can believe that. I hunted my own game and sold lumber. Didn't make much, but I survived. One day I came into town with a haul of wolf pelts and there wasn't anyone there. Everyone had disappeared. Doors were open. Fires still burned in hearths. But the people? They were just gone, Mark. Every last person I'd ever known. Gone."

Mark reeled, leaning his back against the smooth metal wall as he struggled to understand what he was hearing. Eighteen thirty-eight? That would make him, what? A hundred and seventy-five years old. Mohn could have passed for forty.

"A patch of darkness detached from the night. It scooped me up and carried me into the old inn. Next thing I knew, I was plopped into a chair. Then *he* sat down across from me," Mohn explained, eyes distant as he related the tale. "He had leathery skin and glowing green eyes. It was completely foreign to me. I'd never seen anyone like that before. Never seen anyone who didn't look like me. Then he opened his mouth and showed me fangs that could chew the flesh from your bones. I was terrified, Mark. I knew what he was then. A draugr, a creature straight out of Norse legend. I also knew what had befallen my village. This thing had eaten them.

"The draugr gave me a choice. I could serve it in life, growing powerful and outliving everyone around me. Or I could die a swift death. It wasn't a difficult choice, Mark," the Old Man explained, shoulders slumping. "I did things I wasn't proud of. Helped it learn how the world had changed since it had last awoken. I spent the next year as a slave, doing whatever it wished of me. We traveled throughout eastern Europe visiting what he called sites of power."

"Did this monster have a name?" Mark demanded.

"His name was Usir," the Old Man replied. He paused for a long moment before continuing.

"Traveling with him was horrific. We'd blaze through a town in a matter of hours, draining the inhabitants dry. His thirst was unquenchable. Mark, *we* gave rise to the legends of vampires in Europe. I'm sure of it. I even met Stoker, and his accounts were not far off the mark. Then the day came that my master told me he would return to his slumber.

"He demanded that I prepare the way for his eventual awakening. That the day would come when he would emerge to reclaim his rightful place, and that I would be foremost among his servants," he said, unbuttoning his purple shirt and exposing a gold chain. He withdrew the pendant, a clearly Egyptian Eye of Horus with a ruby set in the center. "Usir gave me this. He hung it around my neck himself. The draugr told me he could use it to find me. He also told me it would keep me alive until the world was ready for his return, and that if I deviated in my task, he would know. I'd seen his wrath, Mark. It terrifies me still, almost two centuries later."

"So you sold your soul to this thing?" Mark asked, hurling the words like spears. "This thing could be responsible for the zombie virus, and you're following it?"

"Let me finish," the Old Man growled, eyes tightening. "I never said I agreed. After the draugr left I ran, fast and hard. I headed south, visiting libraries and sharing soup with wizened grandmothers willing to share old tales. There had to be some proof that I wasn't crazy. It took years to find it. There were myths and legends everywhere, but almost nothing tangible. Except for me. I stopped aging, Mark. At first I just thought it was good luck, but when I hadn't changed for a decade I knew. The draugr's amulet was proof of an ancient civilization we couldn't begin to understand. I'd felt its power and beside it, we're nothing. Yet my only chance of beating it lay in understanding it. I needed to harness the same power they used, what I considered magic back then. That was long before the discovery of signals.

"So I used the years to my advantage. I cultivated wealth and influence, because I had the luxury of understanding time in a way very few people can," he explained, pausing to lick his lips. "Mark, over the last two centuries I've gotten the briefest taste of what it's like for them. What it's like to be a god. But all I have is the immortality and a few paltry trinkets I've collected, not the raw power they wield. These things shaped empires that spanned continents. You know what a young werewolf can do. Imagine the power of a millennia-old goddess."

"You were going to tell me about how you weren't selling out humanity," Mark gave back, eyeing the Old Man critically.

"After Usir left I didn't have any compulsion to serve him, but at the same time I knew he'd return," the Old Man explained, shaking his head. "So I went about learning the world. Learning as much about the past as I could. I founded archeological digs and visited ancient ruins. I was a big part of Egyptology back in the nineteen-twenties. I've spent time in South America and India. Always searching for our roots, for some proof of where this thing came from. I found his fingerprints everywhere. He manipulated cultures throughout history; I'm sure of it. From Chichen Itza in the sixth century to Egypt an ocean away. I think the audacious bastard even played Imhotep in third-dynasty Egypt. He taught Djoser how to make pyramids. Always he was found in a culture that created pyramids. Why? What was the significance to a timeless god about the specific shape of a pyramid? Why were they always made of stone?"

Mark was shocked to his core. So much time to learn the world, to study patterns. If you knew what to look for, that is. So many of the company's mysterious operations suddenly made sense.

"My search for the answers led to the founding of this company. I came to understand the galactic procession, that the world would eventually return to the conditions that allowed these gods to flourish. I knew the time was fast approaching, but I hadn't even guessed there might be something like the viruses they unleashed. I did suspect the Arks and even learned where the first one would appear."

"You're talking about Peru," Mark interjected.

"Exactly," the Old Man replied, shaking his head. "I had no idea what we'd find within, but I knew we had to learn all we could before my master returned."

The fact that the Old Man still called this Usir 'master' terrified

Mark. "So what was your goal in the end? You've gathered all this knowledge. Now what? Are we going to fight them?" he asked.

"I honestly don't think we *can* fight them," Mohn said, giving the first shrug Mark had ever seen. "But I'm going to try. We're going to try. I hope you understand what an immense risk I'm taking in trusting you, Mark. I hope I have your continued loyalty."

The whole thing sounded good. Sounded plausible, maybe because of its implausibility. Yet a detail nagged at Mark. If the Old Man wasn't serving this master any longer, why all the calls to London? Mohn was lying, trying to lull Mark into complacency.

"Of course," Mark answered smoothly, dropping his arms to his sides. The last few grains were slipping down the hourglass. Whatever the Old Man's endgame was, Mark was certain he was about to find out. "We're in this together."

61

WHOLE ONCE MORE

The Mother smiled for the first time in a very, very long while. She swept down the ramp into the central chamber, admiring the handiwork of the past several days. Each of the control obelisks shone with a faint inner light, a pale shadow of the energy the rods would one day hold. It wasn't much, but it illuminated the glyphs she'd lovingly painted on the walls all those millennia ago.

The labor had taken her nearly a century, each pictograph lovingly crafted. It was a diary in a way, the remembrance of the events that had led her here. The endless war with the deathless, the desperate struggle to keep them from the shores of this strange continent. Even loss and rebirth of Osiris and the struggle to wrest the secrets left behind by the Builders. She approached one of her favorite scenes, the very first she'd painted.

It showed her standing atop a spire in a massive city. An alien city, one she'd never fully understood in the brief months she'd studied it before it sank beneath the waves. One of the few mysteries remaining to her back then. After all, the world had been her plaything. She'd been a goddess, worshiped by entire peoples under many different names in just as many lands. Isis. Pombo. The Mother. There were so many.

She stroked the cool wall, fingers feeling a familiar electric rush as they brushed the stone. That was why they'd chosen not just stone, but this stone in particular. Quartz contained the energy better than nearly any other substance save Sunsteel. It was easily mined and plentiful throughout the world, making it ideal for the inner core. The outer core was cut from obsidian, etched smooth through shaping. That channeled sun and moon both, feeding the power into the Ark's nearly limitless reserves.

Those reserves were sadly depleted now. It would be years before the place was fully functional. Perhaps decades depending on how much power she used along the way. It was a dangerous time, a time when her stronghold provided far less than it someday would. Yet it was still an improvement over the ruin she'd found when she'd first awoken.

"Where are they now, Yukon?" she asked, stroking her loyal companion's neck as she strode through the inner chamber. It was a mystery she had no way of answering, save for attempting to contact the Ark of the Redwood. That might prove fruitless, or it might reveal the Ark's new owner. Would that be Blair? Or Irakesh?

If it *had* been uncovered, what of the most precious cargo within? What of her daughter, willful and stubborn and beautiful. Jes'Ka was ready for this new world, but was the world ready for her?

The Mother strode through the remainder of the chamber, passing by the Mother's hand and entering the heart. Its white walls pulsed slowly with energy, in time with her heartbeat. How many generations of man had passed while she'd slumbered here?

She rested a hand on the rejuvenator, knowing that somewhere her daughter rested in a similar one. What should she do? She would meditate and pray that the small strength this place gave Blair would be enough to help the Ka-Dun secure the Ark of the Redwood so that she might be reunited with her daughter.

The lights flickered and when they resumed, their illumination had lessened. She whirled, sensing movement behind her. A faint greenish glow came from the central chamber, a familiar glow. The Mother exited the rejuvenation chamber, shifting to her wolf form instinctively as she took in the figure before her.

"By the gods," she whispered, the words the same she'd uttered nearly twenty-five millennia before, when she'd first laid eyes on the shimmering figure. "Ka, how have you come here?"

The translucent figure met her impassively, its flat, black eyes and long, thin neck too alien to be human. It had two hands and two legs, but each hand possessed only four fingers. Its skin was a deep green. Her own age had lacked a word to describe the figure, but this new age supplied it. Ka was a hologram.

"Greetings, Ka-Ken," Ka offered, inclining its head. The hologram flickered, and the lights dimmed further. "I must be brief. Accessing the systems here drains the little power remaining."

"I ask again, how have you come here?" the Mother asked, extending an arm. The reassuring weight of the Primary Access Key coalesced in her hand, its golden length held defensively before her. "You should be imprisoned in the Nexus."

"This was so, until very recently," Ka said, giving another bob of its head. "A hominid recently entered the Nexus and accessed my systems. Doing so drained the primary battery, and the Nexus entered hibernation. When this occurred I was shunted to background systems."

"That doesn't explain how you came to be here," the Mother countered, eyes narrowing. "Explain. Tell me of this hominid."

"Assuredly," Ka said, to all appearances the dutiful servant. The Mother knew just how deceptive that appearance was, memories of the First Ark large in her mind. Ka flickered again. "The Nexus sought to offload my matrix to the first available Ark. When you initiated repairs, the Ark rebooted, which removed the security preventing me from entering. When the Nexus detected this I was automatically shunted here."

"And this hominid?" the Mother asked, stomach twisting in knots. If Set had somehow entered the Nexus...

"Three hominids, in truth," Ka corrected, flickering wildly for a moment before continuing. "Their helixes had been shaped in a manner similar to the mutagen you and I crafted together."

"They're deathless?" the Mother asked, taking a hostile step forward. She growled low in her throat.

"No, Ka-Ken. Their helixes are different. In many ways they are weaker than either the deathless or the champions you have created," Ka explained. It gestured at the air next to it and an image of three people appeared.

One was male, young and handsome with impetuous eyes. He wore black clothing cut from this era, and his gaze lacked the green glow of the deathless. Behind him stood a pair of women. The closer was beautiful and of an age with the man, strong and confident much like Jes'Ka. Her hair was a river of brown cascading down her back, and her skin was darker than the man's. A descendent of the people she'd once ruled on the northern continent?

The last was little more than a child, an auburn-haired female on the eve of adulthood. Her eyes were wide with fear.

"Who shaped them?" she asked. They appeared normal in every way, but then so did she before she shifted.

"The progeny of the Builders," Ka said, dimming until only a bare shade remained. Its voice was tinny and barely above a whisper now. "They have returned to this world, and their plans do not bode well for your species."

The Mother shifted back to human form, leaning heavily on her staff. She knew little of the Builders and nothing of their progeny. She glanced up to ask Ka another question, but the hologram disappeared as the lights of her Ark flickered and died.

62

JES'KA

T revor's hands clenched and unclenched as he paced back and forth just inside the Ark's wide entryway. The massive recess cut into the stone was identical to the pyramid in Peru. An invisible plane held back the ocean, allowing him to gaze out into its black depths. The same depths where he'd watched Cyntia slaughter Blair's friend and possibly Blair himself. Even if he'd survived Cyntia's brutal attack, Blair had probably died when the ocean crashed over him. And it was Trevor's fault.

He hadn't seen what had happened at the end. Just as he'd set the silver box down in the corner, he'd heard a tremendous roar. The ocean had filled the corridor Irakesh had created, obliterating all traces of their passage and leaving them protected within the Ark's entryway. If there was any solace it was that Cyntia had mercifully perished out there somewhere.

"This is the sweetest thing I have tasted in this new age," Irakesh said, stepping up to the water and brushing it with an outstretched hand. "The journey was long, but now the true work can begin."

Trevor looked sidelong at his master, hating him with an intensity that he'd not realized himself capable of. The things he'd been asked to do were unjust in a way no one should ever ask of another. The depths of Irakesh's cruelty continued to amaze him. Yet somehow it wasn't personal or malicious. To Irakesh his victory was all that mattered and Trevor's friends were just casualties. It was the indifferent malevolence of a cat toying with prey.

"Do you want me to carry the nuke inside?" Trevor asked. He needed to escape. He just couldn't be in the same room with this monster anymore.

"No, leave it. Cyntia will carry it," Irakesh replied. He turned a wicked grin on Trevor, ebony skull gleaming under a sheen of condensation.

"Cyntia's dead," Trevor said, gesturing at the water. "There's no way she could have survived that." He was horrified by the alternative.

"Are you so certain? We shall see," Irakesh mused, raising a black eyebrow. He pushed past Trevor and into the corridor leading deeper into the Ark. "Come. Let us explore. I grew up with legends of this place, but have never seen the inside. This is the first Ark Isis ruled wholly by herself, though Ptah had a large hand in its discovery and reshaping."

Trevor trailed after, vaguely curious about these gods Irakesh had mentioned, but mostly consumed by the knot of rage that had been growing since he'd found himself enslaved to the bastard's will.

They entered a corridor with high ceilings, faintly illuminated by silvery glyphs where the walls met the ceiling. They revealed vast scenes of glorious battles between beleaguered silver figures and twisted black ones. The farther they passed the more the shape of those battles grew clear. At first the silver figures had been driven back, but eventually they had allied with four-legged creatures he took to be wolves. Then they had turned the tide, driving the black figures off a cliff and into the ocean.

"Do you see that glow up ahead? That's the central chamber. From there I have complete control over this place," Irakesh said, nearly skipping in his apparent eagerness. It was the happiest Trevor had ever seen him. Like a child clapping its hands as it stood over the corpses of murdered parents.

They entered a wide chamber with high-vaulted ceilings lost in darkness. Five jet-black obelisks dominated the room, one in each corner and a central one that was larger than the rest. Trevor could feel the power they hummed with, though it was so faint he had to strain to catch the echo they gave off.

Beyond the obelisks lay a wide doorway flanked by statues, both female werewolves by the size. Through that doorway came a faint white glow, soft but brighter than the walls in this room or the corridor leading here. Irakesh strode boldly across the floor, clearly aimed at that room.

Trevor followed, gawking at his surroundings despite the numbing horror of all he'd experienced in recent weeks. There was still beauty in the world, even if he could barely appreciate it. They entered the mysterious room, which was empty save for a series of long clear sarcophagi more at home in Stargate than anywhere in their world. They glittered with gemstones along the surface, rubies and emeralds and diamonds. Each held their own inner light, which pulsed and flowed like a heartbeat. The heartbeat of the occupants.

Within the central one lay a black-clothed woman with lustrous blond hair and youthful features. She was beautiful, but something about her was both familiar and troubling. It was impossible that Trevor could know her, but there was something about her. Some sort of mental impression perhaps? His ignorance irritated him.

"By the sun itself," Irakesh breathed, dropping to a crouch next to the sarcophagus. He placed his hands against the amber substance, which glowed faintly at his touch. "Trevor, do you know who this is? Never in my wildest dreams could I have guessed we'd find such a treasure."

"Who is she?" Trevor asked, studying her sleeping face. Another immortal of some kind, one with powers and knowledge he could only guess at.

"Jes'Ka, daughter of Isis. The one you know as the Mother," Irakesh explained, rising and facing Trevor. His eyes were lit with a feverish gleam. "She slumbers because her mother did not trust her with a key. No doubt Isis planned to awaken her after she'd secured this land. Jes'Ka was proud, stubborn, and powerful. If she could be turned to our cause, we could rule this entire continent in a single generation."

"Isn't she a werewolf?" Trevor asked, resting the butt of his rifle on the floor. He knelt to peer into the sarcophagus. He recognized objectively that she was beautiful but the part of him that might have felt anything had died when his heart stopped. "If you let her out, what's to stop her from tearing us apart?"

"I will," came a low growl from behind him. Trevor spun, rifle snapping to his shoulder as he took aim at the speaker. Cyntia stood in her human form, naked and blue from the cold. She was drenched, which wasn't entirely bad since she'd desperately needed a bath. She stood gingerly on her right leg, which was curiously whiter than the left. "Let the bitch out. If she wishes to fight I will gut her and feast on her entrails."

"Oh, Cyntia," Irakesh said, delivering one of the condescending smiles he seemed so good at. "Jes'Ka would end your pitiful existence before you even knew she'd struck. If she wished it, Trevor and I would be dead soon after. She has had centuries to grow in strength, where you have had a bare handful of weeks. You have grown strong and show much potential, but this fight is beyond you."

"So I'll ask again, what's to stop her from tearing us apart?" Trevor asked, lowering the rifle. His finger itched to stroke the trigger, to shoot Cyntia between those fevered blue eyes. Something still held him back. He strained against it, grinding his teeth.

"She has need of me," Irakesh said, rising to his feet. He stared longingly into the sarcophagus and Trevor got the impression it was more than simple infatuation driving him. "I have the key to her Ark. Only a male can control such a structure—a male or the Mother. She cannot use the key and thus needs a male to administer for her."

"Couldn't she kill you and give it to Blair?" Trevor asked, a warm sliver of glee surging through him at the fury that twisted Irakesh's expression.

"Not if the Ka-Dun is dead. If I am her only option then she will see reason. Jes'Ka was always pragmatic and while she generally obeyed her mother's wishes, she was known to think for herself. She didn't have the same blind hatred for the deathless many of her kind had. Perhaps because of her father, Osiris," he said, stroking the glass-like substance.

"Yeah, I don't think that's going to work out," Trevor said, eyes alighting on another rejuvenator. "She's not the only occupant. This one has a male, Irakesh."

63

ESCAPE

Jordan tensed as he stepped from the elevator into controlled chaos. Dozens of techs moved between hundreds of vehicles, everything from helicopters like the X-408 he'd taken to Peru to sleek jets to all-terrain armored vehicles. The entire left side of the hangar was lined with huge crates containing stinger missiles, fifty-caliber rounds and a host of other nasty surprises Mohn could level at its enemies. So much hardware. It might have been at home on a military base, but the idea of a corporation possessing so much was mind boggling. Even for Mohn Corp.

"Jordan, why did they bring us here?" Liz whispered, finally stepping from the elevator into the glow of the halogens. Her hair shone copper. She peered around warily, as if expecting an ambush. He wasn't sure she was wrong to do so.

"Honestly?" Jordan asked, scanning the immediate vicinity. "I haven't the faintest fucking clue. We should have been escorted, at the very least. Even if they reinstated me, you're still a prisoner and they don't let prisoners just wander around. I can't get a read on the situation. This isn't at all like the Director."

"Commander Jordan," a female voice boomed. He turned to see a group of black-clad soldiers trotting up. The one bringing up the rear was pushing a wide metal cart that contained a single black case about two feet wide and nearly six feet long. Sniper rifle? The leader of the soldiers approached, a pretty Asian woman with shoulder-length black hair. She extended a black tablet. "My name is Kristi Benson. Director Phillips asked me to deliver this to you. Please sign here, sir."

Jordan scanned the words on the screen, jaw dropping. "The Director ordered this?"

"Yes, sir. Please sign, sir. I have to get back down to the vault," Benson said, nodding at the tablet. She darted a furtive glance over her shoulder, which spoke volumes. Whatever the Director had set into motion hadn't been blessed by the Old Man.

Jordan used the attached stylus to sign the line at the bottom of the screen, then handed the tablet back. Benson accepted it, snapping a salute. "Thank you, sir. Your ride is on the south side of the hangar, sir, bay thirteen. Crew is waiting." Then she and her companions trotted away, leaving Jordan and Liz standing next to the strange black case.

"What is it?" Liz asked, squatting next to the cart.

"Object Two. The Director sent us the sword, and according to that tablet we've been authorized to make a strike on San Francisco," he said, kneeling and reaching for the twin clasps holding the case shut. He snapped them, flipping open the top. Sure enough, a wide-bladed sword lay on black foam, its golden blade gleaming even in the thin light. "That shouldn't be possible. I attended a board meeting and the Old Man unilaterally denied this mission. Either he had a sudden change of heart or the Director is playing a very dangerous game."

"So that's it? We just walk out of here? Just like that?" Liz asked. Jordan couldn't blame her for being skeptical. He felt the same.

"No, we fly out of here. The Director's given us a pilot and a plane capable of getting us to San Francisco," he explained, snapping the case shut. He picked it up by its handle, muscles straining from the weight. The case was heavy, the blade even heavier. He handed it across to Liz, who took it effortlessly. "Come on. Let's get the hell out of here before they change their minds."

Jordan set off between the wide orange lines marking the area designed for walking. They passed a number of hangar bays on either side, each with a full crew servicing one of the aircraft or land vehicles Mohn had apparently stockpiled. They'd clearly been gearing up for war and had done so for years, if this place was any indication.

They moved in silence, Liz keeping Jordan's brisk pace without effort despite her burden. Some feminist somewhere must be smiling at *that* turn of events. They made their way around a central area where four bombers squatted, each angled towards a single runway that led up a gentle slope into a tube that disappeared into darkness. That must be how they got to the surface.

He passed a black number sixteen painted in huge block letters next to a hangar. The next read fifteen. He scanned down the row as they approached, going slack-jawed at what was waiting there. A sleek black jet, just over seventy feet long. It resembled a Learjet, but there were no windows and the engines hugged the body of the aircraft. It looked faster than diarrhea in Mexico.

"Stop," roared an authoritative voice.

Jordan spun to see two dozen guards spreading out to flank them. All over the hangar personnel stopped what they were doing. Techs took cover, while soldiers looked at tablets as they urgently sought orders.

"I guess this might be a little more complicated than I thought," Jordan said, rolling his arms in their sockets as he unlimbered for combat.

"It can't ever be easy, can it?" Liz asked. She dropped to one knee and flipped the catches on the case, withdrawing the golden sword within.

"Commander Jordan, I've been ordered to take you into custody," a solider near the center of the line called. He didn't approach though, which wasn't surprising. They'd have been briefed on the whole werewolf thing. "Lie face down with your arms behind your back. Any resistance will be met with terminal force."

"How do you want to handle this?" Liz asked, rising into a crouch with the sword held loosely in one hand. She was focused on the soldiers, scanning them like a trained soldier. She'd come a long way.

"Commander," called a thickly accented voice from behind them. "Bay doors overridden. Slow attackers and Yuri can get craft airborne. Need sixty seconds."

"There's your answer," Jordan said, already moving. He blurred forward, not even bothering to shift.

Gunshots cracked around him, but he was simply too fast to track, just like the werewolf back in Peru when this had all started just a few months back. Jordan skidded to a halt next to his first target, grabbing the man's forearm as shell casings spun slowly end over end in the air above the rifle. He yanked it from the man's grasp, slamming the butt of the weapon into the man's groin. It spilled him to the ground and hopefully out of the fight.

Jordan could have done something a lot more permanent, but these men were just following orders.

Liz had no such compunctions, and he couldn't blame her. After all, it had been him who had led the men that had assaulted her first in Peru then later in San Diego. She saw Mohn as the enemy and gave that enemy no quarter.

The copper-haired woman vanished briefly, then abruptly reappeared in the shadow of the soldier who'd called for them to lay down arms. She too moved in slow motion, the blade of her new sword cutting a lethal arc toward the man's throat. Jordan was both repulsed and a bit proud. Liz had correctly surmised that the best way to win was to remove their enemy's commanding officer. That would leave them confused, making it easier to take out the rest.

Jordan blurred to his next target, shattering the man's jaw with a right hook. Then he glided forward to kick another man in the knee. By the time Liz's sword claimed its victim Jordan had downed two more. He kept right on going, blurring through their ranks with nonlethal ferocity. If he could down them all, they'd live. Any he missed would fall to Liz.

Just like that it was over, and Jordan was left blinking at a sea of groaning figures. All were in too much pain to fight, which was just as well for them.

"My god, Jordan," Liz said, trotting in his direction. "I've never seen anyone move like that, not even Blair. And you're not even in wolf form."

"I guess I just needed incentive," Jordan said, turning to sprint back towards the plane. The engines had already started their low howl. He turned to Liz as they ran up the back ramp into the cargo hold. "I wanted to save as many as possible. Not their fault they were ordered to fight us."

Liz eyed him curiously but didn't answer as they darted up the gangplank into the plane. Then the gangplank folded up behind them and the vehicle began moving forward.

"Let's hope San Francisco is just as easy," he muttered.

64

REINFORCEMENTS

B lair stared out the wide bay window at the redwood-covered hills sprawling across the town of Mill Valley. It was beautiful, the towering trees with their thick canopies and the wall of mist clinging to the slopes of Mount Tamalpais. Even the homes were beautiful, a modernist architecture that had been sculpted to blend with nature rather than dominate it. It was exactly the sort of place he'd always dreamed of living, perhaps even in a mansion like the one he now stood in.

Something drifted down the misty road. Or several somethings, to be more precise. A half dozen figures shambled down Miller Avenue towards the freeway. Oddly, they moved with single-minded purpose. That was new. Normally groups of zombies would shamble in roughly the same direction, but often veered off on their own. These walked in a single-file line.

There was movement directly below the window, a flash of orangish red in the high grass. Blair leaned closer to the glass, trying to find the cause. To his surprise he found a large fox staring up at him, ears cocked in his direction. Its gaze met his unflinchingly. It was clearly aware of him and just as clearly fighting to get his attention.

Flee. You must flee.

Blair could only gawk. The idea that he could speak to an animal had never occurred to him. The fox met his gaze unflinchingly, its thoughts tinged with concern for a fellow pack mate. Did foxes even have packs?

Flee. Run far and fast and low. They are slow but they do not tire. Many, many make for the sea, towards the bridge of gold.

"They're heading for the Golden Gate Bridge," Blair muttered, expressing his thanks to the fox. It darted away into the underbrush, gone so quickly he questioned whether he'd seen it at all.

"Did you say something?" Steve called from the kitchen. Blair turned to glance at him. Steve stood next to the marble-covered island with a long-stemmed wine glass in one hand and a hunk of sausage in the other. He took a generous mouthful of a dark red as he awaited Blair's answer.

"The dead, they're all heading in one direction. Towards the Golden Gate Bridge," Blair replied, crossing the hardwood floor and entering the kitchen. It was cold, but not unpleasantly so. This place had lost heat just like every other house, but at least it was well insulated.

"So? Irakesh probably called them there for some reason. All the more reason to stay away," Steve replied, setting his glass on the counter. He withdrew a wickedly sharp knife from the block near the corner, using it to slice the sausage into bite-sized pieces.

"Maybe," Blair said, turning away in disgust. He resumed his position near the window, watching as more undead moved down the four-lane street towards the bay. He counted dozens and this was one little part of Marin County. How many thousands were moving that way? How far did Irakesh's influence extend?

"Do you hear that?" Steve asked. He crossed to the window, wine glass back in his hand and napkin in the other so he could dab at his lips.

Blair listened. There was a low hum in the distance. Familiar, but too distant to identify. "Is that a plane?"

"Yeah," Steve said, swirling the contents of his glass. "Something larger, but not quite a 747. Sounds higher pitched than the plane that got us here. It's definitely approaching."

"So who the hell is it?" Blair wondered, sliding open the glass door and stepping onto the deck. It sat on top of stilts over a steep drop into the heavily wooded valley. "Irakesh is already here. No one else should have a working plane and even if they did, why come here? It's too much of a coincidence."

"It doesn't matter," Steve said, taking another mouthful of wine. He made the action refined. Classy. The bastard had always been able to do that. Steve stepped onto the deck. "We should go back inside. If it has anything to do with us we don't want them to know we're here."

"You can go back inside if you want," Blair said, shifting. His skin tingled as his clothing disappeared. It came so easily now. He turned to stare down at Steve. "I'm going to find out who it is. If they're an ally I want to link up with them. If they're another enemy, we need to know about it."

"Blair, this is madness," Steve said, looking up from his wine. His eyes were so intense, almost glowing. "What if you get killed? You'll be handing whoever it is the key to the Mother's Ark. Is that what you want? You have to be less reckless. Listen, if you're going to do this you really should give me the key first."

Blair hesitated. His head ached. Was it reckless? What if Steve was right? If he ran into another enemy, maybe an ally of Irakesh, he might give up the key and lose *another* Ark. "You're right. I'll stay here. It's not worth the risk."

"There you're wrong," Steve said, taking a step closer. He rested his hand on Blair's arm. The touch was oily, but Blair didn't pull away. "Investigating is a good idea. Bringing the key with you is not. Blair, we've been friends for a long time but I've got to level with you. You've been screwing up. Badly. How many times have we faced Irakesh and how many times have we won? First we lost Liz and Jordan, and now Bridget. I know you cared for her, Blair. If you had turned over the key, maybe she'd still be alive."

A wave of guilt crashed over Blair, and he briefly considered giving over the key. Was that the right choice? Then the beast gave a low, deep growl. There were no words, but the meaning was clear. Be wary.

His gaze snapped up to Steve, and understanding bloomed. This wasn't the first time he'd felt the pressure at the base of his skull. Not the first time he'd doubted himself in the wallowing way the old Blair would have done. Each and every time it happened when Steve was talking. More specifically, when Steve was asking him to give up the key.

"You. Fucking. Bastard," Blair snarled, lunging into a blur. He seized Steve by the neck, hurling him through the sliding glass door and into the side of the refrigerator with bone-crunching force. Steve slumped to the base of the fridge, shirt covered in blood and one rib poking out of the soft silk. "You've been shaping me the whole time, haven't you?"

"How could you think that?" Steve rasped, coughing up a little blood. The rib disappeared back into the shirt with a pop. "We're allies, Blair. I'm just being honest and you're being paranoid."

The tingling started at the base of Blair's skull again, but this time he was prepared. He could see the faint spiderwebs of energy coming from Steve's eyes, settling over him like a net. Blair concentrated and that net shattered into tendrils of light.

"Get up," he roared, taking a step towards Steve's crumpled form. "Fight, you deceitful fucking coward. I'm not falling for your bullshit, not this time."

Steve looked sadly up at him, which didn't surprise Blair in the slightest. He'd always used the lie-and-deny strategy, even after it was obvious that he'd been caught doing something wrong. This was no different.

"I'm not going to fight you, Blair," he said, giving a sigh as he rose shakily to his feet. "I know you're grieving over Bridget's death, but—"

Blair blurred, gliding forward and balling his fist. He punched Steve in the side of the head with so much force that it rebounded off the refrigerator. Then he picked Steve up and hurled him through the plate-glass window onto the deck outside. Blair stalked after him, looming over Steve's shattered and bleeding form.

"You don't get to say her name. Ever," he growled, planting a foot on Steve's back. "This is how we're going to play things. I'm going to go investigate that plane. You're going to wait here. If you try to flee I will hunt you down, and this time I'll kill you, Steve. No more discussion. No more bullshit arguments. I. Will. Kill. You. Do you understand me?"

The last words were breathed into Steve's ear as he leaned down close enough to snap the bastard's neck with his fangs.

"Fine," Steve rasped, not resisting in any way.

"When I get back, we'll discuss our next course of action, but make no mistake. We're going after Irakesh and Cyntia. You're going to help me," Blair said, rising to his feet and stepping away from Steve's body. "Am I making myself clear?"

"That's suicide," Steve said, flipping onto his back and glaring up at him. He'd dropped the mask of civility, and Blair could see the hatred in his eyes.

"That's what you don't understand, Steve," Blair growled, baring his fangs. "You're already dead. I should kill you right now, and if you don't help me, I will. The only way you live through this is by redeeming yourself in the fight with Irakesh."

He spun without waiting for an answer. Blair leapt, bouncing off the trunk of a redwood with a blur-enhanced kick. He landed on top of a house, gouging the roof with clawed feet as he bounded again.

It took several more such hops to cross Mill Valley and then another three to scale the mountain on the far side. Then he was looking down into San Rafael, a patchwork of forested hills broken up by residential neighborhoods. A sleek black jet had slowed and began a gradual descent. It was headed west, towards the oak-dotted hills that lay between the highway and the coast. There must be a runway there.

Blair blurred, streaking down the hill to Highway 37. He followed it west, paralleling the plane's course as best he could. It grew easier as he whipped down the road. The plane was slowing and he had a better idea of where it was going to put down. They'd entered a more sparsely populated area, with long driveways winding up hills. Some of them were flatter than others. One in particular was a good half mile of straight road heading up a gentle slope to a sprawling winery. That was it.

Blair blurred again, leaping to the top of a mighty oak. It provided an excellent vantage of the winery, just in time for the plane's final descent. The military aircraft came down fast and hard, slamming onto the asphalt with a scream of rubber and a shower of sparks. The plane fishtailed, but the pilot was skilled and kept the craft from careening off the makeshift runway.

The stench of burnt rubber and jet fuel made his eyes water, but Blair held perfectly still as the plane rumbled to a halt in a cloud of dust near the rows of grape vines surrounding the villa. Moments later a small door behind the cockpit folded down to reveal three stairs. The first figure to emerge was shrouded in midnight body armor with an all-too-familiar M stenciled on the shoulder. Fucking Mohn. How did they always find him?

Then a second figure descended, her copper hair fluttering in the breeze as she reached the asphalt. It couldn't be, but it was. Liz wore simple black fatigues with the hilt of a golden sword extending over her right shoulder. She looked every inch the warrior princess.

Blair dropped from the tree, trotting toward the plane. He made sure he was in full view, easy for the Mohn goons to spot so they didn't panic when they saw a seven-foot werewolf approaching. Of course maybe that didn't phase this lot, since they were letting Liz roam free. She cocked her head, then slowly spun to face him.

"Blair?" she called when he was perhaps twenty feet distant. Liz lit up, a brilliant smile slipping into place. She ran toward him and he crashed into her, shifting back to human form as he hoisted her into a wonderful hug.

"I can't believe you're alive. How did you get here?" Blair asked, setting her down and turning to half face her companion.

"We had help on the inside," the man said, removing his helmet. It revealed Jordan's familiar chiseled jaw, with his clear blue eyes and blond stubble. "My old boss, actually. He was the only one to recognize the threat Irakesh poses, so he sent Liz and I to help you deal with the situation. Assuming it isn't too late. We saw the Ark in the bay. I'm guessing that means he's already inside?"

"Afraid so," Blair admitted, joy souring as he remembered how dire the situation was. "He quite literally parted the sea and let Trevor and Cyntia inside. So far as I know they're still there. I believe he's gathering zombies on the Golden Gate Bridge, though I haven't the faintest idea why."

"So where are Bridget and Steve?" Liz asked, still wearing that brilliant smile.

"Steve's waiting back at the mansion we confiscated in Mill Valley. Bridget's dead," he said, voice cracking.

65

DIRECTOR NO MORE

"Come in," Mark called, swirling his glass. He leaned back in the chair, feet propped atop his desk as he watched the door slide open.

A pair of black-clad soldiers in Kevlar were the first through, each leveling a submachine gun in his direction. They took positions at either side of the door, faces impassive as the Old Man stepped through behind them. He wore his usual black suit and matching tie, an armor of a different kind.

"That's the second day in a row you've been drinking Scotch," the Old Man said, taking a seat on the corner of Mark's bed. The tone was conversational, but his eyes were deadly serious. "One might think you were losing your edge."

"Or one could surmise that I've already accepted my fate and just want to enjoy myself a little before the end," Mark shot back with an impudent smile. If he was going down, he'd at least tweak the Old Man's nose a little.

"Why don't you pour me one as well?" the Old Man asked. Then he turned to the guards. "Leave us. I want some time alone with the Director."

"Sir?" the soldier on the right said, raising an eyebrow. The Old

Man's gaze tightened, and the soldier hurried from the room. His companion was only a half step behind.

The Old Man waited until the door slid shut before turning back to Mark. He waited patiently as Mark poured a second glass and handed it to him. "You've put me in a difficult position, Mark. Disobeyed a direct order that the entire senior staff witnessed. Freed prisoners who killed one man and wounded eleven others, then stole a very expensive aircraft. All with your direct authorization."

"You left out the part about arming Ms. Gregg with Object Two," Mark interjected, savoring a sip as he smiled at the Old Man. "I could probably add about another two dozen infractions you're probably unaware even exist."

"This attitude isn't like you, Mark," the Old Man said, heaving a heavy sigh. "What happened between us? Where was it exactly that I lost your trust?"

"You lost it the moment you cut me out of the loop, the very instant you started placing calls to London without telling me," Mark said, slamming a fist against the desk as he leaned towards Mohn. "That made it abundantly clear just how little you trusted me. Then you revealed that you worked for one of these immortals. I know you made noises about betraying them and saving humanity, but I don't buy that crap. Your soul was bought and paid for long before I was born."

"Astute to the end," the Old Man said, downing the contents of his glass in a single swallow. "You're right that I never intended to betray my master. It was an expedient lie, because I have no way of convincing you that serving Usir is the single best thing we can do for humanity. The only way our species survives the coming war."

"My god, you actually believe that," Mark said, setting his glass on the desk. "You don't see this as selling out the human race, do you?"

"Of course not," the Old Man replied, setting his own glass on the floor next to the bed. He withdrew the pendant from under his shirt. The ruby blazed, bathing the room scarlet. "It's a pity, really. The actions you've taken are misguided, but they come from a desire to help your fellow man. I recognize that, Mark, though clearly I can't condone them."

"Are you going to kill me with that thing?" Mark asked, nodding at the pendant.

"Goodness, no," the Old Man said, giving a coarse laugh. "Quite the contrary. I have important plans for you, Mark. Very soon, you'll begin to see things my way, once I introduce you to my master."

The ruby flared, its light painfully bright.

66

FINAL PREPARATIONS

I rakesh was dimly aware of his body's primal response to immediate life-threatening circumstances, a vestigial reminder of his mortal beginnings. But he wasn't a mortal any longer. The wall of water bordering the pyramid was thick and dark, alive with tiny shapes darting back and forth. The weight alone could crush a man, and if it did not, the cold and lack of oxygen would finish the grim work. Again, if he were mortal.

Yet he need fear none of that. Not because he was deathless, but because he was master of this place. The ruler of an entire Ark, something only a handful could boast even in his own time. After so many millennia he was finally an Ark Lord.

Not a drop of that water pierced the Ark's protective field, though he knew it could not be sustained forever. The sun was yet weak and did not provide enough strength to charge the Ark. Given time the shield would drain the little power remaining and water would flood the inner chambers. Jes'Ka would die, never having known the wonders of this strange new age.

A predatory grin spread across Irakesh's face. Very soon now power would cease to be a concern. He would finally be a god, an equal to his mother. He turned to Cyntia, who crouched behind him with the silver box cradled in her arms like offspring she planned to whelp. Trevor stood behind her, eyes narrowed and aflame with hatred he no longer bothered to hide. That one was fast becoming a liability.

Yet Irakesh needed him for the coming battle. If he was honest he'd admit he needed him for more than that. What point being a god if you had no one to talk to? It saddened him that Trevor would die today. The final compulsion he had laid would see to that.

For so long he had suppressed the Risen, allowing Irakesh a direct conduit into the part of Trevor's mind it would normally occupy. Every time Trevor struggled, Irakesh had to actively use his own will to stop him. The method was potent because Irakesh was stronger and thus always won. Yet if a struggle came during a critical moment Irakesh would be vulnerable. Such a link terrified him. Its very creation was abhorrent, because it had meant being constantly at risk for the first time in his life. The bond had been necessary to teach Trevor that struggle was futile. He simply could not win, could be made to go against even his most core beliefs. Kill friends or family at Irakesh's whim, powerless to stop himself from committing such vile acts.

In relaxing that control Irakesh was about to risk everything on a bluff. He'd severed the bond, but in its passing left an overriding compulsion within the Risen. Trevor would slay his family even if it cost him his own life. If he demonstrated the same resilience that he had against Irakesh, then he could break that compulsion, but Irakesh doubted he would even try. He'd done his utmost to break Trevor's will, to teach him that he was helpless and that resistance was futile.

Even if he did free himself, it would occur after he was embroiled in combat. By that point, it shouldn't matter. He'd betrayed the Ka-Dun and his pack, and they'd pull Trevor down without the slightest hesitation. He had no choice but to fight.

"Prepare yourselves. We make for the bridge above. An impressive structure, that. It seems your world has produced feats nearly as great as my own," Irakesh said, turning back to face the water. He raised his arms, channeling energy from the Ark's dwindling stores. The water parted, revealing a narrow passage that threaded across the ocean floor towards the bridge's central pylon. "Tell me, Trevor. Why do they call it the Golden Gate Bridge? It is neither golden nor a gate."

"It's the gateway to the bay," Trevor replied. He gave no further words, merely stalked up the muddy trail a few feet behind Irakesh. Yes, his death was for the best.

"Cyntia, walk with me," Irakesh called, pausing until she was even with him. She was back in werewolf form now, dirty blond with deep green splotches. The corruption, they called it. It was thick upon her and grew thicker each day. Madness wouldn't be far behind. Not the aggressive behavior they'd seen, but an all-consuming rage.

She quickened her pace, drawing even with him as he stepped over a curved white chunk of metal. The keel of a boat perhaps. It was hard to know, since he'd devoured few memories of ships in this age.

"What?" Cyntia growled, looming over him as she shifted the silver box to the arm farthest from him.

"What comes next is critical. I can feel the Ka-Dun somewhere to the north. A short distance," Irakesh explained, lifting his sandal as he stepped over a wide puddle of cold sludge. "He will bring whatever allies he has left. They are not strong enough to kill us, but when they try I want you to slay them and devour their corpses. Keep Trevor and me safe. Will you do that?"

"Blair tore off my leg," Cyntia roared, claws flexing. She bared her fangs, eyes wild. "I'm going to eat him, piece by piece. I'll keep him alive, so he can watch me get fat from his flesh."

"Excellent. Visit the same fate on his pack, if he brings them," Irakesh demanded. He expected some sort of protest from Trevor, but the fiery-haired deathless simply watched. Cold. Patient. That was a bad sign. He was marshaling his will, waiting for Irakesh to show sign of weakness.

Just a little longer and neither of his companions would be a threat. *No one* would be a threat. He'd have the strength to dominate the entire continent, building a necropolis to rival the Cradle from his own lost age. By the time his mother learned of his existence he'd be a powerful rival, not an insignificant vassal.

They continued through the sludge, still a shock to Irakesh. In his own time the oceans had been lower. This would have been a well-protected valley on the edge of a calm port. The perfect place to build an Ark that could both dominate the continent and enable passage to other lands. The Builders had chosen an incredible location.

Now that it lay underwater it was even more so, for none of the interesting technical marvels produced in this time could remove the water. That made getting inside the Ark that much more challenging. Assuming it had the power to keep the ocean from flooding it.

A sleek grey form, long and deadly, swam by in the wall of water to his left. The shark sensed that gap in the water and was curious. Excellent predators. He'd need to harness them in defense of this place in case his enemies found a way to plumb the icy depths and reach the entrance of the Ark.

"You're going to blow up San Francisco? Why? There can't be any possible benefit to you," Trevor said. The words dripped acid. Irakesh noticed Cyntia's ears twitch, but she didn't glance back. The madness was close, if even Trevor no longer motivated her. He'd been the life-line to which her sanity had clung.

A corrupted on the verge of the change. A powerful vassal on the verge of becoming a true deathless. Yet by the time the sun sank into the waves Irakesh would be the most powerful being to walk these shores in an age of the world. He must focus on the prize, not the risk.

"What makes you think I intend to blow it up? This is the capital of my new empire, the necropolis from which I will rule this continent," Irakesh stated. It was so, a certain future. He would allow no other possibility.

"Then what is the bomb for?" Trevor asked, slapping the side of the case Cyntia carried. She glowered at him, baring her fangs and giving a low, menacing growl.

Irakesh stopped, turning slowly to face Trevor. His next words were critical. He must allay at least one of his fears or Trevor could attack before the compulsion was even triggered. "Very well, you've earned an explanation. We're going to detonate that bomb. I will use the Ark to harness that energy, drawing it in and filling the vast reservoirs that the ages have drained. It will become the most powerful Ark in the world. The others are all constrained by the weak sun. It will be centuries before they can draw fully from it and in that time I will use this Ark to dominate a continent. Neither Isis nor Ra will be able to unseat me. They'll be too busy sniping at each other, as always."

"Are you sure you can control that much power? What if the Ark overloads?" Trevor asked. Irakesh was generally impressed with Trevor's complete lack of emotion. If the enormity of Irakesh's plan impacted him in any way, he didn't show it.

"If that occurs then the Ark will detonate and the land will be blackened for hundreds of miles," Irakesh said, looking Trevor directly in the eye. "But it will not happen. The Arks were designed by the Builders to withstand the full fury of the sun at its peak, a state of the world you cannot even comprehend. Their reservoirs are nearly limitless."

"Do you know exactly how much power is released by the bomb you're about to detonate? It was designed to annihilate cities," Trevor protested, shaking his head. "Why do I bother? Even if that were a risk, you wouldn't listen. Even though it's your own life at stake. What do you think will happen to you if your plan fails and the nuke destroys this city?"

"I will die," Irakesh answered, again a simple statement of fact. He started back up the path. The wide copper pillar was just a hundred yards distant, its concrete base covered in thick algae. He glanced back at Trevor. "Yet if I succeed, you will have the ability to help shape the future of this land, second only to me. If we fail, then you will no longer have to endure this hellish existence. Look around you. I know the prospect of destroying so much pains you. You are a product from a world that pretends nature isn't horribly vengeful. Yet look what's happened. Those few who cling to life here are huddling in fear as their world gives its last gasp. Surely they'd welcome the freedom oblivion would bring."

Trevor opened his mouth to reply, but then his jaw clicked shut. He shrugged, glancing away from Irakesh. Was that a sign of acceptance? Or that he no longer regarded Irakesh as worthy of communication?

They finally reached the massive pylon, extending hundreds of feet into the air where it met the odd bridge these people had somehow constructed. It rivaled any of the architectural marvels of his own age. How had they suspended so much metal over such a vast expanse of water? The genius required was impressive.

Irakesh focused on his inner reserves, drawing deeply and infusing his entire body with energy. He began to vibrate, faster and faster until he achieved the proper frequency. Then he enacted a change on every molecule, every fiber of his being. He became a cloud of charged energy, a sentient representation of his will. He drifted skyward, admiring the sunset over the ocean.

Cyntia seemed to sense what was required of her, leaping thirty feet up to catch the side of the pylon with her claws. She vaulted again, then a third time. Each leap took her closer to the bridge itself, which bulged above him from the weight of the countless minions he'd used the Ark to summon.

Trevor paused behind him for a long moment. So long that Irakesh thought he might have to offer aid. Then he felt the change in Trevor, watching warily as his protege shifted into a similar cloud. He drifted after Irakesh, following him to the main body of the bridge. The pylon extended into the sky above, wide sweeping cables hanging between it and the next one. They were the color of clay from the deep desert. The builders had mixed copper in that metal. How much of that precious substance had been mined to create so large a structure?

Irakesh allowed the waters to close beneath them once they were above sea level, drifting steadily skyward until he had a vantage of the bridge's main causeway. Excellent. It was thronged with corpses, thousands upon thousands of writhing bodies pressed tightly between abandoned vehicles. There were so many that one was occasionally knocked from the bridge, plummeting to the icy depths below.

"We'll set down near the center, closest to the Ark," Irakesh called over the low wind. He drifted towards the asphalt, willing the milling zombies back and creating a clearing.

Trevor settled on the ground next to him, heavy pistol holstered at his side and a much larger rifle strapped to his back. Irakesh was still growing used to the weapons of this time, much preferring his na-kopesh. Even had it not been forged from Sunsteel, it would still be a weapon he'd wielded for decades. He'd spent countless hours dueling and still more honing his skills in battle.

Cyntia's ungainly form bounded over the side of the bridge, smashing a pair of zombies as she scanned around until she located them. A single bound brought her within the narrow ring Irakesh had created. She looked crazed, still cradling the silver box like her long lost pup. Unease crept up his spine, a cold spider seeking prey.

"Cyntia, the time has come for you to gain your revenge. The Ka-Dun will approach soon and I need you to stalk them," he said, hoping to appeal to her all-consuming rage. "Leave the box there in the center. I will have these minions tend to it while you deal with our foes."

She glared hard at him, no sign of intelligence left in those bestial eyes. Then she finally gave a low growl, setting the box in the center of the ring. She leapt to a nearby cable and scampered up into the fog. Trevor leapt a moment later, scurrying up a cable on the opposite side of the bridge.

All was ready. In a few short hours he would be undisputed master of everything he surveyed.

67

SET US UP THE BOMB

lair's purpose had never been so clear. Cyntia needed to be put down, just like any other rabid animal. He leapt to the top of the hill, peering through shrubs down at the Golden Gate Bridge. The dead clogged the wide structure, so thick they covered abandoned cars like maggots on rotted meat. A dense patch of fog wreathed the top of the bridge and part of the bay, but its familiar red spires poked through.

"Any sign of them?" Liz's disembodied voice startled him from the patch of shadow to his right, between a mossy boulder and a small tree that had been shaped by the wind into a skeletal hand. The sun sank toward the ocean in the west, just an hour before twilight.

"Near the center of the bridge. Do you see that mound?" Blair replied, gesturing towards a massive pile of bodies. It had to be thirty or forty feet high, a writhing mass that drew the eye. Putrid but fascinating.

"I see them. What the hell are they doing?" Liz replied. It was eerie not being able to see her, but Blair had grown used to it. Her presence comforted him, though recent events had left him numb.

"My guess? Irakesh is using them to protect the bomb. He knows we have to go for that first, and if it's buried under zombies we'll have a tough time getting to it. That will give him and Trevor time to strike from the shadows when we approach," Blair said. His hackles rose as another figure blurred into existence next to him, but he was relieved to see Jordan's familiar bulk.

The heavily muscled man was still in human form, shrouded in that strange black armor. The woven fibers could swell to accommodate his wolf form. They even allowed his claws to poke through without damaging the material and included a harness for the arsenal he'd equipped for this fight.

Jordan scanned the bridge and then gave a tight nod. "Blair's right. That pile is where we're likely to find the bomb. Or it's a damned cunning decoy. Could be we search there and find nothing, leaving ourselves vulnerable without Irakesh ever risking the real bomb. Either way we don't have a choice. We have to take his bait."

The high-pitched *whup whup whup* of Yuri's craft sounded from behind. Blair turned to see it rising over the tree line, zipping between the canopy of two giant redwoods as it zoomed parallel with the hillside. The sleek craft was just large enough to hold one person, with rotors embedded in the front and rear like bicycle tires turned on their sides. A sleek black mini-gun was slung under the cockpit, with two boxy missile launchers to either side. The perfect one man fighter.

Steve blurred into a crouch well behind the group, at the edge of the animosity emanating from Jordan and Liz. His midnight fur ruffled in the wind, amber eyes dangerous. It was exactly the sort of look grad student Bridget would have sidled up against, but warrior Bridget would have found disgusting. She'd changed so much in the time he'd known her, become great by the end. Blair clad himself in her loss.

"Jordan, you're the tactical expert," Liz rumbled from the shadows. "How do you want to do this?"

"There are a lot of unknowns, so we'll have to be fluid," Jordan said, still eyeing Steve with scorn. "We'll send Blair in as bait. He'll head straight for the bomb. Either Trevor or Cyntia will attack him, maybe both. When that happens, I engage Trevor and Liz engages Cyntia. At that point, Irakesh may choose to engage. If he does, that's when Steve makes his move. You attack Irakesh. We finish off our respective opponents and help you finish up yours."

"That's acceptable," was all Steve gave back.

"What about Yuri?" Blair asked. He eyed the craft, trying to figure out what the best use might be.

"Yuri will use the fog to hide a strafing run," Jordan replied, gaze growing distant as he spoke. It was a familiar look, but one he'd never seen on Jordan's face. He was touching Yuri's mind. Blair was astonished. Yet proud. "He'll focus on the pile of zombies, knocking off as many as possible."

"Doesn't that mean firing a machine gun at a nuclear bomb? Are we that stupid now?" Liz's voice came from over Blair's shoulder this time. He could almost picture furry hands on her hips.

"The casing was designed to be carried in an airplane," Jordan replied dryly in Liz's direction. "It can withstand a fall from several thousand feet. Crashing. In a plane. A fifty caliber bullet might knock it off the bridge, but it won't detonate it. The best thing that could happen right now is for that bomb to end up on the bottom of the bay. If it's not armed he won't be able to use it, and if it is I'll take any protection I can get before it detonates."

"Can't we disarm it somehow?" Steve asked, taking a step closer. He was still in a crouch, just below the rise shielding them from the bridge.

"This isn't a movie, Steve," Jordan growled. His hands tightened around the body of his rifle, fat black scope affixed to the barrel. "You don't arm a nuke unless you're planning to detonate it. If he's armed the thing a chemical reaction has already started and that thing is going to blow up in the next half hour or so. Nothing we can do about it."

"Shit," was all Blair could muster. "Let's hope he hasn't armed it. The guy is obsessed with power. I can't imagine him blowing himself up or even risking the possibility."

"One way to find out," Jordan said, stepping to the crest of the ridge. He was in plain view for anyone looking up from the bridge. "Liz, if we're going to do this, we need to do it now."

"Then let's do it," Liz growled, hands balling into fists as she joined Jordan on the ridge.

Jordan's eyes took on that glassy look for a moment, then Yuri's strange craft accelerated up over the ridge with a high-pitched whine. It hugged the hillside, dropping low along the grass as it zoomed towards the bridge. It was still nearly a mile distant when the gun slung under the cockpit began to spin. A hail of bright streaks lanced into the mountain of corpses, flinging body parts in all directions as they bored through flesh more efficiently than any drill.

Blair blurred down the hillside, vaulting a boulder and landing near the tunnel entrance leading further north into Marin. The vista point, where countless tourists had snapped photos of the Golden Gate Bridge, was deserted, with not a single car or even a zombie. The latter were all on the bridge. Blair took his bearings and then knelt to blur again. He stopped when he spotted movement on top of one of the bridge's arches. A figure drew a rifle to bear, sighting down a scope towards Yuri. He could make out a shock of almost orange hair and a battered camouflage jacket. The rifle bucked and a gout of flame erupted from the muzzle.

There was a scream of metal as the front rotor of Yuri's craft exploded. It spun wildly out of control, careening away from the bridge towards the Marin side. A second shot punched through the cockpit, shattering the glass just before the copter slammed into the side of the hill. Blair winced, expecting a Michael Bay-style explosion. There wasn't any, just a scream of metal as the frame buckled and slid out of sight.

Blair couldn't see what happened to Yuri and didn't have time to find out. He blurred into motion, leaping on top of one of the cables and running up it until he neared the middle of the bridge. It amazed him how quickly he crossed the distance, wind tugging at his fur as he entered the mist. Then he leapt, falling towards the mound of bodies.

It had diminished considerably after Yuri's attack, but still rose a good twenty feet. His feet sank into the shattered ribcage of an obese man, cushioning his fall. Blair rolled backwards, landing at the base of the mound. Then he began to hurl body parts away as he tunneled towards where he hoped the bomb lay.

68

JORDAN VERSUS GREGG

J ordan's eyes narrowed as he spotted movement on top of the bridge. For a long moment there was nothing, but suddenly a figure appeared with a rifle. God damned shadow dancers. He couldn't make out the model, but that gun was large enough to give a tank pause. He already knew who held it; the red hair was unmistakable. Jordan winced as it fired, the gout of flame from the muzzle visible a split second before the thunder cracked over the bay. Damn but that thing was loud.

Fiery fragments exploded from Yuri's craft, sending it into a tail-spin. Jordan desperately wanted to intervene, but forced himself to adhere to the rules of the engagement he himself had crafted. Instead he drew the stock of his own rifle to his shoulder. The Mohn crafted weapon was state of the art, heavy but reliable. He sighted through the large scope, settling the crosshairs over Trevor's chest. Then he stroked the trigger.

The rifle roared, kicking back against his shoulder like a bucking horse. He raised his chin, relying on his normal vision to ascertain the damage. Trevor had vanished, but the shot had done some damage. The pylon where he'd been standing was drenched in blood, and the rifle he'd been holding plummeted into the mist.

At least Jordan had disarmed him, but that created its own set of problems. Blair was blurring his way onto the bridge and approaching the pile of corpses. If Trevor ambushed him it would be at close range now, and Jordan couldn't react quickly enough. He needed to get closer. It meant deviating from the plan, but he had to gamble that Trevor would see him as a threat and engage if given the chance.

Jordan blurred towards the bridge, shifting as he moved. By the time he reached the base of the bridge he was in full wolf form, eight feet of solid muscle and sharp teeth. He sprinted up one of the wide orange cables, vaulting over the hurdle-like obstructions every ten feet. In moments he'd risen into the mist, finally on even footing with Trevor. Neither one of them could see in this thick soup. Yet he couldn't take advantage of stealth. He needed to be bait, to get Trevor to engage rather than attack Blair from the shadows.

He continued his blur until he emerged from the mist, surrounded by the acrid tang of wet metal and new blood. He wiped the damp from the fur around his eyes, scanning the immediate area. There was no way he could detect Trevor, but it didn't stop him from looking. It was possible Trevor had dropped below the mist and was engaging Blair even now, but Jordan doubted it. That would have meant abandoning the high ground and Trevor was too canny for that.

Pain flared in his back as Trevor's claws bit through the mesh. The armor muted the blow, or he might have had his spine ripped out. Instead it simply knocked him forward into the narrow rope-like cables that paralleled the much larger one he'd run up. He spun quickly, but Trevor had already disappeared back into the shadows.

"I'm sorry, Jordan, about Panama. You're one of the good guys now. I see that. You have to put me down if you want to stop Irakesh," Trevor said from somewhere slightly below him. Right where the mists shrouded the wide cable.

Was that some attempt at a trick? Not at all what he'd expect from previous encounters. Trevor was smarter than that.

"Oh, I will, you ginger bastard," Jordan growled. He flipped to his feet, ripping his .357 from its holster and squeezing off two rounds in the direction of the voice. The cracks were deafening, but he would have heard something if they'd struck home. Dammit. Where was the bastard? He had no choice but to wait for Trevor to engage. Maybe meeting him up here had been a bad idea. Maybe he should have waited for Trevor to attack Blair, but after what he'd done to Yuri Jordan couldn't wait any longer.

"Not like that, you won't," the voice was behind him again. Something struck him in the back of the knees, sending him tumbling from the main cable. Jordan blurred, just barely catching one of the thin ropey cables. He used that to haul himself up, landing in a crouch on the main cable again. Why hadn't Trevor used the opportunity to finish him?

"What are you playing at, Trevor?" Jordan growled, not really expecting an answer.

"Irakesh is controlling me and I can't stop him, but that doesn't mean I want this. If you want to kill Irakesh you have to deal with me first." The voice was above him. Jordan looked up, but too late. Trevor fell on him like a comet, claws raking his armor and the weight of the deathless driving him into the cable. It was all Jordan could do to hold on, to keep from plummeting into the mist.

Jordan opened his jaw and lunged, but Trevor was quick. He ducked out of the way and Jordan's teeth snapped shut mere inches from his throat. Then Trevor's claws slashed at Jordan's throat, tearing open the jugular. Jordan reached up to swat Trevor off, but the deathless batted the blow aside.

"You can't win if you can't find me. You need an answer to my shadow walking," Trevor said, tone maddeningly friendly, as if they were old colleagues discussing a paper. Jordan had had enough of being taunted. Enough of watching friends die and seeing the world burn.

"How about fuck you? How's that for an answer?" Jordan roared. He summoned the strange new power he'd discovered, this telekinesis the beast had told him about. He seized Trevor in an invisible grip, yanking him from the cable and hurling him out over the ocean. He jerked up his .357 and emptied three rounds into Trevor's face, sending out a shower of gore. "Hope you can fly, motherfucker."

Trevor's body arced slowly towards the water, but then something incredible happened. His body became vague and hazy, slowly becoming insubstantial as he melted into a cloud of green mist.

"Are you *serious*?" Jordan roared. The bastard *could* fly.

69

VENGEANCE

L iz danced the shadows, sprinting along the rocky embankment and onto the wide concrete that led to the Golden Gate Bridge. She'd never lived in the Bay Area, but had crossed the bridge several times growing up. It was breathtaking, even given the situation. A modern marvel of architectural brilliance. One that might well hold the fate of the Western Hemisphere. Yet the entire structure seemed tiny next to the massive pyramid now dominating the bay near Angel Island.

She shifted her attention to the throng of undead, their bodies clogging every visible space on the bridge. The stench was awful, the sight grisly even after all she'd witnessed. She briefly considered her options. Move along the railing or take to the wide suspension cables that led up into the mist?

A howl split the dusk, drawing her gaze to the center of the bridge. Blair stood at the mound of bodies, arms drenched in gore as he let loose his anger and loss. It was beautiful and terrifying, a challenge if ever she'd heard one. A challenge that was answered. Cyntia's towering blond form burst from the shadows behind Blair, looming like a linebacker over a grade schooler.

Yet somehow he dodged her first attack, her claws rending the air where he'd been standing. One moment he was there, the next standing atop her shoulders. His claws plunged into her neck so quickly Liz couldn't discern individual movement. Blood spurted skyward, drenching his face and painting him with a fiendish brush. Even at this distance her enhanced vision let her see the unbridled rage consuming his features. He snarled like a beast as he continued his assault.

Cyntia reacted quickly, arms jerking upwards as she sought to grab him. Blair was too quick. He rolled backwards, landing in a crouch near Cyntia. He darted in, jabbing her in the gut with several strikes. Cyntia roared in pain and rage, bull-rushing Blair. This time she had more success, knocking Blair from his feet and coming down on top of him.

"No," Liz cried, the word freeing her from inaction. She leapt forward, bounding from corpse to corpse as she used the zombies like some unstable road. She had to reach Blair.

Thunder rolled from the mist above. No, something louder than thunder. That was a gun being fired. A pistol, like her brother's .357. Jordan had found Trevor. Or Trevor had found Jordan. She froze at the base of the bridge's first pylon, a massive copper spire shooting into the mist on either side of the four-lane charnel house just below her perch on the railing. She glanced upwards, part of her dying as she considered her options.

She could see Trevor, speak to him for the first time since she'd lost him. Maybe she could make him see reason. Make him join their side. If that wasn't possible, if the unthinkable must be done, shouldn't it be her that did it? She owed him that much. But there was Blair, embroiled in a fight he couldn't win without her. It filled her with nausea in the way the stench of the dead never could.

In the end there was only one choice. Stick to the plan.

Liz leapt forward, drawing a gleaming broadsword out of English myth from her shoulder scabbard. Three more bounds took her within range. She grabbed one of the thick steel ropes connecting the suspension bridge to the road, vaulting into the sky above Cyntia.

Blair was holding his own, tearing furiously at Cyntia's face in a blur of claws and teeth. Yet she had a death grip on his right leg, massive claws exposing bone. It must be pure agony, yet it didn't touch Blair. She was awed by what she was seeing, the true melding of beast and man. The only thing she had to compare was the Mother's slaughter of Mohn Corp.'s garrison back in Peru when she'd first awakened.

She came down with the long blade braced against her right leg, both hands gripping the grooved hilt. The move was instinctual, plucked from the beast lurking within her. The blade pierced the back of Cyntia's neck, two feet of gold disappearing as it found bone. Cyntia roared in pain, glaring up at her hatefully from the eye Blair hadn't yet gouged out. She seemed to weigh Liz's attack, but lunged forward to seize Blair in a massive bear hug. Then Cyntia began to squeeze.

Blair's ribs shattered, his brief scream turned into a pitiful wail as Cyntia tightened her grip. Liz lost any semblance of rational thought, at one with her need to kill a woman she'd once called friend. She plunged the blade deeper, her roar echoing over the bay.

A sickly green light burst from Cyntia's wound, burning Liz's skin like a long afternoon asleep in the sun.

This is the true power of the blade, Ka-Ken. Purify her soul and claim it for your own.

Liz tightened her grip on the blade, driving it deeper into Cyntia's back until only the hilt was visible. Liz howled, funneling her rage into the blade. The sickly light grew brighter. Brighter still. Then it flared into the clear white brilliance, a liquid heat. The light began flowing up the blade in rapid pulses, each jolt like a shot of espresso after a long night studying. Strength flooded Liz. Power. Understanding. It was incredible.

A portion of the strength she accumulated is yours, Ka-Ken. A gift from the blade. This is why the weapon is so kingly, so highly prized.

Liz's howl deepened. The sword was vibrating now, a living thing in her hands. Cyntia had stopped struggling, sagging to her knees and dropping Blair's mangled body. He twitched weakly, dragging himself toward a nearby car.

The pulse became a steady stream, a massive burst of something she could only describe as Cyntia's essence. Part memory, but mostly a wash of emotion. Infinite grief but a rage to match it, a blend that could result in no other fate than madness. Liz was flooded with pity, finally understanding the awful struggle Cyntia had undergone; her friend had been driven mad by the death of her world. The only thing she'd held onto was her hope that Trevor could somehow save her. That faith had led her down an ever darkening road, one Liz herself could have walked had their roles been a little different. What she was doing here was a mercy, a last favor for her friend. Cyntia's body went limp, an empty husk of meat and bone. It lay at the base of the pile of zombies, a final insult to her memory.

Liz scanned her surroundings, taking in the relative silence. There were no more gunshots from above. There was no sign of Irakesh. Only the mound of bodies. Liz sheathed the blade. She knelt next to Blair, cradling his mangled body. He was breathing, but his eyes were closed.

She didn't know what he'd been through in their time apart, but it had left him with very little energy. It might be days before he healed enough to rejoin the fight.

70

THE KEY

Blair returned to consciousness by degrees, each shallow breath pressing a shattered rib into his lung. His vision focused and he realized that his body had been propped against the bumper of a Suzuki Swift.

Liz-wolf stood near the mound of corpses lying about her with that golden sword as she danced between shambling bodies. Hundreds of them advanced, forcing her to spend more time dealing with them than she did digging into the mound.

He wanted to help, but he couldn't feel anything below the waist. His useless legs were still mangled, a femur jutting through the skin in his left leg. Experience told him that he'd eventually heal, but not in time to make a difference.

"Blair," a voice hissed from his right. He slowly turned his head to see Steve's midnight form crouched next to the car.

"Help Liz," Blair wheezed. It took everything he had to force the words out.

"I will. I'll help all of us, but I need your help to do it," Steve said, studying him with that calculating gaze.

Blair's mind was foggy, but he knew what Steve was after. The access key. He also knew why Steve had chosen this precise moment to ask for it. Irakesh had yet to show his hand. When he did their only hope was to counter him with the power of the key.

"No," Blair slurred, shaking his head. "I'm not falling for your damned tricks. I'll die first."

"Then we'll all die," Steve hissed, leaning closer. "This time it's no trick, Blair. With you incapacitated the rest of us are screwed. San Francisco is screwed. We aren't going to be able to stop Irakesh, not without the key. I know you hate me, but are you willing to sacrifice everything just to spite me?"

Blair glared at Steve, but didn't reply. Not immediately anyway. Liz's towering form still danced between corpses, but the fight was endless. For every one she cut down another filled its place, and there was an endless sea of waiting bodies. She could do this for days and not kill them all.

"Let's say I give you the key. We kill Irakesh, then what? You'll be just as bad as he is," Blair growled. Weakly, because it hurt like hell.

"Now you're just being dramatic," Steve shot back. He glanced at Liz, then back at Blair. "Listen, make your damned choice, Blair. Give me the key and I'll do everything I can to help us win. Deny me the key, and I'm out of here. I'm not sticking around and dying because of your stubbornness."

Blair was torn. He knew giving Steve the key would be a mistake. Steve was the worst kind of megalomaniac, and if they survived this he'd have centuries to regret this moment. If they survived. That was the deciding factor. They needed Steve, if they wanted to have any chance of victory.

It is a painful choice, Ka-Dun. I support you in this. If we do not give the key to the treacherous one, we will be overwhelmed by the deathless. We will likely be overwhelmed anyway.

"Take it," Blair snarled, extending his hand. The fur was matted with blood, and his arm shook badly as Steve grasped his hand.

"You're making the right decision," Steve said, giving him a confident smile.

"No I'm not," Blair said, closing his eyes and willing the key to flow into Steve.

71

FREE WILL

Trevor floated above the sea of carnage clogging the bridge, every molecule on fire both from the gunshots to the face and from the act of violently transforming his body to a gaseous cloud. The anguish went deeper, of course. He badly wanted to die, to have Jordan or Blair or Liz put him out of his misery. Yet he lacked the power to free himself, a prisoner in his own body.

Trevor gazed beneath him at the mound of bodies, at Blair's broken body and the black-furred werewolf who crouched next to him. At Liz, who was desperately attempting to clear the area around the mound of corpses. She flowed between zombies, hacking off heads as her golden sword hummed through the air.

A shape plummeted past him, sliding down one of the metal ropes that connected the suspension cables to the road below. Jordan. The Commander kicked off the cable to land in a crouch next to Blair's mangled body. To Trevor's immense relief Blair's body spasmed. His friend was still alive, though just barely.

Enough. They are no longer your friends. They are prey and we will slay them.

Trevor drifted silently towards the ground, powerless to control his actions as he stealthily approached. Light warped around him, cloaking him in darkness as he descended. The closest target was Liz, his kid sister. The girl he'd grown up protecting. The one who looked up to him, who believed he could do anything.

He struck, body solidifying even as his clawed hand punched through Liz's lower back. He seized her spine, twisting violently. Liz tumbled forward with a cry of immense agony that harmed Trevor in a way no physical blow could. He seized her golden sword in his free hand, yanking it away and pivoting towards Jordan.

Jordan was fast, but Trevor had caught him in the act of reloading his pistol. The werewolf dropped the weapon and came at Trevor with his claws. It was a mistake. Trevor dropped low, blurring underneath Jordan and using the reach offered by the sword to draw a wicked slash across Jordan's belly.

The Commander yelped as he landed, rolling away from Trevor and coming up in a crouch. Even as he readied another attack, Trevor simply vanished, bending light to confuse his foe. Liz was staggering to her feet, spine already healed. Trevor gave her no quarter, ramming the sword through her back as he reappeared.

"Getting tired of ill-mannered zombies. Give werewolf sword back," a thickly accented voice said. Trevor had enough time to see a man with a metal leg striding in his direction, black armor torn and smoking. One lens of his chrome sunglasses had been shattered, and part of his goatee had been burned away.

An unfamiliar pistol was gripped in both hands. The weapon barked and a round tore through Trevor's shoulder. Then another ripped into his gut. A third punched through his chest.

Allow me, my host, the Risen crooned.

Trevor's free hand came up of its own volition, gesturing at the Russian. A wave of sickly green energy burst forth and sent the man limply to the bridge's cracked asphalt. He twitched and flopped like a fish.

Now, my host, use the blade. Drink the Ka-Ken's essence.

He realized the sword was still embedded in Liz's back, as she struggled weakly to gain her footing. A pulse of clear golden light surged up the blade, filling Trevor with strength. It was more than just energy. It was memory. Essence. He saw her thoughts, a sunny day in Costa Rica. A family trip to Yosemite.

Each pulse brought a fresh memory, and a surge of strength. Liz withered, falling to the ground as he drained the life from her. Trevor exalted in the power, and he hated himself. He was killing his sister, killing what was probably the last living family he had in the world. All so he could serve a monster.

NO. He wouldn't allow it. Whatever he'd become didn't matter. This wasn't going to happen.

You cannot fight it, my host. It is what we are.

"It's what *you* are," Trevor growled, ripping the sword from Liz's back. He tossed it to the asphalt in a clatter, taking a stumbling step back from Liz's body. "I want no part of it."

They will kill you, my host. You must take her essence, or she will take yours. Kill them.

"No," Trevor said aloud. The simple word had enormous power. It freed him from the need to obey the voice, from the need to obey Irakesh. He closed his eyes and forced the Risen into the shadowed depths of his mind. Then he opened his eyes to find the barrel of a .357 just inches away. It was held by a very pissed-off-looking Commander Jordan.

"No," Liz hissed, resting an arm on Jordan's shoulder as she struggled to her feet. She stepped up to Trevor, peering down at him from that wolfish face with the eyes he'd known all his life. They might be set in a face covered with auburn fur, but this was Liz. His sister. "He could have killed me, but he didn't. He dropped the sword, and he's not resisting anymore. Let's at least hear him out. What do you want, Trevor? Make no mistake, if it's some trick I *will* kill you. I love you, but I can't let you help Irakesh come to power. No matter what."

"You *should* kill me," Trevor replied, every bit of him united in thought. "It's the only way. I'm myself for now, but I don't know if Irakesh can exert control again. Keeping me around is a risk you can't afford."

"You don't get off that easy," Liz snarled, glaring down at him. "We can't fight Irakesh alone and you've got a lot to atone for. You don't have the luxury of death yet. Help us, Trevor."

Trevor smiled. "Same fire I remember."

"We can catch up later. Trevor, where is the bomb?" Jordan asked, raising an eyebrow. Trevor doubted the man would ever trust him. The feeling was mutual.

"I can sense Irakesh shaping on the San Francisco side of the bridge. I'll roam ahead and try to locate the bomb. Is this all we have left? What about the black-furred male with Blair earlier?" Trevor asked, looking around for their missing companion. There was no sign of him, at least on the bridge.

"Steve?" Liz asked with a snort. She rolled her eyes. "We might be able to count on him, but I doubt it. It's probably just us three. Blair isn't in any shape to keep fighting."

"Shouldn't we deal with these zombies?" Jordan asked, gesturing at the ring around them. The zombies hadn't approached, though they shuffled around the edge of an invisible ring. A ring with Trevor at its center.

"I can keep them at bay for now. Save your strength for Irakesh," Trevor suggested. He faced the far side of the bridge, which descended towards San Francisco in the distance. "Let me go in first. When Irakesh attacks, and he will, make that opportunity count."

"Yuri will follow behind and look pretty," the Russian said, retrieving his pistol from where it had fallen when Trevor had attacked him.

Trevor smiled at that, the first honest one he could remember in a very, very long time.

72

BOOM

Irakesh smiled as events unfolded before him. He perched on the roof of a small round building that sold gifts, just across the bridge on the side closest the strange city with its garden of towering glass spires. The sounds of combat competed with the low moans of the nascent deathless clogging the causeway onto the bridge.

Cyntia's death was timely, though its nature was troubling. Her growing insanity made her a threat, one he was glad to see eliminated. Particularly as it meant disabling the Ka-Dun Blair. That one no longer possessed the key, but he'd been a dangerous and canny opponent. One Irakesh was pleased to see removed from the battle. It would take several nights under a gibbous moon to recover from the wounds he'd been dealt.

The arrival of the Ka-Ken and her Sunsteel weapon had been a shock. If he was not mistaken that was the blade of Osiris himself, the father of the world he'd left behind in the last age. How had she come to possess it? That seemed an unlikely coincidence. He did not trust such coincidences.

The weapon's origin could be investigated later. First he must complete his task. After that he could take the weapon from the Ka-Ken's lifeless hands, claiming it for himself. If the rumors were true, it was even more powerful than his own na-kopesh. An Emperor's weapon. He would have it and have this continent as well. He'd reached the apex of his plan, after which the rest was only a matter of patient, deliberate plotting.

The sun touched the water to the west, the clouds obscuring its glory as it began its mythical journey through the underworld. Its fading light painted the bridge's copper into burnished gold, and Irakesh finally understood the structure's name. Perhaps that name was more apt than he'd have thought. It was a pity he was about to destroy it.

Some of the mirth faded as he rose from his crouch. Trevor materialized next to the Ka-Ken, attacking viciously. His thrall tore into her pack, driving them back with incredible ferocity. It was an amazing display of power, and truth be told, Irakesh found it more than a little terrifying.

Then, at the very moment of his triumph, Trevor discarded the Sunsteel sword and sank to his knees. Had Irakesh breathed he'd have held his breath, waiting for the blond Ka-Dun to kill Trevor. Then the Ka-Ken gave Trevor...a hug? Trevor had broken the compulsion, and been embraced.

It didn't matter. Irakesh would prevail. No one could stand up to the full fury of an Ark, not even Isis herself. Nothing could touch him when he was close enough to touch the Ark's heart.

A high-pitched whine began beneath him. Irakesh had never heard the like, and neither had any of the unfortunate souls he'd consumed. It was wholly alien, though not unexpected. It must be the bomb, finally ready to unleash its near-limitless energy. Irakesh concentrated, shifting into mist as he readied his will. This would be incredibly delicate work.

The entire structure vibrated for a split second and in that moment Irakesh blurred, accelerating not just his body but his consciousness. He drew deep from the reservoir he rarely touched, gripping the hilt of the na-kopesh as he began to shape. Then the blast came, every molecule of the structure blowing apart like leaves drifting on a lazy wind.

Irakesh harnessed that energy, funneling it towards the tip of the ark. It lanced into the dark stone, washing down the sides of the enormous structure and into the bay. Tendrils spilled out all around him, tearing into boats and houses with equal fury. The area around the building's scattered atoms ceased to exist, torn apart by the unthinkable energy he'd unleashed.

It washed towards the bridge, melting steel and concrete and flesh. The first quarter of the bridge was obliterated before Irakesh gained some semblance of control. He yanked that power away from the bridge, away from the city. It poured into the Ark in a river of liquid fire, the energy disappearing into the white-hot slopes of the ancient structure.

How long the process went on, Irakesh couldn't say. There was an eternity of fire and pain, an unending struggle to contain the uncontainable fury he'd unleashed. Then it was over. The fire was gone, leaving nothing in its wake save smoking ruins. A deep crater filled the area where he'd stood, and the now disconnected cables of the beautiful bridge sagged inward, slamming into the still smoking metal at the first junction with a thunderous crash. Miraculously it still stood, the last three quarters straddling the bay. Marvelous.

Irakesh reached out, touching the power of the brilliant Ark behind him. It was immense on a scale he'd scarcely dreamed of, so far beyond what he'd expected that he understood now why Ra had considered him little more than a child. She'd wielded such power for nearly her entire reign.

Irakesh drifted towards the bridge, an immense green cloud of barely contained fury. His opponents gaped in horror, suitably impressed and appropriately terrified. A late arrival sat near the back of the bridge, the midnight Ka-Dun who'd barely taken part in their previous struggle. The familiar pulsing of a rival access key emanated from the man. This was the one who'd wrested the key from the Ka-Dun Blair.

More than that, the key was active now. The Ark it linked to fed it a small trickle of power, thin but steady. The Mother had repaired the immense damage wrought to her control room. Interesting. Irakesh briefly considered his options. He could eradicate the Ka-Dun with little trouble, but doing so would free the key. If he could instead capture the fool, he could imprison him within the Ark of the Redwood. Doing so would deny the Mother a Ka-Dun to watch over her Ark. That would leave her little choice but to remain close to it, shackled to the structure lest some interloper invade in her absence.

One final obstacle remained, his former vassal and the annoying pups who'd yapped at him since he'd fled Peru. It was time to put them down.

73

TRIUMPH

Blair used the Suzuki's bumper to pull himself to his feet. Breathing was agony. Moving beyond a broken hobble an impossibility. He'd never been this badly hurt, not even when he'd fallen from the plane back in Panama. That memory summoned an image of Bridget smiling, tending to him at his bedside. Of the brief time they'd shared together. He pushed it back, craning his neck to see over the milling zombies just beyond whatever safe zone Trevor was providing.

There was no sign of Irakesh on the bridge, only more zombies. So Blair looked beyond it. A tiny figure crouched atop the odd round building just on the other side, the gift shop that sold tiny replicas of the bridge and postcards with catchy phrases. His familiar bald head shone in the setting sun, flowing white tunic and pants somehow miraculously free of dirt or blood.

Blair had but a moment to watch before Irakesh dissolved into a cloud of sickly green mist with little arcs of lightning shooting through it. Then an enormous flash burst from the building, coming towards him faster than comprehension. He blurred, but even at such accelerated speed the explosion still raced towards him.

Jordan's neighboring blur vibrated the air around Blair, thrumming through him like the piano cord of the universe. The beefy blond werewolf leaped into their center, holding his arms aloft as if bracing an enormous wall. What was he doing? Blair had never seen anything like it, not even from Ahiga or the Mother. It looked as though he'd erected some sort of bubble around them, oily rainbows undulating along its surface where the fire burned hottest.

The inferno raged around them until Jordan collapsed to his knees, arms trembling as he sought to sustain the shelter he'd created. Could he hold on? Blair wished he had strength to lend. Then Liz was there, crouching next to Jordan. She pressed the flat of her golden blade against Jordan's knees. It began to glow, white pulses flowing from the tip to the hilt, each one making Jordan sit a little straighter.

Blair watched as the bubble shrank, just barely covering them now. Sweat matted Jordan's fur to his face, eyes fixed on nothing as he struggled with the powers he'd harnessed. He tilted to the right, only Liz's arm keeping him erect. Then the fire was gone. Blair leaned on the hood, gaping as a river of light flowed into the tip of the Ark. The structure drank it in greedily, absorbing it and leaving the bridge's smoking remains still standing.

The awful scope of Irakesh's plan was finally clear. He'd never intended to destroy anything. The bomb was a power source, and Irakesh had just leapt ahead of every Ark Lord in the world. It was brilliant. If a weakly powered Ark had allowed Irakesh to push Blair out of his mind like a misbehaving toddler, then what could he do with a fully powered one?

"Prepare yourselves," came a growl from behind Blair. He shifted atop the SUV to see Steve crouched on a commuter bus whose paint had been boiled away in the blast. He could still read Route 4 in the windshield. "Irakesh will attack and we have to stand together. If we don't we have no chance."

"Steve?" Liz called, rising from her place next to Jordan and stalking towards the midnight werewolf. "You actually want to stay and fight? I was positive you'd tell us to run, if you hadn't already left us all to die."

"I know you hate me, though I've never done anything to wrong you. I'm not a coward. I'm pragmatic and don't throw my life away in futile gestures. If I didn't think we had a chance, I would have run. But we do have a chance. A damned good one. Irakesh is strong, but there are four of us. Five, if you count Blair. We all want Irakesh dead and unless I'm a bigger fool than Blair that bastard is about to show us his end game," Steve taunted, tone just as acid as Liz's. Blair's eyes narrowed at the insult, but he was in no shape to do anything about it, even if he'd not been a mangled wreck. "You want to stand here bickering, or get ready for a last stand?"

"He's right," Jordan said. Yuri helped him regain his feet, but his chest was heaving as though he'd run a marathon. He used a paw to wipe the sweat from his forehead. "I don't know how much that explosion took out of Irakesh, but as soon as he recovers, he'll attack. We can't afford to give him that chance. We need to go on the offensive."

"It's too late for that," a mocking voice came from above. The mist had boiled away in the blast, leaving half-melted spires jutting into empty air. Between them stood a familiar figure, the white-clad form of Irakesh. He drifted towards the ground, left hand resting on the hilt of his oddly curved sword. The dark-skinned deathless made no other aggressive gesture as he set down just a few dozen yards from the group. He waved a hand and the zombies behind him stepped back as one, leaving him more room.

Irakesh delivered a triumphant smile, thick with a smugness Blair wished he could beat out of him. "I've won. The Ark is mine. The bomb has been detonated, giving me power beyond your limited comprehension. There is nothing you can do. No ability you can summon that will save you. Not even the Ka-Ken's storied weapon poses a threat. I believe I'll take that after I've incinerated the lot of you."

"You think it will be that easy?" Liz growled, slipping into the shadow of the bus.

In that instant Jordan leapt forward, blurring as quickly as Blair had ever seen. He bounded upwards, wrapping his arms around

Irakesh. Or attempting to. Jordan passed through the illusion and sailed beyond, catching himself on a blackened cable just above the wall of zombies. It snapped, dropping him into their midst. Whatever force that had held them at bay dissipated, and they fell upon Jordan as one. He came up swinging, dismembering the first and smashing the next pair's skulls together. He danced away from them, which left him vulnerable. Blair could only watch as a bolt of eldritch fire, the same hideous green of the cloud he'd seen earlier, lanced from the air above Jordan. It caught him in the back, arching the Commander's spine like a cat stepping on a live wire.

Then Steve raised an arm, gesturing at the place where the bolt had originated. His voice thrummed with power. "Peace, Irakesh. There is no need for us to be enemies. I control the Ark to the south. Together we can…"

"Your paltry shaping is nothing, Ka-Dun," Irakesh cut him off. Blair couldn't find the source of the voice. Until Irakesh appeared directly behind Steve. He jammed his hand through the back of Steve's spine, jerking his fist with a hideous crack of bone. Steve's legs went limp, spilling him to the ground like a puppet whose strings had suddenly been cut. "You cannot affect my mind. Even before I had the strength of the Ark, you were no match for me. But now? Now you are nothing. It is well for you that your life has some small worth to me. Lie there or there will be much, much greater pain."

An arc of green lightning shot from the air above Irakesh, crackling through his body in rolling waves. It knocked the deathless to his knees, much as he'd done to Jordan just moments before. Blair had completely forgotten about Trevor. He looked up to see a second green cloud, smaller and less distinct than Irakesh had been.

Irakesh shot to his feet with a roar, snarling at the sky. "So you've thrown in your lot with Isis and her get. You could have been second only to me, a god in the new pantheon that will dominate this world. Yet instead you choose oblivion. Contemplate that as I unravel you."

A bar of solid green light erupted from Irakesh's upturned palm. It shot into the sky, wider than the trunk of any tree. It obscured Trevor's cloud for an instant, then continued its passage into the sky.

Trevor's now solid form dropped onto a Ford Focus with a tremendous boom. His body smoked and smoldered, the scent of cooked flesh overwhelming.

Irakesh's chest erupted as a golden blade burst through his heart in a shower of desiccated gore. He stumbled forward with a cough, blinking rapidly. Then his eyes glowed and he blurred. The movement was far faster than Blair could track. Irakesh slid off the sword, whipping behind Liz with his own blade in hand. It pierced her chest in cruel mockery of Liz's own attack. She gasped, trying to slide loose from the blade jutting from her chest.

Irakesh refused to let her. He blurred again, twisting his arm around her neck and pushing the blade deeper until nothing but the hilt showed. Blair's teeth clenched as the rage built.

"Ah, Ka-Ken, so much spirit. Would that I could convince you to join my cause. You'd be legendary, my wrath made manifest in this world," Irakesh said, bending Liz almost double so her head was near his own. His eyes twinkled malevolently.

There is no hope. As long as Irakesh holds the key, he is as a god, the beast rumbled, sadly.

Blair's eyes widened. What if he no longer held the key? The Mother had designed them. She'd been meticulous in her planning, to the point where she'd modified the racial memory of their entire species. Would she have designed the key so that it could be used by her enemies? Of course not. If Irakesh was able to use the key it must be because the key assumed he one of the Mother's children.

You are cunning, Ka-Dun. I grasp the heart of your plan. It may work. Shape his helixes. Change him, that the key will see the truth.

Blair staggered from the hood of the car, using one partially healed leg to fling himself awkwardly in Irakesh's direction. He nearly missed, straining so that his outstretched hand just barely grasped the deathless's foot. The moment he touched it Blair blurred, accelerating his consciousness for the feat he was about to attempt.

Relax your vigilance, Ka-Dun. Let me guide you. I will show you the way.

Blair did. He allowed the beast to guide him, amazed as his

perceptions shifted. He rode the signal his body somehow broadcast into Irakesh, so intricate that it penetrated his very DNA. It shifted and changed, proteins re-arranging as Blair somehow *altered* the deathless. Irakesh swung to face him, releasing the hilt of the sword he'd rammed through Liz. He reached for Blair, his eyes promising a swift death.

Too late. Blair achieved some sort of critical mass, some change in the very fiber of Irakesh's being. His electromagnetic signature, or maybe aura was a better word. It shifted from a pale blue to a deep, sickly green.

"Nooo," Irakesh shrieked, diving towards Blair. He never made it. Brilliant silver light burst from every pore in the deathless's body, forcing Blair to avert his eyes. It washed over him, somehow familiar and comforting like a night's rest after a day that refused to end.

Blair shielded his gaze, watching in awe as the bits of light drifted skyward. They formed a bright orb about a foot above Irakesh's head, pulsing and flowing like a miniature silver sun. Was that the key? It was breathtaking.

The orb shot towards Blair, searing his chest and face as the energy penetrated him. The agony was incredible. Unforgettable. The only time he'd ever experienced something like this had been in Peru, when he'd first grasped the Mother's hand. When he'd accepted the key to the Ark.

The pain subsided. Blair couldn't remember when he'd felt so alive. He looked down in wonder, finding his body whole and undamaged. Lurking somewhere at the edge of his consciousness was a vast reserve, an ocean of light that he could tap into if he just reached for it.

74

HOPE

The lack of oxygen crowded Liz's vision with black spots. That was hardly a surprise, given the two-foot span of golden steel jutting from her chest. It should have been slick with gore, but a detached part of her realized that the blade was pristine, somehow free of any stain.

She was vaguely aware as the arm slid free of her neck, allowing her to topple onto the charred pavement. Liz pressed her chest against the ground, gritting her teeth as the point of the sword dug into the pavement. The blade was gradually forced from her body, eventually clattering to the ground next to her.

A moment later her chest filled with the familiar fire of healing. Blood began to pump again, sluggishly but enough to keep her conscious. What the hell had happened? She'd been aware of Irakesh's attack, but had no idea why he'd suddenly released her. She shifted her body, turning her head until she was forced to shield her eyes against a brilliant silver glow.

It emanated from Blair, his silver fur composed of light. It should have been impossible to look upon, but the longer she stared the easier it became. Her hand dropped, no longer necessary to shield her eyes. The light was clean and pure, bathing the area in its wonderful warmth. She could feel the strength of it, how similar it was to the light that she'd just pulled through the blade when she had finally laid Cyntia to rest.

He stood noble and majestic like some benevolent god come to heal the world. It was without a doubt the most beautiful thing she'd ever seen. Tears fell unheeded down her cheeks as she sat mesmerized. It took some time to notice the figure at Blair's feet, a familiar dark-skinned man garbed in loose white garments. Irakesh shielded himself with his arms, covering his face and balling up into a fetal position. This was the villain they'd been afraid of for so long?

Liz rose to her feet, still unsteady but markedly better now that the healing had begun. She glanced around, spotting Jordan's crumpled form. He'd been bitten repeatedly by zombies, terrible wounds in his arms and back. Yet the zombies had fallen back, cowering at the edge of the magnificent glow coming from Blair. Jordan groaned, struggling into a sitting position. He was alive.

She caught movement from the other direction, not far from Blair. Steve's battered body lay next to what may have once been a luxury sedan, his face twisted into a mask of hatred and rage. He glared at Blair but didn't seem willing to approach.

Where was Trevor? She craned her neck, peering wildly around the bridge. There. His still smoking body had made an impact crater in the hood of a Focus. She rushed over, feeling his wrist for a pulse. There was none, of course, and she felt like a fool.

"Did...did we win?" Trevor wheezed, tilting his head in her direction. His face was badly burned, the hair charred to ash. It was a miracle he'd survived.

"We won," she said, resisting the urge to put a comforting hand on his charred shoulder. It would probably be agony for him.

"What's that light?" he whispered, trying to peer in the direction of the silver glow. "It hurts."

She glanced in that direction in time to see Blair kneel next to Irakesh. He hoisted the deathless aloft with one hand, peering directly into his eyes. "You've killed my friends. Murdered innocents. All so you could seize control of this Ark and begin your unholy empire. But you failed. How does it feel, Irakesh? How does it feel knowing we beat you, that in the end all of your plans account for nothing?"

"Just kill me and be done with it," Irakesh spit on the ground at Blair's feet.

"I'm not going to kill you." Blair gave a wicked grin, dropping Irakesh. "I'm going to delve your mind until I've gleaned every bit of useful information about this world. Then I'm going to turn you over to the Mother. It's only fitting that she decide your fate."

Irakesh didn't reply, instead glaring sullenly at the ground. He seemed to grasp the futility of his situation, yet Liz could take no joy in it. Not after everything they'd lost.

Blair raised a palm, aiming it towards the zombies clogging the remainder of the bridge. A thousand tendrils of silver flame burst forth, flowing around her and the others. The light spun into the zombies with incredible fury, rivaling the bomb itself. When it faded, nothing remained save piles of ash. The remains of the bridge were completely free of zombies. Liz stared in awe as Blair walked over and picked up Irakesh's sword, examining it for a long moment. Then the weapon melted, flowing up his arm and disappearing as their clothing did when shifting.

Blair turned towards the group, taking them all in. His eyes held a weight she knew must be mirrored in them all. He cleared his throat, pausing for a long moment before speaking. "We've won and I think that entitles us to a little rest. I have a lot to learn about controlling an Ark, but some things have already been explained to me by the beast. Hold still. This will feel a little odd."

A pulse of silver light radiated from Blair, bathing them all. Her skin tingled, warm and prickly like static electricity. Then the flash grew brighter and there was a feeling of vertigo. She was blind. Her heart quickened. She'd always been a little claustrophobic and part of her screamed out to escape.

When the light faded she stood in a wide chamber that mirrored the Ark in Peru, identical to the central chamber save that the statues and murals had clearly been created by a different hand. Blair had teleported them. Was that even scientifically possible? Just how advanced had the ancients really been?

The others gaped openly, Jordan's rifle clattering to the ground as he examined his surroundings. Trevor braced himself against the side of an obelisk, but kept his feet. Steve simply sat down with his hands in his lap. Yuri seemed less phased than the rest of them, removing a candy bar from his jacket and tearing open the wrapper.

It was Trevor who finally broke the silence.

"Listen, everyone. I know that there's no way you can forgive me for everything that happened. I know what you have to do," he said, staggering over to Blair and dropping to his knees. "Before you end it, just know that I'm sorry. For everything. I wish it could have been another way, that I could have fought with you."

"Quit being such a little bitch, Trevor," Liz said, giving an exaggerated eye roll as she slugged her brother in the arm. It made her smile, just a hint of the camaraderie they'd shared during their trip to Peru not so very long ago.

75

BAD NEWS

J ordan allowed himself a smug smile as the thick bronze bars
flowed from the ceiling, trapping Irakesh and Steve in the
same cell. Energy crackled between the bars, little arcs of
unfriendly blue and white lightning. He turned toward the
others, all of them clad in shimmering white clothing. That had been
a neat trick. Blair had simply willed their old clothes out of existence,
and had replaced them with garments similar to those Irakesh wore.
It made him feel like an extra in *The Mummy*, but damn if they
weren't comfortable.

"You're sure you want to leave them alive?" Jordan asked, turning
to glance at their prisoners. Steve stared sullenly at them, but Irakesh
had already slumped against one wall and refused to look at them.

"They're not getting off that easily," Blair said, offering a satisfied
smile. "I'm certain the Mother is going to want to have a word with
each of them. Besides, their combined knowledge could be really
useful. The Ark gives me a lot more power than I had before. I should
be able to delve them easily enough, and I have a feeling we're going
to need what they can teach us."

"If it's knowledge of the past you want, couldn't you get it from the
pair upstairs?" Liz asked, leaning against the wall next to the cell.

That sword was really starting to look as if it belonged over her shoulder.

"She's got a point," Trevor added, folding his arms. Jordan still didn't trust the deathless, but knew telling the others that would be useless. "Can you touch their minds while they're sleeping?"

"Probably," Blair replied, scrubbing at his hair as he considered. "Honestly though, I'd rather wait. I can use the Ark to contact the Mother before we decide anything. It would be nice having her here before we rush to any decisions."

"That's not a bad idea," Liz conceded with a shrug. "How soon do you think she'll arrive?"

"Now that this Ark is active we should be able to light walk to her almost instantly," Blair replied. It was mind-boggling that they could cover thousands of miles in seconds. That kind of tactical advantage would be critical in the days to come. "I figure we head down there, explain the situation and then come back after she's weighed in."

"All right, but I still think killing them both is the smart thing to do," Jordan said. "A dead enemy is no threat. A live enemy has a chance to become one."

"Liz?" Blair asked, turning to the copper-haired woman.

Jordan liked that she'd stepped so seamlessly into a leadership role. They definitely needed one. Democratic discussion got people killed.

"It's a risk, but I think you're right, Blair. It's a minimal one. I think we'll be okay until the Mother arrives to deal with them," she said, rising from the wall and eyeing the prisoners. Steve had sat down on the far side of the cell from Irakesh. He too was ignoring them now.

Beep, beep. Beep, Beep.

Jordan tensed, hand shooting to his breast pocket. He removed the smart phone Yuri had given him just after they'd escaped Mohn. Incoming call, number unknown. He answered it, blinking when he saw the Director's face appear on the tiny screen. The phone was at an awkward angle, as if his hands were bound and he were propping the phone against a leg.

"I don't have long," the Director said, glancing over his shoulder. "I still have a few people loyal to me, but that's not going to save me."

Jordan went cold as the implications set in. "You're a prisoner?"

"The Old Man had me arrested. I'm being transported to London to meet his 'master.' Someone he calls Usir," the Director explained, shooting another glance over his shoulder. He turned back to his phone. "I don't know who or what he serves, but whatever it is this thing controls Mohn Corp. through the Old Man. Something big is going down in London, and I have no idea what."

"We're not in a position to launch any sort of rescue," Jordan replied, still reeling with the news. He was aware of the others clustered around him, totally silent as they listened to the conversation.

"I'm not expecting you to. Apparently, this master is something called a draugr. It can control minds, and I don't expect to be myself for much longer," the Director replied. His face went grim. "From here on out, you need to consider me and Mohn as a whole the enemy."

"Acknowledged," was all Jordan could muster.

"One last thing. Other Arks have returned. The one in Egypt is the largest, and it's also the center of a lot of activity. Whoever controls it is gathering a massive army of the dead," he continued.

There was the rustling of fabric, then the phone canted at a crazy angle. It tumbled to a metal floor, and went black for a moment before it was picked up again. When it stopped moving it showed a different face. A familiar face. "Ahh, Commander. I'm so pleased to see you survived your encounter with Irakesh."

"Mohn," he growled, eyes narrowing at the triumphant smile on the Old Man's face.

"Mark is indisposed at the moment. You'll have to try again in a few hours, after I've introduced him to...an old friend," the Old Man said. His eyes twinkled, then the phone went dead.

Jordan turned to the others. There was a moment of silence before Blair spoke. "Usir is a name I know. It's ancient Egyptian, a synonym for the god of the underworld. Most people know him as Osiris."

EPILOGUE

Steve waited until Blair and the other fools had stridden up the corridor before turning his attention to Irakesh. He studied the deathless, an unassuming black man about an inch shorter than he was. Well, unassuming if you didn't count the razored teeth or glowing eyes.

"I'm guessing you don't want to be here when Isis arrives," Steve said, rising to his feet. The deathless didn't answer. He paused for a long moment, then continued. "I'm not eager to be here, either. So I'm leaving. You're welcome to join me, for a price."

That got his attention. Irakesh's head came up, eyes narrowing as he stared hard at Steve. "How exactly do you propose to do that? We're locked behind a stasis field. Any energy directed at it will simply rebound back at us. There's no way to escape."

"No way that you know of," Steve shot back. He crossed to the bars, raising a hand to within inches of the crackling energy that surrounded them. "Humor me. Let's just say that I had a way to get past the bars. Would you be willing to help me escape?"

"Very well, I'll indulge this folly," Irakesh said, rising to his feet. He stalked to the bars, folding his arms as he stared up at Steve. "Let us say you have a way to open the bars. How would you escape the Ark? We'd be crushed by the ocean if we sought escape."

"Are you familiar with an ability called light walking?" Steve asked, giving Irakesh a sly smile. The deathless's eyes widened.

"I know it, but only Ark Lords possess the ability. How do you even know of it? No one in this age should," Irakesh asked, eyes narrowing again as he eyed Steve with a calculating gaze.

"I *am* an Ark Lord, thanks to Blair," Steve said. "I delved the mind of Isis while she slept, and learned a great many things. Blair is new and untrained. He has locked us in this cell, but if we light walk, then the bars won't matter. We can bypass the stasis field."

"Why would you bring me? We're enemies, you and I," Irakesh replied, but his expression had softened. He was curious.

What you suggest is madness, Ka-Dun. Repent, and the Mother will spare you. Continue with your mad plan, and she will hunt you to the last corner of the world. There will be no escape, his beast rumbled. Steve ignored it, as he often did. The creature was noble, possessed of a morality he simply didn't share.

"We *were* enemies," Steve replied, smiling. "Now we are allies, like it or not. As you can see, Blair and the others are no friends of mine. Nor do I wish to be here when Isis arrives. I'm willing to take you with me, but as I said, there is a price."

The deathless was silent for a long moment before speaking. "Name it."

"Your mother rules the Ark of the Cradle in Egypt, does she not?" Steve asked. He knew the answer, of course, but Irakesh would be less reticent if he felt on equal footing.

"She does, and I begin to grasp your plan," Irakesh said, finally smiling. "You wish me to accompany you, so that my mother will not slay you upon our arrival."

"Precisely," Steve replied, giving his most devious smile. It felt good not having to hide it. "This new world is a far different place than the one you came from. There is much I can offer the mighty Ra, not least of which is the key to the Mother's Ark."

Irakesh blinked once, then extended a hand. Steve shook it. Blair thought he'd won this little encounter, but he was about to find out how wrong he'd been. Steve reached deep into his well of energy, and willed the two of them away from the Ark of the Redwood.

Note to the Reader

Thank you for reading No Mere Zombie. If you enjoyed it I hope you'll consider leaving a review. They're the lifeblood of indie authors, and help me get to a point where I can write full time.

Want to know when future books are available? Sign up to the mailing list here.
You'll receive the Deathless prequel novella *The First Ark* for **FREE** when you do!

Want more info on the series, character artwork and other goodies? Check out my website at chrisfoxwrites.com

If you'd like to visit us on Facebook you can find us at https://www.facebook.com/chrisfoxwrites

Made in the USA
Middletown, DE
23 March 2021

36116879R00219